MARCUS PELEGRIMAS's SKINNERS

"An action-packed, blood-soaked ripsnorter of a monster-hunter series."

—Tom Piccirilli, author of *The Midnight Road*

"Pelegrimas has done the impossible—come up with a fresh and exciting twist on vampire lore."

—Ed Gorman, bestselling co-author of *Dean Koontz's Frankenstein: City of Night*

"Bram Stoker reinvigorated Gothic horror in the late 19th century . . . Pelegrimas [has] the potential to do the same thing here in the 21st century. . . . His storytelling style is utterly readable, his characters are unconventional and endearing, his wry sense of humor priceless."

—Paul Goat Allen

"With a scalpel-sharp eye for detail, Pelegrimas slices open an entirely new kind of street-smart vampire."

—Michael Largo, winner of the Bram Stoker Award

"An amazing talent!"

—Robert J. Randisi

By Marcus Pelegrimas

Blood Blade
Howling Legion
Teeth of Beasts
Vampire Uprising
The Breaking
Extinction Agenda

Extinction Agenda

SKINNERS

MARCUS PELEGRIMAS

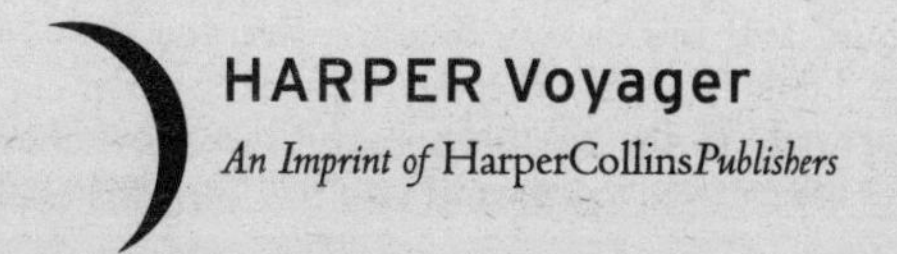

This is a work of fiction. Names, characters, places, and incidents are products of the author's imagination or are used fictitiously and are not to be construed as real. Any resemblance to actual events, locales, organizations, or persons, living or dead, is entirely coincidental.

HARPER Voyager
An Imprint of HarperCollins*Publishers*
10 East 53rd Street
New York, New York 10022-5299

Cover art by Larry Rostant
ISBN 978-0-06-198638-3
www.harpervoyagerbooks.com

First Harper Voyager mass market printing: November 2011

Printed in the U.S.A.

10 9 8 7 6 5 4 3 2 1

Many thanks to everyone who helped me through a very tough year. You listened to me when I ranted and were still there when I ran out of steam. The brownies you sent helped more than you know.

Very special thanks go out to Karen. You're a great editor and an incredible friend.

I wouldn't have wanted to do this without you.

Extinction Agenda

Prologue

The wolves are coming in from the forests,circling the village that is under my protection.
Perhaps they know, perhaps they don't care that I am here.
They move in, lapping up our scent, salivating at the prospect of separating limbs from our bodies.
The wolves don't give a damn about this village or about the hopes, dreams, families, or friends of its people.
They come in from the forests to claim what they see as theirs.
When this siege is over, there will be another.
And another one after that.

—From the journal of Jonah Lancroft, 1867
There is no record of the village referenced in this entry.

In the months following the Breaking Moon, a cold descended upon the world as if to numb it for the carnage of a burgeoning war. That night's victories prevented the Full Bloods from spreading the Half Breed plague across an entire continent in a matter of hours. Only as autumn sank into winter did the Skinners realize how close humanity had been to the brink of its destruction. Although the Full Bloods had been stopped before, using the earth's own energies to spread the Breaking, the Half Breeds had still been unleashed, and their bite was still just as deadly. Angry breaths spewed from the mouths of shapeshifters as they roamed city streets in packs. Humans shivered in their homes, their tired eyes watchful over the barrels of hunting rifles or shotguns. Such weaponry had been bought up rapidly once the werewolves spread throughout the country, despite the fact that normal ammunition was somehow becoming increasingly useless against the creatures that seemed to have grown thicker coats for the winter. When a shot was fired, the noise drew sharp, black eyes toward its source. Even if that bullet had somehow dropped one of the Half Breeds, others would stampede the would-be hunter and decorate the stark white ground in a spattering of dark red.

As the months wore on, local police departments were tasked with keeping order in panicked jurisdictions. Large cities and small towns alike were dragged into what many thought was the end of the world. Monsters charged in from the hills, howled at the moon, tore through families. Overconfident at first, police forces, local militia, and even the military either fed the ranks of the dead or were turned into members of a pack. Whether those people were to be called victims, heroes, or martyrs ceased to matter. Dead was dead, and in this uncompromising winter people wanted to live. Fear led to panic, which settled into the desire to fight. No human emotion mattered to the wolves, however, as they kept running and feeding and killing and maiming. Their numbers grew exponentially, and when some packs were cleaned out, it wasn't until after dozens of locals had been added to their ranks. Just a few stray Half Breeds meant more deaths and casualties. More casualties meant more Half Breeds, and the howling never waned.

The military had been called to action as a way to maintain order in the streets, divvy out the emergency food, and escort medical supplies to where they were needed. When the Full Bloods showed themselves, battles raged. Unfortunately for the cold, frightened world, the Full Bloods showed themselves often.

While the United States suffered the worst of the initial turmoil, the nightmare was not contained by any political border. It swept out from the siege of Atoka, Oklahoma, and the occupation of Raton, New Mexico. Before the media could debate whether the creatures were truly werewolves or just "diseased canines" from previous sightings in Wisconsin and Kansas City, the Half Breeds had made their presence all too clear. As bodies piled up, explanations became scarcer. Before long, nobody seemed to care what the creatures were or where they came from. They just wanted them to go away.

But the beasts weren't going anywhere.

It was going to be a long, brutal winter.

"The Skinners know we're here, Tara. This isn't smart."

Pacing across the front window of a town house on Battery Avenue, a skinny woman with stringy blond hair pulled aside a filmy curtain to get a look at a quiet section of Baltimore. Tara's round face would have been pretty if not for the black tendrils creeping beneath her skin along both cheeks. Although the pattern was more or less random, one half of the markings reacted in perfect synchronicity with the other. They shifted beneath her flesh, sometimes twitching out of hunger. Where one tendril stretched out, another on that side pulled back so neither of her two spores could claim a lion's share of the host. She paused when headlights splashed across the pavement as a car sped past the town house at highway speed. Like the rest of the country, most of Maryland's authorities were too busy elsewhere to worry about traffic violations. "The Skinners already had their shot at you, Cobb," she said. "They came up empty."

The other man in the room stood at average height, his muscular build wrapped in a sweater frayed along the bottom. A thick turtleneck was stretched out enough to display a ring of black wavy markings around his entire neck.

Some of them met the narrow goatee that had been shaved to a point above his Adam's apple. The ones at the back of his neck reached all the way up into a thick crop of light brown hair that would have perfectly suited an edgy businessman from the mid-1990s. Even so, he cared for himself well enough to make the look seem timeless. When he didn't say anything, he ground his teeth and allowed his lids to droop down over crisp green eyes ringed almost imperceptibly with quivering black filaments.

"They *did* come up empty, right?" Tara asked.

"I was told about those two Skinners in Toronto less than an hour before they kicked in my door."

Tara placed a hand against the window as black claws snaked out from beneath her fingertips. "What did they get?"

"One of my personal PCs. It functioned as a small backup server and was used to post updates through ChatterPages.com."

Tara's claws scraped against the glass as she slowly balled her hand into a fist. "So they know how we've been passing our communications? They might even know everything we've been setting up ever since we took control?"

"The ChatterPages stuff has already been changed," Cobb said. "If they have been listening in, they would have put their information to use by now."

Moving in a flicker from the window to where Cobb stood, Tara clamped a hand around his throat and applied just enough pressure to raise him onto the balls of his feet. "That information should have been destroyed," she hissed. "That was the order."

"Right," Cobb said as his two upper sets of fangs eased out from where they were sheathed in his gums. "An order given by Hope. Not you."

"Hope put me in charge of making sure the order was carried out."

"She may have given you some duties during the uprising, but that doesn't mean anything now that she's dead. The others are entrenched within their own cities watching the wretches tear the world apart. Why would they feel the need to obey orders given by a wild-eyed Double Seed?"

Even as Tara tightened her grip on his throat, the tendrils on either side of her face twitched in a way that was just frantic enough to prove his point. While most Nymar were created by a vampire spore attaching to their heart, only a select few could survive the process of having more than one introduced to their system. That feat won no respect with other Nymar, however, who saw only a raging temper brought about by the disproportionate hunger of two separate spores living in the same body.

"I am more than just a Double Seed," she warned. With a thought in the right direction, Tara was able to widen her tendrils into thin stripes that could paint her entire body in a black cloak. "Because of what Hope and I did, all of our kind will soon become Shadow Spore."

"I know that. But without me, the uprising never would have happened."

"If you're talking about a bunch of backstabbing pricks who don't know who to thank for having entire cities to run, I already know about them. Just because the Nymar who followed Hope don't respect me doesn't mean that you shouldn't."

"What I said before is just the consensus," Cobb told her. "That's how they see you. If I saw you that way, I never would have told you where to find me."

"What makes you think I couldn't have tracked you down myself?"

"The Skinners haven't been able to pull off that trick, and that's one of the few things they're good at anymore."

She released him and walked back to the window. Holding her fingers to her lips, she licked the longest of her nails before they retracted. "The plan was to wait until the smoke cleared after the uprising before we started looking for the nymphs. Things may have gotten more out of hand than we thought, but it's still just as good a time as any to hunt those sweet little dancing girls down."

"You got that right. The Skinners that were protecting them before have a lot more to keep them busy now. But," Cobb added, "there are more than Skinners to worry about. Those things that run loose on every street in this country are after us as well. The Full Bloods have something to prove after being kept at bay by our lies for so many years."

"Which is why we need to find the other Shadow Spore."

Cobb shook his head. "That was never the plan. Whatever you and Hope had going, it no longer applies. Hope's gone and I only came out from behind my main terminal to put the Skinners out of the picture for a while. All we need to do is ride out this storm and gain control of whoever's left."

"And what if it's the shapeshifters?" Tara asked. "Only a Nymar seeded with both of the original Shadow Spore can ever defeat a Full Blood."

"We have strength in numbers. That's how it's always been. We turn as many as we need to throw at our enemies so that established Nymar take the least amount of casualties. This may not be the fight we were after, but it's only a matter of scale. When it's time for our kind to step up against the Skinners, the humans, or even the shapeshifters, we'll be ready. I've started recruiting through the Internet and already the Nymar in most major cities have come close to tripling in number."

Lowering her voice as if there were sharper, unseen ears to intrude on her conversation, Tara said, "The Full Bloods won't stop after riling everyone up like this. There's no reason to think they'll even stop after overrunning this country. Even with superior numbers, we can barely hope to withstand the wretches they've been sending after us. We need the other Shadow Spore!"

"How do you even know there is another Shadow Spore?" Cobb asked. "We were lucky to find the one in Lancroft's basement."

"I've seen records from the decades when the Lancroft Reformatory was fully functioning. There were two Shadow Spore, just like we've always been told. And—"

"'And when the two can become one, even the Full Bloods shall quake,'" he recited. "I've heard the stories too. Every species has its stories. You know why? Because none of them wants to admit it's dominated by another. Stories tell us there's always hope, always something to tip the scales. Well you know what, Tara? Sometimes you're just outclassed."

Her features were gaunt, no matter how much blood she might have drunk in the last hour or two. Although the two spores attached to her heart shared a space, there was rarely enough food to go around. She turned toward the window as a distant howl drifted through the air. "You heard about the assassin I sent to find Cole Warnecki after he was dragged to prison?"

"That was right after the uprising," Cobb said. "There was a lot of posturing and plenty of big promises made regarding payback and whatnot. I was the one passing all of that garbage along, remember?"

"It wasn't garbage," she told him. "It took a while, but he found where Cole was being held."

"I could have told you that much. It was the prison in Colorado that was all over the freaking news!"

"And then you never heard about him again," she continued. "He was supposed to be waiting for a trial or being questioned, but *that* was a load of shit!" The more she spoke, the angrier Tara became. "Why is it that we're always supposed to be the liars, when we're the only ones telling the humans exactly what we want? They line up at our Blood Parlors to be bitten. They know what they're getting, but the Skinners decide to burn us down. The Full Bloods act like they're so high and mighty, when they're the ones that have been sneaking among us for centuries like snakes."

Knowing better than to try and calm her down, Cobb held up his hands and walked back to a computer desk set up in what was meant to be the town house's dining room. "No need to tell me about it. I've been spreading that word for years."

"Well it's time to finish what we've started with the Skinners as well as the Full Bloods. There's supposed to be some group that splintered off from the rest."

"You mean the Vigilant?"

She nodded. "I want to hunt down as many as it takes to get to the heart of their operation. Surely they're doing something against these goddamned shapeshifters. We need to get whatever weapons they've got."

"And then what?" Cobb asked as he settled into a creaking office chair. "Stand toe-to-toe with Full Bloods? Leave the insanity to the crazy people. How many times do I have to tell you to just . . . be . . . patient?"

"You can stop telling me right now," she snapped. "Because I'm sick of hearing it. What kind of message does it send if we stay hidden while the Skinners do the fighting? Even if we mop up what's left, nobody will respect someone who leads a battle fought in the dark just to claim the scraps."

Cobb tapped his keyboard and shrugged. Although he knew it wouldn't go over well, he couldn't let his other matter drop. "And what about the killer you hired to take out Cole? I assume he found something, even if he didn't get his job done."

"What makes you think he failed?"

"Because," he replied simply, "you would have reminded me several times by now if that wasn't the case."

Her smile was more like an image from an old reel of moving picture film—unsteady and twitchy. "I guess you're right about that. He did find Cole. And when he checked in before making the kill, he told me that Cole wasn't being held in a prison at all. It may have been one at some other time, but there were only a couple Skinners and a few very special prisoners there."

Cobb thought about that for all of two seconds before shrugging it off and shifting his attention back to the monitor. "It's a crazy time. Just about everything is getting torn down. Wasn't that part of the beauty of our uprising? The

Skinners aren't the same since we set their houses on fire and pitted the humans against them."

"There's more to it than that," she said while tapping the glass. When the claw sprouting from her index finger raked against it, she eased it back as if using the window to shove it under her flesh.

"What did your assassin tell you when he returned?"

"He didn't return."

Cobb chuckled under his breath and typed furiously at his keyboard. "Then it seems like the Skinners are pretty much the same as when we left 'em."

But Tara wasn't convinced. She watched as the people in the town house across the street poked their noses out like a couple of frightened rabbits. They were so timid that she almost hoped to see a wretch scamper across their lawn to tear their wide, doe eyes from their sockets. Since there were no Half Breeds to be found, she got a better idea. "I'm hungry. Be back in a minute."

This wasn't the first time Kansas City had fallen beneath the cruel whims of a monster. Unlike the days when Liam had climbed its towers to claim the city, there was no denying what was happening, and nobody was trying to paint a prettier face upon a siege. As in the rest of the country, the first packs had claimed their victims within two days after the incident in Atoka, Oklahoma. Those wretches were born hungry and they fed to create more. Unlike many cities in America, this one had its protectors.

I-29 was covered with snow. Although it had been plowed well enough to reveal the surface of the concrete, there were drifts on the side of the road where empty cars and pickups were embedded like peanuts wedged into a candy bar. Most of the wrecks were tagged and all of them were empty. A few still blinked their hazard lights onto the pristine surface of the white layers that had collected on the vehicles. In the morning, patrols would come along to check the freshest of the accidents to see if someone either needed to be brought to a shelter or shot before they turned. Those unlucky enough to have crashed without being spotted by the irregular patrols would have to stay inside their cars for the night, lock their doors and pray the only thing to gnaw at their faces was the cold.

As if responding to the panicked thoughts of those stranded motorists, three Half Breeds trotted along the side of the interstate, sniffing wildly at each car. Their gnarled faces twitched with every flake of snow that came to rest upon their snouts or ears. Half Breeds didn't need a reason to flinch, because they were always in pain. Having been born to the sounds of the breaking of their bones before their muscles could stretch out to hold them together, the werewolves were in a constant state of wincing, whining, or snarling. The cold, it seemed, only made them worse.

A man and woman sat huddled inside a blue Dodge, its two right tires buried hopelessly in the slush. Their faces were pressed together and their eyes widened when frightened breaths drifted from their lips to smear against the glass. That hint of movement was enough to catch one Half Breed's eye a second before its companions caught the humans' scent. The trio of werewolves lowered their chests to the snowy ground and stalked toward the car.

Both of the people inside wore glasses. Their lenses were fogged, but not enough to keep them from seeing what was coming. As the unexplainable terrors spread across the country, people had no choice but to either hide or carry on as best they could. Judging by the tears streaming down both sets of reddened cheeks, these two were reconsidering their choice.

As the Half Breeds approached the car, they bared their teeth along with two sets of tusks curving down from one row of teeth and up from another. The tusks were thicker than the rest of their teeth, but thin enough to scrape against each other like scissor blades as the werewolves opened and closed their mouths to sample the frigid, late night air. Once they spread out to form a semicircle around the vehicle, the creatures planted their feet and fixed their eyes upon the trembling humans. After hunkering down for a moment, the Half Breed in the middle of the group lunged forward to ram its head against the car door. It made a dent, but it could tell it wasn't going to get inside like that, so it reared up and began scraping at the window.

From within the car, muffled voices wrapped around each other in much the same way the people's bodies clung together for warmth. When something moved beneath the car and scraped directly below the passenger compartment, the couple began to scream.

By now all three of the Half Breeds were doing their best to find a way inside the car. Thick paws slapped against the frame. Twisted faces pushed against the doors and windows before the weight of a heavy body caused the entire vehicle to groan. The thing that scraped against the bottom of the car quickened its pace toward the side being attacked by the Half Breeds. As soon as it reached the driver's door, the scraping against the window stopped. Soon, the other two Half Breeds were pulled away from the car as well.

When the man inside wiped the frost off the window to get a look outside, he found several shaggy bodies wrestling in the snow. Blood sprayed through the air in a fine mist cast from fangs and claws. It was impossible to tell which creatures were winning or even where one ended and another began, so the man eased away from the window before he was noticed.

"I think we should make a run for it," he told the trembling woman.

"Where are we going to go?"

"I don't know. Just away from here!"

And, as suddenly as the creatures had appeared, the fight was over.

The wind scraped against the car's exterior, its slow rustle the loudest thing in the world at that given moment. Glass creaked and bits of ice rapped against the side of the car as if the winter itself had sprouted claws.

"Should . . . we still run?" the woman asked.

Two sets of claws wedged into the driver's side door, one at the base of the window and another near the handle. With a minimum of effort, the door was separated from its frame and tossed aside. Outside, a tall creature stood wearing a thick coat of light blond fur peppered with streaks of darker brown and encrusted with chunks of snow. Blood was already frozen where it had been spilled. Kayla had presided over Kansas City since her pack had taken part in ending Liam's siege. Although the Mongrels under her command had been thinned out due to treachery within her ranks or combat with the encroaching werewolves, she wasn't about to step aside so any invader could have their way with her territory.

"Yes," she snarled through a snout that seemed just a bit too long for her feline facial structure. "You should run."

The couple within the car pressed themselves against the opposite window and nearly jumped from their sweat-stained coats when another Mongrel appeared outside the passenger window. Ben's appearance was even more disturbing than Kayla's. Being a digger who could practically swim underground, he was accustomed to remaining out of sight. Gill flaps along his neck stretched out and immediately snapped shut after drawing in too much freezing air instead of the soil they were meant to process. Blood and ice stuck to the beak that dominated his face, and his black eyes remained calm beneath their vertical lids as they studied the people within the vehicle. His fingers slipped beneath the door's handle and were strong enough to force it open despite the ice that had sealed it shut. "There is another car further up the road," he said. "White four-door just past a minivan facing the wrong way."

Dazed by the words that came from the Mongrel's beak, the woman stammered, "We can't just . . . steal a car."

"Get away from us!" the man snapped as he tried his best to squirm in the cramped confines in order to put himself between her and the Mongrel.

Ben merely stepped back, allowing the man to play his role as protector without reacting to the threatening tone in his voice or the way he grabbed a long flashlight and wielded it like a club. "It's not stealing," he told them both. "The owners of that car were killed by the same creatures we just chased away. My advice is to take that car and get somewhere safer. Also," he added, while dropping to all fours and scraping away the top layers of snowy earth using long, curved claws, "don't look too hard at the mess in the ditch."

When the man turned to where Kayla had been standing, he found only the bloody remains of two Half Breeds. The third had already bounded down the interstate, chasing after a lean figure that slid gracefully into another lane.

"I think we should go," the woman said.

Taking his eyes from the sight of the chase toward the row of lonely abandoned vehicles on the side of the road, the man swallowed hard and zipped up his coat. "Right. Do you have our suitcase?"

"Just move!"

He followed her order and bolted from the car. Along the way he thought about the fire that had all but consumed Topeka after the werewolves sprung up in the autumn. Only during the drive to KC had he asked his fiancée why they might have been spared. The conversation had lasted until they pulled over to fill the gas tank and their stomachs at a place that had a Subway sandwich shop and Pizza Hut tacked onto it. Every seat was filled, with people of all ages, genders, and nationalities. Each stunned face was focused intently on their meals. The terror implied within their features was all too familiar to the man from Topeka. He'd been wearing it ever since he abandoned his hometown.

It hadn't been an easy decision. When the first werewolves showed up, everyone he knew wanted to fight them. A call to arms swept throughout the entire country at about that same time, encouraging everyone to buy a gun and defend their homes from the animals that meant to do them harm.

Explanations would wait for later. Now was the time to fight.

That lasted for a few weeks.

When the angry voices died down, it wasn't because of victory or fatigue. The people who'd bought their guns and started firing at the wild animals in their yards had been torn to shreds. It wasn't pretty and it wasn't spectacular. Even the few who'd rigged explosives with some degree of success barely managed to do any damage. After that, the wolves had swept in to kill them all.

The police were just more men with guns.

The military was taking a stand, but not in Topeka.

Soon, like most other cities, Topeka burned. Whether the fires had been started by accident or as a last ditch effort to kill the werewolves didn't matter. The flames rose and the people who tried to put them out were set upon by another pack of ravenous beasts. The firefighters that lived to crawl away only howled in pain as their bodies were twisted into one of those things that set out to hunt for food. Like the rest of his family, the man who now clung to his fiancée to keep from slipping on a patch of ice on I-29 hadn't wanted to leave Topeka.

His natural instinct was to stay. For the first several weeks of the crisis, people barricaded themselves indoors to fight for survival. They watched their televisions for news about how far the insanity had spread and what was being done to stop it. Before long, people stopped watching the news and just focused on living for another day. Then, as things got worse, the highways became crowded with cars on their way to someplace better. The people behind the wheels might or might not have known where they were headed, but it was time to go.

The man from Topeka stayed until his friends and family were consumed. That's what people started calling it, since there often wasn't a way to know if they were truly dead. At least that word was better than the thought of seeing a parent, child, or neighbor broken down into a screaming heap to be reforged into something with fangs and wild, pain-filled eyes. The last possible good he could do was take his fiancée away before her pretty face was twisted into something cruel and hungry. They'd made it as far as KC, and he was determined to keep going. When she slipped, he was there to pull her to her feet and urge her onward. They'd passed the minivan which had spun 180 degrees before plowing into a drift. The four-door was directly ahead of them, cleared off and waiting for them like a freshly unwrapped present.

"Stay here and I'll check it out," he said.

The door was unlocked and the keys were on the dash. After fidgeting with fingers that were almost too numb to feel the keys, he slipped the right one into the ignition and started the car. "Come on, honey!"

The woman cautiously stuck her feet into the snow. Tracks that were too large and spaced too far apart to be set down by humans surrounded the car. They converged a bit farther away from the road near a pile of crimson pulp that had been covered by a fine layer of snow. Heeding Ben's advice, she turned her eyes away from the mess and fumbled with the handle of the passenger side door. After she got in, but before she had a chance to pull the door shut, the car lurched forward.

"Where are we going?" she asked while frantically tugging at her safety belt.

"I've got some old friends in St. Louis. We'll go there."

"Can we make it all that way? How far is it?"

Blinking furiously as a Half Breed leapt out from a hole on the side of the road, only to be overtaken by a beaked Mongrel, he sputtered, "I don't know, but we're going. We came this far, we won't stop now." He looked over to her and saw nothing but determination on her trembling features. She swiped some tears from her eyes, nodded, and placed her hand in his.

Smoke rose into the sky. Shapeshifters roamed freely. Corpses lay scattered beneath a stark winter sun. Randolph

Standing Bear could smell all of those things as he pulled long, deep breaths into his lungs. The air also carried more familiar fragrances like pine trees and the crisp, simple purity of snow that lay piled hip deep across most of the Canadian wilderness. The Full Blood cherished winter more than any other time, simply because it was the quietest of the seasons. Considering all that had transpired over the last few months, silence had become the rarest of commodities. Launching off two powerful hind legs, Randolph closed his eyes and lifted his nose toward a sky that seemed to have been painted above him in thick, chalky gray.

His front paws stretched out as his stocky body cleared the highest point of his jump. In his four-legged form he could run fast enough to cross several miles of ground within the space of a minute. Powerful muscles propelled him forward after being tensed during all the time spent on the boat that had brought him from European shores. The soil felt familiar when his paws touched it again. Almost every stone was right where he'd left it. Despite everything that was happening to this continent, it was still his territory. And throughout the trials that lay ahead, he would reclaim it once again.

That had always been his intention. The move to his homeland had been necessary to create enough wretches to keep the humans huddled within their homes and firing their precious guns in every direction. Now he would take steps to reclaim the territory he'd fought so hard to claim all those years ago. And thanks to the chaos cinching around the world like a noose, other territories would change hands as well.

This was a new world, and a new breed was required to live in it. If Liam had been right about anything, it was that Full Bloods were through with hiding. With little or no effort, Randolph could hear the other Full Blood's voice in his mind.

You can take them all, my friend.

Sometimes Liam's voice was hard to block out. It was

strange to miss the other werewolf, considering all the times he'd been ready to kill Liam himself. In the end, Liam's death was just another responsibility that Randolph had allowed to slip from his grasp. But those irresponsible days were over. The Breaking Moon had risen, imbuing all of the Full Bloods gathered at the source of the Torva'ox with more power than they'd ever tasted. Those primal energies now flowed freer than ever, and it was Randolph's intention to find out who among his brethren would put them to use. Then, the Skinners would be dealt with.

For too long he had tried to keep everyone in check. When the Skinners were poised to claim weaponry that would tip the balance in their favor, he was there to take it away from them. When Liam threatened to draw too much ire or shed too much blood, he was there to see it didn't go too far. But no matter how much he tried to rein things in, they spiraled even further out of control.

Not everything's s'posed to be controlled, Liam reminded him, either from memory or beyond the grave.

Perhaps that was true, but he had already given up trying to control things. Ever since he caught the scent of the First Deceiver, Randolph had known there was one last opportunity to set his new homeland back onto its proper course. Kawosa roamed free, opening geysers of the Torva'ox in his wake and imbuing his precious Half Breeds with new strengths, like a craftsman tinkering with a favorite line of toys. Kawosa had one more purpose to serve, and when that was done, there would finally be quiet.

No more humans with their arrogant voices and filthy machines.

No more wretches with their wild, pained cries.

No more Mongrels tunneling and sneaking in the dark.

No more leeches strutting and preening like spoiled children.

Just pure, natural, blissful quiet.

A quiet the world hadn't known for over a thousand years.

Chapter One

St. Louis, Missouri

Paige stood on a highway overpass, wrapped in two T-shirts, a tactical vest, and a light jacket, all of which was all topped off by an olive drab canvas coat that came down to her knees and was tied shut with an old belt. It was just past sundown, and the wind tore across the Mississippi River to become even colder than when it had started rustling on the other side. In the distance, car horns honked and tires screeched across slippery roads that were even more poorly tended now that the salt trucks had been attacked by a large pack of Half Breeds. That alone wasn't enough to call in the heavy artillery, but the Full Blood sighted by the scouts across the border in Cahokia, Illinois, raised all the red flags needed to bring the Skinners there.

"How many times do I have to clean this place out?" she grumbled while checking one of the many handguns strapped beneath her arms or clipped to the mesh belt holding her coat together.

The man lying on the shoulder of the overpass might have gone completely unnoticed by a casual observer if he hadn't shifted on his stomach and scraped his legs against the ground. His back was covered by a thin layer of snow that blew off him like ash. He twisted around to prop himself up on his elbow so he could look up at her. “Wasn’t just you the last time, you know.”

Paige lifted a pair of compact binoculars to her eyes and scowled through them. “Yeah, right, Cole. I also know that you and Rico spent a lot of time at strip bars or in jail. Real productive. Still beats Chicago at this time of year. Sometimes there’s barely any snow around here. Everyone used to panic at the first sign of a flake. One time,” she chuckled, “there were school closings because the forecast was for it to be cold. Wasn’t cold yet. Just forecasted to be cold. Wish it was that easy to get out of class when I was going to school.”

“Little Paige Strobel in her pigtails and backpack. Mmmm.” Cole’s thoughts were cut short by a quick thump of Paige’s boot against his ribs. He could barely feel the blow through his two flannel shirts and T-shirt but wasn’t about to ask for a follow-up shot. Even if she’d put some real mustard behind the blow, his outermost layer would have absorbed it on its own. The long coat he wore was tailored from strips of Full Blood hide and allowed him to shrug off direct shotgun blasts. It was confiscated from him when he was taken into custody, but had recently been returned, thanks to some impressive connections in the official chain of command.

“Look sharp,” Paige announced. “Your boy’s headed for the river.”

Cole stretched out one arm to support the rifle that was held steady by a collapsible stand situated near the edge of the overpass, giving the smooth black barrel of the Brown Precision Tactical Elite plenty of clearance above the snow. The rest of the sniper rifle was coated in a similar black Teflon finish, so only the lenses of the scope would reflect anything from the few functioning streetlights in the area. He gazed through the scope and gripped the rifle behind the trigger so he could slowly pan along the nearby shoreline.

They were on the outskirts of downtown, with the Gateway Arch to their left and several layers of highway overpasses behind them. Not long ago there had been more riverboats connected to illuminated piers. Most were casinos and the rest were restaurants or tourist traps. One of the casinos was still open and even had a good crowd inside. The restaurants were open as well, but not doing a lot of business. In the months following the Breaking Moon, people were still willing to make the occasional attempt at a normal life no matter what else was going on. Still, even for a cold winter night, St. Louis was close to deserted.

"I don't . . . wait a second," Cole said. "Now I see him. Look at that guy move!"

Below the overpass were several low buildings and a wide expanse of parking lots normally used for busy summer days, festivals, or to contain overflow from sporting events. Since the werewolves had claimed the streets, open spaces that backed onto walls or the river were avoided at all costs. Because of that, the figure running from the direction of the arch had nobody to get in his way and only a few derelict cars to vault over as he dashed toward the water. Light from the highway and riverboats gave the snow a dim glow that radiated up to the night sky. When the figure hit the ground and spun around to glance toward the overpass, Cole lifted a hand over his head and waved without taking his eyes from the scope. "Hey, Frankie."

"He doesn't like being called that," Paige reminded him.

"That's why I didn't say it too loud. How many is he bringing to the party?"

She lowered herself to one knee beside and slightly behind him, sighting through the binoculars until she spotted several shapes rustling through the shadows. "Four. Maybe five. They're coming straight for him."

Frank was a Squamatosapien, and like most Lizard Men, didn't enjoy the cold. It wasn't his natural habitat, but he wasn't about to curl up and die after being caught too far away from Florida during the winter months. His heavier breathing and steps might have cut down on his sneaking ability, but the steely chill in the air added fuel to his fire when he ran. Like any other Squam, he could cover plenty of ground in a short amount of time and wasn't hampered by the dark.

Through his scope, Cole could see the vaguely luminescent sheen on Frank's eyes as his tear ducts squirted a substance onto his eyeballs that allowed him to see scents. After snapping his head around to catch sight of the Half Breeds, the Squam crouched down and drew his entire body into a compact bundle. He waited for the last second before exploding in a flailing tangle of arms and legs that extended just a bit farther than human proportions. The moment his first toe touched the ground again, his legs aligned for a perfect landing and his arms swung at his sides to preserve his momentum.

The Half Breeds tore past a squat rectangular building at the edge of one lot that had been used to sell parking passes, then put Frank in their sights, fanning out so two could dart ahead and another three could scramble over a chain-link fence surrounding the lot. The werewolves were moving erratically to swarm around the lot and building, and their target allowed his head to hang in a classic submission gesture that sent a message to any animal with a predatory lineage. Since Half Breeds were among the most powerful predators out there, he knew they would take a straight run at him as soon as they got a clear field in front of them.

"Are those the new rounds?" Paige asked.

"Yep."

"Why aren't you firing yet?"

"Because I want a clean kill," Cole told her.

"You're not just going for head shots, are you?"

"No, ma'am."

"Are you just saying that to shut me up?"

"Yep."

Before Paige had a chance to fire back at that, Cole zeroed in on the Half Breed that looked to be the leader of the pack. Tracking so many of them over the months following the Breaking Moon, he'd come to recognize their behaviors with ease. Just as that creature was about to bark the command to charge, Cole released the breath he'd been holding and squeezed the trigger. The Brown Tactical bucked once against his shoulder and spat its round through the air. Not only was the rifle custom built to fire a .50 caliber round, but the bullets were lovingly crafted by the Skinners themselves.

Although Cole had spent plenty of time at firing ranges when researching the video game shooters he'd helped design, that experience paled next to the crash course he'd been given by the snipers of the Inhuman Response Division. Although refusing to become official members of the IRD, he, Paige, and a few other Skinners had signed on as specialists with the military fire teams assembled to deal with threats like werewolves and Nymar. As it turned out, his video game experience had sharpened his reflexes and eye-hand coordination, making him proficient with sniper rifles. Either that, he'd thought, or his instructor had been boosting his ego by telling him as much. For the moment, his skill level was high enough to put a round just behind the shoulder of the lead Half Breed.

Not only did the werewolf drop, but its front end slapped against the ground and skidded as being smeared against the cement by a cruel, invisible hand. Its front paws scraped the ground and its head twisted around to send a piercing wail through the air. The bullet that caused all the commotion was a Snapper round. Since Teflon-coated rounds could punch a hole through them that was too clean to put a Half Breed down, and hollow points would only flatten against their skin before penetrating, Rico had taken it upon himself to build Snapper rounds. They were Teflon-coated hollow points filled with a mixture of diluted fragments melted down from the Blood Blade. Initial impact triggered an internal support to collapse, which delayed the flattening of the hollow point just long enough for it to crack open after making it through a Half Breed's exceptionally tough hide. Then the round broke open with its titular *snap* and let the

Blood Blade infused poison flow. Combined with the innate punch of a .50 caliber round, it was enough to drop a Half Breed no matter where it hit. Unfortunately, due to the limited supply of the poison and the time it took to craft the rounds, Snappers weren't exactly standard issue.

Cole's mouth formed half of a small grin as he pulled back the lever to chamber the next round. While the other Half Breeds were looking around for the source of the shot, he took quick aim at a cluster of three and fired. It was a grazing shot that didn't allow the Snapper to do its thing, but produced a cool metallic explosion in the snow just past a werewolf's head.

"They're scattering," Paige said.

"Ready on the backup."

Hearing that through her earpiece, Paige dropped her binoculars and picked up an M-4 assault rifle without much of anything by way of special modifications. The overpass was about 250 meters from the Half Breeds, which put them within the weapon's effective range. As soon as Cole fired his third Snapper into the flank of a Half Breed, Paige pulled her trigger in a quick rhythm that sent the M-4 rounds sparking against concrete, thumping into snow, and clipping the occasional werewolf. Blood was spilled, but not nearly enough to put the creatures down. However, she'd accomplished her goal of scattering the creatures before they overwhelmed Frank, which also gave Cole a chance to shove three more rounds into his rifle.

"There's more on the way," Frank said through his matching earpiece.

"Stay put," Cole replied. "Just for two shots."

Without a single word in protest, Frank remained where he was and watched as the Half Breeds scrambled to regroup and charge at the only target they could see. Even from a distance it was obvious that the Squam was coiling for a burst of movement. His entire body compressed until the tips of his splayed fingers dipped beneath the snow like a lineman getting ready for the quarterback to snap the ball.

Rather than try to find a single body through his scope, Cole picked a spot between the Half Breeds and Frank. The Half Breeds were hungry and too riled up to try anything more sophisticated than a head-on run at their target. As soon as Cole spotted something at the lowest edge of his magnified line of sight, he exhaled and squeezed the trigger. By the time the Brown Tactical bucked against his shoulder, a Half Breed was charging across the center of his sights. The Snapper round punched a hole through the back of the creature's head, emptied the contents of its skull onto the ground and sent the werewolf skidding on its chest for another few feet. Cole opened his other eye so he could see the entire shoreline while retaining a hazy view through the scope. His next shot was taken quickly, using pure video game reflexes. His instructor would have slapped him on the back of the head for taking it, and Paige would have given him another jab for wasting a Snapper round, but none of that was necessary. His round tunneled into a Half Breed's shoulder, doing enough damage to send the creature spiraling onto its side as it headed toward Frank.

Now that the two shots had been taken, Frank sprang into action. He leapt straight into the air to avoid the last uninjured Half Breed and came down with one large foot on top of the one Cole had winged. Although they couldn't be seen from a distance, the Squam's nails sprouted into claws, which he drove in between the wounded Half Breed's ribs. The werewolf howled in pain as those claws sank home and the poison from the Snapper ripped through its system.

"You got that last one?" Paige asked.

Cole and Frank answered with a simultaneous, "Yeah."

She set her rifle down and picked up the binoculars. Within seconds she spotted the others Frank had warned them about earlier. "I see two more."

"Only two?" Cole asked. "No prob."

"No. Two more packs," Paige clarified. "One coming in from the arch and the other from those trailers."

Cole looked toward the Gateway Arch and spotted a cluster of werewolves moving along the Riverfront. The other pack was swarming over and around a row of trailers left there after a festival that marked the city of St. Louis's last attempt at conducting business as usual. The festival hadn't been the bloodbath some people predicted, but it was cut short when three people went through the Breaking less than two hours after the music started. They were gunned down before they could hurt anyone, the festival was cancelled, and the trailers set up to sell apple cider and caramel apples were left behind as temporary obstacles for the werewolves that came toward the Riverfront and veered off sharply before getting anywhere close to Frank.

"Shit," Cole grunted. "Frank, try to draw those things to you."

"What more do you want me to do?" the Squam replied as the surviving member of the first pack lunged at him again.

Cole fired his third round at the Half Breed, but only caused a burst of snow to explode within two feet of the creature. "The other packs aren't headed for you anymore. See if you can draw them away from those riverboats!"

The casino and restaurants were the main reason the Skinners were there. Despite added security to protect those who'd decided not to heed the countless warnings from local police and newscasters, packs of Half Breeds had claimed the Riverfront and killed dozens of people. Now, whether there were people in sight or not, the werewolves had become smart enough to know the boats were a perfect source for a quick meal.

After cursing incoherently into his transmitter, Frank leapt away from the Half Breed, dropped into a crouch as soon as he landed, then sprang forward into an even higher jump that carried him along the frozen bank of the river. He barely sounded winded when he said, "The others had better be close."

As soon as Cole was finished reloading, he found Frank through his scope and fired at the first hint of movement to come up behind the Squam. The Half Breeds had gathered too much steam, however, and his shot only caused another pretty pop in the snow. "Shit," he said while lowering the rifle and flipping the safety. "They're moving too fast for me to catch them."

"There's a big cluster behind Frank and to the left," Paige announced.

Cole's thumb flipped the safety off and he pressed his cheek to the rifle while keeping both eyes open. As soon as he found the group she was talking about, he sighted through the scope and fired two quick shots into the mass of fur and gnarled muscle. The Half Breeds scattered amid a series of grating yelps, leaving three of them behind. Two staggered and fell over, while the third hobbled and gnawed at a fresh wound in its flank that must have been put there by a round that went through one of the other two. Cole put it out of its misery with a shot straight through its face, which was a beauty to behold.

"I've got three Snappers left," he said. "Should I load 'em up?"

"Don't bother," Paige told him. "Listen."

A low rumble filled the air, which Cole could feel almost as much as hear. As the rumble became more rhythmic, a voice crackled over their earpieces.

"Raven One approaching. Targets in sight."

Seconds later a sleek helicopter roared over the Skinners' heads, then angled out toward the water. Cole saw that it was the same type of aircraft that had been brought down when he and Jessup had met up with Rico in New Mexico. After working more extensively with the IRD in recent months, he knew it was a modified NH90 Tactical Transport. It roared down to where most of the Half Breeds were gathered, hovering about twenty feet off the ground while a large barrel extended through the third window along the helicopter's curved frame.

"Frank, clear out!" Cole shouted almost loud enough for his message to make it to the Squam without the earpieces.

Frank skidded amid a spray of dirty snow, changed direction and started retracing his steps. The Half Breeds closest to him scrambled and adjusted their course as well. So far, none of the werewolves were paying any attention to the helicopter. Leaping over the Half Breeds, Frank cleared a path for the aircraft's gunner to open fire. The belt-fed machine gun sprayed hot lead onto the Riverfront, hitting more snow than Half Breeds as the helicopter swung around to keep the creatures from racing toward the riverboats anchored less than a block away. Rather than scatter again, the Half Breeds leapt up to sink their claws into the side of the helicopter.

"Can you take any of them out?" Paige asked as she watched the helicopter through her binoculars.

Cole looked through his scope but was having a hard time keeping the bobbing aircraft in view. "It'd be a wild shot. Even if I hit one of them, there's a chance I could punch through the helicopter."

"Shit. This is why we should always work up close," she grunted while packing up the few things she'd brought along. "I told these Army guys not to rely too heavily on guns, but do they listen to me? Nooooo!"

"So they *are* Army?" Cole asked while securing his rifle. "I still haven't gotten a straight answer on that."

"You know what I mean. Let's just get down there before somebody hits Frank."

The Skinners carried their equipment to a four-door car with Illinois plates. Since it wasn't a Cavalier, Paige didn't seem to care whether she drove it into a wall. Since it wasn't their old Cavalier, specifically, she barely seemed to care what model or make it was. Once their stuff was loaded, she climbed in behind the steering wheel and started the engine. The moment his back hit the seat, Cole was reaching for his safety belt.

Near the Riverfront, the chopping sound of the machine gun competed with the thumping of the helicopter's blades as Half Breeds barked and screamed up at the aircraft. Soon those sounds were joined by the screech of metal being peeled away and the whine of an engine straining to compensate for additional weight. Cole looked back and saw several werewolves dangling from the helicopter and kicking as they were lifted farther off the ground.

"They're trying to bring it down," he reported.

Paige shook her head and gritted her teeth while driving to a nearby off-ramp. "Of course they are. They always do. Why the hell do they make us give those stupid briefings if nobody listens to us about little things like how fast Half Breeds are or how high they can jump?"

"Because Adderson already thinks he knows everything?"

Most times, just hearing the name of the man in charge of the IRD was enough to make Paige's mood worse than usual. "Bingo," she said. "Keep them updated on what we're doing. Hopefully that'll keep them from shooting us."

"Raven One, this is Cole. Paige and I are driving down to the Riverfront."

When there was a long pause before he got his answer, Cole rolled his eyes and added, "Over."

"Maintain a safe perimeter until we clear these things out. Over."

"Frank's still down there!"

"I think they know where I am," Frank said through the earpiece. This time his voice was strained, which meant he must have been doing a lot more than running and jumping.

Cole didn't have to search for long before he spotted Frank hanging from the rear leg of a Half Breed that had embedded its claws into the lower edge of the chopper. After a few pulls and a couple sharp jabs from his claws, the Squam convinced the werewolf to let go so it could twist around to snap at him. He pushed away from it as soon as he started to fall. Both he and the Half Breed dropped toward the pavement, but only Frank was agile enough to turn in midair to land on his feet. The Half Breed thumped heavily on its side, and would have broken its legs if they hadn't already been snapped along with the rest of the bones in its body during its initial transformation. Despite the awkward landing, it flopped over and stood up so it could howl and roar along with the rest of the creatures.

"Come and get me," Frank hissed. "Now!"

It was tough to read expressions on a Squam's face or in a voice that sounded like two dry blocks rubbed together, but there was no mistaking Frank's urgency. Paige focused even harder on the road and swerved toward the Riverfront. The helicopter gunner unleashed a steady torrent of automatic fire that should have shredded the Half Breeds. Although some of the creatures fell and were subsequently hacked to pieces by the large caliber rounds, most of them were batted around and enraged by the insistent gunfire. Those were the newer breed that had thicker hides and matching sets of tusks protruding from upper and lower jaws. Paige steered directly toward them, knowing that Cole would brace himself for the inevitable impact. Before they got close enough to worry about scraping creatures off the windshield, the car's headlights splashed over a tall figure that landed in front of them.

Frank was dressed in thick canvas pants and several layers of thermal material that encased his body without doing much to hinder his movement. The headlights illuminated the pale yellow and tan scales covering his arms and glinted off of his darker yellow eyes. When Paige threw the car into a sideways skid, he moved back far enough to clear a path and then opened the rear passenger door to climb inside. "I think this is all we'll flush out tonight," he said, "but that gun won't kill them all."

"I know," Paige replied while slamming the car into a lower gear. She tore away and headed back to the ramp and onto the highway. Not only had the IRD set up roadblocks to keep the overpass clear, but the helicopter swung around to fire at the remaining Half Breeds until the wave of creatures moved away from the Skinners.

Even after the roadblock, traffic was light on I-64. Once

St. Louis and the river were behind them, Illinois stretched out ahead. A year ago Cole would have been glad to be back in the state where he'd spent the initial part of his career as Paige's partner. In more recent times, however, the two of them had wandered so much that it hardly felt as if they had a home anymore. What hit him even harder was that if they returned to Chicago, they wouldn't have anywhere to go. Rasa Hill was gone, and even Steph's Blood Parlor had been torched during the Nymar uprising that resulted in most Skinners being placed on federal and state Most Wanted lists.

After the events surrounding the Breaking Moon, Cole and Paige hadn't settled in one place long enough to call it home. The IRD provided them with quarters when they were close enough to a base within Adderson's jurisdiction. Every now and then Cole found himself thinking back wistfully to the weeks he'd slept in an old walk-in freezer at the condemned restaurant he'd only known as Rasa Hill. To this day he still wasn't certain if the faded lettering on the front of that building spelled Rasa or Raza.

"You are quiet," Frank said.

"I'm driving," Paige snapped.

The Squam pulled in a rasping breath. "You are always quiet. I meant Cole. Being silent this long usually means something's wrong."

Cole looked over to Paige, who seemed to have expected his glance. They didn't have to say a word to each other before she let out a heavy breath and nodded to him.

"Whatever you're thinking, you can say it to me," Frank told them. "I deserve that much for putting my life on the line as living bait for you and those soldiers."

"Not living bait," Paige told him. "Scout."

"Scouts run ahead and look for things," Frank grunted. "I have to dodge bullets and hang from helicopters."

"Scout plus?"

Although Frank's yellow eyes were covered by translucent

lids, they were still capable of conveying plenty of emotion. When Cole glanced back at the Squam, he could relate all too well to the frustration he saw in them.

"The answer to your next question is no," Cole told him. "Being with her never gets any easier."

Chapter Two

The IRD had their mobile outpost set up in Collinsville, which was a short drive from St. Louis. The outpost consisted of two large campers, three covered trucks, and two helicopters. By the time Paige parked between the campers, another helicopter was returning from the St. Louis Riverfront. Its machine gun had been pulled inside and the landing gear lowered so it could touch down and unload the three soldiers who had been riding inside. Judging by the spring in their step, the men hadn't left the helicopter to engage any Half Breeds. Although none of the higher ranking officers acknowledged Frank with more than a careful glare, the soldiers all sought him out so they could give him a grateful nod or wave. Frank's thin, reptilian lips curved into something of a smile when he accepted their show of respect.

Paige and Cole stood outside of the second camper, stomping their feet and enjoying the hot chocolate that had been served to them in a paper cup. It was a thin and watery mix, but Cole preferred it much better than the salty yellow water that was supposed to pass for chicken soup.

Not only was the wind brutally cold, but the sun had been down long enough for the smallest remnants of its light to have been long forgotten. Both Skinners stood in the bracing chill and turned their faces into the wind. Cole closed his eyes and savored the way his nose tingled and the wind whispered directly into his frosted ears. Embracing his humanity by reveling in the simpler things was a habit he'd picked up from Paige. One of the good ones.

"What's wrong with you two?" asked a man who stood in the doorway to one of the campers. "After all that's happening, you want to catch your death in the cold?"

"Be right in, Ma," Cole said.

The man who'd scolded them was somewhere in his early forties, dressed in heavy black and gray fatigues, his light brown hair buzzed down to a perfectly even layer. Although Cole had been clipping his hair to within an inch of its life, the shears he used paled in comparison to the fine military precision that marked Major Adderson's hair as well as everything else he wore, touched, or said. Obviously not threatened by the cold, Adderson scowled at the Skinners and stepped aside while propping the door open with the side of his boot.

Paige and Cole drank their hot chocolate until it was gone, but knew better than to make the major wait long before entering the camper. Inside, the vehicle had been stripped and refurbished with a row of computers and monitors along one side, several televisions bolted to the ceiling used to monitor national and local news broadcasts, and a communications setup on the other side. At the back of the confined quarters was a space that had probably contained a bed. Now there was a small square table with a built-in illuminated touch-sensitive screen. Mainly it was used to display maps and objectives for the various IRD operations in which Cole and Paige had taken part. As soon as the Skinners were inside, Adderson led them back to join the two men who sat there.

"This has been a long couple of days," the major said, "and we all look like hell."

Cole chuckled at that. Compared to Adderson, he and Paige always looked like hell.

Paige crumpled up her paper cup and tossed it into a small

receptacle that Cole hoped was a trash can. "If you guys want our help with these things, you gotta start listening to us!" she declared.

Adderson eased down onto a little stool bolted to the floor and sighed, "Do we, now?"

"Yes. Someone could have been killed. Just ask your pilot."

A skinny young man wearing dark khakis and a baseball cap arched his back to work out a kink. Although the cap bore a Marine Corps emblem, the rest of his uniform was marked only by his rank on one shoulder and an IRD patch on the other. The Inhuman Response Division's insignia was a half skull and half wolf's head beneath crossed assault rifles on a field quartered into red and gray sections surrounded by a gold rope. The letters IRD were stitched on one side, and USA stitched on the other. "I don't know what mission you were on," he said, "but I wasn't about to crash."

"What about when that Half Breed clamped onto your helicopter?"

"That's in my report, lady."

"I'm sure it was. I'm not trying to call you out on anything. Just tell me one thing."

Although Paige had made her intentions clear, the pilot still eyed her as if she were doing her best to get him in trouble in front of his boss. "I bet I can tell you plenty of things, honey."

"Hendricks!" Adderson barked.

The pilot nodded toward his commanding officer and then met Paige's eyes when he said, "I mean . . . ma'am."

Paige walked up to the pilot, stood toe-to-toe with him and then leaned her chin forward just enough to make it seem she might try to bite his nose off. "Tell me how high a Class Two shifter can jump."

When Hendricks looked over to Adderson, all he got was a steely glare. Shifting his eyes to Paige, he said, "Approximately five to six meters."

"That's what you were told when we made that first run into Nevada," she replied. "It was wrong then and it's still wrong now! Cole and I have told you as much as we can, but you still stick to your same damn guidelines."

"We're working on definitive profiles of all of these creatures," Adderson said. "Your input is appreciated, but it's not consistent. Until we can lock in some parameters for what we're dealing with, we'll work with the knowledge we have."

"Aren't you supposed to be able to deal with new intelligence as it comes in?" Paige asked.

"Sure, but when it changes according to who's giving it, we have to take it with a grain of salt. Would you like to debate this further or shall we continue with the debrief?"

After shooting a disgruntled look in Cole's direction, she crossed her arms, leaned against one of the monitors and allowed the soldiers to continue. For the next several minutes the pilot and crew from the helicopter gave their reports on what happened at the Riverfront. Then it was Cole and Paige's turn to let them know what they did as far as the Half Breeds were concerned. When that was done, Adderson wrapped up by clapping his hands against the table and declaring, "We were called in to get a good idea as to how many Class Twos were positioned near the Riverfront and that's what we did. Correct?"

Reluctantly, Paige nodded.

"Don't give us the silent treatment, Miss Strobel. Is that what we did or isn't it?"

"Yeah," she replied. "Half Breeds aren't exactly hard to find. Considering how the balance has shifted over the last few months, it's tough to say what's going on. Cole and I seriously need to get out there and see what's happening so we can pass on some better information to you guys."

"How do you propose to do that?"

Every eye was focused on Paige. Most of the soldiers respected what they did and had a good idea as to what they could offer, but they mainly treated the Skinners as just another thing that had gone wrong with the ecosystem.

"We could use some funding for supplies and weapons," she said. "Maybe some transport to—"

"Our funding is limited as is," Adderson cut in. "If you'd like to sign on as official members of the IRD, you'd have access to transportation as well as resources, including provisions and weaponry."

"We don't need your weaponry," Cole said. "If anything, you need ours."

"What's that mean?" Hendricks asked. "Unless you missed it, we dusted plenty of those dogs tonight."

"Shooting them is one thing," Cole retorted, "killing them is another. Haven't you realized that by now? They can take a lot of damage and shake it off unless you stick around to do the job right." Recognizing the cocky glint in the pilot's eye, he added, "And in case you missed it, I was dropping those things with one shot."

"Enough, Cole," Paige hissed.

"This isn't bragging, Paige. It's fact. These guys act like they're the big men on the block, but we're the ones that have been doing this since before anyone knew what a Half Breed was. And it *is* a Half Breed! Not Class One, Two, Three, Four, or Ten! When we shoot one of those things, it stays down. For every one or two you guys chop up with a thousand rounds fired from a helicopter, you're letting six or seven sneak around to flank you. Half Breeds aren't the smartest, but even they know how to take advantage of an opening when you give it to them."

"Now that you mention it," Adderson said, "some upgrade to our ammunition would be outstanding. I'm sure you could arrange that."

Paige's elbow jabbed Cole's ribs like the business end of a stake.

Adderson slowly approached the Skinners. "I'm sure I don't have to tell you how valuable those rounds would be if they were placed in the hands of one of our elite fire teams. In fact, I believe we could have wiped out every last shifter on that Riverfront. Wouldn't you agree?"

"Maybe, but we can't exactly mass produce those things," Cole explained.

"Perhaps we could. That is, unless you're refusing to help outfit the IRD with supplies that could be considered vital to our long-term success."

So far, despite the suspicion leveled at them by the uniformed soldiers and the constant pressure to sign up with the IRD on a long-term basis, Cole had been proud to serve with them. He couldn't help but feel ashamed when he said, "I can't do that."

"Can't do what?"

"Can't promise more of those rounds. Rico was the one who put them together, and he—"

"Fine," Adderson grunted. "Any more to report?" Since nobody spoke up in the fraction of a second he gave them, the major said, "Then get back to your duties. I want to have a word with our specialists."

There wasn't much space within the camper, but the five soldiers who remained in it sat at workstations or stood in front of monitors as if they were the only things left in their world.

"Walk with me," Adderson said as he led the way outside. Cole and Paige followed him to a spot several paces from any of the other soldiers. The major fished a cigarette from a pack he'd pulled from his breast pocket and lit it with a Zippo.

"Does that thing have the IRD symbol on it?" Cole asked as he nodded toward the lighter. "If so, I want one."

Smirking around the cigarette clamped between his teeth, Adderson held the lighter to show the hula girl engraved on its side. "Sorry, Cole. I can probably have one made up for you if you decide to sign up for the long haul."

"We are in it for the long haul, sir. Couldn't you even throw us one of those patches?"

"Collector, huh?"

"How about a T-shirt?" Paige asked as she rubbed her arms. "Or maybe some action figures? Any other way you guys want to market a supposedly secret organization?"

"Identification is all it is," Adderson told her. "A man needs to know he's part of a unit, and the higher-ups need to be able to identify that unit with a glance. Goes all the way back to . . ." He puffed on the cigarette and shrugged. "Hell, I don't know. Goes back a long ways."

"Plus it looks cool," Cole said.

"That it does."

Although Paige was clearly freezing, she stepped away from the heat spilling out of the vehicles so she could lower her voice when she said, "We can't continue with these hit and run things."

"Agreed. When was the last time you've seen a Class One?"

"A Full Blood? Not since Atoka."

That was a lie and Cole knew it. The last time they'd seen a Full Blood was in Finland when they squared off with Liam. He still had nightmares about just how many times he'd almost been killed that night. Once the adrenaline wore off, it wasn't so easy to say if he'd acted bravely or with extreme stupidity.

"That town is still being held by one of those things," Adderson said. "One of our teams reported one major sighting before we lost contact. From what you've told us and from what we've observed, it seems that those Class Ones are controlling the Class Twos."

"The Full Bloods are creating the Half Breeds," Paige said. "That's how it's always been. Only now they're creating Half Breeds without having to attack and infect each and every victim. The range for that seems to be between a quarter and an eighth of a mile. I told you this when we first agreed to work together."

Adderson wheeled so quickly around to face her that Cole almost grabbed for the spear strapped to his back. Paige was surprised as well, but kept her instincts in check before they got her shot by at least half a dozen Marines.

"We're not working 'together,'" Adderson said. "You two work for me."

"Is that how it is?"

"After all I've done to cover your asses and keep the rest of you Skinners out of the fire where the police, FBI, and ATF are concerned, yes. You'd damn well better believe that's how it is." His next words slid out of him like the cigarette smoke curling from his nostrils. "If you'd sign up with us in an official capacity, then you would of course be assigned a rank and could command specialized troops to help you in any number of missions that you would design."

"Why are you so intent on getting us to sign up?" Cole asked. "Do you get some sort of bonus?"

"Honestly, I'd be able to command this entire team more efficiently. I'd also be able to explain to my superiors why I'm bringing along civilians on highly classified military operations. Funny how the brass tends to get real picky about procedure when the rest of the world is sliding into hell, but if we turn to anarchy, then the whole game's over."

"So you are a recognized branch of the military," Paige said.

Despite the attack helicopters, campers stuffed full of high-tech equipment, Marines and Army personnel behind him, Adderson somehow managed to keep a straight face when he told her, "I'm not able to confirm or deny that."

Shaking her head, Paige said, "He wants to be able to tell us where to go and what to do, Cole. More than that, he wants to study our weapons and probably us as well. Didn't you have your chance when you had Cole on the operating table?"

"He was taken from our facility before we could make an incision."

Those words alone were enough to make Cole's gut clench. More specifically, the memory of what was wrapped around his gut made him clench. The Nymar tendrils were still there, but he'd learned to deal with the cinching pain reflexively tightening around him. He felt better after some rest, but it was still easier if he just didn't think about the part of him that had been infected by the vampire spore.

"And speaking of that procedure," Paige said, "you guys

never did get around to making good on your promise of fixing him up."

"That's all right," Cole said. "Forget it."

"Which is exactly what he told our medics when they approached him to undergo the next proposed operation," Adderson pointed out while holding his cigarette between two fingers and watching the tip smolder.

She looked back and forth between them and finally flapped her hands against her sides. "All right. Fine. You're the one that called us out here, Major. What's on your mind?"

"I asked about the Class Ones because we seem to have lost track of them," Adderson said.

After somehow walking away from being encased in stone, the Full Blood named Esteban had kept himself busy by returning to Colorado and tearing apart two small towns and three correctional facilities in his quest to find more storehouses left behind by Jonah Lancroft. All he'd managed to do back then was create several dozen Half Breeds to keep the humans busy and level the town of Canon City.

"We need a better way to get to those bastards," Adderson said. "Do you have any ideas?"

Although Paige only paused for a few seconds, Adderson bristled as if she'd turned her back to him and walked away. Finally, she said, "There was a weapon called the Blood Blade. It could cut through a Full Blood well enough. We've been working on a way to coat a bullet with melted fragments of it."

"Similar to what's inside those Snapper rounds?"

"That's right. We've had some success, but haven't had a chance to test them in the field."

"With all the wolves running around, you haven't had a chance to test them?" Adderson asked.

"Things have been messy lately," she replied.

That was an understatement. Even with the werewolves running loose, the Skinners had been thrown into disarray with the emergence of the splinter group called the Vigilant.

Professing to subscribe to the beliefs of Jonah Lancroft—known for capturing specimens, chopping them apart over the course of months or years, and mixing up toxins that killed almost as many civilians as monsters all in the name of survival—the Vigilant redefined the term "hardcore." Since Adderson wasn't privy to insider Skinner business, "messy" would have to cover it.

Adderson grinned around his cigarette. "You seem to be losing sight of the whole reason I wanted you people on board. You have the know-how, and we have the manpower and equipment to put that knowledge to work. In exchange for that—"

"No," Paige said sharply, but politely. "We're not signing on to become official military."

"What's your problem with the military?" Adderson asked. "Your daddy in the service and he moved you around too much?"

"We're working with you to get through a tough time. We're not going to hand over everything we are to the government. *Any* government."

"Fine. Believe it or not, that wasn't even what I was going to ask. We've already put together something that should bring the shifters to us. Class Ones and Twos."

"Uh-huh," Paige sighed.

Surely, Cole thought, she was thinking along the same lines as he was: that somebody in the IRD had gotten their hands on one piece of the Amriany device that was used as Full Blood bait in Atoka.

"What do you mean 'should' be able to bring them to us?" Paige asked.

"It's a sonic emitter," the major explained. "Experimental. Works on a frequency that's had some success with the Class Twos. It didn't take a whole lot of tweaking for us to find the frequency for Class Threes."

Getting sick of the cold, Cole summed it up: "So you guys made a dog whistle for Half Breeds and Mongrels?"

"More or less. When cranked up to a certain degree on

test subjects, it seemed to produce some pain." Adderson gripped his cigarette between two fingers, exhaled some smoke and watched it drift up to the frozen stars. "After collecting enough data, we may be able to have a weapon capable of neutralizing these things before more drastic measures become necessary."

"All right," Paige said. "Two questions. First of all, what test subjects?"

"Just some Class Twos we trapped here and there. Despite some differences between the ones that have tusks and the ones that don't, they all seem to have the same ears."

"Second," she growled, "what do you consider to be drastic measures?"

Flicking his cigarette to the ground and stomping it out, Adderson said, "Tactical nukes have been proposed for portions of the country that are overrun, but will only be approved in the event that such areas become complete losses."

"You mean no humans left?" Cole asked. He chuckled more out of discomfort than any sense of humor when he pointed out, "We're still a long ways from that."

"Zero human population is well beyond what we'd consider to be a total loss," Adderson said. "We're looking more at the logistical certainty that we couldn't retake those areas without having to level everything from buildings to shrubbery. We all know that Class Twos move too quickly for air strikes to be effective unless we hit an area at least five times larger than normal. So far, no strikes have had any success against Class Ones. According to spotters, they hear or smell the planes coming and are gone long before the pilots see their target."

"So you want us to do something with those sonic things of yours?" she asked.

"Field testing. We need someone who can track those things down or at least get close enough to test its effectiveness as a viable option in a combat scenario. Seeing as how you know these things so well, you're the ideal choice."

"Plus," Cole said, "we don't have to roll in using helicopters and RVs."

Adderson glanced back at the modified campers and nodded. "You got it."

"Will you be sending anyone along with us?" Paige asked.

"Not unless you'd like it that way."

"Will you be following us?"

"I doubt we could do so without your knowledge," Adderson replied.

"What about satellite tracking?" Cole asked. "Electronic surveillance. Planting any GPS devices on us. That sort of thing."

The major wasn't the sort to twitch when someone struck a nerve, but the pause that followed that question, compared to the snap response he'd given them before, told Cole more than enough. "I'll see to it that no such devices are planted on you. As far as satellite tracking goes, the military's expense account is taking a big enough hit just mobilizing to respond to those new reports across the border."

"You're talking about those attacks in Brazil?" Paige asked, referring to a story that had found its way into the headlines over the last few days. Apparently, creatures resembling Half Breeds had been creeping in from the Amazon jungle led by a Full Blood that didn't match any others photographed over the past few months.

"Correct. With everything escalating the way it has, you can't even imagine the requests we're getting from other countries for assistance."

"How many other countries?" Cole asked.

"I'm not at liberty to divulge those details to civilian contractors," Adderson said, without even trying to be subtle in his constant effort to recruit them. "Let's just say that the U.S. is on the map for the majority of instances that have been made public, but there are plenty more leaking into public awareness from across the globe. Whatever these things are, wherever they came from, they're obviously not contained within American borders. That's what makes it even more pressing to create a more effective way of dealing with them that falls short of melting down or blasting apart large sections of civilian structures and population."

With that, Cole was given a glimpse at why Paige must have agreed to sign on with the IRD in any capacity.

"Fine," she said. "Count us in. Where do we pick up this sonic thing?"

"A mobile version is being put together now," the major said. "I'll have it prepped and ready to go by 0600."

"That's six in the morning, right?" Cole grumbled.

"Affirmative," Adderson said with a sadistic grin.

"We could use some more clothes, some guns, supplies, and a vehicle," Paige said. "Plus some money would be nice since we're probably going to be on our own for a while. It'll take a few days just to get the smell of all this equipment off us."

"What are you talking about?"

"These things track by scent," she told him. "Anything from gun oil, gasoline, to boot polish stands out from the norm. And we've also got to assume that they'll probably see us long before we see them. Look, I can't tell you any of that is certain, but if you want us to do you any good, we need to work our own way. And if you don't trust us to do that, then we're no good to you whether we get to wear the cool patch or not."

Adderson thought that over and nodded. "All right. We've got weapons and ammunition, as well as a few changes of clothes for you. As to the rest, we should be able to scrape something up by morning. Is that good enough or should we air drop it in a field somewhere so you're not seen with us?"

"Where could you drop it?"

The major's tired grin wavered and dropped off. Apparently, he'd already been around Paige long enough to know when she wasn't kidding. "We're not air dropping anything, but if you have to play it that way, we can leave it at a secure location of your choice."

"Perfect," she said with a nod. "I'll write up a list. You can leave it a few miles from here and we can pick it up after you guys roll out. You were planning on leaving soon, right?"

"You know damn well we were scheduled to move our mobile command into Kansas to check on those pack animals you told us about. The Shunkaws?"

"Yep, and you guys shouldn't have any trouble clearing them out. Remember, they like sugar. They're tough, but bullets should bring them down just fine."

Seeing he wasn't going to get any further with her than that, Adderson nodded and turned on his heels to step back into the main camper. When Paige started walking toward the open area, away from everyone else, Cole followed her.

"Whatever vehicle they give us, we'll need to check it from top to bottom just to make sure it wasn't bugged with a tracking device," he said.

"Bugged? Too many movies."

"No, there's about a dozen ways to get the job done using crap you can buy online or at Best Buy. I don't even want to think about what the military could come up with. Actually, since the IRD may be some sort of shadow organization, we should probably insist on renting a car using their cash."

She bent her right arm across her body and rubbed it with her left hand. The injury she'd sustained in Kansas City had been improving ever since she was able to reform her weapons properly. "You really get off on the whole shadow organization thing, don't you?"

"I guess. I've written games about them for years and now I'm in one."

"You're a civvie. Don't forget that. And as far as the whole car thing goes, we only need to drive it around long enough to make sure we're not being followed. After that, we're outta here."

"Outta where?"

"Here," she said, as if the ground itself had become inhospitable. "Away from these people."

"But you're the one that signed up with them."

"That was out of necessity. The way things were headed, military involvement was going to happen whether we liked it or not. At least Adderson seems to be going about it the right way, but this isn't the way Skinners are supposed to operate. I was hoping they might be able to get some surgeons who could help you with your problem."

"I've got vampire tendrils wrapped around my guts," Cole reminded her with a tired chuckle. "That's not exactly the sort of thing you go to the emergency room for."

"I know. It was worth a shot."

"That's not the only reason you started all of this, is it?"

Paige stuffed her hands into her pockets and whispered, "All of this was happening already. Adderson approached me with this whole IRD thing already in place. With everything getting too big to hide anymore, it made sense to help those who looked like they had the best chance of succeeding."

"In the words of the great and wise Daffy Duck, if you can't beat 'em . . . join 'em."

She shook her head. "I thought they could help you, Cole. At the very least, I knew they could get you away from all of those cops who just wanted to string you up after we were framed for all of those cops who were killed by the Nymar."

"You don't have to explain yourself anymore, Paige. I get it." Dropping his voice, he asked, "Where do you want to go once we ditch these guys?"

"We'll field test their sonic thingie somewhere along the line, but I don't think that's going to turn the tide. I think we need to get back to basics and tackle this problem the best way we can. No helicopters. No fire teams. Leave all that for the mopping up."

"What happened to that thing that was in Cecile's arm?" Cole asked. "The Jekhibar. It was important enough for two Full Bloods to hide and another to tear up an entire state looking for it. Do we even know what it's supposed to do?"

"Never got a chance to find out, but there's at least one guy who does know. Didn't Jessup tell you he had it?"

"Yeah. When I talked to him after the Breaking Moon set, he said Cecile was more than happy to get it out of her and that he and the rest of that Lancroft cult had it. The Vigilant."

"That's them. We need to check them out, and we sure as hell can't afford to get close right now. They'll be looking for it after Jessup announced his involvement with them in New Mexico."

"You think Rico's really turned on us?" Cole asked.

"You heard it yourself, didn't you?"

"Yeah, but maybe he's just looking for another way to do things. Just because he's decided to tackle this apocalypse thing a different way than us doesn't mean he's an enemy."

"Apocalypse, huh?" she scoffed. "You've been listening to the news again."

"You've been with Rico longer than I have. Are you telling me you don't trust him just because he decided to tackle the Full Bloods from a more aggressive angle? That's not exactly out of his normal play book."

Paige drew a long breath and chewed on it for a few seconds. It emerged from between her lips in a thin mist as she said, "There's another avenue we've got that I think even the Vigilant won't have, that is unless Lancroft had more foreign contacts than anyone ever thought."

"The Amriany," Cole said, being careful not to mention the name loud enough for it to catch any attention.

"They made the Blood Blades and I'm pretty sure they made the Jekhibar. If they don't have answers about how we can deal with Full Bloods that can create Half Breeds with nothing more than a howl, then maybe we can at least get some more weaponry."

"And if we're going to approach them, I should see what I can learn from the guys around here in regards to what's going on in Europe. Perhaps those satellites picked up Full Bloods, Half Breeds, or some other bit of craziness that the Amriany don't know about yet. Information like that could be one hell of a bargaining chip."

She nodded and rubbed his shoulder. "I have taught you well, young one."

Cole put his hands on her hips and pulled her in close. Before she had a chance to react, he planted a kiss on her that made them both forget about the winter's chill.

"What was that for?" she asked after finally pulling away.

"Seems like we're gonna be busy," he replied. "Just thought I should enjoy the quiet while it lasts."

"You know me. Quiet never lasts very long."

Chapter Three

Sauget, Illinois

The car they'd been given was a two-door, brown Chevy that was so nondescript it might as well have had "Unmarked Vehicle" stenciled on the bumper near the government plates. Paige laughed to herself when she saw it, but didn't waste much more breath on it than that. They didn't intend on driving very far, so it didn't really matter if anyone tracked them. Both of them wore comfortable cargo pants that had been worn into a second skin during all of the time they spent with the IRD. Other than that, Paige wore a dark blue jersey that was so old that its Bears logo was almost invisible. Her hair had been recently trimmed and pulled into a neat tail that brushed against the nape of her neck. Cole looked about the same as always. As far as clothing went, all that had changed was the design on his T-shirt. Today, he wore one depicting the first screen of Donkey Kong.

"When did they reopen this place?" he asked while leaning forward to get a better look into the glare of early morning sun.

Paige pulled to a stop in front of a small club marked by a tall diamond-shaped sign that read, THE EMERALD. "This place wasn't closed during the Mud Flu," she reminded him. "That was Bunn's Lounge. Get that straight before you go in to talk to the management."

"It's not Christov, is it?"

"Sure is."

"Oh," Cole grumbled. "Thanks for the reminder."

They exited the car carrying the bags of gear they'd collected and walked across a nearly deserted parking lot. Even McDonald's didn't have a breakfast rush anymore, which made Cole wonder if the world truly had come to an end. Before they got close enough to knock on the tinted glass of the front door, the shade of a smaller window was pulled aside so a bald man with skin the color of a fish's belly and forward-folded ears could look outside and jab a finger toward the side of the building.

"You told him we were coming, right?" Cole asked.

"Yeah. Why do you think he looks so pissed off?"

He was still laughing at that when the side door was opened by a shapely redhead dressed in flannel pajama pants and a sweatshirt cut to show about a millimeter of her smooth, flat stomach. Since she was a nymph, she made that ensemble look better than ice cream on top of a freshly heated brownie. "Hi guys, come on in."

"Hello, Kate," Cole said, fondly remembering her instantly, even though it had been more than seven months since he laid eyes on her. If only for that reason, it seemed like a harsh winter. The nymph smiled and stepped aside, allowing the Skinners to enter the club as another set of stomping footsteps rushed to meet them.

"You are not welcome here!" Christov said. He was flanked by two young bouncers who looked just as disheveled as he did. Between the three of them, they probably hadn't gotten more than twenty minutes sleep since squaring away the club after the previous night's business.

"We're only passing through," Paige said.

"Then why can't you do it during business hours, eh?" Although bloodshot, his eyes were sharp enough to gleam after waggling back and forth between Cole and Paige. "See? I don't forget. Last time you came, it was to get information about a killer. The next night, my club is infected with the Mud Flu, my customers are tearing it to pieces, and monsters are kicking down my door."

When Cole tried to interrupt, he was cut off by a swiftly upraised hand that moved as if to erase him from existence. *"And,"* Christov continued, "not long after that disaster, my beautiful club is closed down by the state health board."

"But you got another one," Paige said while extending her arms. "All is right with the world."

"No! All is not right. I am still paying off debts I got while buying out former owner of this dump. Now I must try to build it up to something half as good as Bunn's."

"All we need is to talk with Kate here," Paige said. "Then we'll be gone."

"Gone, as in . . ." Christov waggled his fingers in the same way he would to make a coin magically disappear from beneath a handkerchief.

"Right," Paige said. "Gone like that."

"What about your car? I'm not running some kind of garage."

"It's yours," she told him. "Might want to check it over before you use it. It's government issue but I doubt anyone will be looking for it."

"Stolen?" Christov asked, a hint of admiration showing in his eyes.

"No, but strip it for parts, swap the plates, do whatever you like. If anyone comes around asking for it, tell them we stopped by to partake in the buffet and left it here for safekeeping."

"There is still a buffet, right?" Cole asked.

"Of course," Christov huffed. "What kind of a place you think I am running? Fine. Leave the car and have your talk with Kate. If you like, I can get you a drink on the house. Only one."

"Pass on the drink," Paige said as she stepped inside.

The wind seemed especially cold as it blew across Cole's face. He turned his back to the outside world, walked inside and allowed the heavy door to slam shut behind him. The Emerald wasn't a large club and it sure wasn't a deluxe one. It was, however, much different than the last time he and Paige had been there. Apart from an additional stage, there was a longer bar, a larger section curtained off as a VIP area, and bigger speakers bolted to the ceiling. At the moment there was only a pair of smaller bouncers turning the chairs right side up in preparation for the lunch customers.

Kate and Christov had taken Paige to the storage room behind the bar. Although it was the same room that was used as a temporary Dryad temple a while ago, there had been plenty of changes since then. First of all, the walls, floor, and bar were covered with Dryad glyphs that were either painted or burned into surfaces until they looked as if they'd been there since the wooden planks were cut from the forest. It wasn't until he was reaching out for the edge of the door leading into the storage room that Cole noticed an illuminated sign hung up behind the bar that looked like a beer advertisement with a few glyphs worked into the background.

"You will pay for this!" Christov shouted.

Tensing his muscles in preparation for a fight, Cole stormed into the back room and asked, "What's the problem now?"

"The bridge to Louisville," Paige explained. "He wants us to pay for it. A hundred bucks."

"Seems reasonable, considering how much you save in time and gas or plane ticket," Christov said.

Seeing the scowl on both Skinners' faces, Kate said, "It's not too big of a jump. We've got the energy stored up."

"You are *my* employees!" Christov barked. "Times are rough and I must make a living. Do you know how much I needed to spend to get this place up and running properly? Do you have any idea how expensive it is to turn this building into an A-frame?"

"Plus all that purple paint, huh?" Cole scoffed.

The bald man turned as if he was about to take a swing at him. "You're damn right. I don't care what else is going on outside, I have a business to run. I have seen wars in other countries and life must still go on. The people who aren't fighting or dying must still struggle to pay for food and electricity just like before. Only now they must do so while waiting to hear about the next battle or get a call about the next person they know who is dead. I have to make ends meet and now it is harder than ever!"

Cole looked at Paige and asked, "What's the problem?"

"I only have fifty bucks on me."

He dug into his pocket and came up with a few twenties. "We've got ninety between us," he said while extending a hand with the cash in it. "Can't the rest be counted as the car?"

"I was keeping the car in mind." Christov's gaze drifted to the weapons strapped to Cole's back and the ones holstered in Paige's boots. "Why are you going to Louisville?"

"To meet up with some other Skinners who might know something about the creatures that have been tearing us all up."

"You are soldiers," he sighed. "Sometimes I forget. Go ahead and do what you need."

"How'd you come up with that figure anyway?" Cole asked.

Christov shrugged. "The energy my special girls collect is used for some of the regulars who pay top dollar."

"Yeah," Cole said as he slapped the twenties into Christov's hand. "I can only imagine. Hopefully this makes up for some of what you'll lose for not being able to put on one of those shows."

The bald man smiled and nodded. "It does, my friend. Plus, there is some purple paint to buy. Go with God."

"Appreciate it."

Once Christov and the bouncers were gone, Cole was finally able to appreciate the space that had been added to the makeshift temple. Before, the glyphs and beaded curtain marking the entrance to the bridge that allowed someone to instantly travel from one spot to another competed for space with piles of napkins and stacks of chairs. Now, after losing at least one wall, there was enough room for the three of them to stand comfortably with those same supplies piled up to the ceiling on either side of them.

"I'm sorry about him," Kate said. "Christov has been impossible after buying this place from the last owner. He seriously got reamed in that deal, but he's still fighting to rebuild this into a place half as good as the old Bunn's Lounge."

"Step one," Cole said with a grin, "go back to the old name. That's a classic."

"I agree," Kate replied. "I called ahead and there's a club in Louisville waiting for you. The only catch is that you'll need to be quiet about how you got into town. At least, you can't mention us. We're still trying to lay low since you guys are still technically fugitives. Don't you know anyone that can take care of that for you?"

"Sure," Paige grunted. "There's just some major league strings attached with that kind of favor, and our friend isn't ready to cut them just yet."

"Well I can't do anything about that request," Kate said apologetically. "It comes from Tristan herself."

However Dryad society was structured, Tristan was at the top. "How is she?" Cole asked. "I haven't heard from her since the fall of Atoka."

The touch of worry that drifted across Kate's face was like a cloud passing across the sun. "She's better, but still not very good. She had to channel some dark energies to do whatever she did that night and they took their toll."

"Is she sick?"

"Not sick, but not herself either." Kate put on a smile that was inspiring despite being shallow. "She'll be all right soon. Are you ready to go?"

Paige looked over to Cole and saw he had a few large bags hanging from his shoulders and a case in his hand. Picking up the gear she'd been carrying, she nodded and looked at the beaded curtain in front of her as if it was the door to an airplane terminal.

Like most Dryad temples, the room was covered in flowing, curved script that no Skinner had ever come close to deciphering. It was the handwritten equivalent of a tone hummed by an angel: pleasing to the eyes, even if those eyes couldn't tell what was being said. As an accompaniment to those glyphs, Kate arched her back and sang like a whisper drifting in from miles away. As far as Cole could tell, the songs used to activate the Dryad bridges were never the same. Without any real structure, they were simply expressions of the natural power flowing through every nymph. The symbols embedded in the walls and floor gave off a cool green glow that flowed into the archway from which the beads hung.

As soon as Cole and Paige stepped through them, it would take a lot more than digital tracking devices and satellite maps to figure out where they'd gone.

Chapter Four

Louisville, Kentucky

According to Jonah Lancroft, the biggest difference between Skinners and the rest of humanity was vigilance. That might have been a nice term for whatever it took for someone to voluntarily hunt down creatures that could tear through a human body like it was made of tissue paper. Ever since the Breaking Moon, more Skinners had been dropping off the map. Some openly mentioned a group called the Vigilant. Others who never mentioned the Vigilant by name made a point to spout off about how Skinners had lost their way, needed to follow old leaders and resurrect more traditional methods for these desperate times. Wherever he was, Lancroft was smiling.

Cole and Paige wound up at the Lariat Saloon just off of I-65. It was a quaint little place with an Old West motif stuck inside a purple A-frame within a stone's throw from the interstate. As soon as they stepped through the curtain, the Skinners got their bearings, accepted the greetings from the single nymph who'd opened that end of the bridge and arranged for a car they could use to make the short drive into town. Like most nymphs, Shelley had no shortage of regular customers who could provide her with a car to replace the one she loaned them in case something happened. It was Paige's intent that their visit would be short enough to make that offer unnecessary.

"You sure this is the place?" Cole asked.

The Vigilant's newest base of operations was a pair of buildings at the corner of South Spring and Payne streets. The largest of the two structures looked like a barn that had been cut in half and sectioned into large slices. It was three floors high, with a roof that sloped downward at a steep angle before leveling off at the back. The front windows went from large rectangles at street level and shrank down to little squares by the third floor. The building beside it was a quaint little single story house with two front windows and a door beneath a white awning. Both structures were painted the same shade of faded gray. Across the street was a small liquor store, a neighborhood bar on the adjacent corner.

"What were you expecting for a meeting place used by a militant splinter group of Skinners?" Paige asked. "A fort?"

"No, but maybe something more strategic."

"Bars are perfect cover," she explained. "Noisy at night and plenty of places to post lookouts posing as regular customers. The liquor store is a good addition too. Especially if it gets robbed a lot. At the very least, there's enough foot traffic to keep any more from being noticed. You pay the owners of either place enough and they'll keep an eye on your front yard along with theirs."

"You seem to know a lot for a woman who lived in an abandoned restaurant."

"It took a lot of work to scope that place out. Now come on. Let's meet us some heavily armed nut jobs."

As they approached the building on the corner, Cole wasn't exactly sure who would greet them. The fact that they weren't welcomed with open arms, however, was no surprise. The two who showed up first looked to be no more than twenty years old. Skinning werewolves didn't have an age restriction, but even the newest recruits usually had a little more hair on their faces than the two young men who rushed outside carrying shotguns.

"That's close enough," one of them said.

Paige raised her arms, so Cole followed her lead. "We're not going to hurt anyone," she said.

"And you're not about to take any of our supplies neither. What the hell do you want?"

The one who'd done the talking so far was a burly kid who looked like he'd spent his time playing football and partying before the world went to hell. He looked back at his partner, a taller kid with long hair and baggy jeans riding low on bony hips. Both wore matching sweatshirts that had probably been taken from a rack at the same Salvation Army store. Either that or the randomly raggedy look had become fashionable.

"Tell Jessup we're here," Paige replied. "It's not safe to stand out in the open for this long."

The guy spoke into a radio that was slightly bigger than a cell phone. "These two say . . . yeah. Okay." Grudgingly, he looked at them and waved them through. As he moved past them, Cole noticed that neither of the younger men had any scars on their hands that would mark them as having been trained with a Skinner's shifting weaponry.

The main room of the largest building reeked of kerosene, burnt gunpowder, and charred wood. Although Cole couldn't spot whatever traps had been set to turn the entrance into a kill zone, he was fairly sure they'd already been sprung several times. Although his knowledge of Skinner runes was still far from complete, he had no problem picking out the ones etched into the splintered door frame. The room was barely the size of a walk-in closet and was sealed off by a thick wall supported by steel posts. The clatter of teeth braided into leather cords announced Jessup's arrival through a narrow gap between two of the posts on the far side of the room. He was an older man with a grizzled beard and scarred skin. Even without the tanned werewolf hide vest decorated with teeth and claws, he looked like someone who was never meant to leave a desert. He nodded toward the two shotgun-wielding Junior Varsity athletes who'd answered the door and said, "You boys can go check the perimeter. These two are all right."

The ferocity on the younger men's faces was obviously a tired facade, and they didn't do much to keep it up as they turned their backs on the Skinners and headed outside.

Jessup studied Paige with a gaze that had been hardened by more than his share of nightmares. Although most of the people in the country were building a gaze like that, Skinners had been working on theirs for a whole lot longer. "We've tried contacting you two for some time. What brings you here?"

"We came for the Jekhibar," she told him.

"Then you might as well turn right back and go. We went through too much to get our hands on that thing."

"I know," Cole said. "I was right there in New Mexico with you. In fact, I don't think you would've made it out of there if I hadn't been watching your back."

"It's too late in the game to start asking for credit on the battlefield." Jessup sighed. "Too much fighting, too many losses. There ain't hardly anything worth owning up to anymore."

"You told me to contact you if I wanted to learn more about the Jekhibar," Cole said. "Here we are."

"It's been months since I made that offer. You lookin' to join us?" Jessup asked.

"No."

"Then why the hell should I show you a damned thing?"

"Because as long as we're not sprouting fur or fangs, we're on the same team. If you didn't have any intention of doing that much, you never would have made contact with me after New Mexico."

"True enough," Jessup admitted. "You guys hungry?"

Cole and Paige followed him back through the narrow doorway and farther into the building. There were several sticks of dynamite and metal containers that reeked of flammable liquids fastened to the other side of that wall. Wires running from the homemade explosives ran to a set of switches farther inside a round room that had been gutted to make space for several shelves, storage lockers, and chairs. As he surveyed the rest of the area, Cole picked out at least a dozen lines of blocky runic symbols etched into the floor, walls, and ceiling.

Motioning toward a series of scorch marks, bullet holes, and claw marks adorning the floor and walls, Jessup said, "As you can tell, you ain't the first ones to pay us a visit." His long gray hair looked as if it had been scraped up from the ash coating much of the room's surface area. It was held back by a thin leather cord. "We gotta be careful lately," he explained. "If the Full Bloods ain't tryin' to sniff us out, the bloodsuckers are sending in spies to get as deep into this place as they can to plant bugs or any other kind of electronic bullshit."

Without being told, one of the three others in the room stood up and opened a door leading deeper into the building. Until now Cole had barely noticed the other tired faces staring at him from their posts within the foyer. And, thanks to the explosives, he'd all but written off that second door as a possibility of leading anywhere but to the next life. It swung open after a few conventional locks were undone and was held open by a man with an M-16 in his hands and a wooden weapon hanging from one shoulder. The deep patchwork of scars on his hands told Cole that he knew how to put each of those weapons to use.

"So the Nymar know you're here?" Paige asked as she followed Jessup into the next room.

"They've been after us ever since all that business with the dead cops," Jessup explained. "It ain't like they can really back down after something like that, right?"

"We've been stepping up our work against them," Cole said as he stepped through the hidden opening and looked around. "Any Nymar Blood Parlor we've been able to find has been burnt to the ground."

"Just so another can spring up somewhere else. Nope," Jessup grunted definitively. "We're well past the point of keepin' the peace. It's 'us or them' time."

The next room was part living quarters and part bunker. Several walls had been knocked down to open what had to be most of the first floor. Men and women in layers of tattered clothing walked quietly between televisions and computer terminals, sifted through racks of guns and wooden weapons, or rested on cots or chairs situated near the back of the room. Some ate from cans or drank from plastic bottles, obviously more concerned with fueling their muscles instead of enjoying a meal. Every last one of them took notice of Cole and Paige. He recognized some of them as Skinners who had come to Philadelphia to scavenge from Lancroft's old house, but others were strangers with tired, suspicious eyes.

"By the way," Jessup added, "you'd better not be trying to communicate with those friends of yours from the military. If any of them IRD choppers or trucks come along, we'll know it was you that brought 'em here."

"What have you got against them anyway?" Cole asked. "We're all trying to kill the same Half Breeds."

"Sure, but what happens once the fight's over? We know what should be done with those monsters. We know what Lancroft would have done with them. We know what any other Skinners would do. Can you tell me you know exactly what the Army or Marines would do? They might as well be a bunch of excited kids playin' around with the shotgun they just found in their daddy's closet." Rather than show them to any of the other doors near the back of the room or any of the steel lockers guarded by armed men as well as several layers of iron bars, Jessup dropped to one knee and pulled up a thin section of floor to reveal a solid block of runes that fit together into a clump at least twelve inches square. He touched several of the runes with such quick, fleeting motions that Cole didn't have a chance to memorize the sequence. A second later the square shifted and Jessup was able to open a hole that contained a dented metal box. He opened it so Paige and Cole could see inside.

Cole hunkered down to examine a thin wedge of silvery metal that looked like it had been blasted by fire and painted with thin streaks of blood. "That's the Jekhibar?" he asked.

"Yep."

"What does it do?"

"Near as we can figure," Jessup explained, "it stores up whatever power the Full Bloods were after during the rise of the Breaking Moon. Don't know how to tap into it yet, but we'll figure it out."

Paige started to reach for the dirty little rock, but paused with her hand lingering just above the opening to the small hole. "Mind if I take a look?" she asked.

A knowing grin slid across Jessup's face. He tapped another couple of runes, which caused the air within the small hole to crackle before settling down. Fortunately, both Cole and Paige had seen the runes at work enough times to realize they did much more than cover secret panels or warn of approaching vampires. Now that the barrier had been dropped, she reached down to pick up the prize that was important enough to be guarded by at least a dozen armed Skinners, several false fronts within a single building, and multiple arcane rituals that had probably been burning intruders down to the bone for centuries.

Paige used her right hand to pick up the stone, but quickly shifted it to her left. Even though she'd been making huge strides in healing that arm, there was just no way to compare it to what she could do with a hand that hadn't been through the hell of nearly being petrified into a stump.

"You've worked with the Gypsies," Jessup said to them. "Anything you can tell us about this thing? Maybe they keep files you could hack into?"

"Haven't been able to try it without a dozen military techies looking over my shoulder," Cole said. "Even firing up my laptop makes me wonder if someone in a black van is blazing past my firewall to look at how much porn I've got."

"We might be able to scrape up a few computers for you to use." Although Jessup knew exactly which of the others in that room to look at for a response to that, the tall young woman sitting near one small bank of monitors didn't seem particularly happy to return his grin.

"Maybe you'd like to see the main attraction?" Jessup asked as he took the Jekhibar back and placed it in the box. "It may be enough to convince you that we have more to offer than those government jokers who've been doing nothing but shooting up the whole damn country."

"You talkin' about me?" Rico asked as he strode in from one of the two back rooms. "Because if you ain't, I'll be real disappointed."

Chapter Five

"So," Rico said, "how you been?"

The instant Paige stepped toward him, she was flanked by men on either side. "I've been out there fighting. How about you?"

"Unless yer blind, you'd know we're already losing that fight. All you been doing is riding around with the IRD providing cover fire while the military tries to impress the common folk by blasting a few Half Breeds to hell. Then you show up here and figure we'll welcome you with open arms? For all we know, you're settin' us up to be taken down. Which, by the way, would be a very bad move on your part."

Paige stood with every muscle in her body tensed and ready to go. "We're not the only ones fighting with the IRD," she said.

"Right. You also got that Squam playing scout for ya. How's that workin' out?"

"There's a few other Skinners working with them as well," she continued. "Two in Texas and a few in Jersey."

Without missing a beat, Rico said, "The Texas crew is gone. Wiped out when the IRD flew into San Antonio and stirred up all those Half Breeds that were tucked away in the suburbs. Nobody walked out of that cluster fuck. As for the Jersey bunch, I believe Maddy is the only one left there, and she's locked up by the cops on more of that bullshit from the Nymar frame-up."

Paige bristled at that but let it slide.

"So that leaves me with the million dollar question," Rico said. "Why the hell did you decide to drop everything and come here now?"

Cole could see the tension in her neck fading away. It left her looking weary when she said, "You're right. We're losing this battle. Cole and I have been fighting alongside the military and all we've been seeing is soldiers getting killed."

"All they want to do is keep firing weapons at things that barely feel a bullet," Cole said. "And all they want from us is to make them more bullets."

"Did you give them my Snappers?"

"Yeah. They work great."

Rico beamed like a proud papa.

"They put down a Half Breed in one shot," Cole continued. "Doesn't do much against a Full Blood, though. Slows them down, but not long enough for us to finish them off before they jump away to heal."

"So put another one into them when they're runnin'!" Rico snapped. "Jesus, do I have to do everything for you guys?"

"Actually," Paige said, "we were hoping you might be able to give us some more of those Snappers. They go a long way in helping to keep things under control out there."

"I can do that."

"And there's something else."

Jessup let out a short, snorting laugh. "Sounds like you made a whole list of demands. Why not save us some time and let us see it?"

"Where's Cecile?" Cole asked.

That was enough to quiet everyone else in the room. "Why the hell do you wanna know that?" Jessup grunted.

"She's still new to being a Full Blood, and unless she's had a complete change of heart in the last few months, she still hasn't bought in to what they're doing."

"She's one of them," the older man stated. "Plain and simple. The most she can do for us is stay out of the fighting before more of them Half Breeds decide to rally around her. Unless you ain't noticed, those things have been getting tougher to kill and better organized. Some packs have more'n thirty sets of fangs in 'em. That's getting worse every week."

"And you think she's behind it?" Cole asked. "She was just a girl trying to get the hell away from all of this."

"So what makes you think she's got anything to contribute?" Rico asked.

"Because the other Full Bloods must have approached her by now," Paige replied. "According to what Cole told me, she's already been in contact with Randolph Standing Bear. He's the one that gave her the Jekhibar in the first place. She could know where to find him or at least be able to stand still long enough for him to find her."

Jessup looked as if he'd just been forced to drink lemon juice when he asked, "And then what? Your friends in the Army shoot at them some more?"

"No. We take care of them the old fashioned way. I would have thought you guys would be into that sort of thing."

"If we were ready to stand toe-to-toe with Full Bloods, we'd be out there doin' it by now."

"We've got connections to get some improved weaponry," Paige said. "Finding Cecile may take some time, and even if it doesn't, it'll probably take a little while for her to lead us to another Full Blood. When that develops, we'll be back with the weapons needed to kill at least a few of those things. Do you know where she is or not?"

"Yeah," Rico said. "I know just where you can find her."

"Hey!" snapped the woman sitting near the computers. "We don't know if we can trust them!"

When Rico swung his gaze toward that other Skinner,

it was with an intensity that even Cole could feel. "I been working with Bloodhound well before I ever knew who the fuck any of you guys were. I'm takin' these two downstairs. Anyone got any objections," he added while looking primarily at Jessup, "tell me right now."

Nobody said anything. Reluctantly, Jessup nodded and turned to deal with the other Skinners, who converged around him to speak in harsh whispers.

Rico motioned for Cole and Paige to follow him as he headed to the back of the room. "Things have been pretty hectic since we parted ways in New Mexico," he said. "Hope you're not still riled up about that."

"Riled up?" Cole grunted. "You mean since you told us to get bent for not doing anything right over the last few years?"

"I never said that. I just said it was time to take a harder road."

"You mean Jonah Lancroft's road," Paige pointed out.

Nodding as he tapped a few runes on a wall to uncover a small doorway, he replied, "Yeah. Would you have just come along if I asked nicely?"

Neither Cole nor Paige answered him, but Rico grinned as if he'd heard them loud and clear. "Didn't think so," he chuckled.

The stairway was lit by a few bulbs encased in wire frames. They were obviously going down into a basement, and Cole was immediately reminded of when he, Paige, and Rico had descended into Lancroft's cellar another lifetime ago. There was a small landing at the point where a normal staircase might end. The stairs continued down for another eight feet into a room that looked like it had been freshly chiseled from a single block of concrete. It was a space sealed so tightly that he could hear every breath the three of them took. About three-quarters of the way into the room, a set of iron bars was set into the floor and ceiling to turn the rear portion of the room into a large, long cell.

"This looks familiar," Cole mused as he approached the

bars and studied the runes etched into the iron. "You make these markings?"

Rico glanced at the angular script like a carpenter examining one of his own joists. "Nah, but I did a lot of the rune work upstairs."

Cole's attention was so absorbed by the dust-covered writing that he almost didn't notice what was being kept inside the cage. Paige stepped forward, placed her hands on her hips and looked straight past the bars at the rough stone statue of a cowering Full Blood. Cecile's features might have been crude, but there was an underlying intricacy to the lines that crossed her body and limbs in a pattern much too complex to be cracks or imperfections in a sculpture. It was fur that had been plastered down and frozen into place.

"She's in there all right," Paige said as she brushed her fingers against her palms.

Cole could feel the heat in his scars as well. It wasn't as strong as when he was usually in the presence of a Full Blood, but it was there. Muted to a dull ache in his bones that he couldn't feel when he'd been upstairs, the pain snaked beneath his skin as if deftly avoiding the instinctive, probing touches of his fingertips.

"Damn right she's in there," Rico said. "Not like that bastard that walked away from New Mexico."

"You've seen Esteban?" Paige asked.

"We've all seen him, Bloodhound. The others split apart after the fall of Atoka, and he's the one that's been organizing the packs in the States."

"We didn't know for sure," she said, as if hesitant to dispel the hint of pride that had crept into her former trainer's voice. "It seemed a pretty safe bet that you'd at least have her locked up, even if she did manage to crack out of that magic shell. Or that you'd at least have . . . pieces of her."

"Whatever you left back in Oklahoma, it's still in there."

"Have you heard anything from her?"

"Like what?" Rico scoffed. "A squeaky plea for an oil can?"

"No," Paige said. "Like a radio frequency." She looked him straight in the eyes to make sure he wasn't about to make another bad *Wizard of Oz* reference. "Or something from your cell phone. Do they even work around her?"

"Why would you even ask that?"

"Just answer the question," Cole said. "It's important."

"No," Rico grunted. "We're in a subbasement. It don't take a tech genius to figure your cell reception might not be so good down here. Why the hell are you so worried about that?"

"Is anyone listening to us down here?" Cole asked.

"No."

"Are you sure of that?"

Rico drew a deep breath and stepped up to him until he was almost close enough to touch the end of his nose against Cole's face. As creepy as that might have been, Rico maintained the close quarters as he spoke in a voice that was hardly more than a rustle in the back of his throat. "This place was wired up before I got here. Whoever is in charge of the Vigilant ain't seen fit to introduce himself to me even after I hooked these jokers up with the runes upstairs."

"You left us to join up with them and you sound like you barely trust them," Cole said in a similar whisper.

"They're paranoid and a little crazy. Far as I can tell, that's just the sort of thing that's needed since everything's been going to hell."

"But can you trust them?"

"Why do you ask? What do you need to say that you can't just come out and say?"

Paige dropped her right hand onto his shoulder and turned him around. Even though she was strong and that hand was still partially petrified from her injury, she could tell that Rico was allowing himself to be moved. "You may have given up on us, Rico, but that doesn't mean we're ready to give up on you."

"And," he told her, "just because I'm testing the waters somewhere else, that don't mean I'm your enemy."

"Sure seemed that way when you left New Mexico," Cole pointed out.

"A lot happened that day," the big man said. "And even more's happened since. Believe me, if I was your enemy, you woulda gotten a lot more than a gruff tone back at that Army camp in Raton. And speaking of them, and you joining up with the IRD, most of the folks here and plenty more of the Skinners that are still alive think you two are spilling all of our names and everything we ever learned to the government. Look me in the eyes and tell me what you make of that."

Although Paige was ready to speak for them both, Cole knocked Rico's shoulder with his fist just hard enough to turn the big man toward him again. "I think that's just the sort of bullshit that makes working with the IRD seem like such a good idea. What happened when we found Lancroft and that warehouse of Skinner memorabilia in Philadelphia? We contacted everyone else and had a freaking yard sale. And when things got really bad with the Nymar, we drew as much fire as possible so everyone else could pull their own plans together, and when things got even worse, we took the worst fall of anyone. I went to prison, for Christ's sake! A prison," he added while extending an arm to point at the bars in front of him, "with cells that looked a hell of a lot like that."

"I get what you're sayin'," Rico said. "I may not know everyone in this operation just yet, but they all respect what you two have done. When you turn your back on them, it rubs 'em the wrong way. Know what I mean?"

"Awww," Paige said with a mocking sigh. "Is the poor little Skinner militia feeling left out? They can weep about it in their diaries. Right now we need to get a look at what's inside the cage."

And just like that the subject was closed. The most pressing matter stood behind bars of charmed iron, pushing seven feet tall and wielding claws that looked deadly even encased in a layer of stone.

"Most of the gargoyles were either shredded or went back into hiding after the feeding frenzy over the fall," Rico said, "but we pulled together enough of what was left to wrap her up good and tight."

Cole stood quietly looking at her. Even though the young Full Blood's eyes were hidden beneath a stone crust, he found it difficult to look into them. "Her name's Cecile."

"What?" Rico said, looking surprised.

"She trusted us. Asked for our help. Even fought Esteban to give us a chance in New Mexico, and to repay that, she winds up like this behind bars."

"So the least we can do is call her by name?" Rico grunted. "Fine. But you should know that any Full Blood is a danger right now. And you know who else has got a name? Randolph Standing Bear. He's dropped off the map lately, and for something as powerful as him, and considering how visible he used to be, that don't bode well."

"I agree," Paige said. "Bring down the Jekhibar."

"I doubt Jessup will allow it out of his sight. He was the one to bring it in and he's real fidgety when anyone else tries to handle it. I'm surprised he let you see that hole in the floor."

"Just have him bring it down here and stand with it," she said while holding her phone to her ear. "He can fondle it however he wants from there."

Sighing, Rico climbed the lower half of the stairs and yelled for Jessup. While those two were engaged in conversation, Cole stood next to Paige and asked, "What are you expecting to hear?"

"Don't you remember that EVP I caught when I was on the phone with MEG in Atoka?"

"You told me about it. You heard one of the Mongrels talking to you over the cell phone," Cole recalled. "Kind of like a ghost voice."

"That's right. He said he was being controlled by Liam through the power they were all after. It was also through that power that Ben's voice could be transmitted. Maybe it was a psychic connection or something to do with wavelengths mixing with the Torva'ox. I'm really not the expert in that kind of crap. But I do know that the energy the Full Bloods were after is real, and I was able to tap into it somehow using a phone."

"Maybe that's how every other EVP is created," Cole said. "Maybe haunted places are actually located near sources of the Torva'ox, and when ghost hunters catch voices on their recorders it's because of that."

Paige gripped her cell phone tighter and glared at it before smacking it with the palm of her hand. "A phone worked before. This phone, even. It's not working now. Maybe if Jessup brings us that Jekhibar, I'll get what I need."

"Which, again, is what?"

"Weren't you even listening when we talked about this on the way over here?"

"Yeah. You said you'd try talking to Cecile. You never said what you wanted to say. How did you even know she was here?"

After shaking the phone some more and placing it against her ear again, Paige whispered, "Rico's been in contact on and off ever since he hooked up with these guys."

"You mean . . . like a spy?"

"I mean like an old friend who's no stranger to playing with less reputable teams so long as they're shooting at the right things. Honestly, I'm surprised he stuck with us for as long as he did without disappearing. He may not be a team player, but his heart's in the right place. Long as we don't get on his bad side for too long, he'll make sure we don't get hurt."

"These Vigilant assholes locked me up," Cole snarled.

"Can you prove that?"

"Not with a paper trail, but I heard more than enough."

Paige smirked and said, "Well, if you can find some evidence, I'm sure Rico would like to see it. He doesn't exactly have fond memories of prison cells either, and knowing for sure that these guys not only took you away when you were supposed to be treated for that Nymar bite but also slapped together a secret prison facility for Skinners, he won't be too happy."

Shifting his focus to the petrified werewolf, Cole asked, "So what are you going to say to her?"

"Haven't figured that out yet. I'm surprised we got this far. And don't look at me like that. Isn't this better than being carted around by Adderson like just another couple hundred pounds of equipment?"

"Actually, yeah. It is."

"So just . . . Wait a second. I'm getting something."

Ashamed that he'd been about to try and listen in on whatever was coming through Paige's phone instead of listening to his own, Cole fished his from his pocket and asked, "What number did you dial?"

"The old one for Rasa Hill. It's still connected, but there's a recording."

Cole dialed the number from memory and listened to a recorded message that quickly faded out, replaced by static. And then the static was replaced by a voice.

" . . . kill you," it said.

Both Paige and Cole looked at the cage. Cecile was still there, etched in stone and unable to move. Two sets of footsteps stomped against the stairs until both Rico and Jessup stood in the room with them. Cole glanced over at the men to see that Jessup was holding the familiar little metal box.

"You try to make a move for this and you'll regret it," Jessup warned. "There ain't no way you'll make it out." Before he could say more, he was shushed by Paige. He looked over to Rico, who wore an exasperated look that Cole knew all too well.

"Can you hear us, Cecile?" Paige asked.

"I can hear you and every other filthy hick stinking up the rooms above me," she replied. Her voice tapered off, then returned like a timid nudge by a hand in the dark. "You can hear me?"

"Yes," Cole replied. "Can you, Paige?"

"Yes," she said. "I just didn't think I'd be able to. Last time, Stu had to record it and play it back. You know . . . like an EVP."

"What are you two talking about?" Jessup asked. When he stepped forward to get closer to them, the static in Cole's phone cleared like dirt floating in water that had suddenly been scattered by an outboard motor.

Cecile's voice was strained and taut. In an attempt to clear it more, Cole approached the bars of her cell. Using the ear that wasn't flattened against a phone, he could hear a subtle creak similar to what he imagined two tectonic plates might sound like when they rubbed against each other. He backed away from the cage and resisted the urge to back all the way out of the room. "I think she's breaking loose," he said.

That brought all the Skinners to the front of the cell.

"You can hear me," Cecile said through the tinny phone connection. "I can hear you. I can also hear someone else."

"Someone in the building?" Paige asked.

After a short silence, Cecile replied, "No. One of the other Full Bloods. She's screaming. Furious. I think . . . far away."

"That could be Minh," Cole said to Paige.

Jessup knocked into both of them in his haste to get closer. "The female Full Blood that helped rip apart Atoka? Where is she?"

"I don't know," Cole lied. Actually, it was only a partial lie. According to Tristan, Minh had been sent away in the same burst of energy the Dryad had used to transport him, Liam, and Paige to Finland. Tristan told him Minh had been sent to one of the older Dryad temples located somewhere in a Japanese bamboo forest. The nymphs hadn't been eager to tell the Skinners where the temple was located, and as long as Minh was encased in a similar stone shell hidden away from humans, Cole and Paige were content to leave her there. Others, like the Vigilant, on the other hand, wouldn't be so willing to let sleeping dogs lie.

"Who're you talking to on that phone?" Jessup asked as he wedged himself between Cole and Paige. "Tell me!"

"What's wrong with me?" Cecile asked in a voice becoming sharper with every inch that Jessup closed in on the bars. "Why can't I move?"

Cole stepped back and stretched out an arm to shove Jessup back. "Get that thing away from her!"

"You're the ones that wanted me to bring the Jekhibar down here!"

"It's waking her up!"

The creaking that Cole had heard a little while ago became more defined and then took on the sharp, snapping sound of breaking ice.

"Why the hell would I ever listen to you?" Jessup grumbled as he stomped toward the stairs. Rather than climb back to the first floor, he turned to one of the other Skinners who had followed him down and handed the metal box to him. "Take this up to where it belongs and shut it away." Then Jessup pulled a small wooden ax from where it hung at his belt. Now, the creaking from the cell mingled with the sound of wood stretching into a new form as the crude ax took on the shape of a tomahawk with sharper, jagged edges.

When Paige moved to shush him again, she swung her arm at Jessup as if she meant to knock him through a wall. "Cecile, listen to me. Can you hear me?"

"I can hear everything!" she screamed through the connection. If it had been a real electronic signal, those words surely would have caused some major feedback. "Those things are still on me. I can feel them. They're biting me. I'll kill them and then kill those Skinners who brought them here. Kill them all!"

Even after Cole lowered the phone, he could still hear Cecile's crackling voice cursing him. "Jessup, how can we put her back to sleep?" he asked.

The older Skinner stepped up to stand with Cole, Paige, and Rico rather than insinuate himself into the group. Where he had been aggressive and suspicious before, he was now plainly one of them. It was the first glimpse Cole had seen of the man who helped him survive the carnage in New Mexico that marked the beginning of this conflict. "That stuff I took from what was left of all them gargoyles back in New Mex wasn't just the paste that coats their prey in rock. There's something else. A toxin. From what I've been able to piece together, gargoyles inject some sort of paralyzing substance into their prey when they feed. Damn near everything is bigger or stronger than them, so—"

"Real interesting," Paige snapped. "If we can knock Cecile out again, I'm liking that idea."

There was another dry creaking sound, followed by a pop that sent a small mist of gray dust away from Cecile's left shoulder. Little chunks of the stony facade broke away and rolled down her chest, making it obvious just how thin the rock truly was.

"Can this cage hold a Full Blood?" Cole asked.

Rico's eyes danced beneath the thick ridge of his brow. "The bars should hold, but I don't know about the rest of the structure. She'll be able to dig out through any of those other walls without too much effort."

Cole reached over his shoulder to grab the spear harnessed on his back. Since the phone was only broadcasting dead air now that the metal box was out of the room, he stuffed it back into his pocket. "Anyone have any ideas?" he asked.

"Yeah," Rico grunted. "Don't mess with the Full Blood while it's all wrapped up nice and tidy. Guess the boat's sailed on that one."

"What about killing a Full Blood?" Paige asked. "If you Vigilant guys are so great, you must have put something together for that, right?"

"Hey!" Cole shouted. "This isn't Birkyus or any of those others. This is Cecile! She's just a kid!"

"Not anymore," Rico said. "She's a Full Blood, and once she gets her wits about her, she'll be a real pissed off Full Blood. I'd rather take my chances jogging into a tornado than being in the same room with one of those without a goddamn weapon in my hand."

"We don't have to kill her," Cole insisted.

Paige stood beside him with a weapon drawn. "We may not have a choice. Jessup, what have you got?"

"Dr. Lancroft created something that allowed him to kill a Full Blood over the course of several weeks," Jessup replied.

Before Cole could protest, Paige asked, "Do you have it here?"

"Yes, but I'll need to get real close without a weapon in my hand. Someone's going to have to keep that thing still."

Cole smirked. "We may have just the thing."

Chapter Six

Cracks spread across Cecile's face, shoulders, and chest in a chain reaction that quickly marred what had once been a smooth, almost pristine surface. As he stormed back down the stairs after a quick trip to the car, Cole could see layers of the rocky coating flake off and fall to the floor of the cell. It had originally been put on her by batlike creatures preserving their meals for so long that the human race either worshipped the statues left behind or eventually called them gargoyles. The true gargoyles had enveloped Cecile's entire body and entombed her layer by layer. Now, as each layer peeled away, Cole knew it wasn't going to be nearly as easy to get the Full Blood under control again.

"Where did Jessup go?" he asked. The spear in his hands had grown to full length thanks to the thorns in its handle that pierced his palms. Although the weapon was connected to him on several levels, there was no way for it to obey every command he was giving it at that moment. That is, unless a charmed piece of wood could fly him off to a quiet cabin somewhere. When he reminded himself of the bad luck he'd had at the last secluded cabin he visited, he purged that dream from his mind and steeled himself as Rico approached the bars.

"Why hasn't she busted out yet?" Cole asked.

Rico had his Sig Sauer in one hand, aimed at the Full Blood, as he used his other hand to touch various runes etched into the bars. "We been studying this one up close since we got her in custody. That's one reason I joined up with these guys."

"Why didn't you mention that when you stormed out of New Mexico?" Paige asked.

"Because it wouldn't have made a difference. Also, I'm still pissed that you two were so quick to shack up with the military when so many Skinners were still on the run from Nymar or the cops. Did you ever stop to think that those Army assholes were just using you to draw more of us into one big net? The cops are still looking for a lot of us, you know!"

She sighed and shook her head, tightening her grip on the baton that slowly shifted into a weapon with a thin handle and a wide, curved blade extending from it. Just like the main spearhead of Cole's weapon, the edge of Paige's sickle blade was coated in a metallic substance created from melted fragments of a Blood Blade. That portion retained its curved shape after being reformed by a burst of strength that had allowed her to finally stray from the clunky machete she'd been forced to use because it was the only shape she could form with her wounded hand. When she spun the sickle around, the weapon cut through the air before catching light cast from the bulbs on the ceiling. It wasn't as flashy a move as what she'd been able to do before her injury, but it was getting there. "You think I'd round up a bunch of Skinners and hand them over to get in good with the IRD just to save my own skin?"

"Or maybe you weren't thinkin' long and hard enough before jumping over to another side," Rico shot back. "Maybe that's a problem you've had for a while now, which ain't exactly the sort of thing that inspires the rest of us to follow you down that road."

Knowing what he did about Paige's violent introduction to

the Skinners, Cole felt a sympathetic jab when he heard that comment from Rico.

Looking over to Cole, she asked, "Do you have it?"

He shifted his weapon to a one-handed grip with the rear end of the spear trapped beneath his arm so he could make a crude stab if the need arose. With his other hand, he reached into the small satchel he'd brought in from the car while Jessup and the rest of the Skinners had scrambled to try and prepare for Cecile's impending escape attempt. The satchel was a large pouch with clips intended to be hooked onto a belt or some other sort of harness worn by soldiers in field gear. If he'd been given an official name for the experimental device, Cole had already forgotten it. Weighing about the same as his cell phone and housed in a plastic shell bearing two dials and a row of multicolored lights, the device looked more like something carried by MEG team members while scanning for fluctuations in the electromagnetic field.

"What's that supposed to do?" Rico asked.

"We'll find out in a minute."

Behind him, Jessup said, "That's not good enough." When he got a stern glare from Paige, he added, "You're damn lucky I let you in here with that thing."

"It's some sort of sonic transmitter," Cole said. "Supposedly, it can hurt Half Breeds with a high-pitched frequency. This is supposed to be modified to work on Full Bloods."

"Does it work?"

"Don't know yet. We're supposed to be the ones testing it."

Jessup approached the cage holding a thick piece of curved leather in both hands. It was thicker than his finger and long enough to clamp around a light pole with small rings embedded along the outer surface. The interior section was stained and shredded as if it had been gnawed on by a set of teeth large enough to scar the thick leather but not tear it apart. Every piece of metal from the rings to the buckle was embedded with runes. Holding the large strap in a way to confirm Cole's suspicion, Jessup announced, "I need to get this around her neck."

"Why don't you just get in there right now before she breaks out?" Rico asked.

"Already tried it when she was brought here," Jessup replied. "Nothing happened. Must need to make contact with flesh instead of rock."

The IRD tech who gave Cole the sonic device had also given him a quick lesson in using it, but the more he fiddled with it, the more questions sprang to mind regarding its use. When he first got the device running, he could hear something. After a few twists of the little knobs set beneath the lights, the sound became a tone that quickly escaped the range of a human's ear.

Although Paige had been trying to get a closer look at the collar in Jessup's hands, her attention was quickly brought back to the cage as a large chunk of the stony crust fell away to reveal Cecile's furry, muscular chest. The Full Blood's torso swelled with a slow inhalation that sounded powerful enough to suck all of the air from the room. When she twisted her head and began to shake off more of the rock, she let out a roar that filled the room and made it seem about half the size it had been a moment ago.

"Here she comes," Jessup warned. "Brace yourselves."

But there was no way to brace for the coming of a Full Blood. Even in the more recent days when werewolves roamed their territory freely, their presence was still more than enough to make any human reflexively cringe. It was the natural order of things for lesser creatures to fear their betters. Ever since the setting of the Breaking Moon, Cole and every other member of the human race were all too aware of how fragile their existences truly were.

"Hang on," Cole said as he continued fidgeting with the sonic device. "I think I'm right around the Half Breed range. We should see some sort of reaction now if this is gonna work at all."

"Step aside," Rico growled.

Cole did as he was told, guided by Paige's hand as she helped move him to the side of the room where the bars met the solid concrete wall.

As Jessup moved toward the cell, Rico tapped the runes to create a break in the bars. The entrance swung open, causing a surge of Skinners to move into the room from the stairway. Most of them were new to the game. Cole could tell that much with only a quick glance in their direction. Their faces were either petrified or overconfident, without much in between. After all of the time he'd spent riding in helicopters with IRD soldiers going into and out of cities overrun by Half Breeds, he'd seen plenty of faces like those.

When Cecile broke through the last of her form-fitting prison, she shattered the rock layers, sending bits and pieces flying into every corner of the room. Roaring angrily, unable to form a single word, her claws snapped out of her fingers and toes to scrape at the floor of the cell as if the cement was tightly packed Styrofoam.

"Is that the best that machine of yours can do?" Jessup asked.

Cole adjusted the frequency of the device so the needle on its scale waggled between two markings. "This is where the experimentation part comes in," he shouted over the wild snarls of the Full Blood.

Paige watched Cecile carefully. She set her feet into a solid stance, gripped both weapons until the blood was squeezed from between her fingers, and brought the sickles up to waist level. "I don't think she knows where she is yet."

"You're right," Jessup said. "Otherwise she would've made a break for the door by now."

"Then shut the hell up before we give her any ideas," Rico snapped.

Cecile thrashed against the back of the cell as if she'd been tossed there, slapping the walls with the palms of her hands to leave cracks in the concrete. Every powerful movement loosened dust from her fur that had been there ever since the Full Bloods formally introduced themselves to the modern world.

Rico gripped the swinging bars with one hand, steadied the door and then craned his neck to look back at the other Skinners. “You ready?”

Jessup pulled in a breath and stepped forward. His tomahawk hung from his belt again, but it wouldn’t do him any good so long as both of his hands were occupied by the thick leather collar. “Yeah,” he said.

Doing his best to steady himself with a series of deep breaths, Cole turned the dials on the device to adjust the frequency. According to the IRD tech, he needed to be careful not to flip through too many frequencies too quickly, in case he skipped right over the one he needed. When he hit the end of the line as referenced by every light on the device, he swore under his breath and reset it to the Half Breed frequency. Cecile pounded her fist against the bars less than a foot from his head. His only reaction was to take a quick look up to make sure she wasn’t about to reach through and tear his face off. Her eyes swung back and forth within their sockets, looking at her surroundings without taking anything in. And then, when Cole switched his focus to a dial meant for finer adjustments to the device’s frequency, the Full Blood’s eyes clenched shut, her head reared back, and she sent a bellowing howl toward the ceiling.

“I think I got something!” he shouted over the werewolf’s pained voice.

When Rico moved the door open another fraction of an inch, Cecile’s entire body coiled like a spring. Her senses were returning and so was her grasp of her situation. There was some confusion on her face, but no more than what should be expected of anyone waking up to find themselves in a different spot than where they fell asleep.

Before she could pounce, Cole steadied his hands and moved the dials on the device just a little more. One of the lights flickered to show the change he’d made, but Cecile’s reaction was much more drastic. She dropped to all fours while her head swung in a slow, grinding circle and her lips curled back into a terrifying snarl.

After getting no more than a look from Jessup, Paige entered the cage. Much like the Full Blood, she was ready to lash out with the weapons at her disposal should the need arise. Jessup moved in behind her. The teeth tied into the leather fringe of his vest clattered together and could only be heard when Cecile paused to draw another breath.

Cole was getting a feel for the equipment in his hands. Holding it so it was pointed at the cell, he used his thumbs to turn two dials at once. Instead of watching the lights or any of the other sorry excuses for readouts on the device, he watched Cecile's face contort into an agonized mask.

"Let . . . me. . . . go," she wheezed.

Jessup moved to the back of the cell to get behind her. Paige stood ready to attack with both sickles, but hung back since Cecile was focused on Cole so intently that she jammed her face against the bars. The charmed metal hissed angrily against her fur, scorching it without the first hint of smoke.

"Can't keep me here forever, Cole," she said.

Hearing his name come from that horrific mouth was jarring. Cole looked into her hazel eyes, which were glittering as if somehow able to catch sunlight from several feet beneath the surface of the earth. Her pale silver-hued fur was encrusted with powder and small chunks of rocky crust, and her narrow face shifted slowly into something even more feral than the fearsome visage that had been encased in stone. One more slight adjustment from his device tensed all the muscles in her body and made her voice sound as if it were pushed through a strainer when she swore, "Now I see why . . . the others hate you. When . . . when they come for you, I'll be glad. I'll be—"

Jessup's hands appeared on either side of Cecile's head as he reached out and wrapped the collar around her neck. The Full Blood started to turn around, but Cole slowed her by twisting the dials of the sonic device between the two spots that seemed to cause her the most grief. Even though he couldn't hear the sound himself, he swore he felt the same amount of pain it caused.

"That's it," Jessup grunted while twisting the collar around so he could work the buckle without having to reach over her shoulders. "Just a little longer." The collar hissed with even more fury than the bars, a sound that quickly elevated from the crackle of a fire to the enraged exhalation of a cobra trapped beneath someone's boot.

Cecile tried to talk again but was cut short. Between the electronic torture coming from Cole's device and the collar being tightened into place around her neck, she was reduced to a wild beast. Cole couldn't take his eyes off her. There was another transformation rippling beneath her flesh that had nothing to do with her ability to shift her muscle and skeletal structure, and it caused her skin to bubble and expel an unseen substance. He traced the rippling effect to where it was strongest, which was at her neck directly around the leather collar. She arched her back as her skin swelled to the point of bursting. The claws extending from her fingers shrank down to pointed spikes as if to create vents at the tips of her fingers where the invading substance could be spat out like so much foul steam. And still Cole could neither see nor smell anything but the dusty remnants of broken rock and the sweat pouring from the skin of every living thing inside that room. He did, however, feel something wash over him like one of the cold brushes of phantom hands described to him by Abby when she told him about encountering a ghost while on one of MEG's field investigations.

The air became cold.

The hairs on his arm stood on end.

He swore he heard a whisper directly behind him, but he wasn't about to turn away. Cecile's eyes were too captivating to let him go. They were deep, multifaceted treasures colored by the same brushstrokes that had painted the first primordial earthen tones. And then, as her entire body forced out the last bit of whatever immaterial substance had been stirred up by Lancroft's collar, her eyes closed, to keep the last bit of their power from leaking out.

"That's got it," Jessup sighed. "Turn that thing off." When

he saw Cole wasn't moving, he smacked the side of his fist against the bars and said, "Turn that thing off!"

One blink was all it took to break the spell that had overtaken Cole. Suddenly, the stark lighting from the overhead bulbs, the dank smells of the basement, even the rough touch of his own clothes against his skin, dragged him back. Cecile was separated from him once more, slumping against the bars no matter how loudly the runes scalded her skin. It had taken Rico's, Jessup's, and Paige's combined strength to pull her back.

"I don't think she's gonna give us any more trouble," Jessup said. "Not as long as that collar stays on her."

Paige willed one of her weapons to shrink back down enough to be slid back into her boot holster, but she kept the other in her grip. "How does it work?"

"Don't know," Jessup admitted. "Either we don't have the journals where Lancroft describes that part or he kept it a secret. I do know this is what he used to kill the Full Blood that was in Philly."

"He used this on Henry?" Cole asked.

"Yep. Damned if I know how he got it on single-handed. Word's been going around that it took a bunch of Skinners to tame that freak long enough for this beauty to be buckled in place, and that Lancroft was the only one to walk away."

"Or," Cole said as he cocked his head at a skewed angle, as if to honor Henry while also getting a better look at Cecile, "he handed it over and told Henry to put it on."

"Well, I knew it wasn't going to be that easy with this one," Jessup said. Using the back of his hand to wipe some sweat from his brow, he added, "Thought it would be harder than this, though. That sonic transmitter seems to work pretty well."

Paige laughed at that. "It's supposed to incapacitate a Full Blood or possibly even kill them. From where I stood, all it did was drive her crazy enough to rip apart whoever is holding that thing. Don't think that'll do much good unless you just happen to have some special bars in front of you."

"Which is just what we had," Jessup said. "Well done." With that, he motioned for the other Skinners to enter the room.

Even though Cecile was slumped on the floor, seated with her back propped against a wall and her head hanging to one side, the younger Skinners seemed just as afraid of her as when she'd been clawing at the floor and howling like a demon. They carried chains, shackles, and more leather straps, some of which had more engraved rings woven into them, while others were simply thick enough to tie down a Mack truck.

While watching a process vaguely familiar from his time locked up in Colorado, the guilty pangs Cole felt hit him even harder. Cecile's body might have been drained and her eyes were momentarily vacant, but she wasn't dead. That meant somewhere, possibly buried too deeply to see at the moment, there was a spark inside that would only grow the longer it was kept in the dark.

"Come on," Paige said, tapping his arm. She'd stepped out of the cage and was already headed toward the stairs. "Let's let them do their thing."

Since Cecile was preoccupying almost everyone in the building, Cole and Paige had no trouble getting upstairs and outside to where their car was waiting. "So," he said after slamming the door shut behind him, "what do you think?"

Paige had yet to take her eyes off the building on the corner of Spring and Payne. "I think there are at least two people watching us from the windows, and Lord only knows how many cameras taping us right now from a couple different angles."

"You think they can hear us?"

"Just face me when you talk."

That was no problem. In the last several weeks, they'd barely left each other's side. Still, they rarely got much time together where they weren't on the road, refining new combat techniques, or hip deep in a combat zone. Taking a second to stare into her deep brown eyes was a welcome change.

"None of that," she said, reading his thoughts with ease. "They may have lip-readers in their surveillance room."

"I meant what did you think about what we heard in there. Did you pick up the same signal that we've been getting over the last few Half Breed attacks?"

She reached under the seat to fish out a small digital recorder. Holding it below the dashboard so it wouldn't be seen by anyone who wasn't inside the car, she tapped the Play button and turned up the volume. It was a scratchy recording, made by holding the little device up to her earpiece while a battle raged around her. Despite the static and background noise, the clear, keening howl could be heard drifting in and out like a hand-drawn line painted across a mess of digital wavelengths. Paige squinted, closed her eyes and slowly shook her head. "It's hard to say. There was so much going on down there."

"I know, but even if you block that out, I still didn't hear anything downstairs like what we've been hearing around the Half Breed packs."

Reluctantly, Paige said, "Damn it. I thought getting that close to a Full Blood as well as a source of the Torva'ox would allow us to get a fix on that signal."

"It's not a signal, Paige. It's a voice. It's one of *their* voices calling out to the Half Breeds."

"I know," she said. "And we still don't know if that's how the Full Bloods are controlling them or if it's how they're turning humans from a distance."

"I don't think Cecile was giving signals to anyone," Cole said. "She seemed pretty out of it. I don't even think she knew what was going on. It's almost like she was in a coma."

"You're just feeling guilty because it's her," she grunted while turning the digital recorder off, then throwing it to the floor. "But she isn't just some poor little accident victim sleeping off an injury. She's one of the things shredding through the human race. Just when it seems we found some way to get ahead, we wind up right back where we started. That sucks."

"It sure does. But the trip wasn't a complete waste. I found out something important down in that basement."

"What?"

"Those are definitely the assholes who took me away from that first prison in Colorado."

"You're sure about that?"

Cole nodded. "Those bars are the same. Some of the writing was different, but the way it was etched into the metal, the way they were set into the floor and ceiling, everything but the little doggy door—and that's only because they figured they'd have to go in and out of there themselves. Waylon mentioned the Vigilant when Randolph attacked that prison, but I had to be sure. Now, I'm sure."

"So, what about getting that evidence I talked about?"

"I have an idea about that, but Rico would have to be willing to work with me."

"Give you two to one on that," Paige mused.

"For or against?"

Showing him nothing more than a cute grin, she said, "That collar was pretty cool. Not something I'd like to try again, but there's got to be more little tricks that Lancroft saved for his favorite followers." With a subtle shift of her head, she leaned in closer and looked at Cole in a way that assured him she was no longer concerned about who was watching them. "We've already learned some things about these guys. We know they've got Cecile and we know how they're controlling her. You already broke out of a prison like that, so you know you can bust apart the one in their basement. We got a good look at how many are holed up in that place, what's inside, how much security they've got, and who's leading them. We know they've got a lot of Skinners who are still wet behind the ears and probably haven't done much fighting. They've got the Jekhibar and we know where it's kept. As far as I'm concerned, that's more than enough to keep this trip from being a waste of time."

Suddenly, Cole smiled. "Jonah Lancroft may have been a nut job, but he did have some very effective methods. The whole reason for breaking away from Adderson was to do a little mixing and matching, right?"

"Yeah," she sighed. "God help me, I thought about you and your games. When one weapon isn't working out too well, you modify it. If you're shooting a fireball at something and it isn't doing enough damage, you switch to ice. Usually, for thc biggest bosses, you've got to combine every weapon you've got into one big one."

Cole's smile warmed up as he asked, "What game have you been playing while I wasn't looking?"

"Don't have to play anything. After listening to you talk for as long as we've been together, I feel like I've already played them all." Since that wasn't enough, she grumbled, "*Cavern Crawler* on that little portable thing you stashed in the backseat for road trips. Happy?"

"More than you could know. You're right, though. Or, I should say, I was right and you were right for listening to me."

"Don't push it."

Chapter Seven

300 miles north of Montreal, Canada

It was a particularly harsh winter, even for a Full Blood.

Especially for a Full Blood.

The snow felt like jagged little icicles between Randolph's toes as he bounded across wide stretches of open terrain. Winds ranked vengeful claws over his back, sinking deeper than any human bullet could ever go. Sounds normally found in the modern world had ground to a halt, leaving only the churning baritone of breaths pumped by unstoppable lungs to throw a plume of steam into the air directly in front of him.

While mankind scrambled to climb back to its feet and reassert itself, the shapeshifters had become a roiling storm.

Half Breeds charged and fed.

Mongrels burrowed under the ground in erratic patterns, never staying in one place long enough to create a home for themselves.

Full Bloods roamed the New World territories freely. The Torva'ox spilled from North America like a vein of oil that had been tapped by metal fingers. After one Full Blood soaked up some of that power, another crept across a different border to slake its thirst. Every one of them became more powerful, but none were as powerful as those who'd been there during the Breaking Moon. Against them, even the noisiest humans with the biggest machines were toothless and incapable. Randolph narrowed his eyes until his field of vision became a small tunnel through which snowy fields and naked trees streaked past him in a blur. When the scent of the First Deceiver became strongest, he dug his claws into the earth and kicked up a spray of frozen dirt while skidding to a halt.

Kawosa sat on top of a small rise with his front paws casually crossed and his hind legs tucked beneath a lanky body. His form was that of a long, lean coyote, which also happened to be his namesake, thanks to the first humans to have been bent by his flickering tongue. His fur was thinned in parts, perhaps to display the freshest scars. By the time Randolph stopped in front of him, Kawosa had propped himself up and taken a form that eased away from a pure animal and into a vaguely human body with pronounced ribs and limbs that stretched to well beyond natural proportions. "Hello, Birkyus," he said. "I didn't think you'd stay away so long."

"I would have stayed away longer," Randolph replied without any acknowledgment to his true name. "There's no point in seeking refuge when the fire is spreading so quickly to anyplace I might be able to go."

Kawosa's was a trickster's smile; steady and shallow. "You never go anywhere you don't want to be. I trust you completed whatever business you had across the ocean?"

"I did."

"And since you're back now, I trust there is business to be conducted here."

"There is." Randolph lifted his nose to draw a sample of air that seemed to be frozen around him. It smelled of distant fires, clean snow, and dying trees. He closed his eyes and reveled in the comforting familiarity. When he exhaled, the werewolf's snout shrank down and his fangs retracted so as not to impede his speech. Compared to the voice he'd used a moment ago, his next words were spoken with a richer timbre and the hint of an outdated accent. "Liam and Esteban may have acted too quickly, but these events were meant to happen."

"There is no good time for war."

"Violence can be a healing tool if applied at the right time and with the proper amount of force. I've learned that from the humans."

"Cut just deep enough to get the job done, eh?"

"Yes," Randolph said. "Perhaps I had been too easy on the Skinners after all. They were the ones to force these events into motion."

"You'd been taking it easy on the Skinners?" Kawosa scoffed. "From what I overheard while I was in Lancroft's care, you were one of the only things the old man feared."

"Don't try to get on my good side. I barely have one anymore. Where is Esteban?"

"Ever since he acquired the first Shadow Spore, he's been stretching his newfound legs. Has he truly achieved the final stage of our evolution?"

"There is a reason why the Shadow Spore was cast aside. We are not meant to tread in the mists. Did you warn him of the dangers that come from using that gift too much?"

Kawosa's grin wriggled on his face like a worm settling into the fur beneath his nose. "He didn't ask."

"Of course not. And what of the young one? Is she still in the custody of the Skinners?"

"That," Kawosa said with a tone that was as overtly deadly as a Full Blood's snarl, "was a mistake—to send her to them. Why would you betray your own kind that way, Birkyus?"

"I tried to protect her. I warned her about the Skinners. If she had been allowed to run with the others, she would have surely been used as nothing more than a lightning rod to draw attention away from the likes of Liam and Esteban. Once the Breaking Moon had set, she would have been killed before coming to terms with the power she'd acquired."

"Perhaps you're right. If she can't fend for herself using

the gifts she's already got," Kawosa declared, "then perhaps she doesn't deserve to live. Especially in times like these. Or perhaps she can hand back the Jekhibar as a way to get in our good graces." Smirking mischievously, he added, "Oh, that's right. She handed that over to the Skinners as a way to repay her gratitude to them. What a gracious child."

Now it was Randolph's turn to put on a grim, humorless smile. As the expression drifted onto his face, he shifted into a human body that stood in the cold field as if transplanted there from a battleground several centuries in the past. His naked skin was covered in scars, many as fresh and aggravated as the one that marred his face. Thick muscles resided beneath his flesh, honed to a burly stature without the need of any supernatural enhancement. Crouching down to shield himself from a wind that tore across the Canadian landscape, he said, "Times like these. You mean times where the oldest shapeshifter there is, the first shapeshifter there ever was, lends a helping hand to the wretches who've been a thorn in our side since the first human was broken? Or consorted with the leeches who've made it their life's work to nip at us when our backs are turned, or spread lies big enough to keep us away from their precious cities?"

"That's Liam talking."

"He hated the Nymar, as we all do. Perhaps his actions crossed a line, but at least he never went so far as to help them."

"What are you accusing me of?" Kawosa asked in an offended tone.

"I'm accusing you of organizing the Nymar by pointing some of their leaders in the right direction to gain an advantage over the humans."

All of the insulted, self-righteous rage that had flickered across Kawosa's face melted away until only his familiar trickster's grin remained. "Oh. You know about that, do you?"

"Of course I do. It's not as if Esteban was ever very good at covering his tracks. Even in the days before photographs, he was happy to terrorize enough humans to be drawn perfectly in chalk or oils. Now, his scent permeates most of this continent. The only parts that don't reek of him are the cities controlled by Nymar, and those cities reek of you." Randolph dug his fingers into the snow and earth as his body shifted into a thicker frame with an extra layer of muscle and fur.

As Randolph's form swelled, Kawosa's dwindled down into a thin silhouette, like a candle being melted in the sun. His head hung low and his snout tapered to a point "Don't raise your voice to me, boy," he warned. "Just because you got me out of Lancroft's pit doesn't mean I'll live the rest of my days indebted to you."

"I don't need your debt and I don't expect your gratitude," Randolph replied as if he was spitting out every foul-tasting word. "What you owe me is some respect! If not for me, you would still be rotting in Lancroft's basement. Just another one of his amusements to be eventually passed around to the Skinners like a whore."

Kawosa stood on two withered legs that barely seemed able to support him. His words were barely distinguishable beneath a throaty growl as he said, "I am your better, Full Blood. When you speak to me—"

"Shove your platitudes up your bony ass, Ktseena!" Randolph barked. "Your only strength is in your lies, and I never believed a word you said to begin with!"

"Not even when you asked me for the one favor you knew only I could provide?"

"You never had any intention of granting favors unless it benefited you. The reason you were removed from that prison was to upset the balance, draw the Skinners out of hiding and set this war into motion."

"Which I have done."

Leaning down to scowl directly into Kawosa's face, Randolph said, "Look into my eyes and tell me you haven't been guiding the leeches into strengthening their position."

Kawosa shrugged and settled back down onto his haunches. "They intrigue me."

"I know your fondness for the wretches. They grow stronger with every generation."

"And considering how many humans are succumbing to the Breaking, one generation flows into another very quickly. With the Torva'ox flowing, it is easier than ever to shape them. Soon they will be almost as hard to kill as . . ."

"And there we have it," Randolph said with a nod. "I'm actually surprised you even started to say it. And wipe that surprised look off your face. You say nothing that hasn't been plotted, planned, and rearranged."

"Actually, I'm surprised it took you this long to get so upset about the wretches becoming stronger. What kept you so busy? Still plotting your own little attempts to gain more power than your brethren? You kept young Cecile under your wing," Kawosa pointed out. "You wanted to use her to hide the Jekhibar from me."

"From you and all of the others."

"Well you got your wish. At least," Kawosa added, "for the moment."

"That doesn't excuse your involvement with the leeches," Randolph continued. "Perhaps the lies that kept Full Bloods in the forests for so long weren't of their own design."

"Humans do so love the romantic notion of vampire royalty. I think they know how fragile they are as a species and so they want to worship something they see as erotic and desirable. Kind of like a prisoner who convinces themselves that their master is truly worth serving."

"Is that what happened to you where Jonah Lancroft was concerned?" Crouching down a bit lower so he could dig his hind paws into the earth, Randolph asked, "Did you decide that it was better to lick his boots since you couldn't find a way out of that dungeon on your own? The great First Deceiver became nothing more than a lying old fool who got caught by someone who was just a little bit craftier."

"I know what you're doing."

"What's that?"

"You want to earn my admiration so that I will take you into my favor."

Those words rolled out of Kawosa's mouth like a breeze

that was just a bit colder and heavier than the ones already freezing the outermost layers of Randolph's fur to a glistening, icy sheen. They swirled within the Full Blood's head, causing his ears to twitch and his head to twist around as if in reaction to a beetle scurrying toward the interior of his skull. After a few seconds he snapped his head to the side, straightened it out and glared at Kawosa. "Your tricks don't work on us."

"Hmmm. Seems like that one got close. I have set things into motion. It's what I do. Isn't that why you freed me?"

"There's enough in motion now," Randolph said. "You know why I've sought you out this day."

"Ahh yes. There's still the matter of that favor you requested as a condition of my release. You want to find the other Mist Born. You want to seek out *my* brethren." Kawosa's eyes narrowed and his lips peeled back in a mildly disgusted grimace. "Somehow, you don't seem worthy of such a gift. Casting your eyes upon me should be enough for now. Perhaps after you learn some respect for your elders . . ."

As Randolph shook his head, it became shaggier and thicker. Fangs slid in to fill his mouth, slicing through the sides of his face with the ease of a sharp stick piercing a cobweb. "You never intended to grant any favors. Anyone who knows your legend would have figured out as much."

"You'd think so, wouldn't you? Liam never lost sight of the truest nature of things, no matter how terrible it was."

Randolph shook his head as if trying to jog something loose. His blue-gray eyes remained sharp even as his body shifted into its two-legged form. Still crouching, he was able to look down at the coyote creature with ease. When he stood on his hind legs, he might as well have been gazing down from a thousand feet above. "Liam partook in too much of the chaos he created. That's why he's dead."

"He just wanted a change of scenery. What do you want, Randolph?"

After pulling in a deep breath, holding onto it and finally letting it go, the Full Blood told him, "Quiet. All I want is . . . quiet." He started pacing then, circling Kawosa while the trickster only moved the muscles necessary to keep a constant distance between them.

"Even in the deepest woods before any of this started," Randolph said, "I couldn't get any quiet because Liam, the Mongrels, Esteban, the Skinners, the humans, the Nymar, even Minh, wouldn't stop howling with madness and bloodlust. Once the Blood Blades were out of the picture, the Skinners were supposed to go back to their old ways. If nothing else, they were good at maintaining the Balance. After Liam's farce of a siege against that first human city, larger steps needed to be taken."

"Larger steps," Kawosa snarled. "Like freeing me?"

"You are something that every Skinner but one still thought was a legend. When I caught your scent, I hardly believed it. But if Lancroft was keeping you squirreled away from his favorite Skinners, that made you a perfect wild card."

"Ahhh, there's Liam's voice speaking through you once again."

"Stop saying his name," Randolph warned. "I knew him for several lifetimes, which means I've earned the right to speak about him after he's gone. I was the only one among us who had the courage to say those things to his face. Even in the short time you ran at our sides, all you ever did was watch and listen."

"It's all I ever do," Kawosa said in a voice only a bit louder than a whimper.

Randolph shook his head. "No. Even if I did believe any of your lies, I would never believe that one. You stir the pot. Going back to legends spoken in forgotten tongues, that's all you've ever done."

Kawosa's eyelids drooped shut and he lifted his snout. "You were here in those days," he said. "You heard their songs. Heard the rattle of their beads when they danced. So many of those songs were for me."

"Not just for you. They were for all of the Mist Born

elders. I come to you now because I only need to find one of them."

Randolph's statement hung in the air for a minute.

And then another minute.

The wind blew. Branches shook. Finally, the silence became too much for one of them to bear.

"Which one?" Kawosa asked.

"Icanchu."

"You only care to find one of the twins? Chuna will be disappointed."

"Where are they?"

Some of Kawosa's fur settled back down to cover his back, and a hint of the sly grin eased onto his face. "I could have told you as much without all this fanfare. You'll need to ask Jaden. She hasn't left the jungles even with the flap of the Breaking Moon, but you shouldn't have any trouble sniffing her out."

"I'll need you to arrange the meeting," Randolph said. "The Mist Born have remained hidden so well that we don't even know the true name of their species. The only reason you were found was because of your propensity for toying with humans to earn a starring role in their myths."

"They are here. They have never left."

"I didn't come all this way just to swap riddles with you, trickster. I sought you out because I need to know *exactly* where to find Icanchu. I also need to know how to defeat him."

"Defeat Icanchu?" Kawosa chuckled. "I think the high and mighty Full Bloods truly have become full of themselves."

Randolph lunged forward with brutal efficiency. "I know you were toying with me, telling me whatever needed to be said so you could pounce on the chance of freedom I offered. But you've gone too far in spreading Esteban's voice across the world."

None of the menace in Randolph's voice was lost on the other shapeshifter. Kawosa moved like the top layer of snow that was just barely brushed aside from the white-capped field around him. With a minimal amount of effort he kept himself facing the Full Blood while also staying outside of the range of claws or fangs. "I don't know what you're talking about."

"Don't mistake me for one of the idiots who swallow your lies. The Breaking Moon may have given Full Bloods the power to unleash the Breaking at will, but not to the extent that has been ravaging the humans in the recent months. When he howls, humans drop for miles in all directions. They become another generation of wretches, and the only one who benefits from so many generations of wretches is you. You, who crafts them into something you can control. Perhaps you seek to replace the Full Bloods with your Half Breed abominations because you never could quite dominate us the way you do them."

"This isn't the best way to gain my favor," Kawosa warned.

"You mean the favor you would have dangled in front of me until I turned my back long enough for you to sink your claws into it? Keep it."

"If you wish to challenge the likes of Icanchu, then I'm the least of your worries."

"You were a necessary evil," Randolph said. "As long as you were free to roam, my brethren would be watching you, and the humans would be preoccupied with whatever chaos you helped unleash. I thought your manipulation of the wretches' bloodline would take a lot longer, but that doesn't matter anymore. Now is the moment I've known was coming from the instant I freed you from Jonah Lancroft's dungeon. Now is when you pay for your freedom by giving me what I need to steal Icanchu's prize."

"And what happens if I don't do as you ask?"

"Then I'll be forced to assert myself."

"That isn't quite a threat," Kawosa reminded him. "There's a little room before you commit yourself that far. Back away now and I'll assume you're overly enthusiastic. Quite understandable in these volatile times."

"All right. How's this? Give me what I want, make good on repaying a debt that allowed you to smell this fine winter air instead of the dusty rock beneath Lancroft's basement, or I'll tear your head from your shoulders and take it to Icanchu to show that jungle demon I truly mean business. Considering your reputation among the older Mist Born, both of the twins will thank me for silencing you."

"Killing me won't get you anywhere," Kawosa snarled. "That is, if you can even accomplish such a feat."

"You're not a fighter, Ktseena," Randolph warned. "Perhaps you should make good and be done with this. I've gone too far to turn back now."

"Just because you haven't seen me kill doesn't mean I'm inexperienced in that arena. You don't want to do this."

Randolph blinked and cringed as he was assaulted by those last few words. Whatever power Kawosa put behind his lies to make someone immediately believe them, he was using it to its full extent. Somehow, whether through his shared lineage with the shapeshifter or through sheer force of will, Randolph withstood the barrage. "There are ways for us to benefit from ending this war."

"But you want it only to end by your hand. To do that, your hand must be balled into the mightiest fist there has ever been. The quiet you seek will come at the expense of too many lives."

"There are too many lives in this world as is," Randolph growled. "Shapeshifter and human alike. If that number continues to grow, one species will devour the other and the landscape will be forever scarred. Both sides need to be culled, and the Balance needs to be preserved. Esteban is helping you create more wretches, and the wretches are cutting a bloody swath through the humans. When that is over, the wretches will tip the scales through sheer numbers. Esteban thinks he can control them, but I know *you* are the one waiting for your moment to show it is your hand at the reins."

"If you know so much, you should have left me in Lancroft's pit."

Randolph had taken a form that was bristling with raw, elemental might. Saliva flowed off of fangs the size of a man's fingers, only to freeze in the thick fur that hung from his chin. "The noise that fills this modern world has become deafening. In order to silence it, the Full Bloods needed first to be heard above the commotion. Liam knew this, but all he wanted was to rage against them all. The Skinners were a larger obstacle than any of our kind ever realized, but it was the leeches that suppressed them long enough for us to mobilize like never before. The Breaking Moon rose and you were free to make the best of it. But I have read the legends. I know that you are the First Deceiver. The first Full Blood. While your lies may not sink as deeply into our minds, your influence burrows like a worm that sinks further and further in the longer you infect our kind with your presence. That is why I spent most of the Breaking Moon far away from this place.

"I know the Skinners better than anyone. I have learned all there is to know about my brethren. I even knew where to find you when the time came. All I need is a source of the Torva'ox that is stronger than what now flows through even your veins. When I have that, there will be a culling that will silence the yapping population of human and shapeshifter alike."

"And you believe Icanchu will help you do this?" Kawosa asked. "You are a fool."

"I did not start this bloodshed, but I offer you a chance to be one of the survivors after I finish it."

"I'll take my chances on my own. Gambling with Death offers better odds than siding with an angry pup like you."

"And I'm through with taking chances. Since you won't give me what I need, I'll take it from you." Randolph lunged. He dropped to all fours and barely allowed his front paws to touch the ground before springing forward and baring almost every fang in his mouth with a wide, vicious snarl.

Kawosa planted his paws in the snow, bobbing his head down and to the side before rolling away as the Full Blood's jaws clamped shut above him. He might have avoided getting his head snipped off, but a good portion of his fur along with a patch of flesh on the back of his neck were sheared away.

Twisting his head to take another snap at Kawosa, Randolph clamped down on empty air. When he opened his mouth again, he spat out the little piece of Kawosa he'd claimed as if the furry patch of flesh had put a foul taste in his mouth. Then he kicked up a frozen white wave as he scrambled to turn back around and face his opponent. Kawosa was there waiting for him.

The trickster wore a weary smile. His black eyes shifted to a cloudy green and then became perfect crystalline orbs similar to a Full Blood's. Randolph tensed for an attack, and when he'd committed himself to a defense, Kawosa attacked a spot that was left open. Compared to the Full Blood's claws, Kawosa's were like curved, bony needles. They didn't have enough brute force to peel a car down to the frame, but they punctured Randolph's flesh with every swipe.

Knowing it was only a matter of seconds before his flesh was stripped to the bone, Randolph stood up and tried to grab hold of the other shapeshifter. When he got a hold on him, Kawosa bit his hand and shook his head until narrow, pointed fangs met inside the Full Blood's wrist. Howling wildly, Randolph tore Kawosa from his back. The pain from the bite was more than enough to wash away the agony of ripping those claws from where they'd been lodged.

Kawosa landed on all fours, and as soon as his paws were under him, put some distance between himself and Randolph. Once that was done, he circled around and leapt at him.

Having already gotten a taste of Kawosa's speed, Randolph didn't try to dodge the incoming attack. He shifted his muscles into thick bands and planted his feet in preparation for catching the wily shapeshifter. Somehow, Kawosa pivoted in midair so his claws could swipe at him from unexpected angles. The instant Randolph grabbed his midsection, Kawosa slashed at Randolph's face. The Full Blood craned his neck to avoid the deadly weapons, howling as one claw snagged the corner of an eye. It was only a matter of determination mixed with a bit of luck that he wasn't blinded. Realizing this, he flung Kawosa into the air, shifted into his four-legged form and broke into a loping run. Not once did he take his eyes from Kawosa as the shapeshifter turned and kicked through empty space. All he needed to do was keep his prey in sight while gauging where Kawosa would land.

And then the trickster disappeared like a mirage that had been made of cloud vapor and drifting smoke.

Randolph slowed his steps while searching the blue Canadian sky. There was nothing to mask the sight of an airborne shapeshifter. In the distance he heard the impact of something landing in the snow, followed by the scraping of claws against hard, frozen earth. Panting with renewed vigor, Randolph raced in that direction.

"You know nothing of what I can do," Kawosa said while pacing less than fifty yards in front of the Full Blood.

Randolph rushed at him, eyes narrowing to keep out as much of the icy wind as possible. When Kawosa sprang from his hind legs, Randolph jumped to meet him at the top of an arch formed by their two trajectories. Instead of colliding the way two physical bodies should, however, Randolph slashed apart the vision of Kawosa that faded without so much as a hint of anything solid that had been there. Before Randolph could touch the ground again, something slammed against his ribs. It was Kawosa, clinging to him, biting and clawing in a frenzy of sharp edges and insatiable hunger. Peeling him off and casting him away this time was even more painful for Randolph than the last.

"I'll give you one chance to think, pup," Kawosa said upon landing. "Think about what you're doing and maybe you'll come to your senses."

But Randolph wasn't going to be swayed. Although there were no energies trying to assert themselves on his mind, he recognized the feral gleam in the shapeshifter's pale gold eyes. There was too much blood dripping from his tapered snout, too much torn flesh dangling from between his teeth, for him to simply give up now. Any werewolf knew the hunger that came after tasting the tender perfection of freshly shredded meat. Rather than put his insight to the test, Randolph allowed his muscles to relax and his head to hang to one side as if he was truly considering the offer.

Sure enough, Kawosa charged. Although the trickster was the one snapping at the bait dangling in front of him, he didn't go about it recklessly. He covered the small patch of ground between them in a series of darting steps, each one sending him forward at a slightly different angle than the last. Even his head sent mixed signals as it bobbed in the wrong way from the rest of his body. Rather than try to compensate for all of those factors, Randolph stood up and swept both arms out. If another creature had been standing directly in front of him, it would have been ripped in half by both sets of claws that raked out in opposite directions to cover as much area as possible.

The swings were wild enough to clip Kawosa in several places. Having underestimated his quarry, Kawosa now found himself in the midst of an onslaught akin to several sets of propeller blades converging on him at once. He snapped at Randolph's legs and brought the Full Blood down. He then kicked his lower body to an awkward angle so another powerful swing could pass him by, and scrambled away.

Like any predator, Randolph's killer instinct swelled at the sight of his prey trying to flee. His howl was a terrible sound that sent smaller animals fleeing for miles in every direction. After all that had happened, even the humans in nearby towns knew to shut their doors and seek shelter instead of poking their noses out to investigate the unearthly riot.

Kawosa kept his steps swift and glanced over one shoulder to find the other shapeshifter bearing down on him. Shifting into a lean, scraggly canine built for running, he bolted toward the north. But Randolph knew better than to chase after him right away. Instead, he slowed down and strained for his other senses to detect any hint as to something else that might be moving around him.

Kawosa didn't exactly disappear from where he'd been, but he did show up in a spot that Randolph hadn't been expecting. When Randolph tried to follow his prey, he found himself simply looking in the wrong direction. Now that the trickster had built up a head of steam, he had enough speed to put a simple ruse like that to good use. Keeping that in mind, Randolph charged over snowdrifts, leapt over fallen logs, and stormed through forests. Kawosa's ruse bought him enough time to veer away to the south, but the Full Blood surged onward with enough force to catch up to him. Randolph's claws snagged the trickster's tail, but Kawosa ripped himself loose at the expense of his own body and ran away again.

After tossing aside the tail he'd ripped from Kawosa's body, the pursuit began in earnest.

Chapter Eight

Louisville, Kentucky

When the sun went down on a war-torn country, nearly every city felt the same. After the Breaking Moon, dusk became a universal warning for all living things without claws to seek shelter before the monsters emerged from their holes. There was no shame in running anymore. No pride to be lost at jumping when an unexpected noise rang out. People still conducted their lives, trying not to think about the horrors that had engulfed their former lives. A trickle of humanity went out to eat or worked at jobs they could ill afford to quit. Some children went to school where drills were conducted to teach them where to run if Half Breeds charged toward the playground. The rest sat behind bolted doors, praying.

Rico had given up on anything as comforting as prayer. He sat inside the sloped building on the corner of Spring and Payne, hunched over the keyboard of one of many Vigilant computers, angling his head so the other nearby Skinners couldn't easily hear him as he spoke into a hands-free phone receiver. Since the windows were all blacked out and barred, he watched the outside world through a small bank of monitors displaying feeds from cameras set up on posts, rooftops, and windowsills within three square blocks of his location. Every so often he would check the faces of the Skinners watching him, and then look back down to the work he was doing. "All right," he whispered. "What do you want me to do?"

"Are you at the computer?" Cole asked through the headset.

"Yeah, but I ain't no hacker. If anyone's tryin' to hide something about that prison in Colorado, I sure as hell won't be able to find it."

"Just type what I tell you and let me know what you find. Look for Hal Waylon. He was the guy who ran the place where I was locked up."

Rico did as Cole instructed, but Hal Waylon's name wasn't easy to find. A little digging into e-mail histories, downloads, and user interface registrations was enough to pull up the name four times. Denver, Colorado, was mentioned, but mostly in connection to the two Full Bloods who'd leveled a supposedly abandoned packaging facility. It was the same bullshit that had been handed to the press, and mentioned nothing of Cole's escape. The fragments he'd found where Hal Waylon was mentioned were too small to count for anything.

"We need more than that," Rico grunted.

"Hal Waylon was a Skinner," Cole insisted. "He mentioned the Vigilant by name and acted like someone who took his sensitivity training from a douche bag like Jonah Lancroft."

"There are other Vigilant branches out there. I only got a few minutes before I'm noticed here, so make it snappy."

The two closest to him were from the younger batch who'd been called in to help with Cecile. They were twitchy due to frayed nerves, pale after being out of the sunlight for the better part of a month, and never far away from a shotgun or assault rifle. A few more Skinners walked back and forth between other rooms. Most of the activity was centered on the basement now that there was a live Full Blood to cut and prod as they pleased. Rico didn't even want to think about what sorts of experiments were being run on Cecile or what samples were being taken.

"Okay," Cole sighed. "Let's try a few other keywords. What about 'tendrils, infected' or 'spore'?" He then told Rico how to run the search to look for instances where those words showed up in conjunction with his own name.

Leaning back in the squeaky old office chair he'd been given, Rico said, "Nada."

"Hey," one of the younger Skinners said. "You find anything yet?" She usually sat in the spot Rico was using, but wasn't high enough on the totem pole to do much of anything when he waved her off.

He searched for *prison* and *cells*, only to find some notes related to building the holding area in the basement where Cecile was being held.

"Okay," Cole said. "We need to search for something specifically related to that Colorado facility where I was locked up, but isn't a high enough priority to be wiped out in an attempt for these guys to make themselves look innocent. Something not very important in the grand scheme of things but that's still in the system. Maybe something mentioned in low-level messages or a document that wouldn't have been wiped off the hard drive."

"You got ten more seconds," Rico said.

Cole only needed four. "Try 'Lambert.'"

"That's the other prisoner that broke out with you, ain't it?"

"Yep."

"Where's he been?"

"Good question," Cole replied. "Haven't seen him since about a week after Atoka fell. He's probably holed up someplace to stay out of the line of fire."

"Join the damn club," Rico grunted.

Some hits showed up right away. When Rico clicked on them, he got a few e-mails regarding a scrawny man claiming to be a psychic who was brought up on charges for assaulting two people at a bar in West Texas. A half-garbled link to a website brought his attention to a news story about a man arrested for robbing a woman outside a tattoo parlor and trying to escape into the Rocky Mountains.

Cole sifted through his memories of those days he'd spent behind bars. The next few searches were quick and easy.

Frank.

That one came up empty, which wasn't a surprise. Cole doubted anyone running that prison gave a damn about what Frank's name was.

Squamatosapien.

Squam.

Lizard man.

None of those words sparked much of anything either. Rico could feel his time at the computer dwindling. It wouldn't be long before one of the others took it upon themselves to step closer and take a better look at what he was doing. When Cole gave him the next search item, the smile shone through in his voice.

"Try 'Sweet Sarah Sunshine.'"

The computer chugged through its own memories before spitting up one note from a file that resided in a buffer where old documents sat after being placed in a bundle and then stored without being opened for an excessive amount of time. It was an e-mail marked, *Prioner description.* The simple misspelling in the title was probably the only thing that had saved it from being deleted with all of the other prisoner-related stuff.

"We have a winnah," Rico declared. It read:

> *Subject in Holding Cell 4: Adult male, Hispanic, approx. 30-35 years old, 5'9" tall, 168 lbs. Tattoo on rib cage reads "Sweet Sarah Sunshine" adorned with lip marks and ladybugs. Low-level psychic ability at close range. Can read thoughts and short-term memories which make him par-*

ticularly valuable in questioning and categorizing other prisoners. No known family. Recommend he be left in vicinity of cells and terminated when becomes too much trouble. Dissection of brain matter may be useful.

The victory Rico felt at finding something faded the moment he realized what it meant. "You were right," he said under his breath.

"What is it?" Cole asked. "What did you find? Can you e-mail it to me?"

Once quick glance at the young woman who normally haunted that computer was enough to tell Rico that she would be sifting through that terminal the moment he got up. "No," he said as he deleted everything he knew how to delete. "But it's enough. Meet me outside. I got something you need to see."

While going through the motions of shutting the computer down, he jabbed a beefy finger toward the young woman and barked, "Go check on the crow's nest and secure the armory!"

She, along with half of the Skinners in the immediate area, jumped up and hurried upstairs to follow through on the orders. Once they were out of the way, Rico stomped over to the rune-encrusted panel in the floor and dropped to one knee so he could tap some of the runes on the square door that Jessup had opened earlier. When the trapdoor came open, Rico pressed his finger against the earpiece as if about to shove it into his brain. "It's not here," he said in a hushed voice.

Cole's response was measured and calm. "I may know something about that."

"You got a hold of that box?" Rico asked. An ugly smirk crawled across his face when he asked, "How the hell did you manage that one?"

"I don't have it, but I know where it is."

"I'm coming out there and you're givin' it back to me."

"I can't," Cole said. "Paige and I need that thing."

Rico shut the door, set the runes to remain locked no matter who touched them next, then nodded casually to the Skinner on guard duty carrying an AK-47. "You're damn lucky that box is still in there. Were *you* the one that didn't shut it right?"

"No!" The guard reflexively replied. "Wasn't me!"

"Good. Don't go warnin' any of the other newbie twerps," he snarled. "When I find out which it was that did that, I want it to be a surprise."

The expression on the younger man's face showed that he was relieved to be grateful he hadn't touched the floor panel, and his quick turn on the balls of his feet showed how anxious he was to get the hell away from the big man.

Chapter Nine

Cole sat in the car down the street, but still within sight of the Vigilant base. After being cut off so quickly by Rico, he perched on the edge of his seat waiting for him to storm out of the building. Paige had left a few moments ago, but the remains of the Chinese food she'd picked up for lunch was still scattered on the floor and backseat. Even after hell had spilled all over the world, General Tso Chicken still came in those little white boxes. On a very genuine level, that brought Cole some comfort.

Rico walked outside using a stride that seemed powerful enough to smash through any wall unfortunate enough to have been built in his path. After spotting the borrowed car, he motioned for Cole to follow him to the corner. He was headed for the Spring Street Bar and Grill, which had its windows boarded up like every other business in the area. Unlike the miniature fortress created by the Vigilant, the bar showed signs of life. Light filtered through the reinforced shutters, and voices made it outside past doors that were tightly closed in the event any four-legged visitors showed up. As Rico passed the bar, he nodded up toward the spots where Cole already knew the Vigilant cameras were posted.

A pair of figures huddled in the shadows across the street,

where a house sat on a corner lot. Its yard was surrounded by a broken chain-link fence, and the grass had been torn up by so many claw marks that it looked as if it had been run over by a piece of farming equipment. A tall tree leaned toward the tiny house as if to offer the shelter that a pointed awning over the front door couldn't provide. Judging by the broken windows and scratch marks along the walls, whoever owned that house needed a lot more than shade to protect them.

Slowing as he passed in front of a row of little, single-story houses, Rico stepped onto a lawn that was smaller than the house's driveway to examine a satellite dish sporting a large ugly bite mark that had claimed almost a quarter of its radius. "You got that rock?"

"Not on me," Cole replied as he closed in on him.

"Then where is it? I'm puttin' my ass on the line here. Jessup ain't a bad guy, but he's not real big in the trust department."

"So are you with him or us?" Cole asked. "After the hell we went through in New Mexico, the least that guy could do is stick with us."

"He is," Rico said. "Jessup's sticking with all Skinners by ditching his own stomping ground and coming to work for the only core group that has been seriously organized. If you or Paige don't like it, maybe you should have done some organizing yourselves before throwing in with the IRD."

"We all jumped to the sides we thought would do the most damage to the Full Bloods. This fight's just started, though, and we're not far from losing it."

Rico nodded. "You got that right. All we need to do is pull together when it counts. These Vigilant dudes may be drifting toward the whacko end of the spectrum, but they got heart and they got some heavy duty firepower from Jonah Lancroft's personal collection. Somehow, they also got to the best stuff from Philadelphia. And since there ain't hardly any other Skinners answering their phone anymore, the Vigilant are about all there is unless you wanna join the Army."

"You can't find any other Skinners?"

"We been in contact with the ones that survived the raids from the cops, but as of a few days ago, it's been real quiet." Rico drew a measured breath and stared at Cole intently when he asked, "Did you or Paige turn over a list of names to the military?"

At that moment Cole was certain of three things. If he'd betrayed any Skinners who were scooped up by the government, he was in for some serious bodily harm. If he tried to lie about doing such a thing, he would be found out and then subjected to even more serious harm. And finally, there was no doubt which side of the battle Rico was on. Philosophical differences aside, Rico was the same man he'd been the first time they met. "After all the shit we've been through, you can still ask me a question like that?"

Rico eased back just enough to let Cole know the storm had temporarily passed. "I've been level with you the whole time," he rasped. "The problem with you and Paige is that you're still thinkin' in terms of us and them. The only 'us' here is humanity, and 'them' is them furry sons of bitches running wild through our cities. Now, I'm not sayin' everyone under that roof back there shares my views on the matter, but that's where I stand. When I was pissed with you guys in New Mexico, I told you so. Trust me, I've been telling Jessup the same things. All it boils down to is that these guys speak my language and Lancroft knew how to whip monster ass. Right now, though, I need to show you something and I need that rock to do it."

The window of the house swung open to reveal an old man wrapped in a thick burgundy robe. His eyes may have been covered by thick lenses housed in cheap plastic frames, but he didn't have any trouble finding a target for the pump-action shotgun in his hands. "Move it along, you two!"

"We ain't messin' up yer lawn, old man!" Rico barked.

The shotgun was raised to his shoulder and the home owner stared the Skinners down as if they were two Half Breeds pissing on his rosebushes. "I said move it along."

Rico spun around and threw an angry wave at the old man. "We killed a pack of Half Breeds before they could climb through his windows and this is the thanks we get."

"Times are hard," Cole said.

"I got sick of hearin' that shit a long time ago."

"Yeah. Me too."

"What about your Army buddies?" Rico asked. "Can't they check around to see who's left besides us and the Vigilant?"

"They barely know which end is up," Cole said. "The IRD is doing their best to stomp out the fires, but they can't wrap their brains around what's starting them. Soon as we realized they don't have much more than big guns in their pockets, Paige and I got away to find some answers on our own."

"What about that little toy you brought in the basement? Pretty high-tech stuff. Or is that something you whipped up?"

"It's some good tech. We might've been able to put something like it together, though. Still, it's . . ." Cole felt his stomach clench. The tendrils hurt like hell, but that was nothing new. He'd reached an understanding with them. Somehow, he just knew they weren't about to kill him. Even if they weren't connected to a spore, they still had a purpose, and choking out their only food source didn't serve it. No, this clench came from realizing he might just be even dumber than he'd thought. "Shit, I can't believe this."

"Believe what?"

"Paige and I ditched the car the IRD gave us, checked everything we were carrying, just about tore apart the clothes we were issued, and even picked through our boots to make sure we weren't being tracked or bugged by those guys. They gave us that device to field test and we kept it because it could be useful, even as a bargaining chip." Cole shook his head, suddenly feeling every bit of the weight that the last few months had dumped onto his shoulders. "I bet that device has got something else in it. Maybe that was the whole reason Adderson gave it to us."

Clapping him on the shoulder, Rico said, “Could be. I was the one watching the screens when you carried that thing past the sci-fi setup in the front of that house. Our expensive computer shit picked up on a signal right away. Since it was you, I squelched it without raising the alarms.”

“Funny. I guess from being out there stabbing werewolves, getting bitten by vampires, and dodging gargoyles, the more modern ways of being hunted don’t register as much. Should’ve seen that one coming.”

“Maybe, maybe not. I would’ve thought to look for some electronic shit inside the little electronic box, but that’s me. I’ve spent a few more years hanging around with criminals or other sorts who think about wiretaps and that kind of crap.”

“Jessup put you in charge of watching the computers?” Cole asked. “You really have them snowed.”

“Nah. Just told ’em I learned a few things from hanging out with you.”

Those words, coupled with the approving nod from Rico, told him that the big guy actually thought of him as something other than cannon fodder.

“Don’t be so surprised,” Rico said. “Word spreads. That’s how it’s always been with us. With you and Paige stepping up the way you have, the rest of us are bound to know who you are.”

“You were there for a lot of it too.”

“And don’t think I don’t remind them of that whenever they try to pressure me into signing on all the way with these Vigilant creeps.”

“So you don’t trust them?” Cole asked.

Rico glanced down the street toward the Vigilant’s building and then turned away as if he was certain they were looking straight back at him. “Since you told me about that bug, I know I can trust you. Speaking of trust, where’s that rock?”

Cole looked across the street, couldn’t find the figures that had been stalking him previously, then shifted his eyes toward another lot. Soon, the figures stepped out from around another house and stayed there to make sure they were seen. Cole waved at them, which was enough for the two figures to part ways. One came straight at Cole and Rico, while the other doubled back down the street. As soon as the second figure stepped out of the shadows, Paige waved at Cole and continued down the street toward the car.

Rico kept his hand on the butt of his holstered Sig Sauer while watching the first figure approach him. "That's one of the new guys. Waggoner. He one of yours?"

"One of Paige's, is more like it. She met him in Atoka."

Waggoner was a tall man sporting a full beard. He hobbled across the street wearing several layers of jackets, thermal undershirts, and flannel to fight a winter chill that struck Cole as mildly bracing at the worst. Judging by the weight of his clothes, Waggoner seemed to be more concerned, anyway, about having the maximum amount of pockets rather than being warm.

"He's been with us for a few months," Rico said as his eyes narrowed suspiciously. "He's been a spy that whole time?"

"Nope. He just got a little freaked out by some of the stuff he heard in that big clubhouse of yours. When he called Paige a few weeks ago, I was just as surprised as you are."

By now Waggoner had made it across the street. After throwing a quick nod at Rico, he hobbled over to stand out of the big man's reach. "Hey, Cole. Good to see you. I would've said hello earlier, but . . . you know."

"Yeah," Rico said while eyeing the little box in the other man's hands. "I know. You've been busy stealing from us."

"You don't even know me, mister. I've seen you around plenty of times, but you ain't even seen fit to shake my hand."

"You're still wet behind the ears, boy," the big man replied. "Just carved your own weapon, right?"

The man nodded meekly at first, but quickly straightened up and lifted his chin.

"I don't care what anyone else said about him," Cole said evenly, "I can tell you he's a stand-up guy. Even after he got injured in Atoka, he still wanted to ride with Paige to face off against those Full Bloods."

Rico grunted. "Bein' stupid should never be mixed up with bein' brave. I already heard about you saving a bunch of people stuck in a panic room during the Breaking Moon, so I guess you do have some redeeming qualities." Looking down from Waggoner's eyes, he said, "Tell me how you got that."

Waggoner shifted his weight off his left side while pressing a hand against one leg. "Half Breed tore into me in Atoka. Nearly crippled me, but some friends patched me up before steering me toward this place."

"Not that, numb nuts! The fucking box in your hands!"

Waggoner tightened his grip on the metal container. "I was coming down to see if anyone needed help when that Full Blood in the basement broke loose. As soon as I got to the bottom of the stairs, Jessup handed it to me and told me to put it away."

"So instead you sneak out with it? Didn't anyone stop you?"

"They were all too busy trying to get a look at the Full Blood or get to a weapon in case it tried to get upstairs."

Before Rico could get close enough to grab hold of the other man, Cole stepped between them and said, "I told him to try and get ahold of the Jekhibar when we called to let him know we were headed out here. We need that thing."

"And I agree with him," Waggoner said. "I'm a grown man. I don't take orders from much of anyone and I don't need someone else to fight my battles." Looking Rico dead in the eyes, he added, "I've heard plenty of things about you. Why the hell would you pick sides with these crazies?"

"Because there's a fight that needs to be won. We can worry about settling up with each other after that's finished." Rico's gaze didn't lose any of its fire when he shifted it toward Cole. "Why didn't you just come to me with this?"

"Why didn't you answer any of the calls we made when we needed help clearing out St. Louis and Topeka?"

"I left you all the Snappers I had."

"And they work great. We need more than bullets, though. That's why—"

"Yeah, yeah," Rico sighed. "That's why you broke off from the IRD. You gonna give me that box or are you gonna make me take it from you?"

Waggoner didn't look like he was cowed in the slightest by Rico, and he didn't look to Cole for affirmation before handing over the metal box. Rico took it, opened it, and snatched the bent metal wedge from it. Tucking the box under an arm, he reached into one of the pockets of his heavy leather biker jacket. When Cole first met the big man, that jacket had patches of canvas to fill in the spaces that still needed to be covered with tanned Half Breed hide. Now the entire jacket was solid leather, stitched together from several pieces that fit like a puzzle wrapped around his entire upper body. From his pocket, Rico took a small plastic bottle of eye drops. Recognizing the color and oily texture of the fluid inside the bottle, Cole knew it did a lot more than moisturize and rejuvenate.

"Put these in," Rico said. "Both of you."

"What is it?" Waggoner asked.

Taking the bottle and sniffing the top, Cole tipped his head back so he could put a couple drops in each eye. "It lets you see scents," he said. "You can also see certain kinds of energy patterns like whatever flows through the Skinner runes." Handing the bottle over to Waggoner, he asked, "What does flow through those runes, Rico?"

The big man shrugged. "Long as they work, I don't give a crap."

Waggoner sighed in a way that reflected his uncertainty at putting his eyesight in the hands of men who barely seemed able to keep themselves from getting killed. Cole knew as much because he'd let out the same sigh plenty of times. Already in too deep as it was, Waggoner put the drops in his eyes and immediately dropped the bottle. "It burns. Shit, it burns. Wash it out!"

"Keep yer voice down," Rico snarled.

Cole was a little more supportive. "It's supposed to burn. Just let it soak in." Grabbing Waggoner's sleeve, he pulled him away from the street even though there hadn't been a hint of a car since they stepped out of the Vigilant's building. "And do it over here so the cameras don't see."

"You're worried about the goddamn cameras?" Waggoner asked. "I could be going blind and you . . . oh wait. It's feeling a little better."

"When it gets cold, open your eyes."

After a few more seconds Waggoner opened his eyes.

Rico was in the process of blinking in the drops he'd just applied as he pocketed the bottle. "All right," he said. "We need to walk back into that bar and order a drink."

"Doesn't Jessup have that place wired?" Cole asked.

"Yeah, and I'm supposed to be on patrol right now. Most of the times, patrol winds up at that bar. Come on." As they walked back to the Spring Street Bar and Grill, Rico wiped at his eye and told Waggoner, "If anyone realizes that rock is missing, I'm blaming it on you."

"Go right ahead. You think I didn't work out a few stories to tell if I was caught with it?"

Rico's eyebrows waggled upward and he nudged Cole. "This one might work out after all." He knocked on the bar door and said, "Step inside and try not to make a big deal about all the pretty colors you'll see."

When the door to the bar was opened, they were greeted with plenty of colors. First, there was the matted black of the shotgun leveled at them by the doorman. Since they weren't Half Breeds or showing any Nymar markings when they were forced to uncover their necks and wrists, they were allowed inside. On the walls, there were bright red and blue beer signs, pink neon advertising a brand of rum, flashing spectrums thrown from video games and a pinball machine, and of course the sparkling yellow and greens of an old jukebox. More than that, Cole saw something he'd never seen before.

When he used the eye drops on previous occasions, he'd seen green wisps coming from Dryad symbols, dark smoky reds from Nymar, and even a disturbing black from Skinners themselves. What he hadn't seen was the light blue curls of vaguely glowing smoke seeping from the people gathered there. The color streamed off everyone in the bar, swirling about them as they moved and entwining when one person's path crossed another.

"Holy crap," Waggoner said. "This stuff is really messing with me."

"Me too," Cole said. "What's with the blue?"

"That," Rico told him, "comes off of everyone who's not tainted by anything." With a grin, he added, "At least nothing that isn't for sale in a place like this. From what I've seen, it comes off of yer run-of-the-mill human."

"When did this start?" Cole asked.

"Can't say for certain since I don't put this shit in my eyes all the time, but I'd say right about the time of the Breaking Moon."

As he spoke, Cole noticed all of the blue wisps in the room were working their way in one direction. His direction. They converged on him like ghostly fingers that just realized there was some sort of treat in his pocket.

"You think that's weird," Rico said. "Get a load of this." He removed the Jekhibar from his pocket, held it in his hand and let it rest on his palm.

There wasn't much of a change at first, but the blue wisps subtly shifted their direction until they were drifting toward Rico. Upon reaching his outstretched hand, they circled it and brushed against the Jekhibar before pressing into the rough, silvery surface.

"Just wait," Rico said before Cole could ask the question that had popped into his mind.

In a matter of seconds the ghostly smoke emanating from the bodies in that room poured out of them even faster and blended to form a singular current that swept through the room. Although it was still disrupted by the constant motion of the bar's patrons, the glowing haze took on a brighter hue as it flowed into the stone sitting on Rico's palm.

"It's coming from the ground," Waggoner said.

Cole tore his eyes from the sight of the shimmering fog and looked down. Although he couldn't see a definite source, the flow of the ghostly substance moved in such a way that a pattern emerged. It was indeed emanating from the people, but also rushed up from the floor, passing through boards and tile as if they were nothing but a screen. It all went directly to the Jekhibar.

"What is that thing?" Waggoner asked while looking to the lump of silver in Rico's hand.

"Whatever the power was that the Full Bloods were after when they took Atoka," he explained, "it's drawn to this rock. It's also drawn to the Full Bloods. What we didn't know before was that it's also drawn to us. I've done a bit of snooping around and I can tell you it ain't drawn to Nymar. And ever since the Breaking Moon, it's been flowing like a damn river."

Their conversation was interrupted as the stringy woman behind the bar leaned over and asked, "You guys drinkin' or what?"

"One for the road," Rico said. "For each of us."

The bartender reached under the bar and came back up with three matching bottles of cheap domestic, which she opened. "That'll be nine seventy-five."

"Pay her, new guy," Rico grunted as he took a beer for himself.

Since it wasn't light beer, Cole took one and told Waggoner, "I used to be the new guy, so now it's your turn."

"Last time I do a favor for you assholes," Waggoner muttered as he fished out a ten and handed it over. The other two were already headed out the door, so he didn't get a chance to hear the skinny woman unenthusiastically thank him for the pathetic tip before he was outside with them.

"Here's the good part," Rico said as he led the way down the street in the direction of the house marked by the bitten satellite dish. He turned and faced the bar again, having already put the Jekhibar back into its box. "As near as we can figure, that blue energy is the Torva'ox or whatever Paige was talking about back in Oklahoma. It's been surging ever since the Breaking Moon."

"Kind of like when you siphon gas from a truck?" Waggoner asked.

"Yeah. Something like that." Shifting his focus back to Cole, Rico said, "Jessup may look like the leader of the pack around here, but that's just because he's got seniority. He ain't the one calling all the shots and he ain't the asshole you think he is."

"I never said that."

"Didn't have to. You were looking at him like you wanted to plaster him against a wall. Same way you were lookin' at me."

Since Cole knew he couldn't make a convincing argument against that, he let it pass. "Then who is calling the shots?"

"We're workin' on that."

Waggoner shook his head and rubbed his temples. "I don't know if it's everything that's been going on or if it's because of these drops, but I feel a dizzy spell coming on."

"Get used to it," Cole said. "I've been feeling like that ever since I saw my first werewolf. Okay, Rico. So the Torva'ox flows into humans. Can we use it?"

"I don't know and I ain't even sure we'll get a chance to find out. That shit that's flowing through them Full Bloods makes them stronger, and this stone just seems to give the Torva'ox some extra spark so we can see it, or maybe adds more of a kick. I don't know. We didn't even make the damn thing. All I can tell you is that your average human being is sucking away the power that those Full Bloods want. Now if you were one of those big hairy sons of bitches, and you went through all that trouble to get the juices flowing, what would you think about so many little monkeys leeching off of the source?"

"I'd want to get rid of them," Cole said.

Waggoner wanted to rub his eyes, but stopped himself. "Is that why they've come after us so hard?"

Now, Rico slapped Waggoner on the shoulder. "That's the shitty thing about being able to see things from another perspective. Doesn't always paint a pretty picture. Take the Jekhibar," he said to Cole.

"You sure about that?"

"Yeah. It'll be a good long while before anyone figures out a way to get that hatch open anyway, after what I did to mess with those runes. When someone finds out about that, I'll steer the explanation toward interference caused by too many new recruits scuffing up the symbols. Should keep 'em busy for a few weeks. Think you can get it back to me by then?"

"I honestly don't know," Paige replied as she strode toward them. Her Beretta was in hand and ready to provide assistance if Rico stepped out of line, but she'd apparently decided that wasn't necessary. "What will you do if things get too hot for you with the Vigilant?"

Rico showed her a crooked smile and plenty of blocky teeth. "I'll leave. I been hidin' from guys a lot more dangerous than them for a long time. Now that I know they were lyin' to me about not knowin' anything about Cole being locked up, I don't feel too bad about jerkin' them around. Until then, I'll stay in town and see what more I can find about them. Somethin' tells me we'll have enough work to do for me to remain a valuable asset."

Paige holstered her pistol and rubbed his arm. "Take care of yourself, okay?"

"You too, Bloodhound. You owe me for this and I'll collect."

Chapter Ten

Shreveport, Louisiana
Two miles northwest of the Bossier City Reservoir

The NH-90 tactical transport helicopter roared over the flat Louisiana landscape amid a roar of engines. It was only one in a formation of the metallic aerial predators that had been specially modified for service in the IRD. One thing that hadn't needed modification was the thermal imaging camera mounted to its nose. As the helicopter sped toward Shreveport, it scanned the terrain for any sign of its prey.

Inside, Major Adderson hung onto a steel grip bolted over his head so he could remain upright without taking his eyes from the thermal camera's display. Since the sun was still adding some heat to the ground and casting a glare, he adjusted the monitor to a less sensitive setting while also flipping it to black and white. Almost immediately a group of white blobs leapt out at him from the dark gray mass covering most of the screen. "We have contact," he said to the man beside him.

The other man stood with Adderson and the pilot in the front section of the aircraft. He was short with a wiry build tailor-made for the tight confines of jets and attack copters. Hanging from another of the hand grips mounted to the ceiling, he looked over Adderson's shoulder at the display and said, "Looks like a pack of Class Twos. Kind of small, though." He reached over for a little stick set into the console near the bottom right portion of the screen. With a few expert nudges, he panned around to where he wanted despite the helicopter's churning forward movement. "There they are. Looks like two smaller packs running alongside that other one." He reached for the switch of the radio clipped to the front of his flight suit and said, "Veer off to the west and swing back around. Flight pattern Alpha."

"Alpha," Adderson said. "You think there's a Class One out there?"

"Class Twos travel in packs anyway, but when you see little groups working together, that usually means there's a big papa somewhere nearby steering them."

As if responding to that, the pilot spoke through the channel designated for local chatter. "Visual contact on a possible Class One. Please verify. Over."

Adderson allowed the smaller man to work the controls until a huge white blob marking a heat source smeared across the screen. He switched away from the thermal imaging then and got a good look at a massive Full Blood covered in thick layers of silvery gray fur that flowed across its back as it loped on all fours behind at least a dozen Half Breeds. After flipping over to a broader channel, Adderson keyed his radio and announced, "Ravens Two and Three, this is Raven One. Confirmed sighting of a Class One shifter and several packs of Class Twos. Be advised, unknown number of additional Class Twos in the vicinity." After keying off of the open channel, he moved away from the monitor and allowed the smaller man to take his spot back.

The main cabin of the helicopter contained five soldiers who were buckled into seats that folded down from the wall or from a set of posts in the middle of the cramped space. As the NH-90 banked through a wide turn, Adderson shifted his weight to keep from stumbling as he studied his men. The soldiers were dressed in standard black, white, and gray camo fatigues bearing only a name tag and the half-wolf, half-skull patch of the IRD. Each was armed with an HK G36 assault rifle. Adderson claimed one for himself from a rack as he said, "In case you haven't heard, we found the dogs we were after. There's a whole lot of them along with one big papa. Looks like they're headed for Shreveport, but we're not about to let that happen. Am I right?"

Despite being a mix of races, nationalities, and gender, all of the soldiers responded with an affirmative bark that made them sound like their own breed of pack animal. Their rifles were held in steady hands and their eyes reflected just the right mixture of aggression and anxiety.

"Standard drill," Adderson continued. "We land and deploy while the others provide air support and reinforcements if necessary. Our mission is to set explosives and try to draw those things close enough to feel the burn. Our specialists left some of their sniper rounds, but there's not a lot left."

"Do we have any specialists on this mission, sir?" one of the soldiers asked.

Even though the extent of the Skinners' knowledge wasn't commonly known to the IRD rank and file, their contributions had been large enough for their presence to be immediately felt. There were only a handful of Skinners who'd agreed to ride with the IRD on any mission, and only Cole and Paige could be counted on with any consistency. Still, no matter how much a rifleman knew about what Skinners actually did, they were aware that having them along greatly increased their odds of survival. Adderson had plenty of faith in his men, but a morale boost like that was hard to come by. He felt a regretful pang in his gut when he told them, "No specialists this time around, although I was informed by one of them that there's a pair of fighter jets in the air that may be able to rain some hell down on these things."

All of the soldiers nodded slowly as their chins dropped.

"That's no smoke up your ass," Adderson assured them. "Backup should be on the way, but we don't need that. This is just a matter of shooting those Class Twos until they can't move anymore. Drop one, move on to the next. Repeat as necessary."

"What about the Class One?" another soldier asked.

"Leave it to the air support and explosives. We can only do so much, but it's a hell of a lot more than those civvies who'll be watching the show in Shreveport can do."

The soldier grunted. "And on every other goddamn news station there is."

"You're right about that. So instead of letting those fucking dogs rip them to shreds, let's give those civilians something to watch!"

The soldiers shouted their approval several times, and before they were finished, Adderson was shouting right along with them.

All three helicopters poured on one last burst of speed to get as far ahead of the Half Breeds as possible. Since they were able to get ahead of the creatures at all, Adderson knew the wolves were either conserving their strength or slowing down on purpose to meet them. Either way, he didn't like it.

For some, hitting the ground running was just a motivational term. For the IRD, it was a means of staying alive for more than three seconds after being dropped into a hot zone. The helicopter barely touched down before the soldiers streamed out. Adderson was first on the ground, and the instant his boots slapped against the dirt he had his assault rifle in hand and was running toward the other two helicopters that hovered about twenty feet above the swaying brown grass. The remaining soldiers piled out behind him.

The Half Breeds were coming. Their paws made impacts that rumbled through the earth. Their panting breaths formed a current that rolled beneath the wind roaring in from the west. The other two helicopters deployed their men using drop lines, which hung from their doors like weighted tails. As those soldiers were unloaded, the pilots only had to pivot in the air to unleash a stream of fire from the mounted machine guns that poked their muzzles through a modified window. When the first Half Breed leapt up to try and grab it, the NH-90 moved away so it could continue firing. As the drop troops disconnected from their lines and raised their weapons, Adderson and his men opened fire.

All of those weapons formed a singular voice that melded with the thumping chopper blades to create a wave of fury that knocked the first batch of Half Breeds off their feet. None of the IRD soldiers wasted a moment in counting their blessings because the next wave was already upon them.

All three helicopters rose up and fanned out, hovering just above the newly adjusted minimum safe distance to avoid unwanted interruption of flight patterns due to Half Breeds clawing at their fuselage. The belt-fed machine guns pumped round after round into the werewolves farthest from the soldiers so as not to incur any friendly fire. Basically, it amounted to pounding the hell out of the same bunch of dogs until they were paste, which left a whole lot of work to be done.

Adderson knew it helped to think along tactical lines when he was in the mix. He considered a battle from afar even as he was wrapped up in it. That made it easier to go on when his men were knocked over by a gnarled shapeshifter that ripped a previously excited face off of its skull. When Half Breed and IRD lines converged, it was a bloody nightmare. HKs and claws all sent blood into the air. Screams and howls, both human and otherwise, filled his ears.

His focus was narrowed even more when one of those bastards singled him out. It was a long, lanky Half Breed with a face that had already been hit by heavy caliber fire to reveal knots of muscles that were white from the strain of keeping its head together while opening a mouth filled with crooked fangs. He fired in controlled bursts, and when that didn't drop the shaggy fucker, switched to full auto to force it back before it brought him down.

"Grenade out!" a woman behind him shouted. That was followed by the sharp cracking sound of a rifle-mounted launcher sending its explosive round into a target that was hopefully several yards away.

It wasn't.

The grenade thumped into the chest of a Half Breed directly behind the one that had taken a run at Adderson. It went off, opening a sizable hole in the creature, but not as sizable as it should have been. He was still having a hard time getting used to how tough those things were. It seemed as if all of weaponry he'd come to know like the back of his hand had been dialed down. For the moment, however, that Half Breed was down, the creatures around it were staggered, and he'd been thrown to the ground in the explosion.

Adderson was dazed and his ears were ringing. While his brain struggled to pull his thoughts together, his legs and arms fought to bring him to his feet. Three Half Breeds tore through two of his men like they were made of jelly and then feasted on their meat. He fired until his gun ran dry, reloaded, and fired some more. Grabbing the radio that was linked to the longer range frequencies powered by equipment in the helicopters, he shouted, "This is Hunting Party One to Lodge. Come in!"

After a few seconds of crackling static, a voice from a command center in Wyoming replied, "This is Lodge. Go ahead Hunting Party One."

"Where's our goddamn air strike?"

"F-18s are engaging targets outside of New Orleans, Hunting Party."

"Gimme an ETA! We're getting ripped apart and a Class One is set to jump on us!"

"Unknown at this time. F-18s are currently—"

"Explosives are out!"

He didn't know where the advisory had come from, but Adderson rolled onto his belly and covered his head. A moment later there was a deafening thump followed by a blast wave that jammed his nose into the dirt. Something heavy landed beside him, and he looked to see if it was a Half Breed or another soldier caught in the blast. The Full Blood was neither.

Esteban's fur was smoking from the explosion. Caught

somewhere between forms, he kicked four large paws into the air while rolling onto his side. By the time he got there, he had two legs, two arms, and a vaguely human torso. There was nothing even vaguely human, however, about the face that was turned toward the major. "You are their leader," he snarled.

Adderson responded to that by propping himself up, taking aim and clamping his finger on the trigger. The AK rattled in his hands while spouting a choppy current of lead into the Full Blood. Esteban placed a hand in front of his face while climbing to his feet. Sections of his coat were singed all the way down to rough patches of skin, and when some of Adderson's rounds hit him there, they barely left a crease. Every other bullet snagged in his fur or thumped uselessly against his body.

Shifting his gaze toward the soldiers that rushed to Adderson's side, Esteban said, "Watch."

"Get clear, Major!" a soldier shouted.

Although Adderson was a hell of a long way from clear, he replied, "Hit him, hit him!"

Automatic fire came, followed by the thump of a grenade against Esteban's body. The explosive bounced away and went off among the Half Breeds. Fortunately for Adderson, Esteban's body was tough enough to shield him from the blast. When the howling started, the firing stopped.

Rifles clattered as they landed heavily on the ground after being dropped by soldiers who only wanted to press their hands against their faces or clamp them over their ears. Next came the screams.

It wasn't the first time Adderson had seen the Breaking up close. On some level, he wondered if he'd begun leading the charges because he got sick of hanging back at a safe distance while the soldiers he'd sent into battle dropped like flies. He'd heard the crunching bones over earpieces and headphones on missions across the entire country. That sound, along with the screams and howls that followed, meant another member of the IRD had died drowning in a sea of pain. They, like the soldiers who now fell after trying to save his life, could very well be in agony until some lucky shot put them down.

"I've shown you this before," Esteban said in a Spanish accent that gave each of his words an exotic curl. "And still you continue to oppose us. Perhaps you need a closer look."

"Stop it," Adderson said. Even though he knew he was speaking to an animal, he pleaded, "Stop what you're doing, you piece of shit!"

One of Esteban's eyebrows rose as it he was taking a small bit of amusement from the automatic fire chattering through the air and the small explosions thumping all around him. "You would rather they die than be turned? That is more honorable than I would expect from a human. Usually, the rats would rather live no matter what that life entails."

Behind Esteban, more soldiers dropped. The first ones to go down writhed on the ground as their bodies were reshaped and their teeth were knocked out by the tusks that grew in to replace them. In Adderson's ear, a pilot announced, "Raven Two has a shot."

"Take it, Raven Two," Adderson said, before struggling to put as much space as possible between himself and the Full Blood.

The gunner in the helicopter opened fire. Large caliber rounds pummeled the ground in a path that led straight to Esteban and hit with enough force to push the creature back. Esteban dropped to all fours, put his thick back to the NH-90 and stared at Adderson with pure white eyes. The moment he closed them, the helicopter started to wobble. Adderson once more heard screaming through the radio as the pilot's humanity was peeled away to become the broken, knotted form of a Half Breed.

"Deploy explosives!" Adderson commanded on the open channel.

Esteban clenched his eyes shut even tighter, looking more on the verge of a climax than amid so much death. The soldier in charge of detonating the charges that had been meant to turn a group of Half Breeds and hopefully the Full Blood into pulp was turned before she could even acknowledge the order she'd been given.

"Now that I am so close to a fresher source, all I need to do is reach out to them," Esteban said, "and they fall. The wretches can be controlled, and if not, at least they won't become filthy cockroaches that sully the world with their machines."

Another helicopter went down. The pilot of Raven Three swore he could recover, just before losing control of his limbs and taking a nosedive into the ground.

The Full Blood stalked toward Adderson. "Watch and tell the others what is happening here."

"What makes you think they don't know what's happening?" Adderson asked while struggling to reload his assault rifle. "There's no place to hide."

"We are not hiding. And if you told the rest of your army how hopeless your battle truly was, you would have all found better places to run to. Perhaps a better message would be sent if you were to be found scattered across this field."

Adderson slapped another magazine into the AK and chambered the first round. "The more you kill, the harder we'll come after you."

"No," Esteban growled as he rose up to stand well over seven feet tall. "Not you."

Adderson tightened his grip on his rifle and steeled himself for one last burst. If he was going to be sent to hell, he wasn't about to go without doing some damage. Esteban lunged at him with speed that was a surprise even for someone who'd been monitoring Class One movements for months. He barely had enough time to squeeze his trigger, and when his shots cracked through the air, they hit nothing.

A split second before the first bullet sped down Adderson's barrel, something else plowed into Esteban's side. All Adderson could see was a dark blur intersecting another blur. A gust of wind blew across his face and the earth rumbled beneath him. When the rumbling stopped, something other than the Full Blood was within his line of fire. Standing between him and the hulking beast that had been ready to kill him was a third, smaller creature with light brown fur and a more compact frame. Adderson was still trying to pick his target when the smaller of the two creatures that had just appeared looked to him and snarled, "Run!"

There was only one helicopter and a fraction of his men left, so Adderson took the creature's advice. Along the way he keyed the long range radio and prayed that some of the equipment in one of the helicopters was still working. "We need that air strike *now*!"

"Negative, Major," the voice on the other end replied. "F-18s are RTB."

"Why are they returning to base? Who the fuck is this?"

When the voice responded, it was too tired to bother with official protocols. "They made three passes on two separate targets, Major. That's three apiece. Each time, the shifters scattered before the bombs hit the ground. Pilots say the packs were scattered even before they fired a shot. Analysts think they knew they were coming."

"What? Are you telling me those things have spies informing them of our movements? They're fucking animals!"

"Not spies, sir. Looks like they saw the planes coming. Maybe smelled them. Either way, all the planes did was burn civilian structures and run up collateral damages. They're RTB until we can figure something else out. Do you need transpo to get you out of there?"

Steeling himself while surveying what was left of his men, Adderson said, "Negative. We're staying."

Since the human could barely move at a snail's pace, the Mongrel put herself between Adderson and Esteban. She was a lean feline with more bulk than normally found on others of her breed. The ground shifted as diggers burrowed to get a good position around the Full Blood. Esteban had dealt with Mongrels before, but was more intrigued by the tall man who stood beside the Mongrel.

"I heard the reptiles had emerged from their swamps, but hadn't seen any for myself," Esteban said. "Your kind have been hiding for so long, I've forgotten your scent."

"Good for us," Frank replied. His pants were cut from the same material as those worn by the IRD soldiers, but his chest was covered only partially by a harness that held two pistols, a knife, and a few other pieces of equipment.

"So you come out of hiding for this?" Esteban mused. "To protect a bunch of humans who are already dead?"

"They're not dead," he told him with absolute certainty. "Won't be dead today."

"If not today, then tomorrow."

Esteban moved slowly as soldiers continued to scream and thrash around him. The first ones to drop were already climbing onto wobbly legs and yawning to stretch newly weaponized jaws. "If you don't wish to die along with this Mongrel trash, then step aside and be dealt with when the fight is over. I'd say it won't take long for that day to come."

"There have been others saying similar things. We won't allow this to continue. My people, the Mongrels, the humans, we will all stand against you. Things need to go back to the way they were."

"Oh child," he said through a wide, horrific grin. "It's far too late to hope for that. Now that the Torva'ox is flowing, getting rid of you is the only way the rest of us will get what's rightfully ours." With that, Esteban jumped. He stretched out both front paws and opened his mouth as a wild sheen glinted within his milky white eyes.

The Mongrel tried to jump at him as well, but was intercepted before leaving the ground. Esteban was double her weight, and all of that muscle was put to use once she was wrapped up in his embrace and rolling on the ground with him snapping at her face, neck, and shoulders. Her instincts took over then and soon she was returning his attacks in kind. Once they both got their claws involved, the blood started to fly, until both creatures broke away and began pacing around each other.

"The war has already begun," Esteban said. "What good do you think you can do now, apart from drawing the ire of those who could be your greatest allies?"

Rather than try to respond using a mouth filled with blood, the Mongrel curled her lips up in a fierce, protective snarl.

"The Nymar staked their claim," the Full Blood said, "and if we don't take what's ours, there will be nothing left. Those humans you cherish," he added while pivoting to bat Frank aside as the Squam lunged at him. "Do you think they will show their gratitude for what you do here by granting you immunity when the next armed attacks come? Do you think the Skinners will allow you to live peacefully in your swamps with whatever is left of your family?"

The Mongrel's teeth were not only bared, but elongated, as her snarl became a wild, rasping groan.

"Ahhh," Esteban mused. "So there is not much left of your family. A regrettable certainty among our kind, I'm afraid. They would have died off soon enough no matter what you did to try and save them. Just like these humans here. And since we now see that humans are the only thing preventing us from fully absorbing the Torva'ox, we must put them out of our way. It is the nature of things. The cream will always rise. These loud, filthy creatures and their machines were simply too stupid or too arrogant to realize they're not the cream."

Frank had been using every one of his senses to pick the opportune moment to strike. He could hear, see, even smell the overconfidence within Esteban as he spoke. And when it seemed the Full Blood had regarded him as nothing more than one of the insects to which he'd referred, Frank launched his next attack.

The werewolf made no move to avoid him. He stood his ground, watching him and the Mongrel carefully as clawed hands reached up from beneath the ground to grab his legs. The IRD soldiers who'd been broken had already turned to attack their former comrades, leaving the Full Blood to deal with Frank and the Mongrels. Now that they'd snagged Esteban, the diggers emerged to grab any part of him they could, and when the Full Blood's limbs were ensnared, Frank and the feline Mongrel charged. The Mongrel darted straight at Esteban while Frank leapt high to throw himself at and quickly through the massive werewolf.

When he passed through the space that Esteban had occupied, Frank felt a chill move in a wave through his body. Unlike the winter chill that barely made it through his scaly flesh, this was a cold that seeped all the way down to the bone. But it was more than a change in temperature. There was something insinuating the cold upon him like a thousand little needles injecting it directly into his core. Beside him, the Mongrel seemed equally confused as she landed and was thrown off her feet by her long tail.

Esteban flung her through the air and turned toward Frank. "I have taken the form that had been all but forgotten by our kind. I have mastered not only changing my shape, but shifting between form and shadow. The few weapons that could kill a Full Blood will now pass through me just as you did. Just as I passed through the stone shell the Skinners used to take Minh prisoner. Flee now or take your chances with these humans once they eventually take you prisoner as well. They are getting stronger and will eventually find a way to bring the fighting to a level that will make this world uninhabitable. Although," he added while glancing around at the field, now filled with wreckage, charred mounds of dirt, and milling Half Breeds, "today brings only death."

Frank launched a flurry of attacks while the few remaining soldiers piled into the last helicopter. His claws either scraped against a body that was almost as solid as steel or passed completely though a form with less substance than a memory. After brushing him aside with a few clubbing swings, Esteban clamped his jaws around a Mongrel that had reached up to grab him from underground and tore a large piece of the digger off, to be spat out. Then he calmly walked toward the Half Breeds that had clustered reflexively out of striking distance.

"There is much to do," he announced casually. "I have heard Cecile's cry, which means she has finally broken free. Perhaps she will be more open to the truth than you."

The Mongrel struggled to stand as she shifted into a mostly human form. Now a woman somewhere in her early forties, she enclosed her arms around herself more as a way to stanch the flow of blood from her wounds than to try to cover her naked body. "It's not supposed to happen like this," she said. "I know the Full Bloods and Mongrels have never fared well together, but now is a time we can hold a council or—"

"Council?" Esteban snapped. "Why would I care what you or any of these others have to say? I would rather tear the face of this world apart than bargain with the likes of you."

"What about Randolph Standing Bear?"

That name stopped Esteban in his tracks. When some of the Half Breeds began approaching him, he warned them off with a brutish snarl that sent them scattering, to nip at each and establish a crude pecking order within the newly formed pack.

"Randolph has not been seen since . . ." Esteban's voice trailed off as a slow breeze brought new scents to his nose. "But I know now that he has recently returned. And he's found the trickster. Do you expect me to believe he's suddenly overcome his distaste for your kind?"

"If he's still with Kawosa, he's not striking any deals," she told him with absolute certainty. "He is scheming while this war rages. At a time like this, someone like that is the most dangerous of all."

Esteban took another slow sample from the air and frowned his disapproval. The helicopter blades of the last remaining AH-90 roared to a crescendo as the steel bird rose. "You can do nothing against me, child," he said. "Best for you to find a place to hide or think of the best way to please me before it's worth my time to end your life." And then he broke into a run. The howl that exploded from his throat caught the attention of every Half Breed, a churning mass of bodies in his wake as they all ran for the nearby city.

The remaining Mongrels bolted after Esteban, leaving Frank alone with the dead and dying in that field. He reached down for a nylon belt clipped around his waist, removed a phone from a small pack and found he'd gotten a call. After pressing one of the preset speed dials, he was quickly connected to a familiar voice.

"Cole," Frank said. "It's me."

"Where are you? Did you find any Mongrels to help Adderson?"

"Caught up with them outside of Shreveport, Louisiana. So did Esteban and a whole lot of Half Breeds."

"How many Half Breeds?"

Looking around at the carnage, he told him, "I don't know, but after Esteban howled at these soldiers, there were a whole lot more. Now they're all running into the city."

"Can you do anything about it?" Cole asked.

"We tried to stop Esteban, but he found a way to turn into a ghost, and I don't think I or the Mongrels will be able to touch him."

"Wait . . . what?" Cole stammered.

Frank explained what happened in quick, choppy sentences while jogging toward the city. Even after he was finished, Cole still seemed confused. Then again, in the time he'd known the Skinner, Cole seemed like that a lot. "Just ask your Skinner friends about Full Bloods being able to pass into shadow. That's what he called it. What aren't you telling me about him?"

"You think I'm hiding anything from you?" Cole asked.

"About Esteban," Frank said in a snarl that surprised even him as it rumbled out of his throat. "You told me plenty about Randolph Standing Bear and Liam and even something about the female, Minh. Add the young Full Blood you and Jessup met in New Mexico . . ."

"Cecile," Cole said with a regretful tone in his voice.

"Right. It seems you and Paige know a lot of these Full

Bloods on a first name basis. Why is it you haven't told me much of anything about Esteban?"

When Cole responded to that, his voice was more grating and intense, as if he was practically chewing on his phone: "Because we know next to nothing about him, that's why!"

"He was the one at that prison where you, me, and Lambert were being held," Frank offered.

"I remember." Cole pulled in a deep breath and let it out. "From what you've told me, it sounds like Esteban said more to you a few minutes ago than he has to anyone else. He's not like the other Full Bloods. He's not making demands or finding one of us to threaten. Liam, Randolph, even Henry hunted us down, but this one just wants to kill. He didn't say anything to us when he showed up in Colorado."

"He was there for whatever was being held beneath that prison," Frank said. "And judging by his newfound ability, he found it."

"I don't know about all of them, but Esteban and any shapeshifters following him are way past the stage of calling us out or forcing us to hand anything over. They want us dead. Plain and simple."

"Have you learned something along those lines?"

"Yeah," Cole said. "It's too much to get into now, but the Full Bloods just want to wipe us out because they're sick of sharing space with us and they don't need to bargain or explain a damn thing to anyone else."

Frank's tan and yellow scales flattened against his face, and his creamy yellow eyes fixed upon the distant cityscape. "I'm going to see what I can do in Shreveport."

"Thanks, Frank. Whatever you can do to help will go a long way."

"Just make sure I'm not here on my own for long." With that, he hung up, stuffed the phone into his pack and broke into a run to make up for lost time.

Chapter Eleven

Louisville, Kentucky

Cole hung up and was immediately slapped on the shoulder from the seat behind him.

"What did he say?" Paige asked. "What happened? Where are they? Is Adderson still alive?"

They were driving in the car they'd taken from the Lariat Club. Cole was behind the wheel, Waggoner beside him, and Paige in the back. It was an uncharacteristic move for her to opt out of the driver's seat, but that way she could keep an eye on Waggoner while checking over their weaponry.

"Adderson and the IRD were deployed to Shreveport, Louisiana," he told her. "It got pretty rough. Esteban showed up and turned most of the soldiers."

"Didn't they get a shot off?" Waggoner asked.

"Doesn't matter," Cole replied. "He's powerful enough to turn a human without having to bite them. With Full Bloods being so fast, it's hard to say if Esteban is the only one who can pull off that trick. From what we've seen, he can do it from anywhere within fifty to sixty yards. Usually goes for the heavy equipment first. Helicopters, large caliber mounted guns. Tanks."

"They can take down tanks?" Waggoner asked.

"They turn the drivers. Adderson mentioned something about using remote controlled drones on loan from the Air Force, but they can't come anywhere close to a Full Blood's speed. It's a joke."

"So what happened in Louisiana?"

Cole gave them the short version as the scenery rolled past his window. Louisville, like any other city, was quiet during the day and quieter at night. There were still cars going about their business, but they moved swiftly and drivers gripped the steering wheel as if something would jump out at them at any moment. A few months ago that would have been excessively paranoid. Now it seemed about right.

"So you got some other shapeshifters to work with you?" Waggoner asked.

"Mongrels were against the Full Bloods way before any of this crap happened," Paige said. "Frank signed on after Cole helped break him out of a prison, and he's trying to get the rest of the Squams to join the cause." Before Waggoner asked, she added, "Squamatosapiens are lizard people."

"And the whole prison thing?"

"Long story. Right now, you just need to worry about getting back to your buddies before you're gone for too long."

Waggoner looked out the window, even though they'd driven several miles from the Vigilant base. "Some of the men I knew back in Oklahoma swore by these fellas, but now I'm not so sure about them."

"Then leave."

"And go where? I can handle myself and I've been practicing with the whole stick thing, but I can't exactly run like a lot of these younger men. Sticking with a group seemed to be a good move for me. The men I really trusted back home were killed when Atoka was overrun, and now I find out the Vigilant may be backstabbing pricks."

"Maybe not all of them," Cole offered.

"Oh, that makes me feel a whole lot better." Waggoner shifted in his seat. The closer the car got to Spring and

Payne, the more nervous he became. "The only ones that haven't given me reason to distrust them are you two. Mind if I tag along for a while?"

Paige watched him carefully from the backseat, as she had for most of the drive. Much to Cole's surprise, she said, "We could get you out of town if you like, but I'm not talking about deputizing you."

"Why not?"

"Yeah," Cole said. "Why not? I mean, he's already gotten this far. What's the worst that could happen if he tries to screw us over or doesn't work out? The world ends? Too late for that."

"Nice," she said. Looking at Waggoner, she finally slumped back into her seat, resigned. "Fine. He comes along for now, but I'm too tired to train anyone for a while. If he can't take care of himself, we leave him wherever he drops."

"He likes that idea just fine," Waggoner said. "From what I heard, it ain't too healthy to stay with you two for long anyhow."

"You got that right," Paige said while leaning forward to nudge Cole's shoulder. "We also need to talk to someone who knows a lot more about the Torva'ox than we do. Someone who's already used to working with it or at least storing it."

"Someone who might have created the Jekhibar?"

"Yep. Someone other than the military or a bunch of radical Lancroft fanatics, who might be able to lend us a hand in fighting the Full Bloods. Someone, I might add, who owes us a few big favors."

"You want to make the call or should I?"

Chapter Twelve

Sixty miles west of Great Falls, Montana

The two powerful beasts had been running in ever-widening circles. Randolph did his best to keep Kawosa's scent fresh in his nose, but had lost it on a few occasions. Whenever that happened, the trickster snuck up on him to attack from another angle. Claws slashed through flesh and fangs ripped meat from the bone of both creatures as they circled and launched themselves into the next onslaught. Kawosa was always the one to break off when things got too rough. He needed to find some way to lose Randolph or defeat him. There was no third alternative.

When the Full Blood slowed his pace again and the snowy terrain became more than a white and gray blur, the peaks of the Rocky Mountains loomed before him. Blood surged through Randolph's body, feeding his senses with an elemental fire that allowed him to see in total darkness or stare straight up into the sun. At the moment, he simply took his bearings by looking at the sky and allowed the wind to spill across his panting tongue.

"You . . . *can't* . . . find me."

Despite the power entwined within those words, which

would have made them believable to almost any living thing, Randolph continued his search. But the force of that suggestion had a weight that made his head droop and his next breath seep like tar all the way back down to his lungs. Yet still he searched.

"And you can't escape me!" he bellowed. "If there was a way, you would have taken it already. Step out and face me!"

"To what end? So you can test your might against a god?"

"You are no god, trickster. You are old and powerful, but so am I."

The reaction came swiftly and without mercy. Kawosa exploded into Randolph's field of vision as if he'd been taking refuge behind a veil of falling snowflakes two feet away. He charged to get in close and clamp his jaws around the Full Blood's neck.

Randolph turned his head to one side and then snapped it along with his entire body in the opposite direction. Since Kawosa had latched onto him, the trickster was cracked like a whip. He lost his grip on Randolph's neck with a pained yelp and raced toward the mountains. When Randolph tore after him, Kawosa stopped and pivoted in a way that spat gleefully at the laws of physics and inertia. Shifting into a creature with skin of glistening oil and wings of tattered canvas, he left the ground and sank curved talons into Randolph's back. The more Randolph struggled against the grip that lifted him off the ground, the deeper those talons sank into him. With every powerful flap of Kawosa's wings, he was lifted higher.

"You compare yourself to me?" Kawosa snarled through a wide, twisted beak. "You are a lesser creature! The only reason I've helped you at all was because of your passion to deal with other lesser creatures."

"And this lesser creature," Randolph said while straining to shift into his two-legged form without scraping too many of his muscles against Kawosa's talons, "has forced the First Deceiver to show his true form. How long has it been since you've worn a body that isn't a lie?"

"I don't have to explain myself to you, Full Blood. I've done more than enough to repay you for breaking me from Lancroft's cage. I helped combine the new Half Breeds with your bloodline to track down the newest pup among your kind, and then paved the way for you to escape with her while all of your brethren cried out for your death."

Randolph was being carried toward the mountains, and after a few more flaps of Kawosa's wings, they were there. Jagged slopes and frozen peaks sped beneath them as Randolph finally settled into a form that hung more naturally from the trickster's painful grasp. Without the bulk of his four-legged body, and thanks to his newly elongated limbs, he was able to reach for Kawosa while pulling his lower half up.

"Even Liam wanted you killed," Kawosa continued. "And I steered him away so you could pursue your own course."

"Liam wanted you killed as well," Randolph grunted. "He wanted to see everyone dead at one time or another. It was one of his many flaws."

"And now this nonsense with Icanchu," Kawosa said, as if merely talking to himself. "Now that I see you may actually be persistent enough to find another Mist Born, I must bring an end to this little game you've started."

"Game? Look below you!"

Kawosa shifted his half-blue, half-orange eyes toward the earth, where a battle raged on the other side of the mountains. A small town was in flames, gunshots crackled through the air, and Half Breeds bayed at the skies. The other voice that lent itself to the wild collection of noises belonged to a Full Blood. It was the pure howl of one of Randolph's brethren, but he didn't have the wherewithal to put a name to the cry. Louder explosions rocked the town and were quickly silenced as the humans pulling those triggers were subjected to the agonies of the Breaking.

"It is because of *me* that the Full Bloods gained so much power during the Breaking Moon," Kawosa shrieked. "Your kind still have to be close to a source of the Torva'ox for the effects to be felt, but the more of my children that exist, the wider the howls spread. When one as powerful as Esteban sends out the call, a few unlucky humans on the other side of the world drop to their knees in agony. Did you foresee that, Birkyus?"

"You couldn't have wanted the world to turn into this!" Randolph roared as the wind beat against his face. "Of all the Mist Born, you have always been closest with the humans. Some say you even taught them to speak. The slate needs to be wiped clean. Purged of everything that has sullied it. It's too late for anything else. There must be a drastic change!"

"This is not drastic enough for you?"

"Your wretches are nothing but wild hunger, much like the Nymar. Both of those bloodlines need to be severed. I know of a way to continue the work that has begun and steer it toward something better for those who truly deserve it."

The wet grinding sound in Kawosa's neck made it seem as if his throat had been cut when he turned to look into Randolph's eyes. "I've heard talk similar to that," he said. "When I was locked in Lancroft's dungeon."

"He spoke of murderous humans. I speak of the species that first graced this earth with the touch of their feet."

"That was not your species either, young one. And don't play word games with me. I invented them. All you want to do is paint a horrific picture and then convince someone that you're the only one who knows how to clean it up again. Very crude." Flapping his wings without gaining any altitude, Kawosa eventually dropped toward the stark landscape. "If you want to take a stand against my kind, then your best outcome is to die now before you are ripped asunder by what you find in the jungles to the south. You may be able to give me a brisk run, but Icanchu is more ruthless than you can conceive. The only reason I've shown you my true form is to let you know there are still things in this world that even the mighty Full Bloods haven't seen. Learn your lesson and try to be thankful for what is left of your world."

Randolph hung from Kawosa's talons like a worm curling in upon itself at the end of a line. He craned his neck to get an upside-down view of the mountains they'd left behind. He drank in the sight of all that comforting open ground for what could very well have been the final time, then dug his claws into Kawosa's side. "Thankful?" he roared. "What is there to be thankful about?"

"You live."

Now that Randolph had a firm grip, he used all of his might to tear himself free of Kawosa's talons. The curved nails had sunk in even deeper than he'd thought, but once he started ripping, there was nothing to do but continue along that hellish road until he was free. "I live. In the filthy pit my world has become?" he asked once one shoulder came away amid a spray of blood and fur. "If living in this was my plan, then yes I'd be thankful."

"You can still see tomorrow. Be thankful I have not yet taken that away from you."

"Keep your thanks," Randolph snarled as he dug his claws higher up on Kawosa's back. When the second set of talons ripped away, the pain almost sent Randolph toppling into unconsciousness. It was a glorious, unfamiliar sensation he hadn't felt since his youthful body was first reshaped into the beast. For one who'd felt countless bullets thump against his hide and endured agony that would have shattered any other creature, reaching a previously unknown level of suffering was as much a gift as being taken to higher realms of pleasure.

"You are still a Full Blood," Kawosa said in a wheezing voice that was somehow unaffected by the buffeting winds. "Savor your power and take what is given to you. When this war is over, you can start anew."

Icy fingers of air raked all the way down Randolph's throat, shaking him back into full awareness. "Don't think you can coddle me by dangling the future in front of my nose! You can't distract me with vague notions of brighter horizons! I've been plummeting for a long time, and now," he added while closing a hand around the base of Kawosa's wing, "so are you." With that, he focused every bit of his strength into that arm and pulled.

"You can't do this!" Kawosa cried.

Once Randolph broke through the trickster's outer shell, the tendons, muscle, and sinew connecting wing to torso unraveled. "Another lie," he growled.

Kawosa's appendage tore like wet burlap. The sound of it could barely be heard beneath the overture of his screams and the mounting currents of air marking their swift descent. "We'll both die!"

"Then that's how it shall be," Randolph said. "Perhaps you should be thankful for the view while you still have it."

Chapter Thirteen

Louisville, Kentucky

The phone rang a few times, and just when Cole thought it was headed for voice mail, he heard a strained yet familiar voice.

"Hello?"

"Hey, Daniels. It's Cole."

"Oh. What a surprise," the Nymar chemist replied in a way that registered more nervousness than surprise. "Haven't heard from you in a while. Staying out of prison? Heh."

"Yeah. Good one. I'm in Louisville."

"Is that so?"

"Yeah. Have you found anything more on the Torva'ox?"

"I've been on it for months," Daniels replied, obviously put out by the very notion that he might have been doing otherwise. "All I've been able to find in books or just about anywhere else are a bunch of obscure legends about energies flowing through the earth, which made me think of ley lines, which made me think of the earth's natural electromagnetic field, which made me think of a person's supposed *soul* . . ." When he said that last word, he dragged it out and stressed it as if framing it in air quotes. "All of which can be measured by several different means."

"What sort of means?" Cole asked.

"I've got my theories, but none of it's been proven yet. Every living thing gives off some sort of charge, but that's fairly common knowledge. The brain works by sending electrical impulses to cross synapses and relay basic commands along with higher functions. That's an extremely simplified version, but—"

"How about an even more simplified version?" Cole said sharply.

Daniels sighed and very likely gave the head shake/eye roll combo platter to the phone in his hand. "The Breaking Moon allowed the Full Bloods to draw on massive amounts of that power, whatever you want to call it. Even from where I was, I could measure a dip in the electromagnetic field as it was pulled toward those big hairy magnets."

"With all your research into the Torva'ox," Cole said, "how easy would it be to manipulate it?"

"Easy? We're talking electromagnetic fields," Daniels replied. "And theoretical ones at that. Remember, my information may be pretty conclusive in some aspects, but that doesn't mean I know exactly what field it is. I'm just basing my hypotheses on blanks or extremely low numbers across all the measurements I took. In order to manipulate something, I'd have to know exactly what it is."

Cole was sitting in the car parked in front of a gas station. Outside, Paige and Waggoner emerged from the building carrying hot coffee and a lunch that was still steaming from its time spent in a microwave. She was already tearing into a burrito, dropped it and immediately launched into a tirade while stooping to pick it up. Already knowing his place in the pecking order, Waggoner wasted no time in lending her a hand.

"What would you need to figure that out?" Cole asked.

Daniels sighed and let out a breath that became the sound of exasperated lips flapping against one another in a bad imitation of a speedboat motor. "First of all, I'd need some purer samples. Something that we know for certain is the real Torva'ox and not something I may think is close."

"Got it. What else?"

"Seriously?" Daniels squeaked.

"Yes. That's one of the reasons I've been asking about all of this. What else do you need?"

"I'd need a budget for some new equipment once I narrow down what I'm actually trying to measure, but all of this would still only bring me to the start of a real process."

"How long before you get results?" Cole asked.

"There's no way for me to—"

"We need them quickly. Waste too much time and we might as well hand over the world to the Full Bloods. The military is getting thinned out every day, and the only way for them to survive is for them to hit harder and find some way to know where the Full Bloods may be going before they get there. Unless we can help them with that, the Half Breeds will keep thinning out the human race."

Daniels griped plenty, but he knew when to suck it up and focus on an important task. The voice that came through the digital connection now cut straight through everything else that might have bothered him. "The best possible thing you could do is to put me in touch with an expert in this field. Someone who knows enough about the Torva'ox to point me in the right direction so I can attempt to figure out what to do with that sample you collected. If you know someone like that, bring them to me. I'll get them briefed and we can work toward solving your—"

"How about I bring you to them?"

Daniels made a noise that could have been a word being cut short or half a grunt accompanying what had to be one of his patented sour looks. "All of my equipment is here."

"Would talking to them over the phone be enough?"

"Don't they at least have an Internet connection?" Daniels whined.

"Probably. But I need you to drop whatever you're doing and keep working no matter what happens. As far as the funding or equipment needs go, get what you can, borrow whatever you need, and get it done."

"Will I be reimbursed?"

"That doesn't matter. Humans aren't the only ones on the line here."

Daniels sighed. "Well, seeing as how this work could have a direct impact on the werewolf apocalypse . . ."

"Is someone seriously calling it the werewolf apocalypse?"

"Yes. Channel 7 and one of the correspondents on CNN."

Now it was Cole's turn to sigh. "Whatever the hell it's being called, yes, this will have a direct effect on it. We also need anything you can make us to prep for a fight."

"More?"

Cole went on as if he hadn't heard the grating protest. After all the time he'd known Daniels, he had a lot of practice. "Paige's ink, Ned's eye drops, a whole bunch of healing serum, and as many of those Blood Blade bullets as you can make."

"We'll need more Blood Blades to melt for that, so you're out of luck on that last one."

"Considering where we're going, maybe not. Get it ready as quickly as you can. We'll be there soon."

"How soon?" Daniels whined. "Who's coming? Don't you know I'm being watched? You guys *must* be attracting attention now more than ever and this is *no* time for me to start getting sloppy where security is concerned."

"How's Sally, by the way?"

Mentioning Daniels's girlfriend always brought the Nymar's heart rate down a few notches, and this time was no exception. "She's good," he sighed. "Still getting comfortable after moving in with me. It's an ongoing process."

"I can imagine."

Chapter Fourteen

Chicago, Illinois

It was a long drive along County Road 18 to the suburb of Schaumburg. Waggoner had been stunned to step through the beaded curtain and into a flash across a bright green threshold that sent him to a West Chicago club called Pinups. One of the dancers there let them borrow her car. It was a silver Accent that still smelled gloriously new, and the group hit the road without as much as a glance at the buffet.

"So where are we going now?" Waggoner asked.

"We're meeting a friend of ours and then taking a trip," Paige said.

The newly recruited Skinner looked out the window, but wasn't impressed. In the dead of the night, one stretch of deserted highway looked like any other.

Daniels buzzed Cole in as soon as he tapped the panel outside the apartment building's front entrance. Several sections of the wall as well as a few of the tenants' doors had been replaced due to a run-in with Randolph back in the good old days when Full Bloods weren't headline news and Skinners still made attempts to keep their activities discreet.

Now, Cole strode into the building with his spear strapped to his back and his jacket unbuttoned so the holster on his hip could be seen. Upon reaching one of Daniels's doors, he knocked. There was no answer, so he fished a key ring from his pocket and fit one of them into the lock.

The apartment was one of three Daniels rented on different floors in the building. Although this one was roomy, it wasn't supposed to have more than one level. Most of the floor space was taken by boxes, shelving, and cabinets storing everything from medical equipment to back issues of old Justice League comic books. Cole had been there before, so he wasn't shocked to hear a voice from the closet say, "Upstairs!"

Instead of coats or a vacuum cleaner, the hall closet contained a ladder up to a unit on the next floor. A similar ladder led to the apartment on the third floor. It was an expensive way for the Nymar chemist to get a lot of extra space and indulge an even bigger helping of paranoia.

Cole climbed up to the second floor, which was normally where Daniels did his work. While there were still plenty of test tube racks, bottles of chemicals, and other lab equipment in the kitchen and dining room, the rest of the apartment had been spruced up considerably. The reason for the change was currently seated on the couch. "Hello, Sally," he said with a friendly wave.

Sally sat nestled with her feet curled beneath her on a faded cushion that hugged her rounded frame. Her blond hair, cut just above the shoulders, was held back by a pink scrunchie. Her clothes were brightly colored, moderately fashionable, and were featured on the same shopping channel that she currently watched on a thirty-six-inch TV. "Hi, Cole. Where's Paige?"

"She's in the car keeping her eye on a new recruit. Doing something different with your hair?"

"A little. Thanks for noticing."

"I'm glad you weren't scared away after what happened a while ago."

Sally shrugged and tried to hide a wince. Considering she'd been attacked by a hungry Nymar while a werewolf tore its way between all three of Daniels's apartments, it was a pretty brave reaction. "Scared, yes. Scared *away* . . . not quite. Doesn't seem like a lot compared to everything that's been going on since then."

"How do you like living here?"

She opened her arms as if to embrace the area around her, which was dust free and noticeably tidier than the rest of the cobbled-together complex. It was a perfectly arranged space with clean carpet and newer furniture. More than anything else, the reduced amount of clutter made it clear that someone other than Daniels had been set loose in that place. "What's there not to like? Anything that brings me closer to Danny makes everything else worth the trouble."

"Really?" Cole asked. "I mean . . . that's great. At least you convinced your boyfriend to keep the heat on. Any other time I came up here during a cold snap, he had the windows cracked open. Said something about keeping his samples fresher."

"That was easy. When the insurance and maintenance people came through after all the damage was done, he told them the holes in the floor were made by that creature that ripped through everything. We agreed to fix the holes ourselves and take the cost out of our rent. Since he's not going to fix the holes, the lower rent more than makes up for keeping all three places nice and toasty."

Cole looked from the TV to the woman watching it. Although she could have been anywhere from her early forties to mid-fifties, Sally's eyes made her seem a bit older. They weren't wrinkled or cloudy, but were very weary. "Are you all right?" he asked. "Paige told me things got pretty rough when that Nymar broke into your place."

Nodding slowly, she said, "It was rough, but she killed that son of a bitch. Thank her again for that, will you?"

"She's in the car if you'd like to talk to her."

Her lips pressed together in a way that made it clear she

had plenty to say but no desire to delve any further into the subject matter. "How are you feeling? Last time you were here was pretty rough."

The last time he'd been there, he was nearly killed by his own partner after the Nymar spore was freshly implanted inside of him. Sometimes when he was drifting between wakefulness and asleep, he could still see Paige looming over him with that stake in her hand. "I'm fine," he lied. "Better, anyway."

"It's still inside you, isn't it?"

He wanted to lie, if only to distract himself from the cinching pain that had become a part of his everyday life, but knew better. The look in Sally's eyes told him that she didn't need him to answer the question anyway.

"I know how hard it can get," she said. "Danny gets so cranky when he's hungry. I've heard that it can hurt."

"Yeah, well, me and Paige have to deal with more than our share of scars."

Sally stood up, a picture of softness from the fuzzy slippers on her feet to the bulky sweater wrapped around her body. Her pants were faded green cotton, and little gold earrings hung from her lobes; pretty and comforting in a way that made it easy for Cole to imagine her smiling while handing over a plate of freshly baked cookies. Perhaps that last part was a stretch, but it had been a long time since he'd eaten and even longer since he'd had freshly baked cookies.

"I can help you," she said.

Before he could stop himself, Cole asked, "Do you have any cookies?"

Her smile was warmer than her sweater as she walked to the kitchen. "No, but there's some blood in the fridge."

"You keep blood in the fridge? I thought that was just some campy gimmick on television shows."

"It is, but it also works to keep the hunger down for a while. Daniels says it tastes different when it's not fresh, and most Nymar won't even touch it unless it's straight from a—" She looked at him then as if just realizing she'd tried offering a hash brownie to a cop. "Unless it's fresh."

"Keep it," Cole said. "And don't worry. You get used to the weirdness eventually."

Once again she motioned to her surroundings. This time, however, it wasn't in a fond manner. "My boyfriend rents three apartments and uses the bottom one as a lookout station. Instead of using the stairs outside, he knocked holes in the closets so he could climb between them without exposing himself to outside threats. He twitches whenever the phone rings and installed his own cameras to watch the parking lot. Anyone in my spot would have either run away screaming by now or kept a bag packed for the inevitable moment when he asked me to jump into a cab and leave town for a while. Fortunately, weird rolls off me like water off a duck's back."

"Me too," Cole said. "And just to be fair, Daniels twitches a lot anyway."

"I know. It's cute." Sally didn't ask about the specifics of his visit. Having sat back down and tucked her legs in again, she was content to watch the parade of discount jewelry on TV.

Cole climbed up to the third floor. It had always been the Nymar's main residence, but since he'd last been there, the apartment had fallen more into the "man cave" category. The furniture was the same, although stained with a few more spots of spilled pop and pizza sauce. The television was larger than the one downstairs and bristling with wires leading to four different video game systems. Even the DVDs in the racks beside the TV reeked of a single man's tastes, including bad science fiction, campy fantasy movies from the eighties, and a large chunk of shelf space dedicated to comic book inspired movies from the last few decades, both animated and live action.

Daniels stormed down a short hallway. His arms were wrapped around a bundle of papers and books large enough to cover all but the top of his head. The thick tendrils covering his scalp shifted slightly, as if they were just another part of him that couldn't stop fidgeting. It seem as if he wore a cheap toupee that was hassled by a stiff breeze. "You guys are real jerks, you know that?"

"Hi, Daniels. Haven't seen you on any *Sniper Ranger* death matches in a while. Been busy?"

"Ha ha. Very funny. Between all the projects I've got going for you and Paige, I barely have any time to do much of anything anymore."

"Your fridge is stocked," Cole pointed out. "Seems like you haven't been too busy to keep on top of that."

Daniels blinked a few times as a few stray notes fell from the pile in his arms. "Right. I was going to see if you needed to feed. Those tendrils must be constricting in a most . . . uncomfortable way."

"You could say that. Where'd you get the blood? Out hunting, or is that payment from Stephanie in exchange for keeping an eye on us?"

"Payment from Stephanie? No offense, but she's too busy counting her money to worry about you."

"What money?" Cole asked as his temper flared high enough for him to feel the flush of heat in his face. "We burned her Blood Parlor to the ground before we left."

"You burned one of her Blood Parlors down. She's built more. Do you have that sample for me?"

They got down to business then. After Cole handed over the Jekhibar, he watched diligently as Daniels studied it from every angle, took readings using some of the equipment he'd brought in, wrote his findings in his notes and compared them to other findings he must have gotten earlier. The process took just over an hour, and only when he had the Jekhibar back in his pocket did Cole pick up an old gym bag and start filling it with the supplies he'd requested.

"This it?" he asked.

"That's all the healing serum and ink on hand," Daniels replied while still scribbling on his notepad.

"What about this?" Cole asked as he tossed over the sonic emitter.

Daniels looked it over and grunted. "What about it?"

"There may be a tracker in it. Can you—" Before he finished the question, Daniels had the device popped open and was jamming his sausage fingers into the innards. In a few seconds he'd singled out a circuit and pulled it out as far as the wires would allow.

"This is a small GPS tracker," the Nymar said. "You just want to know if it's there or do you want it reprogrammed?"

"I want it gone."

Daniels plucked the circuit out as if removing a splinter. "Done."

"Now what about tracking the Torva'ox? I was thinking maybe you could use a device like that to create some sort of feedback that could be sent all they way through the system to maybe damage whatever is drawing from it the most. Since that would be a Full Blood or maybe even the Half Breeds, that could . . . What?" Cole stopped because Daniels was gawking at him with even more exasperation than normal.

"This isn't one of your games, Cole. It's not like I can just flip a switch to make that stuff happen. There's readings to be taken, testing to be done, frequencies to find, possibly frequencies to *create.* And even if I could create some kind of feedback, that doesn't mean it's an all-purpose shapeshifter blaster."

"I didn't think that!" Seeing Daniels's raised eyebrow, Cole admitted, "Well, maybe I thought that a little. Do you think you can do anything at all along those lines?"

Regarding the emitter and then tossing it back, he said, "Sure, but I'd be better off starting from scratch. Since I have this circuit, I should be able to mess with that signal if you want."

"Okay. Get to work on that. Any progress on something to use against Esteban when he's in his ghost body?"

Daniels brightened when he said, "Actually, that wasn't so tough. I mixed some of that Blood Blade varnish for your weapons into a compound that can be added to an aerosol.

As long as you spray it into the incorporeal Full Blood's center of mass, it should do some major damage. Can't say if it'll kill him, but it should hurt enough to discourage him from fading away for a while."

"We can call it Wolf-B-Gone," Cole said, which was met by a prompt eye roll from the Nymar. "I'll take it."

"Should be ready soon."

"We need it now!"

Paige had joined them by then. She tapped Daniels on the arm with a hand still feeling the aftereffects of using one of his mixtures before it was ready. "How much time do you need?" she asked.

"Not much. Mostly, I need to get it loaded into a proper container so it can be administered . . . er . . . properly."

"What about a toxin that will work on the Shadow Spore?"

"You want me to tamper with a previously unknown planetary energy field, fidget with government security measures, find a way to damage a ghost, or figure out a way to poison Nymar that even you guys can't poison? I'm already running on next to no sleep, so you'll just have to pick one."

"You think that tracking device is from the government?" Cole asked.

"I got a crash course in justified paranoia from some very talented people. Which will it be?"

"I'll take tampering with unknown planetary fields for a thousand, Alex."

"That's what I thought."

An hour later Cole was pulling to a stop in front of Pinups. The nymph who pushed open the side door was Taylor. She wore a long, heavy robe and was accompanied by the dancer who'd loaned the Skinners her Accent. "What took you so long?" the second nymph asked. "It's almost morning."

The other dancer rushed outside to examine her car, but was stopped by a breeze that kicked up a torrent of snow from a drift that had almost grown tall enough to reach halfway up the side of the building. She wore a short yellow coat, but the legs emerging from the bottom of it were wrapped in nothing but white stockings. "Did you dent my fender?"

"No," Cole grunted as he was loaded up like a pack mule.

Paige was the one doing the loading, and when Cole couldn't carry any more of the supplies they'd either brought with them or gotten from Daniels, she started piling them into Waggoner's arms. "The car's all yours, but we'll be needing one more trip."

"For all of you?" the nymph asked.

"Yes."

"We should be able to get you through," Taylor said with a smile. "Ever since the cold weather hit, we've been busy almost every night. Could be the turkey and egg nog we added to the buffet." Just then another gust of wind blew open her robe to reveal a curvaceous body that could have been sculpted by a pornographic mastermind. She was wrapped up like the best present ever in a light blue thong and a chain of little ornamental snowflakes wrapped around a smooth stomach.

"Yeah," Paige said as she walked around the car and dug her chirping phone from her pocket. "I'm sure that's it." She spoke on her phone while the rest of the luggage was unloaded from the car. When she was done, she grabbed a duffel containing her own weapons and gear and joined the others inside the back portion of the club. "That was Milosh," she said to Cole. "None of the Amriany are in the States anymore."

"The Gypsies moved on, huh?" Waggoner grunted. "Big surprise. Things get too hot for them around here?"

"Full Bloods are wandering back to their own territories," she explained. "The Amriany think some of the other shape-shifters are moving in on the ones that have decided to stay here. They think Esteban left a good portion of Spain and Europe unguarded and another one has come along to claim it. They've never seen her before."

"Her?" Cole asked. "Is Minh still locked up?"

"She's supposed to be somewhere in Japan," Paige said. "There's no reason to distrust the person who told me that, and there haven't been any confirmed sightings of her there or in any other region yet."

Waggoner crossed his arms and said, "That's a whole lot of vague talk. You don't trust me?"

"Don't take offense to it," Paige said. "It's hard to trust anyone. Besides, we've got a whole lot of vague information. From what you've seen regarding your Vigilant buddies, you can't blame us for being a little cautious."

"I suppose not."

Paige stood just inside the door and told Taylor, "I was thinking we'd only have to go to Texas to meet our friends, but it looks like we may have to go farther."

"How much farther?"

Wincing, Paige replied, "Hungary. Do you have enough energy stored up to get us all that far?"

Taylor shook her head and rubbed the smooth slopes of her arms. "I'm afraid not. Why don't I get you guys something hot to drink?"

That sounded good to Cole, but since his partner wasn't moving, neither was he.

"If we can't get what we need here, then we can't stay long," Paige said. "I'm not a huge believer in signs, but even I can't deny that every single one of them is pointing us toward the Amriany. We need to get someone we can trust on our side who knows how to deal with Full Bloods. They're the ones who designed the Jekhibar. We know we need their expertise on that."

"You have a Jekhibar?" Taylor asked.

Cole recognized the awe in Taylor's eyes. Considering that expression was on the face of a Dryad, it held more weight than usual. "Yes," he said.

"And what do you expect to use it for?" There was an unmistakable sternness to Taylor's question that made it clear she required an answer before she made them regret they'd even considered coming to a Dryad temple.

"The Torva'ox is how the Full Bloods got so powerful," Paige explained. She wrapped her arms around herself as if she'd just discovered the cold. "The Jekhibar is the only thing I know of that can let us manipulate it."

"The Unity Stone cannot manipulate the Torva'ox," she said. "It can only store it." Taylor's eyes narrowed and she drew in a breath. When a wind came along to tug at her robe and rustle the jewelry around her waist, she didn't even shiver. In fact, Cole wondered if every twitch or vaguely human response the nymphs had shown was merely another dance they performed in order to blend in with the world around them. "Do you know about the Mist Born?"

"I never even heard of a Unity Stone," Cole said.

Smirking as if to a child, Taylor said, "It's just a translation for Jekhibar. As for the Mist Born, that is what they are called as a group. They are elder beings that have gone unnoticed ever since humans stopped writing legends in favor of reporting simple facts."

"Great," Paige sighed. "More problems to deal with. Where have these guys been hiding?"

"The Mist Born hide from no one. They go where they please and do what they will. It is just not in their nature to interfere so blatantly in the affairs of humans. Well, it is not in most of their natures. I believe you know of a Mist Born that was captured by one of your founding fathers and recently released."

"Kawosa," Cole said, as if the name itself was a curse.

Taylor nodded. "The First Deceiver has always enjoyed toying with your kind. That is why he appears in so many of your legends. The natives of this country know him as Coyote. Some of your early religious texts depict him as a serpent, but they may have confused him with another."

Paige chuckled. "You mean like the serpent that tempted Eve with the forbidden apple?"

Taylor nodded again. One time, leaving no room for misinterpretation. "Neither he nor any of his kind are interested in your religions. They simply . . . are. Human storytellers put the rest of the pieces together."

"We already know about Kawosa," Cole said. "Do you know of another one like him that may help us?"

"You want to manipulate the Torva'ox," Taylor continued. "Since you already have a Jekhibar and know well enough to seek out your Amriany brethren, then you are close enough to be given a name." She closed her eyes and slowly shifted the angle of her head as if hearing a distant song or feeling a lover's touch beneath the flimsy material wrapped around her flawless body. Finally, she said, "Chuna."

"That's his name?" Paige asked.

"Chuna isn't a him. Chuna isn't a her."

"Can you tell us where to find Chuna?"

The Dryad turned and walked farther into the club, speaking in a voice that required the Skinners to follow her if they wanted to hear what she had to say. "I can tell you you're headed in the right direction. Chuna was last seen in the Amriany regions. I don't know a lot more than that."

"Then we're back to needing a ride to Hungary."

"I can't send you from here," Taylor said, "but I can get you to the Hub."

"What's the Hub?" Cole asked.

Taylor patted his cheek and spoke in a voice that was perfectly suited to the sparkling lips that breathed life into every word. "The Hub is where it's at, baby."

Chapter Fifteen

Shreveport, Louisiana

It had been the better part of a day since Adderson lost most of his unit on the outskirts of the city. He'd already joined up with the surviving forces of Ravens One through Three and set up a base camp inside an electronics store with metal shutters over the windows. The werewolves had caused more hardship than the recession and taken a similar toll on local businesses. The shelves had nothing on them but dust, and the storerooms were partially filled with empty boxes. Even so, there was still power flowing through the nearby mains, which one of the IRD techs was able to splice and divert into the store's back room.

It was early morning by the time Adderson stretched his back and worked the kinks from his legs. He made his way to the soldier hunched over the dented metal case containing enough equipment to hack local wireless networks and use them to send and receive encrypted messages. Adderson ignored all the other miniaturized displays as he extended a hand to the squat young Marine with the headset wrapped over his ears. The Marine handed over an earpiece along with a quick warning. "Wasn't able to raise Command, sir. Got patched straight through to one of the other field units, though."

"This is Adderson," he said as soon as the earpiece was fitted in place.

"There's significant movement southeast of your position."

"Who am I speaking to?"

"Sergeant Tate, sir."

The voice wasn't what Adderson had been expecting. It was almost as tired as his, several years younger, and female. "Where did you get this intel?"

"We're entrenched in Carthage, Texas, tracking the shifters via satellite."

"You're able to keep a fix on them?"

"Upgraded the positioning systems yesterday morning," she said with a faint hint of relief in her voice. "Got them online about three hours ago. They're still not quick enough to track the Class Ones, but we can keep a closer eye on the larger packs. There's three of those headed your way."

"How many are with you there?"

"Just me, a private, and a sniper. We've got a Humvee with a mounted .50 cal but don't want to gun the engine until it's time to abandon this position."

"Are there any Class Twos there to keep you company?"

"For now, no sir. But there's no way of knowing how many more are on their way."

"Abandon your position and rendezvous with us in Shreveport," Adderson said.

"Where in Shreveport, sir?"

After giving her the coordinates, Adderson told her, "Come to us ASAP. Monitor the Delta frequency once you get within range, and if you hear me issue the command to break formation, turn around and head for a safer position. Until then use that .50 cal to chop up as many of those things as you can. Focus on the Class Twos."

"We've heard about sightings of at least one Class One shifter in the area, sir."

"You heard the command. Focus on thinning out those packs. If you find any wounded, all Priority Cleanup Protocols are in effect."

There was a longer pause before Tate gave another tired affirmative. After that, Adderson signaled for the connection to be cut and handed back the earpiece.

No matter what he'd seen since the beasts came in from the woods, he felt sickest when enforcing the Cleanup Protocols. Every instinct he had was to either help the wounded or find a way to move them to where they could be helped. Those instincts had to be squelched after the first wave of police officers were attacked and turned in Kansas City. There had been rumors about werewolves before then, but most of them relied on whatever was cranked out of Hollywood or fairy tales. For a man who'd been polishing his boots since the third grade, that sort of thing simply didn't cut it. Adderson was a military man brought up by military men. Even his grandmother had done her part by serving as a gunnery instructor in World War Two. His uncle had been in 'Nam and used to get drunk and brag how his skin was the same color as his jungle fatigues. All of them held one solid belief where battlefield ethics were concerned: nobody was supposed to be left behind.

Cleanup Protocols mandated that those attacked by any class of shifter couldn't be allowed to change into one of them. Plenty of the medics and lab coats still wanted to do their research, but when times got bad, the protocols stated very plainly that no chances should be taken. The wounded were put down. No exceptions. Adderson hated that order, and he hated himself for giving it, but there just wasn't anything else to be done.

Looking out between the cold wooden slats nailed in place over the electronic store's front door, he watched the shadows pull away to reveal an empty street. If he squinted hard enough, he could make out the scratches left behind by a pack of shifters. Their claws had dug into the concrete and spilled blood that dried into cold, dark stains on the curbs and sidewalks. The sounds of panting, barking, and scraping reached his ears. They came from the other side of the window, and as he closed his eyes to savor one last moment of morning sun brushing his face, he could tell the sounds were getting closer.

"Do you have any details on where the survivors are taking shelter?" he asked.

The Marine at the keyboard searched a few files and said, "There are a few local postings about a gym a few blocks away. Other than that, it's just the usual scattered basements patrolled by Neighborhood Watch."

"Send some men to that gym."

"Should they be ready for cleanup?"

"Only if absolutely necessary. The shifters may try to sniff them out. Rather than move any survivors into the open, let's post some explosives at the safest minimum distance and vaporize some of those Class Twos."

"Yes, sir!" the Marine said with a grateful smile.

"There are packs moving into the area," Adderson announced to everyone in the room, without taking his eyes from the window. "A scouting team has picked them up thanks to the new satellite relays, but we all know there could be a lot more than that. We also know there's at least one Class One in the vicinity and no reason to think it would have left just so we could go out for breakfast."

Despite every soldier feeling the same fighter's twitch that accompanied the thought of running away, none of them could argue with the fact that Esteban had allowed them to survive. One of the pilots who'd escaped from a downed NH-90 had something else to say.

"What about those Class Threes? I saw them burrowing underground when my crew was turned. I think it was attacking the Class One."

"Just set the explosives and get ready for a fight. If those things are turning on each other, we'll let them rip each other to pieces. Stay back and give them room. Our top priority is in keeping this city from falling. If we can't do that, we've got to at least keep those Class Ones in one spot long enough for an artillery strike."

"Those things are too fast to be hit by artillery," one of the soldiers pointed out. Adderson recognized the man's voice but was too tired to come up with a name.

"Then we'll have to get creative and find a way to keep them in position. Nobody will turn their noses up at a target if we can make it juicy enough."

All the soldiers could muster up by way of enthusiasm was a few nods scattered among the dirty faces.

The wolves were coming in from the forests.

Chapter Sixteen

Randolph awoke at the bottom of a small crater. Several feet of drifted snow had broken his and Kawosa's fall, but the impact of their bodies was still enough to put a dent in the ground. The trickster was gone. Judging by the tracks left behind, Kawosa had dragged himself up less than a minute before he came around. The Full Blood's head ached and there were thick layers of blood frozen into his fur. He pulled in a deep breath and found a few promising hints residing within the currents of air. The trickster's scent was fresh. More than that, Kawosa was wounded.

Both of Randolph's feet were buried in the snowy wall of the hole, and his hands formed fists around solid clumps of ice that had been loosened on impact. After a short search, he found one curved talon stretching up from the center of the flattened area where his back had been resting. Not only did it explain the nagging pain at the base of his spine, but also why Kawosa hadn't reclaimed the piece of him that had been lost. Although the First Deceiver would more than likely be able to recover from the loss, having the missing wing would speed the process along nicely. Randolph stuck his hand into the packed snow and removed the wing he'd pulled from Kawosa's back.

It was lighter than a tree branch and stank like lard that left to burn for too long at the bottom of a poorly made lantern. Still, as the tattered flaps of skin ruffled in the breeze, Randolph couldn't help but smile. Finding the trickster was the most difficult part. Freeing him from Lancroft had been a trial. Getting Kawosa to trust him well enough to stay close until an opportunity like this arose was a small miracle. If not for the recent Breaking Moon, he might not have had the strength to chase the wily Mist Born down. While Esteban, Liam, and Minh were channeling their share of the Torva'ox into newly awakened powers, he had added to his foundation. Speed and strength. Two things that every Full Blood had at their disposal, but not in the amount necessary to run down an elder shapeshifter, survive an encounter with its purest form, and claim a piece for himself.

After bounding up the side of a nearby mountain, Randolph buried the wing beneath enough cold rocks to keep it safe for the short time he needed to hunt. It didn't take long for him to find a small family of mountain lions consisting of a mother and two cubs. He chased them down easily, weathered a brief but intense flurry of claws and teeth from the panicked mother, and was soon feasting on warm, bloody meat. He scooped out the carcasses, discarded what he couldn't consume, and fashioned a crude sling by knotting the hides together. When he retuned to where he'd buried the wing, he was able to strap it across his back within the sling. That way he could shift into his four-legged form and run at full speed without having to worry about losing his precious cargo.

He ran south through Wyoming and Colorado, skirting the Rockies until they led him to the southernmost portion of the state. Cold wind blasted across his face, broken occasionally by the scent of burning buildings. He did his best to avoid civilization, simply because he no longer had any business there. Human screams and Half Breed howls reached his ears in a mush, entwined with the rustling breezes like a few noteworthy strands in an otherwise uniform bolt of fabric.

Using his instincts along with knowledge gained from centuries of patrolling the same territory, Randolph knew when to point his nose to the east and run toward Kansas. Confronting the trickster was no small feat, but there was much more business to conduct before he could get the quiet he so desperately wanted.

Slowing his pace, he allowed himself to drink in the calm tranquility of a dawn where the humans were too frightened to stick their noses into the daylight. There were no longer any planes crossing overhead. When the other Full Bloods were aided by Kawosa to extend their howls in every direction, dozens of the flying machines had dropped from the sky, their pilots and passengers randomly subjected to the Breaking. Jet planes had plowed nose first into the ground. Randolph passed several wrecks that had been turned into metallic dens by the wretches that survived the crashes.

There was a bare minimum of vehicles on the roads. Although Randolph had grown accustomed to the constant roar and stench of trucks, cars, and motorcycles, being without them was infinitely better. The air was easier to ingest, and the humans were forced to keep their piercing screams and grating music within the confines of whatever shelter they could find. When the wretches got hungry enough to make their rounds among the humans, even those annoyances were silenced.

In the distance he could hear gunfire. There was always gunfire.

Humans fought to protect their homes or keep the wretches at bay.

Soon, none of that would matter.

The quiet Randolph sought would be a complete one. No more gunfire. No more belching machines in the skies or on the roads. No more overconfident howls from the likes of Esteban or others of his kind flexing powers that had lain dormant for very good reasons. No more soldiers. No more Skinners.

Maybe . . . no more Randolph.

That last possibility had kept him from playing his hand until now. Ever since the humans became strong enough to pave over the earth and spread their young like locusts, he'd thought of ways to do away with them. Perhaps that was his natural instinct as a predator, or perhaps there was something within the human race that made them louder and more insufferable than other species. Whatever the reason, he'd held back his growing intolerance.

There was a Balance to be maintained, and extinction was no way to serve it. But through meddling on both sides of the scale, human and shapeshifter alike had upset the order of things. It was within human nature to strive for more, but the Full Bloods needed to be above that. Humans built their structures, forged their metals, and eventually whittled their own numbers down through sheer stupidity and greed. The power within a Full Blood's grasp was much greater, however, and needed to be guarded. It had to be preserved, not wielded. Once something so beautiful was forged into a weapon, the Full Bloods became no better than the strutting humans.

Randolph covered another few miles in an easy, loping stride. He found another plane wreck he'd smelled a while ago, as well as a line of cars that had crashed into each other along a stretch of highway. Judging by the bones and flaking bloodstains on the cars, most of the drivers had been attacked by Half Breeds rather than turned into them. More than likely the people in the cars, distracted by the wreckage, had slammed into each other. Even after their world had crumbled, mankind could still find a way to shame itself.

Doing his best to filter out the stink of dead flesh and rusted steel, Randolph shrugged the makeshift sling to a more secure spot over his shoulder. As soon as he felt the slight weight of the torn wing against his back, he quickened his pace into a run that would make him almost impossible for mortal eyes to spot.

Extinction had already sunk its teeth into the living things of this land. The only question was if it was to be a quick or slow process.

Chapter Seventeen

The tendrils wrapped around Cole's insides changed the experience of teleportation into something that left him dizzy. Mystic natural forces tugged at his clothes, pulled at his skin, and drew him forward like a massive intake of breath. Not only did he feel like he was falling from one temple to another, but it seemed as if something was shoving him forward even faster than anything as commonplace as inertia. The sounds he heard didn't just assault his ears. The pulsing rhythms invaded his skull, slid against the back of his tongue and extended probing fingers beneath his clothes and rib cage to stroke his heart until his next breaths welled up and finally exploded outward into . . .

"What in the *hell* was that?" Waggoner shouted.

He had to shout because that was the only way to be heard over the driving beats coming from no fewer than ten towers of speakers situated strategically around the perimeter of a cavernous room. Soon, Paige staggered through the curtain as well, to grab her ears and wince.

Theirs was one of a dozen curtains, each at the edge of a large stage teeming with dancers of all shapes, sizes, colors, and states of undress. When Cole looked around at them, all of the dancers' bodies congealed into a writhing mass of smooth, glittering flesh. There were definitely several bodies on all the stages, and he knew they weren't combined into a single entity, but between all the writhing arms, strutting legs, and twirling hair, his eyes simply didn't know where to start.

"I think we got fried in transit," he said to anyone within earshot. "Because if this isn't heaven, then I don't want to know what is."

Normally, when Cole felt the Dryad influence tugging at every Y chromosome in his body, he looked to Paige for support or at least a swift knock upside his head. This time even she was speechless as they were approached by a group of four girls dressed in nothing but ankle bracelets and streaks of metallic paint applied expertly to make it seem as if their skin had flaked away to reveal solid gold chassis. These women may not have been robots, but they were anything but human.

One of the dancers, a thin Hispanic nymph with a narrow upper body and perfectly rounded hips, smiled and said, "Oh my. Looks like Taylor wasn't kidding. The new guy's cute. Think you can keep him under control?"

"To be honest," Cole said, "I doubt if I'll be able to keep myself under control."

The other three dancers consisted of a taller woman with coffee-colored skin and a full, generous figure; a petite young blonde; and a more mature blonde who seemed to have stepped out of the pages of *Playboy*'s golden years. The floor beneath their feet pulsed in time to the music, and the patrons occupying seats around the stage gazed up intently to see what would happen next.

Cole followed the tallest nymph toward a corner at the back of the room. It was tough taking his eyes from the swaying perfection of the Hispanic nymph's backside, but there was plenty more to catch his attention. Women climbed poles that stretched down from the heights of a cathedral ceiling, or they crawled along horizontal bars without the slightest lapse in balance. The entire latticework glowed with colors that shot through the structure to illuminate it like pipes filled with blue and green luminescent water. Three cocktail bars were worked by six tenders, all of whom were human women, still gorgeous despite the supernatural competition around them. They smiled at the Skinners who passed, not seeming to notice the weapons strapped to their bodies or the gear they carried.

"Where the hell are we?" Cole asked.

The tall Hispanic Dryad pivoted toward him, which did nothing to break the line of her stride. "Didn't Taylor tell you?"

"She said something about a hub."

"There you go," she replied with a flourishing wave toward a sign hanging above a towering wine rack made of gnarled wood. The sign looked to have been pulled from a vein of ore and crudely bent into two words: THE HUB. It was spelled out in smooth, yet rugged letters accentuated by the curving glyphs Cole had come to know as Dryad script. Now that he'd seen those markings, more of the symbols could be found etched into the walls, floor, and pillars stretching up past the poles from which several nymphs swung or twirled. If he could see the ceiling through the bank of milling steam hanging like a smoky layer of clouds, he guessed there would be markings on it as well.

Now that the smaller Hispanic nymph was closer, Cole couldn't tell if she might actually have a Middle Eastern background. The more he looked at her, the more he wanted to learn. Being an expert in every sort of worshipping stare, she took his hand, shook it and said, "I'm Marissa. I know you're probably a little dizzy right now, so just keep your eyes on me and we'll take you to somewhere you can think straight."

Since his eyes were already glued to Marissa's swaying hips, Waggoner said, "That ain't a problem, sweet thing." Three of the nymphs pretended to think that was funny, as the tallest of the group cut a path through the crowd. When Waggoner was distracted from where he was walking, the younger blond nymph placed a hand on his back and kept him from walking straight into a group of businessmen. "What should I call you, honey?" he asked.

"Alyssa," the blonde said with a smile.

The Hub was massive. Even more impressive was the amount of business it was doing. As far as Cole could tell, nearly all of the seats were filled, every stage was working to capacity, and there was plenty going on in the VIP lounges alongside the main room. The place was even big enough to have more than one climate. As he and the others were led toward the back, the air became cooler and the thumping bass lines of the music gave way to softer jazz tracks played from speakers embedded in the walls and ceiling of an insulated room.

"This is one of our private suites," the taller Hispanic nymph said as she turned around and extended both hands to encompass the space around her. Generous curves tested the limits of her flimsy outfit and a wide smile put the Skinners at ease. The room felt like a plush cave that was insulated well enough to keep all but the lowest bass lines from seeping in. Dark red velvet lined the walls, and tastefully subdued carpeting muffled all footsteps into soft, whispering impacts. There was barely enough space for the Skinners to stand without crowding each other or bumping their shins against low, sumptuously overstuffed couches along both sides of the room. Another door, outlined in dimly glowing green neon, was at the opposite wall.

"I'm Lexi," the tall Hispanic beauty said. "If there's anything you need, just ask for me."

"What we need is to get to Hungary," Paige said.

"It's being arranged," Lexi replied. "Wait here and make yourselves comfortable."

"I thought the arrangements were already made. We're on a schedule here."

"You're also on our ground, Skinner," Lexi said. "Mind your manners or we'll mind them for you."

Temporarily stunned by the tone in her voice, Cole moved toward the group of nymphs. He was immediately cut short by armed men who'd swarmed into the room from behind the other three girls. Although dressed in windbreakers bearing the Hub's logo, they carried assault rifles rivaling the ordnance carried by the IRD.

"What the hell?" Paige said. "When did this shit start?"

The other blonde moved forward to directly challenge Paige. A gold one-piece swimsuit wrapped around her as if painted on by a narrow roller that had been placed on one shoulder then moved across her large breasts and over her stomach to barely cover her below the waist. Despite the lack of clothing, her eyes gleamed even brighter than the necklace that spelled the word STARR in gold letters. "It started when you took advantage of our gratitude by corrupting one of our most beloved sisters!"

"You must have us mixed up with someone else," Cole said.

"No," said a woman who eased past the armed men as if they were just another pair of slack-jawed customers. "They know exactly who you are, but their anger may be somewhat misdirected."

Then Tristan, one of the leading members of the Dryad sisterhood, stepped into the room. She moved gracefully on high heels and wore her flowing chestnut hair loose over both shoulders. A flawless body sculpted from skin that begged to be caressed was wrapped in a relatively modest purple dress that gleamed like water hugging her breasts and hips to flow freely across her torso and legs. Something about her wasn't the same, however. Her usual shine was diminished and her presence didn't radiate the same effortless exuberance. Cole was drawn immediately to her eyes, and when she moved closer, he could tell they were now the color of moss that had never been touched by daylight.

"What happened was my choice," Tristan announced. Since the other nymphs weren't backing down, she approached Lexi and placed a hand on her smooth shoulder. "A choice that couldn't have been forced upon me no matter who was asking me to make it."

"The Skinners never stop asking," Lexi said. "They're never satisfied with what they're given, and now we've all been corrupted."

Waggoner shook his head and rubbed the back of his neck. "In case you haven't looked outside lately, there's a whole lot of corruption going on. From where we stand, it seems you ladies are doing better than most."

Cole hadn't taken his eyes off of Tristan, which had nothing to do with the beauty that still made every other beautiful thing in the world pale by comparison. She was one of the first supernatural beings Cole had met who hadn't tried to kill him. He didn't exactly swap greeting cards with the Dryad, but there was a connection between them similar to the one between a boy and the experienced older woman who'd lovingly given him one hell of a first time. "What's the matter?" he asked her earnestly.

His tone, more than the words themselves, had an effect on Tristan. Her exterior crumbled just enough for him to see how much work was required to keep it in place. "Everyone," she said with supreme authority, "leave us."

"Who stays?" one of the armed guards asked.

"Cole and Paige," Tristan told him. "Everyone else can move into the next room. There's food there," she said to Waggoner in a less severe tone. "Help yourself. If you're going as far as you say you are, you'll need all the nutrition you can get."

After several affirming nods were passed between those concerned, the nymphs escorted Waggoner through a door at the opposite side of the room.

"The one with the beard seems new to the game," Tristan mused as they left.

"That's Waggoner," Paige said. "He's still wet behind the ears but stood up for me and a whole lot of people when things went to hell in Atoka." She waited for the other two to sit down before making herself comfortable next to Cole on one of the couches.

"I heard about your home in Chicago burning down," Tristan said. "That's terrible."

"What were those other girls talking about when they said you were corrupted?" Cole asked. "That is, if they were talking about you."

"They were," Tristan said with a single nod. "I was glad to help you in Atoka when the Breaking Moon rose, but I told you there would be a cost. I had to tap into darker energies, such as fear, hate, and rage." When she said those words, her eyes took on an accusatory glint that was aimed at both Skinners. "There's a reason we don't use those energies. They change us."

"But you'll get better, right?" Cole asked. "I mean, you can't have been the first Dryad to do something like that."

"Definitely not. The only problem is that this sort of corruption makes us into something that isn't Dryad. Human legends are filled with my kind as well as theirs. We are known as muses, mermaids, and sprites, while those others are commonly known as hags, cannibals, and . . ."

"Witches," Paige said.

Tristan nodded and wrapped her arms tightly around herself. The sight of her purposely dimming her own light made Cole feel ashamed for asking her to go through the ordeal. It had been necessary, but that didn't take anything away from the burden he now felt.

"The reason I detained you here isn't to make you feel guilty," Tristan explained. "And it's not to show you what you've done to me. It's to explain that your actions have consequences. Sometimes, I wonder if Skinners fully appreciate that."

"Believe me," Paige said, "we know plenty about consequences."

"Can you know how the actions of every Skinner before you have impacted the world in which we live?"

Picking up on the new edge in her voice, Cole said, "I've only been doing this for a year or two . . . maybe more." Images of his time as a Skinner rushed through his mind in a flash, leaving him feeling older than before they'd arrived. "I may not know a lot, but I know we're not trying to leave anything worse than it was before we got there. It wasn't even our choice for all of this crap to go public. Paige and I did our best to keep people thinking werewolves and vampires were just hoaxes and perverts trolling the Internet."

"I know you mean well," Tristan said as a patient smile eased across her face. "I also know you are trying to do good. That's why I've agreed to help you as much as I have, even when it meant sacrificing a part of myself that I may never regain." She shifted on the overstuffed cushions, drawing her legs in close. "I'm referring to all Skinner activity. The animals you kill have a place in our world. When too many of one species are lost, another takes its place. If one predator falls, another fills the gap. If no other predators fill the gap, more of the smaller creatures emerge."

"Yeah, like Chupacabra," Cole grunted. "I've still got the scars from those little bastards. The gargoyles seem to have gone back into hibernation for the winter, though."

"You killed a Full Blood during the Breaking Moon," Tristan continued. "Another will rise to take his place, just as one arose to fill the void left by Henry."

"So what should we do?" Paige asked. "Just let them all go about their business so they can wipe us out?"

"It's too late for that, I know," Tristan said. "But you have to know that you cannot continue dealing with each individual fire that is started. You either need to commit yourselves to the larger struggle or step back and let the fires burn."

Reflexively lowering her voice, Paige told her, "That's why we're going to Hungary. The Amriany are about to have the same problems we have here. For all we know, they may have already started."

"Yes, things are just as bad there as they are here," Tristan mused. "The Travelers have always been better at keeping things quiet. Why Hungary? Is that just where you intend on meeting the Amriany?"

"I thought Milosh and Nadya were based in the Czech Republic," Paige said. "But they said they wanted to meet us in Hungary."

"Do you know why?"

"Not yet," Cole said, "but you do. Isn't that right?" Seeing the guarded expression on Tristan's face, he leaned toward her and ignored the tension he sensed from the armed guard that had remained posted near the door. "Does this have something to do with Chuna?"

Slowly, Tristan nodded.

"Chuna is one of the Mist Born," Paige said. "That's what Taylor told us. We don't even know what that means. So far, a lot of this seems like just a bunch of disconnected pieces."

"And yet you know well enough to leave the place where it seems you're needed the most, so you can find the meaning to this particular piece?"

Knowing he was speaking for both of them, Cole said, "There's really not a lot else for us to do."

"Sure there is," Tristan said. "You could keep chopping Half Breeds into pulp like the Army. You could follow the Nymar's lead and sit in buildings purchased at a significant discount from frightened owners who are only thinking of surviving for one more day or are too enraptured to refuse the pittance they were given. You could even draw yourselves into a heavily armed cult with strongholds in three different cities like your fellow Skinners."

"You mean the Vigilant?"

Tristan nodded.

Paige kept her voice level and quiet, so as not to further upset the guard, when she asked, "The Vigilant have strongholds in more than one city?"

"Yes," Tristan replied, looking as if she was fully aware of the bomb she was dropping. "Three. At least, those are the ones I know about. The Vigilant have been trying to capture my sisters much like Jonah Lancroft did. As far as I can tell, it's for the same reason. They want use of our temples as well as a fresh supply of Memory Water."

Suddenly, Cole's head snapped up and he drew in a quick breath.

"I'm sorry, Cole," Tristan said. "But Memory Water won't help rid you of the tendrils inside of you. Otherwise I would have offered you some when I helped get that spore out of you."

Before he could stop himself, he asked, "It kept Jonah Lancroft alive for a couple hundred years, but it won't help me? Why?" He'd already bared himself, he thought, so the least he could get was an answer to his question.

"Lancroft was a monster," Tristan said. "Do you even know what's involved in making Memory Water?"

"No, but it can't be too bad or you'd never make it at all. Right?"

"We can collect it," Tristan said. "I won't get into the particulars, but it's a process that has become a sacred ritual among my sisterhood. To speed up the ritual involves torturing my kind and wringing the very essence of our soul from the fabric of our bodies. If Memory Water could help you, I would have gladly given you what little I can spare. It restores the physical body to a point in the past when it was more vital. Youth can be granted. Mortal lives, as you already know, can be extended for centuries." Focusing on Cole, she added, "You may think of it as bringing your body to its default setting."

There was something undeniably sweet about hearing Tristan put things into geek terms for him.

"But," she continued, "it only affects you, and that thing inside you isn't actually a part of you. Memory Water could revitalize your body to a point before that spore was injected, but that doesn't mean the tendrils would be erased. You'd be revitalized and the tendrils would remain, just like clothes or jewelry or any other foreign thing attached or wrapped around you."

"Couldn't we give it a shot?" Paige asked.

"If we had any Memory Water on hand, perhaps," Tristan replied. "But most of our reserves were plundered by Jonah Lancroft, and the rest have been stolen from us by his followers."

Cole sat bolt upright. "The Vigilant have attacked you?"

"Not me, personally, and I haven't heard of any of my sisters that were taken. Lancroft must have passed on the location of our hidden stores, because those were looted within months after the Nymar rose to—" She blinked and looked around at the two Skinners. "Well . . . you know what happened."

"No need to worry about manners," Paige said. "A little salt in that wound really doesn't matter anymore. As far as Cole goes, do you think there might be anything at all the Memory Water could do for him if you could make some changes?"

She shook her head. "It's not a formula we can tweak. It is what it is. My sisters and I have been hunted by Nymar since they decided to dwell within human bodies. Obviously, we don't have much cause to find ways to help ease their pain. Not that we wouldn't if there was a way, but . . ."

"But you'd be dead the moment you got close enough to try," Cole said. "I get it."

"We could help your arm, though," Tristan said to Paige. "Why didn't you drink the Memory Water I gave you when you were hunting Lancroft before?"

"I needed it for other things," Paige told her. "Besides, Skinners need to learn from their mistakes, and there's not a lot to learn by just erasing them and starting clean." Looking to Cole, she added, "We can deal with our wounds. Just because we're hurt doesn't mean we're . . ." Suddenly, her eyes widened. " . . . broken. Can Memory Water cure a Half Breed?"

Tristan's expression clouded over, leaving no doubt in Cole's mind that she'd witnessed a Breaking firsthand when she said, "No. Something about that change is deeper than anything I've ever seen. A human is no longer human after they become a Half Breed, and drinking the Water only brings them back to the earliest point in their life as a Half Breed. The only thing worse than seeing them broken once is watching a human live through it a second time. I will never subject another living thing to that kind of torture."

"What about a Full Blood?" Cole asked. "They can go

back and forth. Randolph and Liam talk as if they've been around forever and were never anything but Full Bloods."

"Right," Paige said. "Which means bringing them back to square one won't make a lot of difference."

Cole shrugged. "Could it bring them back to how they were before the Breaking Moon?"

For the first time since the conversation began, Tristan didn't hold herself as if every part of her ached. There was a glimmer in her eyes again. Though it wasn't quite the same as the nights when she'd been twirling on stage, that it was there at all brightened the atmosphere in the room. "I . . . don't know. We've never had a reason to try anything like that."

"The Full Bloods aren't after you, are they?" Paige asked.

"Not as such, but they don't hold us in high regard. Things were just never the same between our kind after I sent the Full Blood elder Gorren from a forest in Romania to our temple in Antarctica." Seeing the expression on the Skinners' faces, she waved it off and said, "Long story. If you want to try Memory Water on a Full Blood, you'll have to capture one yourselves."

"That may not be as tough as you think," Cole said. "But what if there was a way to get that stuff to all of them at once?"

"You mean through the Torva'ox?" Tristan asked.

"Could Chuna help us with that?"

"I don't know that either. These aren't exactly the sort of things anyone has ever considered doing before."

"But can they be done?" Cole asked as he scooted to the edge of his seat so he could use his hands while speaking. "We've got a Jekhibar, which can hold the Torva'ox. From what Taylor said back in Louisville, this Chuna guy or woman or whatever can help us do even more with it. What was she talking about?"

"Everything within the earth passes through Chuna," Tristan said.

Paige winced. "That sounds kind of gross."

"Chuna is a Mist Born," she continued. "Their existence

is real, but most of them don't choose to interact with other beings. Some say they are the only true sentient forces of nature." Since Cole looked like he was ready to start jumping in anticipation, she held him back with a single outstretched hand. "That doesn't mean Chuna is the answer. The Amriany are thought to have more knowledge of Chuna, just like your Dr. Lancroft had knowledge of Kawosa. According to legend, the Torva'ox flows from Chuna's veins. Like all legends, this may be exaggerated. But every legend connects Chuna to the Torva'ox. If any of the Mist Born would know about that power, be able to manipulate it or anything else along those lines, it is Chuna."

"So," Cole sighed, "we just need to find him . . . or her."

"Finding Chuna may be next to impossible," Tristan told him. "And you cannot just speak to a Mist Born. They are powerful creatures, dangerous beyond your comprehension. I believe they grew tired of dealing with humans simply because your minds were too flimsy to bear the weight of the meeting."

"I met Clint Eastwood once at a press event back when I was with Digital Dreamers," Cole said fondly. "It was kind of like that."

Knowing when it was better to just ignore him, Paige said, "We're meeting up with some Amriany friends of ours. They've worked with the Jekhibar and they're on good terms with the rest of their clan, so we'll see what they can tell us about Chuna. In the meantime, though, the Full Bloods are able to turn humans into Half Breeds with nothing more than a howl at some special frequency or . . . I don't even know how they're doing it."

"They are reaching through the Torva'ox," Tristan said. "Although humans only draw a small bit of that life force, it's enough of a connection for the Full Bloods to reach through and break them."

"This wasn't the first Breaking Moon to rise," Cole said. "Why didn't this all happen before?"

"Because the Full Bloods didn't have the help of a Mist

Born. Kawosa created the first Half Breeds and now he strives to perfect the recipe. Perhaps it's his way of making sure he has more soldiers on the field than anyone else. Heaven help us all if one of the Full Bloods is truly able to steer the wretches."

"Memory Water is the only thing I know of that has a chance of taking that power away from the Full Bloods," Paige said. "Maybe then Kawosa will be willing to go back to the way things were."

"Or he could just back off and watch the fighting," Cole said. "He seems to enjoy dealing with humans and shape-shifters, so at least we can take our chances with him. Either way, it's dealing with one threat instead of . . . however many Full Bloods there are."

Tristan sighed. "Even one Mist Born may be more than enough to make these days even darker, but at least it's a course of action with some promise. Since you're talking about a plan that requires Memory Water, I'll be busy enough just collecting more than what it would take to fill a thimble. When I have more than that, I'll let you know."

"All right, then," Paige said. "What about getting us to Hungary? Think you've got enough juice stored up in this place to pull that off?"

Tristan nodded and struggled to get off the couch. She seemed frailer than ever as she motioned toward the guards. "If you intend on manipulating the Torva'ox as well as tracking down a Mist Born, then I don't doubt your intentions are still good."

"About what happened to you," Cole said, "all I can say is, I'm sorry. That seems so useless, but it's all I've got."

The Dryad touched his cheek and smiled. "It's more than enough. I just needed to make sure you mean to take aggressive action to put an end to this madness instead of doing anything that might contribute to it."

Paige smirked and helped the Dryad to her feet. "Aggressive action is what we're all about. Any chance we can get something to eat before we leave?"

"I'll make the arrangements," Tristan said. "It may take some time to make contact with the other temple, so why don't you all get some sleep in one of our executive suites?" She whispered a few short sentences to the guard. By the time she was through, the big, armed man looked more like a guide and less like an executioner. "You can walk through there to an elevator that will take you to the next floor."

"Next floor?" Cole marveled. "Just how tall is this purple A-frame anyway?"

"You'll see for yourself soon enough. Now if you'll excuse me," Tristan said in a voice that sounded every bit as tired as she looked, "there are many preparations to make." The Dryad walked back to the door that opened into the main room. Along the way, she straightened up and pulled her shoulders back to give her more of a regal posture. That simple transition made her look like a goddess. The gray pallor was still in her skin, and there was a definite lack of energy in her stride, but it didn't take away from the reaction she got when reintroducing herself to the room full of overeager mortals waving money at the rest of the nymphs.

"She's still got it," Cole said as he moved close to the door that was held open, so he could watch Tristan's exit. Then, when Waggoner was escorted to the same spot, the trio of Skinners entered a room that was a smaller version of the VIP lounge, complete with a small wet bar in one corner, a pair of love seats upholstered in luxurious velvet, and a single pole extending from the ceiling like a perfectly symmetrical stalactite.

"What's the plan?" Waggoner asked.

"She's gonna help us," Paige replied, "but it's going to take some time to arrange for transport."

"All the way to Hungary?"

"Yep."

A soft *ding* drifted through the room, and part of a glyph-encrusted wall slid aside to reveal what looked to be a dimly illuminated space just a bit smaller than a car used to carry freight to the upper floors of a warehouse. "Step into the elevator," one of the guards said. "It'll take you to a private suite."

One of the guards had already reached inside to push a button that was camouflaged by the swirling designs on the elevator walls. The glyphs were everywhere. Cole saw symbols flashing with subdued light that could easily be mistaken as a reflection off shiny paint, but he knew better. Every temple was made to harness and focus the energies drawn from human emotion, and the glyphs were the arteries that carried the flow to wherever it needed to go. He could feel the power thrumming beneath his feet and pressing against him like a ghostly dancer grinding against his body.

Waggoner and Paige were closest, so they were the first to pile in. Almost immediately they stopped, their backs blocking the door. Paige was a few steps ahead of him, but Cole was already close enough to see the cool glow coming from the interior of the elevator. Lights flashed and some blinked in quick succession as if to mesmerize the passengers within the elevator.

"Move it," Cole grunted. "I'm hungry."

The instant he stepped inside the elevator, his breath was dragged from his lungs.

The car was made of thick glass, inlaid with Dryad markings trapped between transparent layers like ripples frozen into ice. Beyond the glass, a magnificently discombobulated city lay sprawled beneath and around them. The Statue of Liberty and Eiffel Tower lay nestled between massive glittering buildings, mammoth fountains, and spotlights that exploded from a street bustling with cars and people. When Cole looked down, he saw the side of the building to which the elevator was attached. It was shimmering purple Plexiglas that sloped to a pinnacle several stories over his head.

"Been a while since I been to Vegas," Waggoner said. "Never fails to impress."

"Don't get too comfortable," Paige told him. "We won't be staying long."

"Aw come on," Cole gasped. "This looks like the closest thing to business as usual that we've seen in months. There's actually more than three people on that street!"

Waggoner laughed and shifted his weight. "It'd take a lot more than the werewolf apocalypse to shut Vegas down. Gotta love it."

Chapter Eighteen

Chicago, Illinois

Rush Street used to be the place for discerning customers to go for their more exotic thrills. There were other Blood Parlors in the city, but the place Steph ran atop a standard sports bar was at the center of them all. At least, it had been before getting torched by the Skinners on their way out of town. As a way to show that nothing as simple as a fire could put her out of business, Steph not only reopened her Blood Parlor in the same location but spent a small fortune in repairs to make sure it looked exactly as it had before Cole, Paige, and Rico got their hands on it.

After a push to squeeze everyone on her regular client list for funds using everything from promises for freebies from her best girls to threatening rich men's families, Steph had opened her Parlor and remodeled the bar beneath it. Instead of catering to the few Cubs and Bears fans who'd decided to buy their beer at a place situated beneath a gothic second floor bristling with candles and statuary, she reinforced every wall and door, packing the bar with employees armed with large caliber pistols and shotguns who were posted at the entrances. Anyone else seen sitting at the bar or around any of the tables were waiting for their turn to go upstairs and be fed upon by scantily clad parasites with smooth skin, overly friendly smiles, and unending appetites. Fortunately for anyone involved in the Nymar skin trade, nobody thought twice anymore when someone left their home and didn't return.

It wasn't much past ten o'clock, but the sky had the thick, inky texture of the witching hour. A sleek two-door Mazda pulled to a stop at the curb on Superior Street and let two passengers out to make the short walk to the parlor's front door. Steph watched their progress on monitors that received a constant live stream from cameras set in windows of every adjacent building. As she marched toward the parlor, Tara looked as if she not only knew she was being watched but that she knew who was watching.

"Shit," Steph grunted as she stood up and grabbed a short coat that looked as if it had been made from a mix of wool and puppet skin. "What the hell does she want?"

"What does who want?"

The question had been asked in a cultured English accent by a tall Nymar with smooth dark skin and black hair pulled back into a short tail. Astin had begun his service as a bouncer for the Blood Parlor, worked his way up to own the bar beneath the vampire brothel and now filled the space vacated by the Nymar who'd formerly run Chicago at Steph's side. Astin might have had a refined wardrobe and spoke as if he'd gotten his bouncer credentials at Oxford, but he had a long way to go before gaining the respect Steph had occasionally given her late partner, Ace.

"Shut up and clear out the bar," she snapped.

As reflected by the unwavering expression on Astin's face, he was used to being treated that way by her. "Even the customers?"

"Are they regulars?"

"Yes."

"High end?"

After a moment's contemplation, he replied, "Not really."

A buzzer sounded through a recessed speaker in the security room, forcing Steph to pick and tug her dark purple hair as if she couldn't decide between arranging it or ripping it out. "Tara's here. Last time I checked, she was supposed to be in Baltimore."

"Maybe she's bringing more Shadow Spore?"

"We've already gotten our share. Chicago's supposed to be under my jurisdiction only, so she'd better not have any bright ideas." When the buzzer went off again, it sounded as angry as an electronic burst of noise possibly could. Steph looked up at the speaker as if she expected to find a living thing screaming down at her. "Get two of the others. New guys. Nobody she could have seen the last time she was here. Give them shotguns, put them in the back room downstairs and tell them to come out shooting if I give the signal."

"Why would you want to shoot Tara?"

Steph wheeled around on the balls of feet, wrapped in thick wool socks that looked like they'd been pulled off the Wicked Witch of the East after Dorothy's house fell on her. The top two sets of fangs emerged from beneath her gums as nearly every muscle in her body tensed. "I built up these Blood Parlors real good since we ran the Skinners out of town, and I won't hand them over to some bitch just because she was Hope's lackey during the uprising. We're already kicking back a percentage to the cause, and if she thinks she's getting more . . ." The buzzer sounded again, this time causing Steph's eyes to pinch shut, and she spoke in a hissing snarl. "If she thinks any of that is gonna happen, then she's in for a surprise."

Astin gave her a crisp nod. "And I know exactly what surprise you have in mind."

"You think?"

The moment Astin stepped back into the hall, all he needed to do was point at a few of the Nymar looking to see what was going to be done about the visitors waiting to be let inside. A few clean-shaven faces bearing the subtle hint of tendrils beneath the surface fell into step behind Astin and followed him down a set of narrow stairs at the back of the hall. By the time they'd descended to the first floor, Steph emerged from the security room and plastered a wide, garishly painted smile onto her face. The other doors along that hallway opened into rooms used by customers who paid for the experience of being fed upon by whatever Nymar vixen or pretty boy they'd pointed to in the catalog in the lobby.

"Everyone just go about your thing," she said cheerily to the few faces that peeked out from the rooms. "Just so you know, there may be someone watching you other than me, so keep on your best behavior."

That might have answered a few unspoken questions, but didn't do much to alleviate the tension written across the other Nymar faces. Steph preferred to keep everyone guessing, along with her own employees, so she practically skipped past them down the hall and swept her hair back to make a grand entrance down the wider stairs at the front end of the building.

Standing outside the front of the bar, accompanied by four Nymar wearing their markings like war paint, Tara was obviously not concerned about drawing attention. She and her escorts all stared through the windows as if pooling their efforts to melt the glass using the power of their minds. Astin ushered the last of the customers behind the bar and through a doorway leading to the alley. When Steph looked at him, he nodded discreetly to assure her that backup was in place.

Rattling the knobs to unlock the doors just long enough for Astin to take a good position behind the bar, Steph finally pulled the door open and held it in place. "Wasn't expecting you," she said cheerfully. "Need a place to stay while you're in Chicago or will you be moving along soon?"

"Tell me what you know about the Skinners that used to live here," Tara said as she entered the bar. Once she cleared the doorway, her escort came in and fanned out to make sure they could watch every inch of the bar while keeping clear of the windows and stairs.

"They used to stay at a run-down shithole over on West

Twenty-Fifth and Laramie," Steph said. "I think it used to be some old Greek restaurant. Why?"

"What else?"

Crossing her arms petulantly, Steph snapped, "Whatever they didn't take with them was either busted up or burnt when we put it to the match. What else do you need?"

"Where have they gone since?"

"Don't you watch the news? Kansas City, Philly, Oklahoma, anywhere there's been a big blow-up with the shape-shifters, you'll find the Skinners. Christ, I've even seen Cole getting arrested on the national news! Not that anyone seems to care about that since the furries have taken over." The belligerence in her features dissolved into a wistful smile. "Can't really blame the cops or press for that one, though."

Tara wore a simple overcoat wrapped around her narrow frame. Several layers of thermal shirts, flannel and wool, were revealed when she unbuttoned it. Sunlight might not have hurt Nymar in the slightest, but cold weather played havoc on a body with such limited circulation. "Did you ever see the unedited footage from those prison attacks?" she asked while settling into one of the recently vacated chairs.

"No," Steph replied eagerly. "I just heard all the trouble that started when someone made the stupid decision to leave the prisoners where they were while other good, taxpaying folks were evacuated to shelters."

Tara shifted in her seat while peeling off another few layers. In the light, her skin looked pale, yet clear. As more of that light was taken away or blocked, the tendrils beneath her flesh widened into markings that were only slightly fatter than those found on Nymar infected by the earlier model spore. "Official statements from the Department of Corrections say that nobody intended the prisoners to come to any harm. Angry families and human rights activists say otherwise. After the Full Bloods set those things loose, just about every prison in the country became a giant meat locker, and we all know that Half Breeds don't have any qualms with taking down the easy prey first."

"And there was footage?" Steph asked, as if being tempted by a sneak preview of the newest blockbuster a month before its release.

"You need to know where to go to find it, but yes. It's not pretty." One of her guards had made himself at home enough to step behind the bar, grab one of the bottles of imported beer, and set it down on the table in front of her. Once Tara had a chance to sip the dark ale, she smirked and added, "Well, some of it was a little pretty."

"Nice. So what else do you expect me to tell you about the Skinners? If you know anything about them moving back into Chicago, then you should be the one telling me." When she didn't get a response to that, Steph narrowed her eyes and asked, "Are they moving back into Chicago?"

"I don't think so. Paige and Cole have been quite busy, but they don't seem to have any reason to come back."

"Because they know they'd be risking their own necks in coming here," Steph said firmly.

"No. Because they have no business in Chicago."

"I torched their home when Cole was in it. Him and that bounty hunter couldn't get away quick enough."

"Was that before or after they came back to burn this establishment to the ground?" Steph was still seething when Tara looked around at the silently glowing television screens and said, "Just because you tried to duplicate the old place doesn't mean anyone will forget what happened to it. The Skinners sent you a real good message before they left."

"And you were here for that, weren't you?" Steph growled as her multicolored nails dug into the edges of the table between her and the other Nymar. "Hope set that up and I played along. Only, I didn't know I would lose my parlor along the way."

"Neither did we. I probably knew less than you."

Although none of the anger left Steph's face, she tempered it for a moment so she could study the woman in front of her. "Something's different about you. You're not so . . . snarly."

"That's one way you could put it."

"You're still multiseeded?"

"There's no way to do anything about that. It does take a little while for the two spore to settle into a rhythm." Glancing at the second floor above her, Tara added, "I'm sure you can think of plenty of colorful comparisons to make in that regard. One of the reasons I came was to check on you, since you're one of the few I know who haven't accepted the Shadow Spore."

"I accepted the first treatment," Steph said.

"Why not the others?"

"Because I just wanted to experiment. This one turned out like those few years I thought I was only into chicks. Tastes great for a while, but I started yearning for the good ol' meat and potatoes, you know?"

Tara sighed heavily enough for everyone in the bar as well as anyone standing outside to hear it. "Did Hope seriously leave you in charge of an entire city?"

"You wanna change that?" Steph asked as her fangs reflexively slid partially from where they were hidden. "You're welcome to try."

"So you can cut loose however many dogs you've got hiding in a back room or up those stairs?" Tara asked. "Even when I was in my deepest, hate-filled, self-destructive emotional pit, I would have known better than to walk into your little castle, sit down, and say something like that."

"So what did you mean about checking up on me?"

"I wanted to see if you felt what happened during the Breaking Moon."

"You're damn right I felt it!" Steph said as she leaned back into her chair and drummed her fingers on the table. "Now that people spend every day being scared shitless, my business is booming. I've heard that alcohol, gambling, and gun sales are the only things benefiting from this whole shapeshifter mess. Them and the travel industry." Leaning forward and flashing a fang-filled grin, she said, "Too bad all those people who packed up and left this country will only have about another week or so of peace and quiet before they're dragged right back into it. And when they come home, the price for me taking away some of that misery will be double."

Tara studied her with eyes darkened by threadlike filaments that crept in on all sides to meet at her pupils. "You obviously haven't felt it."

"Let me guess. It was something that cleared some of that double-seeded craziness from your brain?" Seeing she'd struck a nerve, Steph bounced her legs excitedly upon the balls of her feet. "Seems like only yesterday you were climbing the walls and shaking like a junkie when the blood from your last kill was still dripping from your lips. Now you sit there looking all smart and forming complete sentences."

"Hope said the Breaking Moon would let my body catch up to both spores inside of me. All I had to do was live long enough to see it." Holding up her hand to show Steph as well as herself that it wasn't shaking, she added, "Looks like she was right." Placing her hand upon the table as if it had suddenly turned into a lead weight, she asked, "You haven't felt any difference with your spores?"

"No."

"Are there any other double-seeded Nymar in the city?"

"No, but that's not all of what you wanted to talk about." When Tara stiffened, Steph said, "I'm in a line of work that benefits from knowing when someone is beating around the bush. Some people walk right up and tell you they want to get their dick sucked and then get bitten by a girl wearing a miniskirt with her hair in pigtails."

"Who doesn't?" grunted one of Tara's guards.

"But most of my customers," she continued, "probably the best ones, need a little coaxing. They come up to you, but don't quite know what to say. Or maybe they don't want to say it . . . for whatever reason. I doubt you're nervous about anything."

"It's the Skinners," Tara snapped before she was led any further along that road.

"Gotchya. Someone on the rise like you doesn't want to

know how important it is for someone like me to help you."

Tara sighed again. It was shorter than the others. More embarrassed than disgusted. "Have you heard from them or not?"

"No."

"Do you know where they may be? *Specifically*?"

Without doing the first thing to hide how much she was enjoying herself, Steph replied, "Like I already said. Just what I pieced together from the news."

"Do you have anything of theirs they left behind?"

"Like what? An address book? Something they touched so you can get vibes off it? Don't laugh. I actually have a regular customer who thinks we can do that kind of shit. God bless those stupid movies for making the rest of the planet think we're superheroes."

One more sigh from Tara. This time it was a short, intolerant exhalation that had been trapped for too long within an angry body. "What about anyone who might know where they are?" She snapped her black, violated eyes up to lock onto Steph and stun the Nymar into silence. "Think there might be any chance of you knowing someone like that?"

"There are tons of Nymar in Chicago."

"And on the outskirts, but only one who works for the Skinners. Only one who mixes up the Skinner's poisons and builds new weapons for them to use to kill us. Only one who's been getting away with that kind of thing for . . . how many years?"

Knowing it was useless to lie, Steph adjusted her posture so she was sitting properly in her chair. "His name is Daniels."

"There we go."

"How long did Hope know about him?"

"I don't know," Tara replied. "That was back when I was crawling the walls and licking my lips."

"Right. Sorry about that. I was just—"

"I know," Tara cut in. "And if there was any hint that you'd found him by now, you'd already be nailed to a wall, hanging upside down so you could taste everything that leaked out of you before it dripped into a pot on the floor."

Normally, Steph didn't respond very well to threats. The only people who'd talked to her like that on a regular basis had been burned from their home and nearly torn apart. But things had changed in the Nymar pecking order. Tara wasn't at the top, but she had influence that spread much farther than Chicago. As much as it galled her to do so, Steph choked down what she'd wanted to say and slowly stood up. "I may know where you could look for him."

"Where?"

"He used to live in an apartment in the 'burbs. We think he relocated a while ago, but we haven't been able to nail it down. Daniels was paranoid back when he mixed drinks to knock out the kids who came wandering into the clubs we used to run in the nineties. Ever since he broke away from us and ran to kiss Skinner ass, he's been worse."

"How much worse?"

"Worse as in full-on conspiracy theories, electronic security, false identities." She chuckled and added, "The last time Ace spotted him, Daniels was wearing some kind of goofy disguise. Pathetic, really."

"Was Ace able to follow Daniels back to where he lived?"

Reluctantly, Steph said, "No."

"That is pathetic." Tara stood up and stepped away from the table. Her guards hadn't moved from their spots, but she didn't seem concerned with them. "Is he paying you? Did you let him live as some sort of deal you had with the Skinners?"

"I told you, I'm not sure if—"

"I didn't have to ask around very long to find out you steered a man from New York to Daniels around the time of the riots in Kansas City. Even supplied him with a few hitters to tear down some apartment buildings. Did that slip your mind or was there a good reason you failed to mention it?"

Steph chewed on the side of her tongue for a moment before saying, "Daniels mixes poison for them, but it's nothing they can't do without him. He does more work against the Full Bloods than against us. Killing him would have brought too much heat from the Skinners. More heat than setting their house on fire."

"That heat doesn't matter anymore. Can Daniels lead us to the Skinners or not?"

"If he doesn't know where they are, he'll be able to reach them. Paige and Cole are on his speed dial. But it's not a good idea to just go crashing in there," she warned. "He's got protection. He's still valuable to the Skinners and knows it."

"Paige and Cole aren't a threat," Tara said.

"Can you guarantee that?"

Tara raised an eyebrow, which was enough to put a confident edge into her words when she said, "Just because we came out on top after the uprising doesn't mean we can sit back and relax. The Skinners and every other human have their backs to the wall, which means now is the time to make the moves necessary to put the Nymar where they should always have been."

"Things are good for us right now," Steph said evenly. "Why push it?"

"Because the shapeshifters are ripping through humans like wet newspaper. When they're done, they'll come for us. If we're not ready when that happens, we'll take even heavier damages."

"Daniels is too important to be killed. He was researching the spore, trying to find a way to survive on less blood without getting strung out. It's been a few years. Who knows what else he may have come up with in that time?"

Tara's eyes narrowed and she motioned toward one of her guards. "Tell me where he is. Now."

Steph knocked her fist against the table, which was the signal for Astin to come out from the back room, "I don't take orders from you."

As Astin and another Nymar emerged from the back room with their guns drawn, the guards that Tara brought with her raised their weapons.

"Give me the address to those apartments," Tara said calmly.

"His spore research will be important for all of us. When it's done, it's mine."

"Agreed."

Steph told her where to find Daniels in Schaumberg.

"Thanks," Tara said as she started walking toward the door. Before leaving the bar, she glanced over her shoulder and said, "Just so you know, if you still feel this rebellious when the bigger orders start coming . . . you might want to pick out your favorite wall because I'll do the nailing myself."

Chapter Nineteen

Las Vegas, Nevada
Morning

They weren't kept prisoner within the massive temple, but none of them had the energy to leave. The beds in their suites were contained within crooked, driftwood frames. Huge, overstuffed cushions could barely be called mattresses, but they gave Cole the best night's sleep he'd had in a long time. Even though he and Paige shared a bed, they were too exhausted to take full advantage of it. When they woke up, however, he climbed between her legs and worked up an appetite. There hadn't been many times for them to be alone together without passing out from exhaustion or needing to sleep off some kind of injury. Her body was warm and familiar beneath his scarred palms. She closed her eyes, leaned back and accepted him inside of her without the slightest bit of hesitation.

Over the last several months, Cole had been betrayed and rescued by her. He'd stood by her side and they fought on opposite ends of the country. Sometimes he thought he had a better chance of translating the Dryad glyphs through sheer luck than understanding what was going on inside of her head. And then there were times when he knew she felt the same way about him. The simple fact was that it would be impossible to know why she did every little thing she did. He sure as hell didn't intend on sitting her down and explaining all of his actions to her. Now that their lives depended on it, they had to trust each other implicitly. Times like these, when he was allowed to clasp his hands in hers and pin her to the flowing surface of a luxury bed while pumping into her at whatever pace he desired were one of the many payoffs of that trust.

He returned it by allowing her to roll on top of him, straddle his hips, and do whatever she pleased for as long as they could afford. He knew she wasn't about to hurt him, but she came close a few times. Those few, brief tastes of pain that came from her teeth or nails scraping against his skin were worth every second. After that, he and Paige shared a long hot shower and indulged in some scented soaps that were probably more expensive than all of their clothing combined.

Breakfast was served in a dining room lit only by a wall of solid glass built to either catch the sun's rays or the electric glow of the Strip. Cole felt the former on his face as he piled sausages, eggs, French toast sticks, and a heaping portion of corned beef hash onto a large, light green platter. Before he could ask for Tabasco sauce, he found three flavors on a smaller table along with utensils. The meal was still warm in his belly when he and the others headed back into the main room of the Hub.

Nobody was surprised to find the club only slightly less busy now than when they arrived. Even if the rest of the planet crumbled, there would still be plenty of people drawn to the dancing nymphs. It had been that way for thousands of years, so why should it stop now?

Alyssa and Lexi were on hand to greet them. Both wore short dresses that showed plenty of leg without being too revealing. Even so, the nymphs attracted plenty of attention from the customers as they walked over to greet the disheveled Skinners. "Was everything all right?" Lexi asked.

"It was great," Waggoner beamed. "Maybe I'll stay here for another few weeks."

Just as Cole was about to make a comment about resisting temptation, he felt a cinching pain in his gut that cut all the way down to his spinal cord. Normally, the clenching tendrils inside eased up after a few hours of sleep, but not this time. They tightened, held, and then tightened some more. "I agree," he said in a strained voice. "We should get going."

As before, Tristan made her entrance without a lot of fanfare. She wore a simple dress made of a filmy green material enhanced with a minimum of small jewels sewn into the fabric. Her face was timeless, beautiful and free of makeup. Her posture didn't seem as forced as it had been the other day, and her voice was almost up to its normal clarity when she asked, "Have you changed your mind on your destination?"

Paige reached under her jacket to tighten the straps on her holster without being noticed. It would take more than a few armed customers to create a distraction powerful enough to make a difference inside the Hub, but none of the Skinners were about to take chances. "No. Why do you ask?"

"I've made contact with our temple in Trizs," she replied, pronouncing the last word with a roll of the tongue that every human within earshot could feel at the nape of their neck. "There's already trouble there."

"What kind of trouble?"

"The Amriany must have been discovered as they were on their way to meet you. They've been fighting since late afternoon their time."

Cole looked at his watch. "Is that yesterday or today?"

"It's been about four hours," Tristan told him with a patient smirk. "The Amriany are holding their position, but it's rough. There's another temple several hundred miles from there, but it's even farther from where you need to go once you arrive. I just thought I'd warn you before sending you into a war zone. Or, you could go to the other temple."

"This is the first time in months that we've been out of

a war zone," Paige said. "Might as well stick to the plan. Besides, if we're trying to win some points with the Amriany, abandoning them to fight when they were waiting for us wouldn't do the trick."

"All right, then." With that, Tristan nodded once to Alyssa, who put on a smile that lit her up like a fireworks display.

The young blond nymph's face brightened with a beaming smile as she raised both arms in the air. No further prompting was needed before her name was spoken by a sultry voice through the loudspeakers. Unlike most clubs, this one didn't need an overly boisterous DJ. There was only an announcement of who was next up so the fans of that particular girl could fight for a front row seat before she made it to her spot. Alyssa stepped onto a large circular stage with two poles connected by a set of uneven parallel bars. As she cast off the little jacket she'd been wearing, she was hit by a beam of light reflected in myriad directions by the sequins sewn into her light blue thong and bikini top.

"Damn," Waggoner breathed. "Now I really don't wanna leave."

The lights dimmed for a second, then flared back up to the driving beats of ZZ Top's "Legs." Alyssa strutted perfectly to that bass line before ascending one of the poles to climb along a cross bar. From the first crackle of electric guitar, the beads hanging from the rail behind her began to glow. As the light became more and more powerful, the crowd reacted as if it was just a part of the show.

"All right," the sultry announcer said. "Who wants to join Alyssa for a special VIP party?"

"That's your cue," Tristan said. "When they call the numbers, just act surprised and go on up."

The announcer made a point of aiming the spotlight at Starr as she pranced to the booth holding a large velvet bag that was supposed to be filled with numbers corresponding to tickets that every customer was given as they'd entered the club. The booth door opened and Starr went inside.

Energized from his breakfast and all the activity that led

up to it, Cole approached Tristan without feeling the weight of the gear he carried in the bags strapped over both shoulders and hanging from one hand. "You doing okay?" he asked.

The Dryad turned to face him and him alone, fixing Cole with a set of eyes that singled him out amid an entire city of distractions. "Almost."

"I'm sorry," he said.

"For what?"

"For asking you to sacrifice so much just to help us."

"Many others have sacrificed much more," she told him while reaching out to place a hand tenderly upon his arm. In her silence, Tristan no longer looked like a Dryad who might very well have been alive long enough to tempt sailors to the edges of maps scribbled on stained parchment. She'd never told him her age, but the longer Cole knew her, the more depth he saw in her eyes. It could very well be that hers was a sun that didn't blind a man who gazed at it for too long. Instead, that man was granted a good look at a real celestial wonder.

"When you need to come back, either go to the club where we're sending you or any of the other temples," she said. "I'll leave word with all of them in that region to grant you passage back home."

"Should I drop your name to Chuna?"

"It wouldn't help." And then she leaned forward to place both hands on his face and hold him steady as she kissed him. It was a lingering, gentle kiss placed upon his lower lip, and when it was done, she held him in place to whisper, "You can't let her feed you anymore, Cole. No matter how much it hurts. You can't let her keep those things alive while the Nymar are watching."

"What?"

"Think about it."

As Cole's ears filled with the sound of rushing blood, the air around him sprang to life in a pure white halo. A spotlight swept over him and the rest of the group, idly making its way along that portion of the room. The announcer called out some numbers, named a group that was supposed to be there for some stranger's bachelor party. Whatever names or numbers were given, Cole was sure there were enough to cover everyone in the group. Tristan hadn't screwed up any flight plans yet and he doubted she'd start now.

"Just don't think too hard," she said while gently rubbing his cheek. "The answers will be there when you get a moment to take a breath."

"What do I do until then?" he asked.

She pointed him toward a stage glowing with light coming from spotlights as well as an intensifying green radiance emanating from the beaded curtain hanging from the ceiling. That same color pulsed constantly throughout the club as beautiful women stepped through other curtains hanging throughout the Hub. Some could have been entering the room from backstage, while others could have been coming in from anywhere else in the world. "Try to stay alive long enough to put the Memory Water to use," she told him. "I don't know what you've got in mind or if any plan can work at this point, but I learned a long time ago to never underestimate a Skinner."

Cole had never felt as vulnerable as when he'd been about to step away from the comforting sphere of Tristan's embrace. "What if we just screw things up even worse than they are now?"

"It would be quite a feat to make them any worse."

Suddenly, he wasn't so comforted anymore. "You remind me of the other brunette in my life."

She patted his cheek, perhaps just a bit too hard, as if to pay a second tribute to Paige. "That's the good thing about being on the bottom of the mountain. Nowhere to go but up."

The numbers had all been read, the spotlight had found them, and the crowd was cheering them on. Paige and Waggoner bowed their heads and walked toward the stage while Cole waved and pumped his fists as if he truly had won the jackpot. Just another wild day in Vegas.

Chapter Twenty

Trizs, Hungary

Cole had taken a long jump through a Dryad bridge only once before. Unlike the mildly dizzying couple of steps that characterized most trips, his first international trip felt like plummeting through space with a giant fan at his back to push him along even faster. That was due to the nature of the bridge, which had also put the unhealthy tone into Tristan's skin. This time he felt as if he'd closed his eyes and stepped off the edge of the stage into a pit. There was no sound or any sensation apart from the yawning in his gut that made him certain he was about to hit a brick wall at any second.

After several minutes of that, he staggered through another curtain, accompanied by the uneven bass line of a song he didn't recognize. The others were there as well, holding their heads and opening their mouths wide as if on an airplane and trying to get their eardrums to pop. Whatever music he heard in his head was merely an echo from the Hub, resonating in the thrum of passing through the Dryad bridge. The bass lines were really there, however. All the pounding notes and reverberations weren't in time to any music, but instead came from outside the thin walls of what Cole could now see was a substandard strip club.

"Holy shit!" Waggoner said as he looked outside through the smoked glass of a narrow window.

The other man must have been one of the first ones through, because Paige and Cole were still trying to get their heads to stop rattling. Another thump filled the small building, causing glasses to rattle behind a dirty bar and cheap imitation crystals to knock against each other while dangling from a ceiling made to look like a night sky.

Cole rubbed his temples and looked around. The curtain was set up only a few inches in front of a wall adorned with vaguely familiar Dryad glyphs written in chipped white paint covering a corner of the club. Two raised platforms on that side of the room were barely high enough to be called stages, and the poles leaning precariously in the middle didn't look secure enough to hold a child. Two men wearing heavy coats waved furiously at the Skinners and spoke in voices that were partially lost amid the commotion.

Now that he knew someone was yelling at him, he could make out the haggard voices shouting in a Slavic dialect. He might not have known what the men were saying, but he could read flailing arms well enough to know he was supposed to come down from the stage. As soon as he hopped over the edge of the platform, glass shattered and a piercing shriek filled the room. Cole recognized that shriek well enough to drop the moment his feet touched the floor. Paige had been around gargoyles as well, which meant she was quick to follow his lead and pull Waggoner down seconds before the flapping creatures crashed through the window and circled crazily near the ceiling.

As his wits slowly returned, Cole enjoyed the view of tracked-in dirt, cigarette butts, and loose change littering the club's floor. Warped boards rattled against each other as one of the locals made his way over to the side of the stage. "You speak English?" the man asked.

"Yeah."

"You are Skinners from America?"

Before Cole could answer, he accidentally locked eyes with one of the creatures stuck to the ceiling with a set of hooklike talons. The gargoyle had stretched its flat body so it could survey the club using the narrow black eyes wedged near the front of its body. Those were the sharper of its two sets of eyes, the ones it used in flight. The gargoyle let go of the ceiling to slice through the air like a piece of paper taking a pendulous path toward the floor. "Above you!" he shouted.

The man had the solid build of a farmer, complete with muscles that were too big and bulky to have been sculpted in a gym. He swung himself around while spouting words in his native tongue, which had the sharp tone and rough edges of profanity. Although he had a rifle in his hands, he knew better than to fire a shot at the gargoyle. Instead, he used the stock of the weapon to swat the creature away. Since none of the creature's blood was spilled, the others flapped near the ceiling like oversized bats. Disturbing, but no immediate threat.

"Milosh is outside with the others," the man with the rifle said.

"What's going on here?" Paige asked.

"Same thing as everywhere. The wolves are staking their claim and we are in their way."

Cole's scars had been burning since the moment he stepped through the beads, but now they flared up enough for him to reflexively reach for the spear strapped to his back. The man with the rifle didn't need an early warning system to tell him there was trouble nearby. The rasping snarls coming through the broken window did that job well enough. The two dancers who'd been near the stage, who had the flawless beauty of nymphs, hurried to seek shelter behind the bar as the bartender pulled a shotgun from where he'd stashed it. Both he and the man with the rifle fired at the window, sending a curious Half Breed away.

"That won't hold them for long," the man with the rifle

said. "You must leave now and take those things with you."

"Care to lend us a hand?" Waggoner asked.

The man looked at him and let out a single, scoffing breath. "If you need my help, then you won't be any use to Milosh."

Paige stood up, brushed herself off, and pulled the Beretta from under her jacket. Her other hand wrapped around the wooden weapon holstered in her boot, which she gripped tight enough to cause blood to well up between her fingers. "Where are they?"

"Step outside and look down the road. If you miss them, you are blind." When a burst of automatic gunfire set off a chorus of vicious howls, he added, "And deaf."

"Is there a back door to this place?"

The man pointed in the direction the nymphs had gone and then placed the rifle stock on his shoulder so he could sight along the top of its barrel. While stepping toward the window, he fired three careful shots that were much too high to be aimed at any werewolf. Cole took a quick look in that direction to confirm his suspicion. The shots had been fired at a pair of gargoyles flapping their skinny, bony arms to gain some altitude using the thin layers of skin stretched on their bony frame. Hooked talons scraped at the darkened sky when one of the shots caught one through the middle of its body. The creature didn't make a sound until it dove straight down and the wind passed between the layers of its flesh. A small group of Half Breeds that had been approaching the club dug their claws into the dirt and snarled at the rifleman. Some of the blood from the wounded gargoyle spattered upon their backs, which didn't distracted them at all until the creature glided into their line of sight. One Half Breed attacked the gargoyle, tearing its thin body to shreds. The scent of one gargoyle's blood brought down the others that had been circling overhead.

One by one the gargoyles descended. They spread their bodies out to catch the wind, which slowed their fall while putting them in prime position to wrap around the Half

Breeds. Talons dug into the werewolves' ribs and chests. Howls became muffled as they were enveloped, and Cole knew he wouldn't get a better chance to leave the club. "Will our stuff be safe here?" he asked the bartender.

The man with the shotgun laughed heartily. "Nothing is safe anywhere, my friend."

Cole felt a solid slap on his shoulder as Waggoner stepped up to the bar. "I like this man's outlook. How about one for the road?"

Apparently, the bartender was willing to part with some liquor as long as it meant clearing the Skinners from his place. Either that or it was his way of supporting the troops, because he splashed some vodka into shot glasses so they could toss it back. But before Cole could indulge, he and Waggoner were dragged outside by Paige.

"Maybe we should try another angle," Cole said.

Paige led the charge, with Waggoner reluctantly bringing up the rear. "If you're thinking about sneaking up on anyone," she said, "I doubt that's much of an option."

The road leading to the club was lonely and unpaved. Apart from a few cars that were upended along the side of the road, there were only power lines and a few packs of werewolves rushing in different directions, like sections of shadow ripped away from the night and tossed into a blender. They were far enough away from a town that the stars themselves provided enough light for the Skinners once their eyes became acclimated. "I think I see them!" Cole said.

There was movement farther down the road, which amounted to a confusing mess of shadows lunging at each other. Suddenly, that group was illuminated by the strobe effect of an assault rifle fired at full auto into the faces of an impending werewolf horde.

"Yep," Paige said. "That's them all right." Without another word, she gripped her weapons and ran into the fray.

Fueled by the vodka still warming his system, Waggoner took off as well. He had his curved wooden weapon in hand but wasn't gripping it nearly tight enough to draw blood. The expression on his wide face drifted between eagerness and terror. "Do you know how to use that thing?" Cole asked.

That question was enough of a challenge to tighten Waggoner's fists around the weapon until blood flowed from his hands. "Damn right I do."

"Then prove it." It wasn't the most inspiring speech to send a man into battle, but it was all Cole could afford to give before Paige got too far ahead of him. It was enough to get the other man trotting alongside him.

Turning to his right, he saw the vague outline of a shaggy body behind a pair of eyes that caught the dim glow from above. The thorns of Cole's weapon burrowed into his palms as he willed the spear to stretch to its normal size. Its metallic spearhead glinted in the moonlight, and the forked end reached toward the ground like a serpent's tongue. When the Half Breed bared its teeth and leapt at him, Cole threw himself to the ground and twisted around to hit the dirt on his right side. He dug the forked end of the spear into the earth and propped it up so the metallic end was waiting for the Half Breed. Without a way to defy the laws of gravity, the werewolf landed on the spearhead and its weight forced the sharpened point to emerge from its back.

Lying on the ground like that meant he could feel the approach of the other werewolves. Two of them thundered toward him. The one at the front of the group lowered its head and opened its mouth. Saliva poured from crooked fangs in anticipation of the tender meat it intended on ripping from Cole's neck and face. Before it got close enough to have its meal, however, the Half Breed was knocked off its stride by a narrow projectile that hit its upper body with a solid thump. It rolled onto its side and slid the rest of the way toward Cole, who scooted away and jerked the spear free. A third Half Breed leapt over that one, but Cole was ready for it. He bent at the knees and brought his spear up to catch it in the chest. Although the Half Breed was fast enough to keep from impaling itself, it still received a nasty gash along its left side as the spearhead raked across its rib cage.

"On your right," Waggoner said from behind Cole.

When he tried to step aside to clear a path for the other Skinner, a set of jaws clamped down on his ankle. He felt the fangs press against the thick leather of his boots. Willing the forked end of his spear to pinch shut, he slid that end of the weapon along his trapped leg into the werewolf's mouth and then willed it to open again. The wooden tines weren't strong enough to brace the Half Breed's powerful jaws apart, but the smaller splinters that Cole brought up from the wooden surface made the creature think twice before tearing his foot off. The Half Breed pulled its head back and then drew its weight down onto its haunches in preparation for a lunge. It was held in place by a narrow piece of wood that hissed through the air to drive into the creature's chest.

At first Cole thought the werewolf had somehow been stuck by a piece of flying debris. The object lodged in its chest looked like nothing more than a stick with one end that had several pieces cracked away as if it splintered while being crudely ripped from a branch. That's when he realized the stick was identical to the projectile that caught one of the other Half Breeds a few moments ago. Waggoner stepped up to grab it by the splintered end and clench his fist around it. His other hand was wrapped around the middle of his weapon, which still had the string tied from end to end. Cole could now see the string wasn't just there to keep it in place when strapped across his back.

The Half Breed reared its head back and began clawing at the ground. Waggoner pulled the stick out from where it had landed. It came loose amid a bloody spray caused by a sharpened end that had split apart to form two hooks where a single tip had once been. With a little more effort, Waggoner willed the hooks to curl back together to form an arrowhead. He notched the stick on the string, drew it back, and fired it into the third Half Breed.

"Damn," Cole said as he drilled the metallic spearhead through the first creature's eye before pulling it out to pivot and deal with the second. "I haven't seen that one before."

Waggoner's shot sailed true, and the arrow hit the Half Breed in the eye. Because it was made from specially prepared wood, it went all the way through and was stopped only when the splintered end snagged something within the beast's skull. He then put the Half Breed down by cracking the end of his longbow against its temple so Cole could impale it through the top of its skull. "Still some kinks to work out," Waggoner said, "but it works pretty well." He retrieved his arrow and reached over his shoulder to place it in the leather harness, which was just big enough to hold four more of the arrows flat against his back, where they could go all but unnoticed.

Farther down the road, Paige and some of others were firing their guns at a group of Half Breeds. The pack was being thinned out by a cluster of people who took a stand near a pair of SUVs parked in the grass about 150 yards away from the club. Four of them were illuminated by headlights, but there was enough commotion in the shadows to convince Cole there had to be a fight going on there as well.

He and Waggoner ran to catch up with the others. When he heard the telltale screeches coming from above, Cole shouted, "Down!" and threw himself face first to the dirt. Gargoyles might not have been sturdy, but they were fast, their cry a way to catch their prey's attention, not to warn them. If anyone on the ground stopped to look at where that sound was coming from, they would be too late to do anything to avoid the airborne attack. Unfortunately, Waggoner had forgotten about that.

The gargoyle's body hit him with a wet slap, wrapping his arms and torso within a layer of writhing skin. Talons dug into his chest, piercing his jacket and jabbing into his flesh to give the gargoyle a firm grip. He dropped to his knees and yelped in pain, but his attempt to break loose only caused the talons to rip him open even more.

Cole knew better that to simply cut the gargoyle apart. When it was wrapped around its prey, the creature's sole purpose was to administer a fluid from glands on its tongue and beneath its wings and smear it over its prey using the flat surface of its body. After a few seconds the fluid would begin to harden into a stony crust so the victim could be immobilized, preserved, and eaten slowly over an undetermined period of time. The statues left behind had historically been mistaken as gargoyles, while the real things were free to tuck themselves away in corners of buildings or hide in trees where they were again mistaken as hanging moss or large bats.

"Keep still," Cole grunted as he wrapped his arms around Waggoner and the gargoyle encapsulating him. "Struggling only makes it worse."

"Worse?" Waggoner asked. "How the hell could this get worse? It's stabbing me!"

The gargoyle's black eyes gazed up at Cole without a hint of consciousness. Either they were incapable of expressing anything close to emotion or the creature was focused intently on what its other eyes were seeing. The creature's second face was similar to a crude black chalk drawing on its belly. When Cole saw it the first time, he was reminded of a stingray. He couldn't see it now, but could imagine all too well how its narrow mouth was silently opening and closing to administer the hardening fluid.

As if to confirm those suspicions, Waggoner said, "Holy shit, it *is* worse! I think it's biting me!"

"Stay still!"

Waggoner closed his eyes and clenched every muscle in his body like a robot that had blown a gasket and seized up. Hearing the shrieking overhead from another gargoyle, Cole swung his spear with one hand toward the sound and cut the incoming flier in half. Its fluids spattered in a wider, less concentrated arc, which formed a thin, brittle crust where it landed. The sounds of battle were slackening in the distance, but Cole only paid partial attention. Even an army of Full Bloods was headed his way, he needed to drop his weapon and grab both talons that were digging into Waggoner's upper chest.

"This is gonna sting," he said. Without any more warning

than that, he pulled the curved talons as straight as possible from the holes they'd dug in the other man's flesh. They were long and sharp, but also thin and didn't do any significant damage. He pulled the gargoyle back and cracked its frame in half with a quick twist.

Extending his arms and then reaching back to pull the smaller set of talons from his lower back, Waggoner said, "That did the trick. Nice one."

"Actually I didn't mean to do that, but you're welcome anyway."

The lower set of talons were connected to the closest thing a gargoyle had to feet. The long toenails had barely punctured Waggoner's clothing before digging into him. Once they were pulled away, the entire creature fell off him like a second skin that had been shed.

Before Waggoner could stomp on the gargoyle, Cole said, "Wait! Grab it by the head."

"Grab what?"

"You heard me," Cole snapped in a sharp tone that left no room for misinterpretation. "Grab it by the head, reach into its mouth and pull out its tongue."

Confused disgust flashed across Waggoner's face, but he'd been training with Skinners long enough to have heard stranger requests from his superiors. He looked around for a good excuse to ignore the order, but the fighting had tapered off to a few random yelps as some Half Breeds were put down for good. The rush of retreating footsteps flowed away from the road like a wind rustling through tall weeds. Grudgingly, he grabbed the gargoyle by the head and did as he was told. The tongue and bladder to which it was connected came out after no small amount of work.

"Tie a knot in those tubes and keep that sac safe," Cole said.

"You plan on using some of that stuff to turn something into stone?"

"If we have to. Otherwise, we'll keep it for later."

When he was through, Waggoner offered it to Cole.

"No," Cole told him. "Keep hold of it and make sure it doesn't leak."

"But it stinks like hell."

"Yes it does, but you already got that crap all over you. Holding onto a little more won't make things any worse."

Waggoner looked down at the front of his jacket where portions of the rocky crust still clung to him. The rest had left behind a mess of gray, dusty globs that stuck to him like dried glue. Already he smelled as if he'd been doused in rotten eggs and vinegar before being rolled on the floor of an old movie theater.

"Sucks to be the new guy," Cole told him.

"Cole!" Paige shouted from the spot where the SUVs had been parked. "Stop messing around. You and John get to the club and bring all of our stuff over here."

Cole sighed and looked around for any trace of gargoyles or Half Breeds. There was nothing else in the vicinity, which left him no reason to ignore the orders he'd been given. Turning toward the club, he jabbed a finger at Waggoner and said, "Not a word."

Chapter Twenty-One

"How is it that the nymphs usher you around, but not us?" asked a slim black man wearing a dark gray hooded sweatshirt and frayed jeans. He was behind the wheel of the SUV Cole, Paige, and Waggoner had been piled into, and when he looked at them in the rearview mirror, a sour expression twisted the goatee that covered the lower portion of his face. Sharp features made him look even more severe when he said, "We're supposed to be working together, so I think they should put in a good word for us with those ladies."

"You are Russian," Milosh said from the passenger seat. "So nobody cares what you think." He was a stocky man with a full beard that would have spread like a bandito mask across the bottom of his face if not for the two scars running along his cheeks to part the whiskers like smoke.

The driver shot Milosh a piercing glare, which became friendlier when he shifted his eyes toward the Skinners. "Since he is a Czech pig with no manners, I will introduce myself. I am George."

"And that," Milosh cut in, "is Paige and Cole. The other one, I do not know." Settling back into his seat, he grunted, "Pig, indeed."

"So what happened back there?" Paige asked.

George and Milosh both looked into the closest mirror they could find as it they thought there might be werewolves nipping at the SUV's bumper. "Ever since the Breaking Moon," Milosh explained, "the Vitsaruuv have all been crazy."

"Like they were ever sane," George grunted.

"They are changed now. The ones with the tusks. They showed up in America first, but now they are here. Even the Kushtime are changed."

George glanced back at the Skinners. "He means Mongrels."

Milosh nodded and carried on. "At first we thought the Weshruuv all move over to America."

"And you didn't mind that, huh?" Paige asked. "As long as the Full Bloods are gathered on our turf, you guys just don't care?"

"Maybe you forget that I was *there* during the Breaking Moon!" Milosh roared. "Drina and Gunari were killed when that insane Weshruuv brought our plane down. Tobar is still behind bars in your country! He may be dead for all we know." Milosh shifted in his seat. The left sleeve of his jacket had been cut off and stapled shut because there was no arm inside it. He'd lost it to Minh when they fought in Atoka, but the Amriany seemed less concerned about that than he did about his next question. "Is he dead?"

Paige looked over to Cole, deferring to him since he'd taken it upon himself to keep up on the research. As much as he wanted to say otherwise, Cole replied, "I don't know. The prisons were hit hard when the Half Breeds showed up. There just wasn't enough time to move everyone and—"

"And a foreigner being held captive doesn't matter to your police," Milosh said.

"Lots of men and women were killed when those things started to swarm everywhere," Cole replied tersely. "The Half Breeds were hungry, and prisons were just big buildings full of meat to them. Hospitals got hit just as badly. Lots of lives were lost, just like they're being lost everywhere else. You want to focus on what we're doing here or would you rather spout off some more?"

"You must excuse him," George said. "He makes everything so political. All Czechs are like that."

"You want to know what all Russians are like?" Milosh asked.

And, as further proof that the world was indeed going crazy, Paige took the role of peacemaker. "So you and your men were attacked outside of that club. I take it that wasn't random?"

Drawing a knife from a shoulder holster that had been modified to carry it instead of a gun, Milosh said, "No. Not random. Someone knows our networks. Our codes. Everything they might need to guess where we might be and what we might be doing."

Cole winced and pushed himself as far back into his seat as the cushions would allow before saying, "I hate to ask this, but is there any chance that one of your people is leaking the information? Like . . . maybe someone who was captured and questioned?"

Judging by the wariness in his voice and the lack of a knife shoved in his general direction, Cole suspected that Milosh had considered the possibility as well. "Tobar doesn't know enough to have caused this kind of damage. And even if he did, he wouldn't have lived long enough to have gotten it to the right people."

"Who the hell are the right people?" George snapped. "The Full Bloods? They're not people. They're animals!"

"You've only dealt with one of them," Milosh scolded. "Esteban isn't like the others."

Paige and Cole both sprung to attention. "What do you know about Esteban?" she asked.

"My country's in his territory. Has been for over a century. He's an animal that prefers to walk on all fours and would rather eat five children before bothering to bring down a grown man."

"I don't care which Full Blood it is," Cole said. "They're

not the kind to take prisoners and they sure aren't the kind to question anyone about anything. They don't have to. That sounds more like a Nymar tactic."

Milosh grimaced as if he'd suddenly gotten a taste of sour milk. "Old tactics don't mean shit anymore. All of the animals have started playing by different rules."

"No," Cole said sternly. "They've just upped their game. The Full Bloods have their own thing going and it's on a much bigger scale than sniffing out each specific thorn in their side. They've started engaging the military and winning. If you haven't had that sort of thing over here yet, it's only a matter of time."

"Cole's right," Paige added. "You have to see what's going on back home to get just how little the Full Bloods need subtlety right now."

The Amriany in the front seats shared a few quick but loaded glances before Milosh nodded and began using the tip of his blade to pick something out from beneath a fingernail.

"Maybe it has been happening here," George said while looking at them in the rearview mirror.

"Jesus Christ almighty," Milosh growled. "It *has* been happening. No maybes about it." When he wheeled around, he used his knife as the world's most dangerous pointer. "You Skinners don't give a damn about the rest of us. That's the problem."

"We've been kind of busy!" Paige said.

"You're goddamn right you have. Unleashing God knows what!"

"Since when did you become so religious?" Cole asked.

The question was so simple and spoken so calmly that it threw the volatile hunter for a loop. Having reset his temperament, Milosh placed his knife flat on his knee so he could steady himself using the back of George's seat as the SUV rattled over a stretch of rough road. "I know what happened during the Breaking Moon. I'm not talking about that. By then it was too late to do much more than contain the storm. I'm talking about all the years before when you Skinners insisted on doing things your own way by tearing apart the monsters and making them a part of you. Then you made them a part of your cities! Then your whole damn country!"

"What in the hell is he talking about?" Cole asked.

"He's talking about the reason Skinners and Amriany have been working separately for so long," George said. When all he got was silence from the backseat, he asked, "Don't you know your own history?"

"Spare me the old-school feuding bullshit," Paige grunted with a wave of her hand. "This isn't the time for it."

"No," Milosh told her. "Now is definitely the time because those differences from the past still hold up today. If you bothered reading anything from your own Jonah Lancroft or anyone else's journals from centuries past, you'd know that we warned you something like this would happen."

"I read a lot of Lancroft's journals," Cole said. "And he didn't mention specifics about any feud between Skinners and Amriany."

Milosh grumbled something in his own language as he flopped back around to sit in his seat without contorting to look at the people behind him. Finally, he said, "The Amriany have been warning since the first settlers went to hunt Full Bloods in the New World that using vampire blood and werewolf skin was a mistake. It's unnatural and it's disgraceful."

"He's right," George said as he nodded. "Taking the blood of a monster, wearing their flesh, adorning yourselves with their teeth and claws, is savage."

"Disgraceful?" Paige sneered. "People are dying, those things are running around *eating* them, and you're calling *us* savages?"

"See, my friend?" Milosh said to the driver. "Skinners didn't listen to us then and they don't listen now."

Paige grabbed the back of both front seats and pulled herself forward as if she intended to crawl all the way up to the windshield. "I know some of our history. For example, you guys wouldn't part with your precious secrets, so we had to make do on our own. And if you're worried about us being disgraceful savages, maybe you should talk to some of the people who died because you were too busy sitting over here hoarding weapons that could have saved them!"

"You want more Blood Blades?" Milosh asked. "Then why don't you tell us how you bond your weapons to your hands?"

"Why bother?" Paige snapped. "You'll just stick whatever we give you into a storehouse somewhere and use it when you decide someone is *worth* saving."

"It is not nature's way for everything to live!"

Cole leaned back in his seat. "I'm beginning to get an idea of why we haven't formed a monster hunting supergroup in all these years."

Milosh went back to picking at his nails with the knife, and Paige slumped back into her cushions with an exasperated sigh.

They drove for another hour, only slowing down to traverse an exceptionally bumpy road or skirt an area that seemed quieter than anything Cole had ever experienced. When he looked out the windows on Paige's side, he could see a few lights shining down from posts or inside small buildings. There were open fields of tall, frosted grass and the rare movement of other automobiles. The view on his side was another story entirely.

That side of the road had a rugged shoulder and a short stretch of field leading directly into an ominous forest pulled directly from every Grimm's fairy tale he had ever been told. Trees stripped all but bare by the harsh winter reached up to a clear sky as if to rake bony fingers across a gleaming black slate. Although Cole couldn't make out a lot of details due to the speed of the SUV and the dense shadows, he saw no hint of the forest opening up past the first layer of trees. The more he looked at it, the more he felt it was looking back.

He, Waggoner, and Paige shared some coffee that was strong enough to melt through cast iron. It was kept hot in a thermos that, like the SUVs in their caravan and the Amriany driving them, was dented, battered, and hardened. Nobody felt much like talking, so Cole used his phone to check on some Internet news sites to see how things were back home. No big surprise there. Things were bad.

He was jostled from his own little world when the SUV's tires rattled over a bridge and across a cobblestone street. They'd entered a small town that was a distinctly European mix of old and new. Small cottages and pubs lined the narrow streets alongside a few gas stations and convenience stores that would have been at home on any modern street corner. For some reason he couldn't quite pinpoint, Cole felt a distinct calmness here. The signs weren't quite as bright. The windows weren't filled with as many advertisements. The few people who were out and about kept to themselves while projecting a friendly aura.

Before much longer the SUVs pulled to a stop outside a narrow two-story brick building with shuttered windows and a steeply angled roof. The Amriany piled out of their vehicles and didn't make the first effort to conceal the weapons they carried inside. They also didn't make an effort to help the Skinners carry their belongings into the building.

Unlike most of the Skinner safe houses Cole had seen, this one wasn't a hollowed-out structure refurbished to meet their needs. It looked and felt like a home, complete with old, comfortable furniture, quiet conversation, and the smell of freshly baked bread. In that regard, it was more like his grandma's home.

The woman who'd ridden in one of the other vehicles walked down a short hall to confer with the squat man cradling an automatic shotgun who was watching the back door. After she said something to him and patted his shoulder, he lowered the shotgun. She was thin and looked to be somewhere in her late fifties. Her long brown hair was loosely braided and held in place by a small, oval piece of leather with what looked like a wooden knitting needle stuck straight through it as well as the hair beneath it. The vaguely fashionable 'do, combined with the dark green sweater and combat harness underneath a leather coat that stopped just short of her knees, was a strange combination of earthy and military sensibilities. When she removed her coat and hung it on one of the hooks near the door, he saw that the harness held more than the pair of Glocks holstered under her arms. There was a sword too, strapped to her back and almost as long as her torso. The handle was straight and bound in leather straps, the blade was slightly angled as it moved away from the guard, but then took a sharp curve back, down, and around to form a single barb at the end of a large hook. In the short glimpse he had before she turned around again, Cole could see that the blade was dark brown and might have been copper. Also, there were symbols etched into the metal that had more than a passing resemblance to those found on a Blood Blade.

"So," she said in a polite, conversational tone, "did Milosh tell you what happened while we were waiting for you to arrive?"

Cole stepped up and spoke before Paige had a chance to voice her opinion of their guide. "We didn't get around to that."

Her eyes narrowed as she fixed them on Milosh. He winced and veered off to go into another room. When she looked back to Cole, her expression was cordial if not overly friendly. "Some of the Half Breeds were circling that village when we got there. They showed up on infrared cameras but weren't making a move toward any of the buildings on the outskirts. They perked up once we showed up and came running. It leads us to believe they were being guided somehow."

"Guided?"

She nodded. "We brought some bodies back with us. Figured you'd want to be there when we examine them."

"Right, but first things first." Stepping forward, Paige extended a hand, smiled, and introduced herself.

The woman was hesitant before letting out a tired breath. "I'm so sorry about that," she said in a voice tinted by an accent Cole couldn't quite place. "I'm Sophie, and this," she added while sweeping a hand to another of the Amriany who was just as disheveled as the others who were in the fight outside the club, "is Emil."

Emil was short and wiry, with a scraggly clump of black hair sprouting at odd angles beneath a cap that came down just enough to protect the upper portions of his ears. He still had his weapons strapped over his shoulders, only they were more within Cole's area of expertise. The Benelli M-4 was a twelve-gauge semiautomatic shotgun, and the MP-5 was a submachine gun crafted by Heckler & Koch used by many branches of the military around the world. Considering what he'd heard about the Amriany methods for crafting metals, he could only guess what they could do with hardware like that. Smirking as if he could read the envy in Cole's eyes, Emil eased the guns onto a table and shook his hand. "I get to be the pack mule tonight," he said.

"Been there," Cole told him. "How'd those things do against the Half Breeds?"

"You stay around here for much longer and you'll see for yourself."

There was some more firepower strapped onto Emil, but Cole didn't get a chance to see it before it was all wrapped up and carried away.

"Are you hungry?" Sophie asked. "There's still some dinner left. We also can make some tea."

Paige spoke for all of the Skinners when she said, "We ate a late breakfast. Was that just an hour or two ago? I don't even know."

"Must be nice being favored by the Dryad. That's something my people wouldn't know too much about."

"Don't get defensive. It's something new for us too. Before that we were driving ourselves around in beater cars and sneaking onto airplanes to travel with livestock and shipments of auto parts."

Somehow, Waggoner had found his way back to the kitchen and back again. "Yeah," he grunted through a mouthful of what looked like bread. "I've heard you guys are the ones with the private jets. How'd you manage that?"

"Old money," Sophie replied. "Come with me. Let's talk in more comforting surroundings."

Her choice of words was more than accurate. Although the chairs weren't big on padding and the floors creaked beneath their feet, the fireplace crackling in the corner of a large room filled with bookshelves and wooden racks of rifles and shotguns was very comforting indeed.

Paige grinned and approached the fire with her hands outstretched. "Did you say something about tea?"

For a moment, Sophie watched Paige make herself comfortable. After taking deeper stock of the Skinners, she signaled for one of the younger Amriany. "Bring us all some tea."

"All right," Cole said. "Real warm in here. Nice place. Real civilized. But we didn't come all this way for tea."

"So I've heard. I will start by telling you there should have been no reason for those Vitsaruuv to come to that village, and even less reason for them to pace in one spot until we got there. Someone knew we would be there and wanted those things to hit us when we arrived." There were five Amriany in the room other than Sophie, and they all had their weapons within easy reach. "Before we go any further, you'll tell us who could have known we would be there."

"This is your country," Paige said. "We heard all about it on the ride over. We also heard about why you guys want to keep us so far away from you, so how are we supposed to know about local problems?"

Sophie held up both hands to concede the point. "There's also the matter of the Jekhibar. It was stolen from us, so I trust you're here to return it."

"We didn't steal it," Cole pointed out.

One of the other Amriany said something in their own language. Cole couldn't translate it, but he could read the disgust in that one's face well enough to get the gist of it.

"We've got more than enough going on back home to keep us busy," he said. "Stealing from you isn't a priority. At least, it hasn't been ever since I've been around."

"And were you around when the Blood Blades were brought to your country?"

Suddenly, Cole regretted opening his big mouth. Judging by the looks on Paige's face, he wasn't the only one thinking along those lines.

"That's what I thought," Sophie said.

"We've got the Jekhibar," Paige told her. "That's part of why we came. We think we can use the power stored in it to knock the Full Bloods down a few pegs. And not just Esteban, but all the Full Bloods. Even the ones in your neck of the woods."

Milosh staggered into the room carrying a bottle in one hand and a hunk of bread in the other. "If you think you can loot us for more, then you're mistaken!"

"Enough!" George said. It was the first thing he'd said since leaving the SUV, and his words appeared to carry plenty of weight among the others. "We've already let them know how much we don't appreciate what Skinners do or have done. They've heard it. But they haven't come all this way just to try and steal from us. They need to speak to a Chokesari."

Either Milosh wasn't drinking alcohol or he sobered up very quickly when he heard that. "Why does he need to talk to a metalsmith?"

"Because they're the ones who make the Blood Blades and they're the ones who work with the Jekhibar," Sophie replied.

Paige nodded. "Then that's who we need to see. When can you set it up?"

The Amriany began speaking among themselves in harsh voices that Cole still couldn't understand. Sophie calmed them down by striding over to the fireplace and placing her hands on a long sword that looked too pristine to be anything but ceremonial. One hand rested upon a blade adorned with meticulously carved symbols, and the other brushed against a handle fashioned from superbly polished wood. Although the Amriany didn't fall completely silent, they settled down so she could be heard without having to shout.

"This," she said reverently, "is how things used to be. When our two peoples were one. Before the maiden voyage to the New World. Before your founders communed with the native tribes in what is now called America. Before the discontent within our ranks became a chasm that would split Amriany from those who would become Skinners, we used to work together to create what was needed to keep the shadows at bay."

Cole couldn't take his eyes off the sword on the mantel. There were no thorns in the handle, but the craftsmanship and coloration of the varnish were all too familiar to anyone who wielded a Skinner weapon. Both elements, wood and metal, entwined beautifully to create a weapon unlike anything he'd seen. And considering all he'd seen over the past year or two, that was saying a lot.

"Since we have split," Sophie continued, taking her hand away from the sword, "both of our peoples have guarded our secrets carefully. There have been infractions on both sides making this not only reasonable, but necessary." Before anyone could refute that, she squared her shoulders to the room in an unspoken challenge to anyone who might interrupt her. None came. "Because of this, it is no simple matter to just bring a Skinner to see one of our Chokesari. They have been forging our steel for generations and were rare even when the Amriany were not. Without them, there can be no Blood Blades, and if even one metalsmith is lost, their entire craft will be threatened."

Any Skinner understood as much without needing further explanation. Everything from their fighting methods and recipes for mixing the varnish, which allowed their weapons to bond with its bearer or change shape to their will, was passed along through one Skinner teaching another. The few written records of exactly how to brew Nymar antidote, mix weapon varnish, or carve a weapon itself were sparse and closely guarded. It was a subtle system that made it crucial for Skinners to guard their partners almost as staunchly as they guarded themselves.

"Do you honestly think we came all this way to kill one of your blade forgers?" Paige asked.

Sophie's eyebrows rose as she coolly regarded her and Cole. "Maybe it's not something you'd do consciously. But we've heard about a group that may fracture your structure just as the Skinners fractured ours all those years ago."

Straightening into a more defensive posture, Waggoner drew a deep breath to fuel what would surely be a whole lot of unfriendly words.

"Hold it," Cole said preemptively. "The Vigilant have set themselves up in strongholds around the country. Our country," he added when he reminded himself of where he was. "They've even made a move against the military by breaking me and others out of prison. That's been on the news! It's got to be plastered all over official records in police and government agencies all over the place, so it's not like it's too hard for someone to piece together enough to know that the Skinners are having some internal conflicts at the moment."

"Internal conflicts," Milosh grunted. "I love the American sweet talk."

"How's this for sweet talk?" Waggoner snarled. "Up. Yer. Ass."

Even though that wasn't as bad as Cole had anticipated, he jumped in before it could be spiced up anymore. "The point is, it's understandable why these guys might not be so anxious to escort us straight into their hidden base or whatever."

"Yes," Paige said. "But we're the ones at a disadvantage here. We're on your turf while ours is burning, and the longer we're away, the more it'll burn." Pointing to Milosh, she said, "I was with him in Atoka. Nadya and I were the ones to risk our asses running through a field of Full Bloods to keep him from turning into a Half Breed. If he can't vouch for me after all of that, I don't know what else you want from us."

When Sophie looked over to him, it didn't take long for Milosh to nod his approval. "My issue isn't with you," she said, "or Cole. It's with the company you keep. We know you work with Nymar, and we can't afford to have the American vampires infecting any more of ours with the Shadow Spore. For all we know, they could be watching you. Or," she added while focusing on Waggoner, "using you as spies."

"Having a bit of an uprising here, huh?" Cole chided. Although he'd thrown the comment out offhandedly, he could tell by the looks on the Amriany faces around him that he'd struck one hell of a nerve.

Sophie's next words came very deliberately and weighed heavily as she spoke them. "The European Nymar have been taking lessons from the Americans. Already, several police officials as well as military personnel have been killed in a way that would implicate Amriany involvement."

Paige chuckled. "Now there's some classic sweet talk. So your Nymar are stepping out of line. That just means now is the time to act before things get as bad here as they are back home."

"The Full Bloods were always going to return," George said. "That's never been a question. Esteban is only the first."

"Which is why we all need to figure out a way to keep it from getting worse," Paige insisted. "The Nymar can be dealt with just as long as there are people willing to take them on. Unless things change where the Full Bloods are concerned, we could be looking at extinction. Not just Skinners. Humans."

Sophie placed a hand on the mantel, less than an inch away from the sword. After looking around to the other Amriany, she spoke a few words in their language, got a few words back from each one, then shifted her attention back to the Skinners. "You'll have your meeting with the Chokesari."

Cole let out a tired breath. It might have been a small victory, but it felt good to have one at all.

Chapter Twenty-Two

The Amriany proved to be gracious hosts, offering their guests a place to sleep and food to eat. Due to the instant time change they'd experienced in their unusual travel method, the Skinners were barely able to fall asleep long enough for it to be considered a nap. The rest of the time was spent varnishing weapons, cleaning guns, and limbering up with the normal exercise routines. Paige mixed up some more healing serum and prepared a batch of the tattooing ink she'd invented. Even though Cole had given the stuff its first successful field test when fighting Lancroft, she was still unable to use it. Daniels couldn't be sure if the good ink would interact with whatever remained of the bad ink that still might be trapped in her wounded arm, and she wasn't about to risk it by being as impatient as he'd been when her arm was wounded in the first place.

Cole had just finished taking inventory on what Daniels sent along with him when he found Paige standing outside going through a series of steps with her weapons, intended to strengthen her arm. He stood behind her and to one side, taking in the sight of her lithe body going through its well-practiced motions against a backdrop of a red and orange sky. Being so far away from a big city, his breaths were like a spray of cold water cleaning the grit from lungs infected by too many years of urban living. "Tristan told me something interesting before we left," he said.

Paige's weapons were in their blunted form, but she swung them as if they'd sprouted the deadly blades that had cut short so many werewolves' lives. "Let me guess. Pole climbing tips? Be sure to let me know when you're gonna attempt that."

"Not exactly. She told me not to let you feed me anymore. What's that mean?"

Her next swing snapped to a sharp conclusion with the right-handed weapon pointing directly in front of her. "I'm not the one who said it, Cole."

"But you know what it means."

She resumed her exercises, launching into a series of circular swings that turned both weapons into a blur as they struck and parried an invisible opponent.

"Let me see your arm."

It wasn't an unfamiliar request, and Paige had long ago given up discouraging him from checking on her from time to time. Allowing her one-sided sparring match to point her in his direction, she extended her right arm and said, "It's been doing a lot better ever since I've been able to get my weapon to make the right shape again. Maybe it's got something to do with the Breaking Moon. Didn't you say that Skinners draw from the Torva'ox too?"

Cole wasn't interested in what she was saying and he didn't bother looking at the arm she'd offered. "Not that arm."

"There's nothing wrong with the other one," she said with a grin that dissolved as she took her arm back. Standing in a way that kept her left side away from him, she asked, "What's this about?"

"I thought I'd just gotten used to the pain," Cole said. "Thought I'd toughened up enough to keep it from bothering me."

"You have toughened up," she mused. "Don't think I haven't noticed, big boy." He grabbed her wrist then. Though she pulled against his grip, it took her two tries to break lose. That meant he had indeed been toughening up. "Let go of me," she snapped.

He felt the tendrils inside him constrict, which sent a jolt of adrenaline through his system, allowing him to snag her again. Knowing he wasn't going to get much of a chance to examine her, he took advantage of this opportunity by twisting her arm so her wrist was exposed. There was nothing to mar her skin apart from a few little scars that had been there since a childhood run-in with a broken window.

"Happy?" she asked while pulling away and turning her back to him.

"You healed," he told her. "And since you fought me so much just now, it means you were thinking there was a chance that I might have found something." Walking around so he could see her face again, Cole asked, "What might I have found, Paige?"

She let out a strained breath. "There wasn't much of a choice. It was either help you or let you feed the normal way."

"What do I need help with? You know how much I like to eat."

"That's not what I'm talking about! I mean the shit inside of you that Hope's Shadow Spore flunkie left behind."

"Yeah," Cole said. "I just needed to hear you say it. So," he sighed, "you've been feeding me blood when I wasn't looking?"

"When you're asleep."

"Please tell me it was your blood."

"Yes," she replied while looking down at her left wrist. "And usually from this arm. How'd you guess?"

"Because I know how you feel about the right. Even though it's healing, you still look like you want to saw it off sometimes. I'd like to think you'd give me the good stuff instead of blood you might think is tainted somehow."

"If the blood in my arm is tainted, it's all tainted. It was a stupid idea to begin with."

The sun crested the horizon and spread its rays out as if to embrace the landscape below. A cold wind sliced across Cole's face, bringing with it the taste of fresh dew along with a harsh seasonal chill. "And what was your idea, exactly? Keep those things alive inside of me while I thought I was getting better?"

"I was keeping *you* alive, Cole. And in case you haven't noticed, you weren't getting any better." Bringing up one of her weapons, she tightened her grip until the sickle blade formed into an implement she might use to take on a Full Blood. When she looked over at the weapon, it seemed as if the blade's appearance was more of a surprise to her than it was to Cole. She snapped her arm down to send the weapon into the ground. A second later the other weapon was driven into the dirt directly beside it. "That wasn't supposed to happen to you."

"Was it supposed to happen to you?"

Ignoring that, she put her hands on her hips and stared at the sky as if waiting for the sun to challenge her. "We tried taking it out of you. Then I tried handing you over to someone who was supposed to help. That almost got you killed."

"You didn't know I would be taken away from that first prison," Cole reminded her. "Believe me, when we narrow down exactly who in the Vigilant was responsible for that, you'll have to wait your turn to kick their ass."

"I still don't even know if Rico had anything to do with it."

"He didn't."

She looked at him with critical eyes. "Are you sure about that?"

"There's no good reason to think he joined up with the Vigilant until after I broke out of that place in Colorado. He probably just decided they were the way to go after everything went to hell."

"Went to hell which time?" she asked with a tired laugh.

For once, Cole didn't reflect the slightest bit of humor after seeing her smile. "The most recent time," he said. "If he wanted to hurt me, he would've just taken a swing at me in Louisville . . . or worse."

"Definitely worse," she said with a nod, "but it would have been face-to-face."

"So why did you do it, Paige?"

Either she was convinced there was no getting around it anymore or was too tired to try. "It wasn't much. Just a little of my blood to keep the pain away whenever you were sleeping. After all I've done to you, all the pain I caused and shit I've put you through, I figured I owed you at least a little bit of comfort."

"What if I was trying to starve them out? Did you ever think of that? What if I was trying to get a handle on it?" With each question, Cole moved closer. His hands balled into fists out of sheer frustration with her, the conversation and everything else connected to the subject of the broken tendrils wrapped around his innards. "What if I was dealing with it myself?"

"Dealing how? By feeding only when you absolutely had to? Look me in the eyes and tell me you've never fed on anyone."

Images flashed through Cole's mind. He saw faces an inch away, staring at him in horror as he revealed himself to be the monster that every Skinner swore to destroy. It started with Hope back in Colorado, continued with an inmate when he was incarcerated, and included a few others who'd been cornered or knocked out at a time when he was simply too weak to resist and the tendrils cinched in like piano wire cutting into his intestinal tract. Maybe they'd even crept in to squeeze the arteries connected to his heart where the spore had been, but they somehow knew just how much pressure to apply without killing him. He'd had plenty of time to think of such things when he was alone or just about to drift off to sleep. That brought him back to the present and to the one person who was supposed to be the single constant in his life. "You've brought me more than just a little comfort just by being with me," he told her.

"And you've fed," she whispered, as if the words themselves were forbidden. "You'll keep feeding until we can find a way to fix you up."

"You can live with your wound. Why won't you let me live with mine?"

"Why won't you let me help you?"

Suddenly, Cole's voice took a fierce tone: "Because I didn't ask for it. Why were you ready to kill me when we all thought there was no way to get the spore out of me? Because you didn't want me to become one of those bloodsuckers? What the hell does it make me, with you feeding me whether I know about it or not?"

"It's different, Cole. Right now . . . there's just no more to be done. I even asked Tristan if she could donate more blood to draw the rest of those things out, but she said it wouldn't do any good. I threatened her to get me some nymph blood, but she held her ground. She said she wouldn't hand over a piece of herself or her sisters on such a dangerous whim. Her words. The crappy part is that I think she's right. Those tendrils don't have a brain attached to them anymore. You seemed hell-bent on letting them rip you apart inside until you snapped and fed again, but I couldn't stand for either one of those things to happen so I told her I'd take care of you myself." She pressed her fingers to her temples and rubbed while muttering, "I never should have said anything about it to anyone."

"When was that?"

"I don't know, Cole. A while ago. And take that angry look off your face. She didn't like keeping a secret from you, but trusted me to know what I was doing."

"She specifically told me to stop letting you feed me," he reminded her. "Why do you think that is?"

Paige sighed and reached down to pick up her weapons. There were signs of life coming from the Amriany house as well as the rest of the little homes scattered nearby. Once the weapons were shrunk back down to their smallest size, she placed them into the holsters on her boots. "She's probably worried about them growing."

"*Growing?*" Suddenly, Cole felt the need to sit down. Since there wasn't anyplace for him to do so, he squatted so he could put his elbows on his bent knees. "Growing into what? A full Nymar?"

"I doubt it but I'm not sure. The plan was to get those things out of you before that happened. Be honest with me. Was it such a bad idea for me to do what I did? I mean, you don't appear to be hurting nearly as much, and you barely even seem to think about the tendrils anymore. Maybe just a little bit of blood from a willing donor is all you need. I'm more than willing."

"That's not the point! The point is that you did it without telling me!"

"Would you have accepted it if I'd offered?" she asked. After a few seconds of silence between them, Paige said, "Didn't think so. Part of that may be my fault. You know what I went through before I was a Skinner, and you would have never asked me to do something like this. And after the uprising, anything to do with Nymar kinda leaves a bad taste in our mouths."

"I don't want to become one of those things, Paige," he whispered. "Sometimes I can still feel that spore rooting around inside of me. It's . . ."

"Yeah. I know. It's another reason I took the choice away from you. I've been asking anyone I know if there's a way to fix someone in your condition, but I can't ask around too much. Between the IRD and those Vigilant creeps, there are a whole lot of heavily armed paranoid people who don't need much of an excuse to kill a vampire in their ranks."

"Oh Christ. Do you think Rico mentioned it to Jessup or any of those others in Louisville?"

"No," she said with absolute certainty. "If he had, you wouldn't have been allowed to leave that place without a fight. And since we got out more or less like any other Skinner, I'm thinking Rico hasn't crossed over into paranoid asshole territory. Well, no farther than when he threw a college kid through a window for having a tattoo and fake fangs one

Halloween a few years ago. That also gives me a lot of hope that he hasn't fully signed on with the Vigilant in general."

Cole laughed at the vivid image he'd been given.

"I don't know a way to cure you," she continued, "and handing you over to outsiders didn't work out so good. Daniels has been working on it ever since I almost staked you in his apartment, and if you knew of any way to get rid of those things, I'm sure you would have told me. You've told me of a few times when you were hurting and that time in prison when you fed, which means there must be other times in both categories that you didn't tell me about. Am I right?"

Once again Cole didn't have a good answer for her. "So what would have happened if I never found out what you were doing? You just spring it on me when those tendrils get big enough to turn me into a proper Nymar?"

"That wouldn't have happened. Without a spore, the most they could do would be to get bigger or strangle you from the inside."

"Oh, that's a relief," Cole growled.

"We'll find a way out of this. I promise."

"And what if we don't?"

"Then you can nibble on me in your sleep. Or," Paige added with a smirk, "you could try it when you're awake."

For once Cole didn't even begin to rise up to that occasion. As much as he loved it when she smiled that way, there was something else that made it impossible for him to enjoy the moment or the offer attached to it. "Let's just not let it come to that, okay?"

"It'll get worse if you don't feed," she said. "It may not get as bad as if you had an actual spore inside you, but it'll get worse. Daniels studied the tendrils on his own way before this happened, and he says they reflexively tighten when they go without blood from a source other than their host for too long."

"You don't have to tell me that. You just have to trust that I'm strong enough to manage on my own."

She looked into his eyes in a way that made Cole feel as if

she was staring all the way down to the thoughts he'd tried to cover. Placing a hand on his stomach and holding it there, she said, "It's not a question of strength. It'll hurt. A lot."

When he took hold of her wrist, he intended on moving her hand away, but changed his mind. Her skin felt too good against his fingers, and they'd both learned to take their comfort whenever they could get it.

Chapter Twenty-Three

When they'd piled into the SUVs again, Cole thought the Amriany were taking him, Paige, and Waggoner back to the club where they were ushered into the country. But the small caravan turned eastward and headed into a small town called Imola. Although the rural setting was much different than what he was used to, the occasional glimpses of Half Breeds running to the right of the vehicles reminded him very much of home. To the left, however, there was once again nothing but trees.

"What's over there?" he asked while tapping the window.

Sophie was behind the wheel, and she only had to look at where Cole was pointing before replying, "We avoid that place."

"Is it a forest?"

Her interest sufficiently piqued, Paige leaned across him to get a look out Cole's window. "Doesn't look like enough trees to be a forest. Pretty, though."

Milosh sat in the passenger seat and chuckled. "Yes. Real pretty. Perhaps you will find out for yourself."

He was silenced by a few terse words from Sophie.

The landscape that had caught Cole's attention consisted of rolling hills covered in grass and thin layers of snow.

Large clusters of barren trees were spaced unevenly to make the terrain look densely packed in some spots and wide-open in others. There were roads that led between the trees, and every now and then he caught sight of buildings that looked to be no bigger than two or maybe three stories tall. It was a tranquil scene, especially because he had yet to see any Half Breeds roaming on that side of the road. Having spotted packs or the occasional stray roaming the countryside, he had a good idea about the extent of the Amriany shapeshifter problem. Yet, this other side of the road presented a different picture. Not only did it look clearer, but his scars burned less as they drove closer to those trees. Neither of the Amriany seemed ready to talk, so he let it drop for the time being. Paige did too, and they enjoyed the rest of their trip across the cold Hungarian terrain.

On the outskirts of Imola, Sophie pulled to a stop in front of a cottage near what could have been a small farm. Once the motors of both vehicles had been cut, the air became deathly still. No sounds came from the cottage. No voices greeted the Amriany or their guests. No hinges creaked to announce the opening of a single door or window. Milosh led the Skinners to a shed only slightly smaller than the main cottage. The Amriany in the other SUV approached from another direction.

The instant Sophie got close enough to reach out for the cottage's door, Cole felt his scars flare up. "Get back!" he shouted.

But even though Sophie moved away from the door, she wasn't quick enough to keep from getting hit by it as a Half Breed exploded out of the cottage amid a shower of splinters and broken wood. She, Milosh, and George all drew their weapons, and Cole, Paige, and Waggoner already had their weapons in hand. There were more Half Breeds inside. Cole's scars didn't burn until they were almost on top of him.

Normally, three Half Breeds would have been enough to give a few Skinners a run for their money. But this wasn't a normal situation. These werewolves were thinner and shorter than the normal breed. Also, they were overzealous and charged out through the doorway to knock aside the one that had smashed through it.

Cole hopped to one side and didn't bother expanding his spear to its full length before driving it into the side of a passing creature. The Half Breed's momentum carried it forward, opening a gash in its side as the spearhead raked along its ribs. Paige put a few rounds into it from her Beretta as soon as he had a clear shot, and after that, it was the Amriany's turn. Milosh threw one of his knives into a werewolf's eye while it was in mid-jump. As soon as it hit the dirt in front of him, he grabbed the handle protruding from the Half Breed's face and started twisting.

Then two more Half Breeds emerged and went through a similar gauntlet. Paige caught the first by dropping the curved sickle blade down behind its head with a blow almost precise enough to put it down then and there. Its front paws crumbled beneath it, dropping it out of Waggoner's range before he could swing the sharpened end of his longbow. It regained its balance as soon as Paige's weapon was pulled loose, and by the time it climbed to its feet, George was there to meet it. His weapon was a collapsible steel pole almost as tall as he was. One end had a flat weight to counter the weight of the iron claw at the other end. Forged into something that wasn't quite animal or human, the claw was capped with points at the end of each finger that ripped through the Half Breed's flesh before the weighted end was spun back around to knock against the side of the creature's head. George planted his feet and went to work with the claw as another Half Breed sprang through the doorway.

Cole jabbed at it with his spear but only managed to land a glancing blow.

One of Paige's sickles would have finished it if the creature hadn't dropped its head beneath it and kept running.

Waggoner loosed a hastily notched arrow that parted the

fur on the werewolf's back but wasn't enough to prevent it from charging at Sophie.

She stood calmly with her bronze sword drawn. The Half Breed's eyes were focused intently on her as Amriany bullets thumped into its gnarled body, using pain from the glancing wounds to drive it forward. With the last bit of strength it had, the Half Breed lunged. Long fangs dripped with saliva as they were bared and a hungry growl erupted from its throat. Sophie stepped back with one foot, scraped the curved end of her sword blade along the ground and then swept the weapon up to catch the werewolf in the chest. The strength in her arm as well as the momentum of the heavier end of the sword knocked the werewolf up off its front paws to land heavily onto its back. She finished it off with a downward swing and plunged the blade into the creature's heart.

She issued orders in her own language to George, who moved in to clear the place out. When she saw Paige and Cole start to enter the cottage, Sophie barked, "Stay put! This isn't Skinner business."

"Soon as we came over here, this became our business," Paige said as she shouldered past the remains of the door that hung from the top hinge.

George held the steel staff so it ran along the back of his arm, the clawed end resting behind his shoulder. He moved into the cottage, leaving Waggoner outside with the other two Amriany.

Inside, the cottage was just as messed up as anyone might expect after Half Breeds had torn through the place. Cole and Paige held their weapons at the ready as their eyes darted to every corner and behind every piece of overturned furniture. There was one room with two small doors on the opposite wall leading to what looked to be a small bedroom and a bathroom. When the Skinners tried to take another step, they were stopped by a length of rounded steel placed in front of them.

"Hold on," George said while holding his weapon out to block their way.

Although she remained where she was, the look on Paige's face made it clear that it was on a temporary basis. "We're on the same team here. Always have been, whatever screwed up history we—"

"Shush."

"Did you just shush me?"

"Oh boy," Cole moaned.

To make matters worse, George pointed a finger at her as if threatening a child with a time-out. Then, before she exploded, he raised that finger toward the ceiling. Both of the Skinners looked up to find one shadow squirming among the others within an exposed section of roof just above a series of old rafters. Cole could barely make out a human shape, but had been familiar enough with the Nymar infected by the Shadow Spore to recognize one when he saw it.

The vampire hissed from the shadows. It might have known it had been spotted, but there weren't a lot of choices for a quick escape. Dropping to the floor would put it into dangerous territory, and the little window built into the apex of the roof's peak was too far away for it to be a convenient escape route. Light cast by lamps in the cottage glinted off its fangs as it began to shimmy backward along the roof like a giant, coal-black spider.

"I'll pull it down and you sweep it up," George whispered. "One . . . two . . ."

"Three," Paige said as she raised her Beretta and fired at the ceiling.

The rounds hit the Nymar in one arm, forcing it to let go and dangle upside down from where it had sunk its claws. George was quick to swing the weighted end of his weapon, connecting with a solid blow that dropped the vampire onto the floor. As soon as it hit, Cole was there to pin its neck in place beneath the forked end of his spear.

"He's just a scout," George said. "Indentured to Vasily, the Nymar who controls most of northern Hungary."

"You have Nymar that control that much territory?" Cole asked.

"They're not like the American Nymar. They work quietly and have made it their business to breed the Vitsaruuv into things that can be used. Just like the ones we saw here."

"These are just like the ones that attacked you at the club," said a shaky voice from outside.

Paige turned toward the door and looked out to find Nadya hunkering down next to one of the dead Half Breeds. Her light brown hair had been allowed to grow out since Paige fought alongside her in Atoka. She'd been wounded in that battle, but the Amriany woman seemed to have healed up well enough since then. Her sharply angled features appeared more weathered since Oklahoma was overrun, but her light brown eyes still showed a hint of warm familiarity when she cast a quick glance at Cole and Paige. That was all she gave by way of a greeting before announcing, "They're infected with the Shadow Spore."

Cole leaned against his spear. That wasn't enough to keep the Nymar on the floor from squirming, so he pressed a boot down on its chest. "Is that even possible?"

"We've found some similarities between the pure Shadow Spore and shapeshifters. There may be some shared lineage."

Paige stood by one of the dead Half Breeds and used the tip of a sickle blade to move aside a clump of its fur and take a look at the pale skin beneath it. While most Half Breeds had fairly thick coats, these looked mangy. Beneath the patchy coat was an intricate black design that looked tattooed onto the creature's hide. Since its mouth was hanging open, she already had a good enough look to say, "They don't have Nymar fangs, so why would they bother with a spore?"

Even though he had a few ideas of his own, Cole went straight to the source. He leaned down harder both on the boot that was pressed against the fallen Nymar's chest as well as the spear pinning its head to the floor. "Answer her," he demanded. "Why bother with the spore?"

"It . . . connects us," the Nymar replied in a thick Slavic accent. "Just like the spore connect me to our own kind."

"So that's how you command them?"

"Yes."

The Nymar was male, and because of the sporadic lighting from a few sputtering lamps, his tendrils had widened into stripes that moved beneath his skin like seaweed swaying in a gentle tide. The tendrils were spread evenly over most of his body, even crossing his face as if drawn there in camouflage paint. He wore a pair of black pants and a tight black shirt beneath a heavy cotton shirt. Judging by the trembling Cole could feel through the spear, the cold was getting to the Nymar as he remained pinned to the chilled wooden floor.

"Who sent you?" Cole asked. He didn't expect the answer to come right away and wasn't surprised when the Nymar smirked and looked silently up at him. Tightening his grip on the spear, Cole forced a slow trickle of blood to swell between his fingers and run down along the weapon. The Nymar's eyes narrowed as he looked at the Skinner's hands with a mix of confusion and hunger. Panic was added to the mix when the inner edges of the tines became sharp and started moving together like a pair of scissors.

Milosh stomped into the cottage, dropped to one knee and leaned down to snarl almost directly into the Nymar's face. "You never seen a Skinner before, eh?"

The Nymar tried to shake his head and reached out to grab the spear. Milosh stabbed a blade through the back of his hand, twisted to angle it toward the floor, then nailed it into one of the wooden slats. For a one-armed man, it was a very impressive move. He maintained a grip on the knife as he spoke to the vampire in a steady flow of words that Cole couldn't understand. Due to the sharp texture of the Amriany's native language combined with the occasional twist of the knife used to punctuate certain words, the conversation seemed to be dragged straight back into the Dark Ages.

Before too long Milosh stood up and retrieved his knife with a quick, merciless pull. "Vasily sent him. This was the same one who sent those dogs after us when we were waiting to meet the Skinners at that club."

"How'd they know we were coming?" Paige asked.

All it took was a mental nudge on Cole's part to tighten the forked end of the spear against either side of the Nymar's neck. Once the blood began to trickle from the wounds, the vampire started talking in a quick flow of broken English.

"We get call . . . Vasily get the call . . . from America!"

"Who called him?" Paige snarled.

When the Nymar turned wide, tendril-edged eyes up toward him, Cole winked and tightened the spear a little more.

"I never talk on those calls," the Nymar insisted. "Vasily. He say it was from America."

"Who?"

"Cobb . . . Dirty Egg. Something like this. I only heard a little."

"Cobb38," Cole grunted. The rage that sparked inside of him upon hearing that name caused the spear to tighten even more. When he heard the Nymar yelp, he willed the tines to separate.

George was there to grab the Nymar's stringy black hair and drag him to his feet once Cole stepped back. "Where is your phone?" the Amriany asked.

Although the Nymar had gone silent again, Paige didn't need to search long to find one of the few things the Nymar carried in his pockets. She took the phone and tossed it to Cole. "Can you find anything on that?" she asked.

"I'll need a few minutes."

"Take them later," Milosh said. "Right now, this *mulosheka* needs to call Vasily and tell him everything went according to plan."

Waggoner stood in the doorway with his back against the splintered frame so he could see inside the cottage as easily as he could see outside. "Doesn't he have any backup or someone watching him?"

"The Vitsaruuv herders need to work alone so their beasts

don't turn on the other Nymar. Isn't that right?" George asked as he swatted the side of the Nymar's head. "Vasily is waiting for the good news, so this one will give it to him."

The Nymar spat a few words at the Amriany, which were cut short by another swat.

"I don't care if he finds out. Right now, I just care that he gets good news." George slid the steel pole under one of the vampire's arms, across his chest, and against the front of one shoulder. With a bit of subtle maneuvering, he could twist either arm against its joint using the cumbersome yet effective hold.

Once Milosh stepped forward to press a blade to the Nymar's throat, the vampire grunted, "All right. I will call."

Milosh nodded to Cole, who asked for the number. When he dialed it, he waited before pressing the Send button. "You sure this is the right number?"

"It is," Sophie said from the doorway.

Waggoner looked her up and down before asking, "What's *mulosheka* mean?"

She looked him up and down as well. "Roughly, it means piece of vampire horseshit."

"Nice. I'll have to remember that one."

George kept the Nymar in place while Cole held the phone in front of him and Milosh held a knife to the vampire's throat. The conversation was brief and well outside of Cole's linguistic capabilities, but Milosh nodded until he motioned for Cole to take the phone away. After the connection was cut, Milosh said, "Should buy us an hour for sure. Any more than that is a risk."

"How much time do we need?" Cole asked. "Your guy obviously isn't here."

Looking over to George, Milosh said, "We will search this place and move on." To the Nymar, he said something in his own language that brought a response that needed no translation. The Nymar spat in his face, prompting George to twist the steel pole and wrench the Nymar's arm from its socket. As soon as the vampire was allowed to drop to one knee, Milosh raked the blade across his throat, kicked him over, and spat an even juicier wad onto him.

The tendrils reached out from its wound to close it as Milosh put the knife back into its scabbard and removed another one with a darker blade encrusted with wide symbols wrapped all the way around its edge. He waited for the Nymar to look up at him before placing the tip of the blade under his chin and driving it up into its skull. The vampire grunted and flopped at the end of the weapon as his skin hissed angrily where it touched the blade. Cole saw that it was actually the Nymar's blood that hissed and boiled when it made contact with what had to be specially crafted metal.

"We could have just tied him up or something," Cole said.

"Why? So he can call another pack of Vitsaruuv or one of his bosses? This is how we deal with the Nymar here. You don't have to like it."

The two Amriany knew what they were looking for, so the Skinners allowed them to go through the cottage. Cole and Paige stepped outside, where Sophie, Nadya, and a few others who'd arrived in a different SUV waited. "It looked like you found a way to poison the Shadow Spore," Paige said. "I'd like to know your recipe."

"I can pass a few basic ingredients along," Sophie replied. "And we should be able to put something together for use fairly quickly. That is, once we get a chance to work on it."

"Work here if you like. Ira wouldn't mind."

"Ira's your blacksmith?" Paige asked.

"They are called Chokesari, but yes."

Cole looked at the cottage and then down to the dead Half Breeds. "This, uh, doesn't seem safe."

Already the Amriany inside the cottage were making less noise. They'd either found something or were taking a breather.

"I'm surprised you were so squeamish in there," Sophie said to Cole. "Have the Skinners been easing up on the Nymar even after their uprising?"

"No. We just don't kill them without good reason."

"Perhaps that's why they've gotten out of line. Here, the moment they drink another human's blood, that is good reason."

"Must be nice to have that kind of leeway," Paige said. "That and all the fancy jets."

"Yes, well that has changed. We, like you, have been forced to cut some corners."

Milosh and George stepped out of the cottage. "Ira left a marker behind," George announced. "He's headed north and isn't answering his phone, but he may just be too deep into the forest for coverage."

"You guys need a better calling plan," Cole said.

"Are you sure your guy is still alive?" Paige asked.

Walking straight past them to put his weapon into the closest SUV, George replied, "He left the marker, which means he's still alive. Even if he isn't, there's nowhere else to go but north from here. Vasily has already burned down our safe house in Trizs."

"You mean the place we slept last night?" Cole asked.

"Yes."

He blinked away a series of fiery memories that had been in the back of his head since he narrowly escaped the burning remains of the old Chicago restaurant that he and Paige once called home. Those thoughts were jammed in a mental corner along with the rest of the things that would haunt him until he grew too old to recall them.

Sophie lifted her face to a breeze that shook the cottage's shutters as well as the chunks of broken door still hanging in the frame. There were lights behind some of the windows of the houses and shops in the distant town, but they might as well have been bright spots on a rustic painting.

"Is Chuna in those forests?" Cole asked.

"Yes," Sophie told him. "Chuna is there, but still sleeps. If that has changed as well, you Skinners will get more old school than you might have wanted."

Chapter Twenty-Four

Sixty-five miles northeast of Atalaya, Peru

The journey into South America was one of the longest runs Randolph had taken.

It was glorious.

He was able to run as fast as he could go without holding back. The ground flew beneath his paws without him really feeling it, voices trailed past his ears without having a chance to sink in, and his eyes only needed to focus on what was directly in front of him. If he was human, he might have called it therapeutic. Covering more ground in a series of leaps between runs, he gazed around to notice the landscape changing from mountains to desert to wetlands and back to desert before finally becoming a lush green that stretched up to surround him on all sides. Perhaps the trip had taken hours. Maybe the better part of a day. Perhaps more than one day. All that mattered was that the air rushing over him carried scents he hadn't experienced in decades. The water splashing against his belly was cool and wild. Creatures snapped at his heels as he passed, and exotic insects buzzed in his ears.

Jungle surrounded him on all sides until it became the

only thing capable of slowing him down. Even if he'd wanted to, he would have had a rough time breaking free consistently enough to regain his former speed. He was in his four-legged form, prowling beneath a green canopy as a thousand eyes watched from above, below, and within the waters of the Amazon. Propping himself onto his hind legs, the Full Blood craned his neck while drawing in a breath that not only swelled his lungs, but caused his muscles and skeleton to realign. When he exhaled, he stood upon two legs with thick claws stretching from his fingers.

Something heavy moved nearby. If not for the distinctive scent, he might have allowed the sound to blend in with the constant movement of his surroundings. Even though he could feel the familiar weight against his back, Randolph placed a hand on his chest to touch the strap of the sling he'd fashioned. It was still there, as was the cargo he'd gone through so much trouble to collect and bring to this place that was as far away from human civilization as he was from their species. He turned while crouching down and bared his teeth at the other Full Blood emerging from the thick wall of trees on the opposite side of the river.

She made no attempt to hide from him. Moving comfortably in her upright form, her muscles writhed beneath protective layers of thick, dark yellow fur that might allow her to be mistaken for a cheetah from a great distance. Long legs and a lithe body might have furthered that illusion if not for the thick musculature and tapered snout of a werewolf. As she walked toward him, the animal features melted away, leaving a woman with dark, bronzed skin and flowing black hair long enough to cover her firm breasts, if not for the whims of a restless breeze. Coming to a stop several paces in front of Randolph, she bore the countenance of a sentinel that was more than capable of fending off him or anyone else who dared take another step. Reflexively, Randolph came to a halt.

"If you're seeking refuge from the storm to the north," she said in a musky voice that was colored with accents from several different cultures, "you can keep running. There are still some quiet places in Panama where the military and wretches aren't such an eyesore."

"I'm not running away, Jaden," Randolph said.

"Good. After all you've done to brew that storm, the least you could do is sit in it." Propping her hands on rounded hips, she said, "You'd better not be thinking about reversing my deal to trade territories with Liam. If you have a problem with the arrangement, you'll have better luck bargaining with him than me."

"That's quite an amusing prospect. Liam never was much for speaking reasonably with anyone. Perhaps that's why he's dead."

Claws eased from beneath her fingernails, but only enough to be seen. More than likely they'd appeared as an unbidden reflex, along with the tension showing beneath her skin. "He's dead? Did you kill him?"

"That does seem the likeliest scenario," Randolph said with no small amount of sadness. "He fell to the Skinners."

This time Jaden didn't try to hide what she felt. Her hands hung at her sides, ready to put her curved, daggerlike claws to use. Wide eyes, the color of polished gold, flicked back and forth to study the trees along the riverbank. "The Skinners have acquired more Blood Blades?"

"Not yet, but they did organize well enough to take a stand. Not that the others left them any alternative. You heard about what happened with the Breaking Moon?"

"I'm out of touch lately," she said. "Rarely leave the jungle. Only see the occasional human, and that's easily avoidable most times. I knew there were others of our kind in America. Liam told me about the Mongrels taking a more active part in defending their homes. I honestly don't know what took them so long to rise up like that."

Randolph's brow furrowed as he asked, "You're sympathizing with them now?"

"No. We've been tearing at each other for so many years that it's a wonder they haven't grown sick of hiding or pulling up their dens when one of us gets too close for their comfort."

"Perhaps they're one of the few that always knew their place."

"Now that," Jaden pointed out, "is Liam speaking. Despite your differences, you two always were more like brothers."

"I often wanted to kill him myself."

"As I said. Like true brothers. So how did the Skinners manage to defeat him? Did he try to clear out another city?"

Randolph's mouth formed a smile that opened at the edges to reveal teeth that had partially formed into fangs. "He brought the others together so they could draw more of the Torva'ox, empowering himself as well as a few of them with the ability to spark the Breaking within humans at will."

"I haven't heard of that happening since Gorren purged almost every other Full Blood from the planet just so he could have a Breaking Moon to himself. But that was long before my time."

"Mine as well," Randolph said. "The Skinners weren't working alone. They had help from the Gypsies as well as the military. Minh was even encased by gargoyles and spirited away by the Dryad."

Some of Jaden's defensiveness was replaced by wonder as she asked, "Gargoyles?"

Randolph nodded. "They must have gotten stirred up amid all the confusion that brought everything else to the surface.. Have you ever seen them before?"

"I've found a few old statues in the depths of the jungle and spotted some fleeting shapes in the upper tree cover, but not enough to be certain it was a gargoyle. I don't know if anyone's seen one of those dreadful things for ages."

"They caught Liam, Esteban, and Minh by surprise, I can tell you that much. I might have been caught as well if I hadn't distanced myself from all of that. It took more than gargoyles to bring Liam down, but he was taken down eventually. Probably poisoned or hobbled by some other Skinner trick." His entire body shifted closer to the savage end of the spectrum as he added, "Knowing those ghouls, they've probably already chopped Liam into pieces and will be wearing his pelt while adorning their weapons with his teeth. With him gone, the humans have become brave enough to stand against the wretches even when it is clear the Breaking will claim them no matter how many guns or machines are at their disposal."

"Such is the way of things, Randolph. You and Liam were always spoiled when it came to the harshness of the Balance. So much proud, self-righteous talk when it tipped your way. So much venom and contempt when it didn't. The humans are simply doing what they do. Armies will fight and Skinners will sharpen their sticks. Shame about Minh. I know that you two had something of a history. Have you freed her?"

"I don't even know where she is."

Skepticism crossed Jaden's finely sculpted features, but she let it pass. "So you came to warn me about the military?"

"No," he chuckled. "If you need someone to warn you when those soldiers are packed into enough trucks and helicopters to announce their presence hours before they arrive, you've got bigger problems. I came because I have important business in your territory."

"Asking permission for passage? Now there's a courtesy I'd all but forgotten about. Sure you're not seeking refuge?" Judging purely by the tone in her voice, Jaden was more than aware how much those words would grate on the ears for which they were intended.

"You know that's not it."

She sniffed the air and fixed her golden eyes on the strap crossing Randolph's chest. "Then it is about what you've brought with you. If you intend on taking one more step into my lands, you'll have to be rid of that filth."

Randolph's hand drifted to the sling and closed protectively around it. "A lot of trouble went into procuring this. Trouble, time, and sacrifice."

"Don't try to paint a prettier face on it, Randolph. I know what you're carrying, although I must admit it's hard to believe."

"I swear to you, it's not intended to harm you or your territory."

"What else could you do with it? What else but evil could come from one such as him?"

In a firm voice, spoken through a mouth that was slowly forming into a snout as if to match Jaden's partial transformation, he replied, "It's an offering. To a Mist Born. Icanchu is here. I have studied the legends, followed the broken trails, and listened to enough of our own elders to know as much. And if he is not here—"

"Icanchu is here," she said.

"You've . . . seen him?"

"That's the beauty of the Mist Born. When you open your eyes and know what to look for, it's more difficult to miss them. Searching for them is an understandable pastime, but trying to gain their favor or seek an audience with beings like them is more of a human quest. After all," she added with a wry smirk, "there are more of them to replace the ones that go missing in such a pursuit. Like these trees, humans have some value, possess some beauty, but can replenish their numbers easily. Full Bloods should know better than to push the boundaries of their longevity. If nothing else, didn't Kawosa teach us that the Mist Born are better left wherever they may be?"

"Kawosa will be dealt with if he decides to show himself again. For now, it is more important that he remain among the humans where he can wreak all the petty havoc he likes. That has always been his way."

"Has it become his way to shed his limbs?" Jaden asked.

Shrugging beneath the sling as if he could feel its weight upon such a meaty shoulder, Randolph told her, "Perhaps it is no longer time to be satisfied with the Balance. Perhaps it is time to set things on a different path. Find a new way."

She strode forward, almost casual in her steps and the smooth sway of her arms. "You've always painted such beautiful pictures with your words. Is that how you convinced the young one to follow your lead during the Breaking Moon?"

"Cecile knew it was better to follow me than the others."

"And where has it gotten her?"

Randolph snarled. "She has been shown firsthand why it was a mistake to trust the Skinners. And she has also seen how we can take care of ourselves. What she does from now on is her choice."

"We are the only ones qualified to act as our keepers. As for the rest of your business," she said cautiously. "I still haven't heard why you want to speak with Icanchu."

"Do you know where he is?"

Randolph followed the path her golden eyes took when they glanced up at the low-hanging branches above and behind him. The leaves were always in motion, due to the wind or any number of creatures that lived among them. Insects filled the air, gathering in numbers great enough to shake the leaves even more. There were too many living things nearby for him to separate each individual scent, but his eyes were sharp enough to pick up on movement ranging from animals scurrying along the dirt floor to the writhing bodies of serpents hanging from thicker branches.

"I need to see Icanchu now," he said. "There isn't time for riddles or territorial disputes. This goes well beyond even Full Blood claims."

"Why? Because you say it does?"

Randolph exhaled a breath that was accompanied by a rumble emanating from deep within his chest.

Stepping close enough to reach out and place a clawed hand upon his face, Jaden ran it gently along the jagged scar left behind when a strip of the Blood Blade had cut into his cheek. "Spending so much time this close to a Mist Born changes your perspective, Randolph," she said in a soothing purr. "Even though I can sometimes hear the screams as the wretches and leeches tear the old world apart, I know there is one that is much older and will survive whatever fires are set by human or Full Blood."

Another serpent moved through the trees behind her. This one's scales were bright green as opposed to the light brown ones covering the body of the one Randolph had spotted before. Leathery bodies swam through the river, giving the werewolves a wide berth. The more he looked, the more living things he saw. They surrounded and enveloped them in a way that was foreign and unwelcome to one accustomed to open plains, snowcapped mountains, or mile upon mile of swaying grasslands. Even the cities were no longer as congested as that small piece of real estate. It was much easier for him to focus on Jaden's smooth face and the simple, deadly purity of the fangs protruding from her mouth.

"I came to speak with Icanchu," he told her. "And that is what I will do. Please don't waste my time with trite sentiments like the Mist Born can always see us and all we need to do is speak to be heard."

"I wouldn't presume to deflect you with spirituality, Randolph. I will tell you that I have spoken with Icanchu more than once since claiming this territory from Liam. The Mist Born are short on tolerance and they don't suffer fools. I think the only thing that kept Liam from being taught a very painful lesson is that he preferred to terrorize the locals and run along the river instead of venturing into the trees to take a long look at what was there."

Upon hearing Liam's name, Randolph smirked. Every now and then he could still hear his friend's voice whispering some bit of bad advice into his ear or planting a disruptive notion into his thoughts. "Kawosa said you'd know where to find Icanchu. Obviously, the trickster was telling the truth."

"Not," Jaden said while tracing a claw beneath the sling and through the fur sprouting from Randolph's chest, "without some persuasion, I see."

"Icanchu must see that I am nothing to be taken lightly."

"You never have been, Birkyus."

Doing his best to ignore the hunger in her voice or the warmth of a female's touch, Randolph said, "I also know Icanchu and Kawosa were never on friendly terms."

"Kawosa wasn't on friendly terms with most of the Mist Born. That much is common knowledge to anyone who knows the legends. As for what you brought with you . . . no offering will make a difference," she warned. "Not against a Mist Born."

"Take me to him." The voice in which those words were spoken had dropped to a fierce growl. Randolph stood before her in his towering, nightmarish form. His chest swelled with an intake of jungle air that was pushed out from his nostrils amid a curling trace of steam.

Jaden had shifted into her full werewolf form as well. Perhaps playing to her strengths, she'd chosen her four-legged body. Having been freshly pushed through the pores of her skin, her fur was clean and glistening as if it had been freshly bathed in the Amazonian waters. "He may kill you," she said.

"I'd rather meet my death howling into the face of a god while trying to set my world straight than spend the rest of my days waiting timidly for it in a world I've grown to despise."

"And," she said with a ferocity in her voice that turned her eyes into orbs of molten ore, "know that I do not intend on giving up my territory. Not to you, not to Liam's ghost, not to anyone."

"I would expect nothing less."

"Good."

With that, she bounded into the trees from which she'd first emerged. Randolph ran after her, but soon saw why she'd chosen to make the journey on four legs. Rather than follow her lead in every way, he kept the body he currently wore and traversed the increasingly dense foliage as best he could. As Jaden ran close to the ground, ducking under obstacles or leaping over them, Randolph climbed the largest trees so he could watch her progress. Even with the keen senses at his disposal, it wasn't an easy task.

He scaled one moss-covered giant, launched himself from another, and sank his claws into a third as if the bark were flesh he was tearing from an enemy's body. It was near-impossible to track her by scent because the jungle was alive with enough competing odors to keep his nose busy for months. Whenever he shook a tree down to its roots with the impact of his most recent jump, he sent several more enticing aromas into the air. So Randolph relied on his eyes and ears. Jaden's paws pressed against the soil or slapped against fallen logs as she ran ever deeper into the wilds. Her breath still churned within a Full Blood's powerful lungs, and her heart thudded like a machine that the finest human engineer could only hope to mimic. Whenever Randolph lost sight of her tracks, or the sound of her steps amid the chaos within the rain forest, he moved on pure instinct.

She'd always been an exotic beauty, even when she was human. Now that she'd joined the elite ranks of the Full Blood, every one of her assets was enhanced into a natural wonder. This wasn't the first time they'd danced this way, her leading him through a seemingly impossible maze. Randolph kept that in mind as he leapt from tree to tree, savoring every fleeting glimpse of her and each flicker of gold when she looked back to see if she could find him.

As they went deeper into the trees and farther from the river or any overgrown path, he could sense other predators around him. He felt them watching, waiting for him to slip or land too close to the wrong set of hungry jaws. Spiders clung to his fur. Primate voices screeched at him as he passed. Creatures that had never been detected by human eyes waited within hidden dens, plotting escape and attack routes should either possibility arise. But what caught his attention most were the serpents.

Snakes of all shapes and colors reclined on branches or dangled from trees that were low enough to grant them access to slow-moving prey. Colorful scales twitched as the werewolf's paws thumped nearby. Long, muscular bodies wrapped around his ankles in an attempt to drag him down. Full Blood or not, Randolph was a stranger in those trees. That made him vulnerable to any number of carefully orchestrated attacks or well-timed bites. All those possibilities gave him a rush of excitement that had been absent after so many years of dancing with the same hunters across the same patches of land.

Eventually, Jaden slowed down. Randolph caught up to her right away and tightened his grip on the next tree he could wrap his arms around. Sinking his claws into the aged bark, he looked down at her as one of the snakes slid across his knuckles.

"Here is where we wait," she announced.

The clearing was small and could very well disappear or be reshaped by a storm. She remained on all fours, keeping her head low either out of deference to the being that approached or to watch for whatever threats might be lurking beneath the thick carpeting of fallen leaves and topsoil. Randolph felt the urge to climb even higher just to survey his surroundings but didn't want to ruin what might be a singular chance to meet Icanchu. There would be time for sightseeing later. For now, there was business to discuss.

Chapter Twenty-Five

Shreveport, Louisiana

The sirens wailed throughout the city. Whoever didn't heed the warning they provided were either directed into shelter by passing soldiers or cut down by the increasing number of Half Breeds that swarmed through every alley, neighborhood, and suburb. Whenever Esteban raised his voice to howl above the din of the sirens, more locals dropped to their knees, clawed at their faces and screamed as they were cruelly introduced to the Breaking.

Adderson cringed every time he heard the Full Blood. On the occasions when the agonized cries were too far away to affect him or his men, he felt shame for being relieved that he hadn't lost anyone to the random slaughter inflicted by the whims of a monster. He didn't know why some were broken and others weren't. He didn't know why he hadn't even felt a twitch of pain during any of those howls. As a soldier, however, he was all too familiar with the terrible randomness that struck some down and left others standing to view the carnage.

After taking silent stock of the soldiers in the Humvee with him, Adderson ordered the vehicle to stop. The driver was a tall kid who'd just turned twenty after being transferred to the IRD from an infantry post in the Army. Myles may have been young, but he'd proven himself under pressure in Afghanistan and a few times already when cleaning up various cities after the wolves started showing up.

"Take a look up top, Warren," Adderson said to a Marine on her second tour of duty in a war zone. "And be careful. There may be some following close enough to the Humvee that we can't see them through the windows."

Jennifer Warren had put twice as much time into her career as the young driver and carried herself like a true warrior. "Yes sir," she said. "Just like in Memphis." In Memphis some of the Half Breeds had gotten smart enough to slink alongside IRD vehicles and wait for soldiers to stick their heads out so they could be pulled to the street and devoured. Even though she still had nightmares about those deaths, she stood up through the hatch in the roof that put her behind a mounted .50 caliber machine gun. "Looks like there's some activity down this alley, sir," she reported.

Keying his radio, Adderson said, "Turning down the alley. Be ready."

The drivers of the two Humvees behind him acknowledged, and gunners emerged from their roofs.

After getting the nod from Adderson, Myles hit the gas and turned down the alley. Almost immediately four Half Breeds exploded from behind a row of trash cans to attack the convoy. Warren opened fire with the .50 cal, and the Humvee behind her followed suit. The third gunner waited until two of the Half Breeds circled around before opening up on them.

The first pair of Half Breeds caught Warren's barrage in the face and chest. She knew well enough to aim low and lead the werewolves rather than wasting ammo trying to hit a target that was too fast to be pinned down with normal fire. Even after their front paws were knocked out from beneath them, they kept coming. The first time she'd seen creatures get up and continue to function after being hit by .50 caliber rounds, Warren had been stupefied. That was just enough time for two of the men in her unit to be taken down and another to be turned. Ever since then, she just fired at them until they stopped moving.

When the driver started to get anxious, Adderson told him, "Steady. We'll get our chance."

That didn't seem to calm the kid's nerves as machine guns kept blazing and chunks of pavement were blasted apart on either side of his vehicle. For a few jarring seconds all three of the .50 cals were firing in unison. Adderson's brain rattled in his skull, but he focused on the alley from which the Half Breeds had emerged. There was more movement down there and what looked to be someone on all fours crawling out from the shadows. That figure, along with a few others, still seemed human.

One Half Breed propped itself up to scratch its claws against Myles's window. A few rounds from the second Humvee knocked it to the ground, where several more holes were blasted through its body. Once that one stopped moving, the gunfire fell silent.

"That does it for that pack, sir," one of the other gunners said through Adderson's radio. "Moving on?"

"Negative," Adderson replied. "I need a recon unit to accompany me into that alley. Looks like there may be casualties."

"Yes sir."

One of the weapons issued to Adderson and the rest of the IRD troops had been an HK-G36. The lightweight assault rifles were modified to carry extended magazines as well as grenade launchers under the barrel. Not long after the IRD's first mission, incendiary rounds were also issued, but it turned out that the only thing worse than a rampaging pack of werewolves was a rampaging pack of werewolves on fire. For now, hollow points intermixed with standard rounds were the flavor of the week. Enough of that mixture on full auto usually put down a Half Breed. Of course, a good amount of prayer didn't hurt.

A few comforting verses drifted through Adderson's mind

as he led the way down that alley. Snarls came from all sides. Some came from above. He kept his focus on the path directly ahead and pointed toward the rooftops so the Marines behind him could keep watch on that area. Someone was crying. He couldn't tell whether it was a man or woman, child or adult. When someone was in that much pain and terrified, they were all brought down to the same level.

"Wolves up top," was all one of the Marines said before he and another soldier opened fire.

Adderson barely flinched at the chattering gunshots. He was close enough to an alcove to see a woman and a boy who looked to be around ten years old huddled against a building's side door that remained shut no matter how hard they pushed against it. She was missing an arm and he was lying on his side along with her severed limb. They were both covered in blood.

"Help her," the boy cried.

The woman's eyes were glazed over and her body was still.

"Help her! Please!"

"She's gone, son," Adderson said.

"No," the boy wailed. "I can hear her."

The woman's chest was moving. Adderson could see that and could hear her as well. The wet crunch of bones breaking inside of her was very distinctive. "Come here by me," he said to the kid.

The kid wouldn't budge. "No! You're supposed to help us. Help my mom!"

"Mosier, come take this kid into one of the Humvees."

A Marine stepped forward to carry out the order. He'd been with the IRD since its inception and seen enough to recognize the danger signs where the boy's mother was concerned. His instincts were so finely honed that his HK never wavered from her as she began to jerk and twitch under heavier convulsions. His grip on the kid's arm was firm but gentle at first. It became uncompromising when the boy planted his feet and held onto the woman's dirty wool cardigan.

The woman's eyes snapped open. Her jaw dropped and her back arched as the Breaking moved through her spine and ribs.

"Mommy!"

"Get that kid away from here!" Adderson roared.

Despite Mosier's best efforts, the kid would not be taken easily. Adderson waited until the boy was out of the alley, but could still hear his screams when he aimed at the woman's head and sent a three-shot burst through her brain. The kid screamed, and his voice was soon joined by others. Even though the woman's twitching had stopped, he kept his assault rifle pointed at her when he said, "Scout ahead to see who else is here."

Three soldiers replied in the affirmative, two Army Rangers and one Marine. They hurried down the alley in a shoulder-to-shoulder formation so all three of them could open fire if the need arose. Adderson couldn't see much past them, but the shooting started almost immediately. All three of the soldiers fired in controlled bursts before going any farther. Since they hadn't called for reinforcements, he knew they'd probably found a smaller pack than the one that attacked the convoy.

Adderson's ears picked up on the howl right away. He heard its rising and falling tone woven in with a distant set of sirens. "There'll be more coming," he said to the others.

No response came.

"Take the kid back to the Humvees and get him out of here."

Still no response.

Swiveling around, Adderson found one of the soldiers on his knees, hanging onto the kid's wrist in a grip that caused the boy to squirm in pain. Mosier must have handed him off but now was fighting to get him back. From the Humvees, muffled cries could be heard along with the thrashing of boots or fists pounding against the interior of the vehicles.

More shots were fired by the scouting team in the alley, which meant they were unaffected by the most recent howl.

The growls coming from that direction were definitely being made by Class Twos. Mosier struggled to pull the kid back while keeping his aim on the soldier who was being broken. "Come on, kid. Just relax and let me pull you loose."

The kid jerked his hand free, but also let out a bloodcurdling scream as his head twisted to one side and the bones in his legs began to pop. Having seen more than his share of action, Mosier dropped the kid's hand and took aim. Because he was a father of three, he wasn't able to pull the trigger right away. Because he was a human being, he wasn't about to let the kid suffer once his bones began to snap and the wolf's teeth ripped through tender, pink gums. He fired, knowing he would remember every shot until the last day of his life.

"All teams in Delta Sector report!" Adderson shouted into his radio.

Two of the groups didn't report back. The Humvee closest to the street opened fire with its .50 cal, causing a torrent of pained growls to fill the air. Soon, the grating sound of claws scraping against metal pierced Adderson's ears.

"Hunter One, this is Duck Blind, do you copy?"

At that moment those names felt all too appropriate. While Adderson and his troops waded hip deep in blood, the IRD brass stayed where it was safe and watched the fighting through satellite feeds and online relays. Jamming his finger against the radio's Talk button as if he wanted to smash it into the box itself, Adderson replied, "This is Hunter One. My convoy has been compromised. There's been civilian casualties. We're downtown on—"

"Pull your team back. We're pulling the plug on this one. Over."

"No, sir! We're already embedded. The Class One is staying nearby. We won't get a better chance than this to take it out. Over."

"Do you have any specialists on site? Over."

Adderson clenched his jaw while weighing the pros and cons of lying about the Skinners being there along with his team. In the end he knew their presence wouldn't make much difference. If anything, having the Skinners at his side when things swirled this far down the bowl would only make the higher-ups think twice about allowing the specialists on another operation. "No specialists on site," he said. "Over."

"Then we're out of options in dealing with that Class One. Pull your men out of there and clear a path for the bombers."

"What about the civilians, sir?"

"We've already ordered them to take cover. The ones who haven't are probably dead already. Now pull out, Major."

Adderson stood so he could see his men in the fire team as well as the bodies on the pavement nearby. Mosier took up position beside him with his rife held at the ready. The fire team was alternating fire so they could reload, but were holding their ground. A few were enforcing the Cleanup Protocols on the troops who'd fallen to the last howl. After another burst of fire, the alley was quiet once again. Keying his radio, Adderson said, "Negative, sir."

"What was that, Major?"

Although Mosier didn't speak up, he looked over to his commanding officer with surprise written across his hard-edged features.

Gunfire had died down in the streets as well, and the howling had stopped, leaving the city with a silent pall and a gritty texture that left the taste of blood and burnt cordite in the back of Adderson's throat. "Bombing runs haven't worked on a Class One yet, sir. Soon as they hear the planes, they run away. Even if we get this one to stand still long enough for the bombs to drop, there's no proof they'll do any damage. This one is different, sir."

"How so?"

Rather than try to explain how Esteban had faded in and out of a solid form, Adderson said, "It's not like the others. I'll file a report when I'm out of Shreveport, but I won't be leaving until we put up a real fight."

"A real fight? What the hell do you call what we've been doing?"

"We've been doing what we could while trying to remain safe, sir. It'll take more than that to put these things down."

"And if we don't play our cards right, those things may just wipe us off the map. We just got a report that Hunter Four's team was compromised by an unknown number of Class Twos in South Dakota. The entire platoon is gone."

"All of them?"

"Affirmative. And there wasn't even a Class One present."

"Not that we know of, anyway."

"That's just a matter of checking one box or another on the reports, Major. All those soldiers are either dead or running around the Badlands with the rest of those fucking wolves, and I won't have that happen to your unit as well!"

Adderson drew a breath and held it as he thought about the last time he'd seen the commanding officer of Hunter Four. Mark Jones had bought a round of drinks and charged it to the federal account under Essential Provisions. Adderson had promised to buy the next round. "We can't pull back, sir," he said. "These Class Ones are smart and they're getting braver. This one's staying in Shreveport just because it can."

"Come again?"

"We've tracked its heat signature and it hasn't been searching any particular part of town, chasing any specific scouting unit, or even tearing into a specific batch of civvies. It's just pacing, sir."

After a pause, the voice on the other end of the radio asked, "Pacing? What the hell does that even mean?"

"Just like I said. It's circling the city, keeping out of our range, turning us at random intervals and engaging whenever it feels like it. Some of this is a judgment call on my part, but I've engaged enough of these things to know when they're trying to wipe us out or hit a particular target. This one's just staying here because it knows it can. I think it's trying to turn the entire city to add more wolves to the outbreak."

"Jesus Christ. Have you taken losses?"

"Some of my men were turned by the last howl, but it's still random. The Class Twos that were made will attack more targets who will either be killed or turned." Steeling himself, Adderson said, "It's only a matter of time before it gets every human being in Shreveport."

"That's what our analysts say. This problem is spreading exponentially across the globe, which is why I'm recalling you, Major. I can't afford to lose another Hunter platoon. Especially not yours."

"Have the tech crews come up with anything better to fight these things?"

"The specialists left us some of those Snapper rounds, but they're a bitch to manufacture on a large scale. We've already allocated all of those Silver Bullet rounds to the Hunter platoons, and whatever that stuff is that's attached to those rounds, the specialists either don't have any more or aren't willing to share."

"So that's a negative on new equipment," Adderson stated.

"For now. Do you have an ETA on when those specialists will be returning?" When Adderson didn't respond right away, the next question was, "Are the specialists returning?"

"With or without them, we can't afford to retreat now," Adderson said.

"You have your orders, Major. This isn't a discussion."

"This Class One isn't just an animal, sir. It's watching, and we have to assume that it'll tell the other Class Ones what it sees here today. If I pull my men out of here, we not only lose Shreveport and take more civilian casualties, but we add to the number of wolves out there. On top of all that, we're sending a very dangerous message to everyone watching."

"That's what the press is for. They can spin it however we need them to."

"The press doesn't see how many homes my men and I have found that are filled with families who've committed mass suicide to get out of this godforsaken hell. Or how many have gotten themselves killed because they went out to fight a pack of Class Twos with nothing but shotguns or fucking .22s. Or how many are dropped from friendly fire because they're caught outside after the damn sirens have been going for hours on end!" With every word that came out of his mouth, Adderson gripped his radio tighter. "People need to see that we're fighting so they don't give up. They need to see we're pulling our weight so they keep their heads down and let us do our jobs. They need to know we're doing everything possible to win this without the reports being some DC-spun bullshit.

"The last intelligence reports I saw showed a three hundred percent spike in shifter activity worldwide," he continued. "The least we can do is provide an example of how to fight these things instead of showing CNN a good picture of us retreating every time a Class One decides to step up to us. But the most important thing we need to do is show those Full Bloods that they fucked up by sticking their noses out of the forests in the first place."

Notably more weary than it had been a moment ago, the voice on the radio said, "We can't afford to lose you or your team. You've been out there the longest, so you've got to know how important it is for the IRD to establish an upper hierarchy among its own ranks."

"I have been out here since the jump, which is how I know we're losing this fight and will take even heavier losses once these things smell weakness. They already think they can grind us into the dirt. They've been doing it. The only way to slow the bleeding is to let them know we won't just hand over our cities to the bastards that roar the loudest. Maybe we don't take Shreveport back, but committing to a fight here and now will at least make the Class Ones take a moment to think before going after the next city. We might even buy enough time for the tech division or our specialists to put together something that'll make a difference. Bottom line is that retreating from here will only increase the Class Two population, and we can't afford that."

As the man at the other end of the connection chewed on

those words, Adderson motioned for his surviving soldiers to load into the Humvees. Finally, the man asked, "You're not even waiting for me to agree, are you?"

"No, sir."

"I'll want full status reports every step of the way."

"Will do."

"And Major . . ."

Adderson stopped what he was doing and listened carefully even though he had a pretty good idea what was coming. "Yes sir?"

"Look forward to a court-martial in your future. You're not the only one that needs to discourage certain behaviors in the field."

"I understand, sir. Any chance I can expect reinforcements?"

"Everything I can spare and then some. Duck Blind out."

Chapter Twenty-Six

Slovakia
Eight hours later

They'd driven north using whatever roads they could find after leaving Hungary. Judging by the ease at which the Amriany made the crossing, the guards who'd checked their paperwork were accustomed to letting them pass no matter what they were carrying or who was with them. Paige and Cole weren't surprised by that, since Skinners knew plenty of officials at various U.S. borders who were sympathetic to the cause after a near miss involving some supernatural creature or another.

Almost immediately after driving into Slovakia, the weather felt colder. Other motorists were more difficult to find and signs of life in the buildings they passed was hit and miss. Cole hadn't seen many Half Breeds in the fields or gargoyles in the skies, but the fear he felt in the few people they did find as well as the strange statues he spotted along the side of the road were evidence that it hadn't been long since they were visited by either of those creatures.

After covering over fifty miles of nondescript highway, the view from Cole's window shifted to a wall of dead browns and dirty whites. There was just enough snow on the ground for it to have fallen anywhere from a day to a month ago. The trees were tall and close together, giving the area a stark, lonely quality. After another fifty miles or so, the trees formed walls on either side of the road, and the few buildings they passed were either dark or completely boarded up. "What's the deal with this place?" he asked. "Does anyone live here?"

"This village was abandoned a year ago," Nadya replied. "Werewolf attacks."

"A year ago? Why didn't anyone say anything?"

"They've been saying it for generations. Nobody listens. Now, their complaints don't matter. Once the gargoyles were stirred up, it's become difficult for anyone to live here."

"I saw a few lights on back there," Paige said. "Must be some people sticking it out."

"Cheap rent," Nadya said with a shrug. "Times are hard."

They continued driving. Eventually the road became a dirt path and then a set of shallow ruts. By then all traces of civilization were far behind them. In those surroundings, it seemed strange to Cole that Nadya was on a cell phone. The sight of her speaking to the little device appeared as out of place as a television set in an Old West saloon.

She hung up and tucked the phone away. "Ira is alive and he's here."

"Good thing," Paige said. "Especially since I wasn't about to make the drive back empty-handed."

"Sophie and our clan are the ones who are at risk. We're supposed to get the permission of at least two other clans before bringing anyone to this place. Considering you are Skinners, we probably would have needed agreement from all of the clans to avoid any problems."

Cole turned away from the continuous loop of trees flashing past his window. "We still don't even know where here is."

"You wanted to see Chuna." Using a short sweeping motion with one hand to encompass everything in front of them, Nadya said, "Chuna is here."

"What is Chuna?" Paige asked. "Nobody will say anything other than he's the one who has a direct connection to the Torva'ox. Is he one of your blacksmiths? Is he even a he?"

"Not blacksmith," Milosh grunted from the passenger seat. "Chokesari."

"You were so much better when you were asleep."

"How can I sleep when you keep talking about one of the most sacred members of the Amriany like they put shoes on horses?"

"So anyway," Cole said, "the nymphs talked about Chuna as if he was more than just a choke-a-sarry."

Milosh wanted to correct his pronunciation but didn't. Cole figured he was close enough or the Amriany was just tired of griping.

"Chuna is a spirit of the earth," Nadya explained. "Some call him a demon. And no," she said to Paige, "I'm not sure if Chuna is really a he or she. What I do know is that he is very old. Older than humans. Older than Full Bloods. The only thing older than Chuna and the others of his kind may be the Torva'ox itself."

"What's the connection between the choke . . ." Knowing he couldn't pull off the pronunciation without making it sound like a bad Bela Lugosi impersonation, Cole switched gears by saying, "Between Ira and Chuna?"

"Ira's craft requires him to be close to the Torva'ox," Nadya replied. "To forge things like the Jekhibar or even a Blood Blade, he must use what Chuna has left behind."

"Gross," Paige muttered. "And you call Skinners savages for putting blood into our mixtures?"

"That's fair enough," Nadya said. "But you should know that the first to break away from the clans and make the voyage to the New World, the first who would become Skinners, were fluent in this craft as well. It's how they got started in putting these things to use. And it's not as gross as using blood or wearing skins with flesh still attached."

Milosh sat up and adjusted his seat, abandoning all hope of drifting back into sleep. "And not nearly as savage as swinging sticks embedded with teeth and claws."

After scolding him with a short-lived glare, Nadya slowed down so she could follow the vehicle in front of her onto an even rougher stretch of ruts worn into the cold dirt. "In recent years, Chuna has become angry. Impatient. Still, Chuna knows where the Torva'ox flows, and when it flows close to buried metals or certain kinds of stone, a skilled Chokesari can use those in his craft. A Chokesari must know where to find Chuna. Since the Vitsaruuv were sent after him, the closer to Chuna he goes, the safer Ira would be. The Weshruuv keep their distance from Chuna's kind."

"But you guys have a working relationship?" Paige asked.

"No. We keep our distance as well. But this is an extreme circumstance for all of us. After what the Weshruuv did during the last Breaking Moon, I have a feeling Chuna will not mind helping us extract some form of payback."

They drove for another half hour before the ruts simply wandered into the forest as if the grooves in the ground had grown sick of running side by side. The Amriany parked and climbed out of the SUVs. After emerging from the second vehicle, Waggoner looked over and received a reassuring nod from Paige. It was going to be a long hike, so each person only took what they could carry on their back.

Cole wondered if Daniels was making any progress. He hadn't been able to connect to a network for some time. The Amriany's phones held out a bit longer, but even they'd become nothing more than glorified clocks. With no modern conveniences to distract him, he carried his gear as well as all the thoughts racing through his head into the woods. It was tough to decide which was heavier.

Chapter Twenty-Seven

Schaumberg, Illinois

The Nymar had torn through the entire building. Guided by Steph via cell phone, Tara led the group of shooters from the top to the bottom of the structure. Even though the Half Breeds hadn't hit the Chicago suburb as badly as other places, people still barricaded themselves into their homes behind multiple levels of chains, dead bolts, and bars set directly into the floor. Because of that, when the vampires started pounding on doors, they had a tough time getting in. Half an hour later the cops arrived and were promptly ripped apart by Tara and her crew. It would be a while before they were missed, and even then it was a safe bet that nobody would look any further than the werewolves to explain their disappearance. Yet another advantage of life after the apocalypse.

"So," Steph said when she got the call from Tara, "did you find the bald little jerk?"

"Not yet. Are you sure you told us the right building?"

"Do I have to do everything for you?" Before the inevitable demand came, Steph added, "The address I gave you is on the first floor. Try the apartment directly over it. Sometimes we've seen him peeking out of that window too."

"He's friendly with the neighbors?"

"Either that or he just moved up a floor. It's worth a shot, though. Just remember to leave whatever he's working on in one piece. That stuff still belongs to me."

Tara hung up and tucked the phone away. The building was a shambles. The parking lot was filled with empty cop cars that were spattered with blood from the people who'd driven them. Two Nymar had been killed in the fight as well, adding to the mess on the vehicles and pavement. One set of lights still flashed, but the radios were eerily silent, since gutting them had been the Nymar's first move. The building's front door had been torn from its hinges, along with two of the five doors on the first floor apartments. The door to one second floor apartment had been ripped off and was lying on the landing halfway between the first and second floors. Terrified voices could still be heard behind the doors that withstood the assault, but they quieted down as the remaining Nymar walked up the stairs.

Tara approached the apartment directly above the first floor address she'd been given. Of all the doors they couldn't knock down, this was one that hadn't even budged. Standing to the side to avoid any potential gunshots that might be fired through the door, she shouted, "I know you're here, Daniels! I also know about your connection to the Skinners. Steph might have tolerated it before, but that's over now. Hand over whatever you've got on them and we walk away." After a few seconds of silence she added, "Make us work any harder to get in there and we'll tear you apart and then search your place to find what we wanted anyway."

Still no response.

"So far we've done this the easy way," she went on. "Plenty of noise. Plenty of warning. Plenty of chances for you to see how serious I am. Even though you work with the Skinners, you're one of us. Steph overlooked your transgressions because she was afraid of retaliation and you were useful. After the uprising, you stopped mattering and weren't worth the effort of destroying. You matter again, but have no protectors. The Skinners abandoned you, which means you have no reason to protect them. Hand over your work and contact information so you can matter to the right people. What happened before the uprising is history. All that's left is the future. Same for you as it is for the rest of us. Don't throw yours away by maintaining loyalties to the losing side."

One of the doors opened barely a crack, but it wasn't the one Tara had been watching. Instead of the balding Nymar, a man with a full head of graying hair peeked out. The only thing that protruded far enough to make it past the reinforced frame of the entrance was the barrel of a shotgun. "Whoever you are, get out," he said over the urgent protests of a woman inside the apartment who desperately wanted him to get back inside.

Tara shifted her gaze in his direction just long enough to evaluate him. Tossing an off-handed wave to one of the other Nymar that had accompanied her to the apartment complex, she said, "Shut him up."

Her enforcer stood just over six feet tall, had buzzed hair, a full goatee, and tendrils that were concentrated on his left arm. As he approached the door, he passed beneath a light set into the ceiling that caused the tendrils to constrict into barely perceptible lines. At the last possible second he jumped over to one side while reaching the shotgun barrel. The trigger was pulled, sending its rounds into the wall between the doors of the shooter's and the neighboring apartments. Still holding onto the shotgun, the Nymar placed his hand on the door and eased it open while moving the man aside with minimum effort.

"See what you're doing?" Tara said to Daniels's door. "If you'd cooperated, none of this would have happened."

Screams came from the shotgunner's apartment. Most of them were from the woman who'd begged for the door to be shut in the first place, but these were soon followed by the pained cries of the man who'd attempted to drive the Nymar away.

"I know you're working on something for the Skinners," Tara continued, speaking to the closed door. "I also know it must be something important for you to hold out this long to protect it. Does this project mean enough for you to sacrifice yourself and the woman you have in there with you? That's right," she added with a smile, as if she could somehow see Daniels's reaction to that bit of information. "We know about your friend. Or is it wife by now? Maybe fiancée? If you make us work any harder to get to you, you'll have to watch as we feed on whoever she is until she begs for us to kill her. And you can't even imagine what we'll do to her from there. You're good at math, right? Think you can count how many ways we know to violate a woman using broken glass?"

As if to punctuate that threat, the woman in the neighboring apartment screeched a few syllables before she was suddenly silenced. The man shouted as well, but was cut off by a roar from the shotgun.

Inside his apartment, Daniels crouched down so he could hold onto both of Sally's hands while looking into her eyes. His face was less than an inch from hers as Tara's voice drifted through the apartment. "Don't listen to her," he said. "She doesn't know what's here, including us."

"She knows," Sally said in a whisper he could barely hear. "She said so."

"They say a lot of things. That doesn't make them true."

"What are you working on? What's so important?"

"It's . . . nothing we need to talk about right now."

"You don't trust me," she said.

"It's not that. It's . . ." When he heard a scraping sound, Daniels placed his hands on her cheeks to form a barrier between them and the rest of the world. That way, their faces were the only things they could see and their voices were confined to an even tighter space in front of them. "It's not about trust. What I'm working on is important. It has to continue no matter what happens to either of us."

"You mean . . . no matter what happens to me."

Daniels closed his eyes, but forced them open again. However tough it was to look at her, it was the least he could do, considering the things he needed to say. "That's right, sweetie. If they get to us, they'll do terrible things. You're too smart to believe anything other than that. They might kill you, but they probably won't kill me. I'm too valuable to them."

"If this is supposed to comfort me, you really missed the boat."

"No," he said with a stifled laugh. "If it comes to that, I'll make sure they don't follow through on what they're threatening."

She winced and glanced in the direction of the door. "What is she saying? I can't make it all out from in here."

"Never mind that. Just know that I won't let it get bad for you. If the worst possible thing happens, I'll end it for both of us."

"I know you would, dumplin'."

It was a strange moment, accented by the sound of claws scratching against the walls and pained screams coming from other parts of the building, but romantic nonetheless. They looked into each other's eyes, his hands on her face and hers holding them in place, smiling as if they were sharing a picnic blanket in the middle of a noisy park. Hearing her call him by that name made it easier for him to relax until his forehead bumped against hers.

"It won't come to that, you know," he said.

The scratching stopped, but was then replaced by the scraping of those same claws against glass. Some of the gifts of the Shadow Spore were the claws, lighter build, and leaner muscular structure that allowed the Nymar to grab onto ceilings like giant, hungry spiders. Some of Tara's enforcers were bypassing the security measures Daniels had set up by scaling the exterior walls and trying their luck with the windows.

"But if it does," she said quietly, "you'll take care of me. I like it when you bite me."

"I know you do, cutie."

Outside, something hissed. Inside, something cracked and splintered. They'd found his patio window and were forcing it open.

In those early years after agreeing to help the Skinners, Daniels had felt some degree of shame for equipping humans to kill his kind. But after the things the Nymar had done to him before his first meeting with Paige—as well as everything he'd seen them do to innocent people all along the way—Daniels knew he was on the right side. Some of the Skinners might have been crazy, but Paige always had a good plan in mind. More important, those plans were never easy. The easy plans never amounted to much good, and in fact often led to plenty of bad. He'd had his doubts when Cole was brought into the picture, but they faded after his first meeting. Now, with Steph making herself comfortable by sullying the city that had been his home for so long, and Tara leading the charge to make the Nymar an even bigger threat than the shapeshifters, he was even more confident in his allegiances. One of those choices still resided in a nearby syringe.

The very act of connecting his apartments into a fortified structure within the secondary structure of the building had been to provide ways out in case one of his many paranoid scenarios actually came to pass. That syringe, now covered with caked-on dust, was another. Unfortunately, it wasn't valid. The files Tara wanted were hidden and protected. There hadn't been enough time to destroy them, and he couldn't allow his work to become just another device used to undo human society.

Daniels pressed Sally's cheeks just hard enough to get her eyes to open again. "I know things are bad. They're horrible right now, but I've never been the one to accept that, and neither are you."

"If I was, I would've moved back to Aurora after the first time those things busted into my place. Even seeing Paige kill one of them was almost enough to send me packing."

"But you didn't go anywhere. You stayed with me, and I need you to know how grateful I am that you did."

All she needed to do to kiss him was stretch her neck out and pucker until her lips touched his. That bit of playful contact led to deeper kisses, which were less about passion than about savoring their proximity to one another. The scratches outside were growing, and culminated in the shattering of glass.

They were inside.

Chapter Twenty-Eight

Peru

As the hours passed, the clearing Jaden had chosen slowly shrank. The wind blew, while countless animals above and below them encroached like a living fist. If Randolph remained silent, he could hear the trees creaking beneath their weight. He remained in his upright form but allowed his fangs to retreat beneath his gums so they weren't piercing his cheeks in a gruesome show of force. His claws stretched out to their full length and drove deep into the fertile soil when he crouched down to bury them as well as the powerful hands from which they grew.

"I don't suppose there is a need to let him know we are here?" he inquired.

Jaden laughed under her breath. "No."

"Legends say, no matter what any living thing does, one of the Mist Born will know about it."

"Those are legends. We above all creatures know how convoluted those can be."

"The legends of the Mist Born are beyond convoluted," Randolph said. "They become muddier every time another group of humans tries to figure them out. Tales of Icanchu refer to twins. Is there another Mist Born within these trees?"

"There is only enough room for one," she said while gazing up at the dense greenery that closed in on her from all sides. "Does that ruin your plans?"

"The only thing that would ruin my plan is if Icanchu himself is nothing more than a story."

Something rustled in the leaves near Randolph's feet and something else shook the branches over his head as well as behind Jaden. While he stood up to get a look at what might be creeping in on him, she closed her eyes and lifted her chin as if to smell the wind or bare her throat to an all-encompassing opponent.

Reflexively, Randolph shifted into a form that he would have shown to the Skinners or the human military. Fangs extended from bloody gums. Muscle swelled into layers equally suited for protection or combat. Although the Full Blood didn't know what Icanchu might look like, he knew the legends that told of a demon in a body of fog, a creature with a thousand mouths or a serpent lord that could crush the life out of the mightiest warrior if the mood struck him. He had already dealt with one Mist Born, and knew they were not demons or ghosts. Kawosa had his limitations, but if only a fraction of the legends were believed, Icanchu was mighty even by Mist Born standards.

"Where are you?" Randolph roared. "Show yourself!"

The trees shook. Not just some or most of them, but all. No matter which direction Randolph chose to look, he found quaking branches and leaves fluttering toward the ground. Smaller animals bolted from dens or whatever cover they'd taken to hide from the pair of Full Bloods, only to be swept up by opportunistic snakes that dipped their long bodies down and captured the frantic creatures within inescapable coils.

"Stay still, Birkyus," Jaden urged.

Having given himself over to the primal survival instincts that always fought for dominion within him, he bellowed, "Point me toward the Mist Born or hold your tongue!"

She knew better than to try and calm him, so she just made

certain to stay out of his reach. When the snakes dropped down to wrap around her arms and brush against the side of her face, she pulled in a breath and forced herself to remain calm no matter how badly she wanted to join Randolph in his display.

The blood surged through his veins, powering his mighty form like a steam engine. Every time he raised his fists and brought them down, they slammed against the dirt to shake even more leaves from their branches. The touch of a serpent's body against his ankles unleashed a desperate howl that raked against his throat and thundered to the narrow strips of sky he could see through the jungle's leafy canopy. One of the serpents encircled his leg and tightened, so Randolph tore it apart with a swipe of claws that also ripped into his own flesh. Another snake wriggled between his toes, only to be crushed when he shifted the shape of his foot so it could clench shut like a knot within a rope. And still the snakes came. Bodies of varying lengths, color, and texture rose up from the earthen floor and dropped down from the trees. Randolph slashed at them until he realized he was wasting his strength. The blood he'd spilled didn't smell like anything he'd ever encountered. He stopped then, pressed his palm against his fur and lifted it to his nose so he could draw the scent even deeper into his lungs. Something about it was familiar. He'd last smelled it when the wing was torn from Kawosa's shoulder.

The snakes gripped his legs but didn't try to drag Randolph down.

They slithered through his fur but didn't sink their fangs into his flesh.

Leathery bodies emerged from the soil and every tree to form a living, writhing wall between the Full Bloods and the outside world. Once that wall closed in around them, the world they knew disappeared. Randolph enjoyed the solitude of the jungle, but this was something else.

"Move your scouts away from me before I shred them all," Randolph warned.

A breath rolled through the jungle. The inhalation caused every one of the snakes to expand, and when those serpents exhaled, they expelled the stink of mold that had grown on the bottom of a thousand year-old rock. Closing his fingers around the snake that wriggled over his palm, Randolph realized it swelled with the same heartbeat that echoed within all of them. A chill rolled through his body when he felt dozens of forked tongues flutter against his fur.

Now that his instincts had settled, he studied the serpents surrounding him. They weren't unlike other snakes he'd seen in other forests, deserts, or prairies, apart from one major difference. None of these had a tail. Serpent bodies hung from above and wriggled below, but he couldn't see where any of them ended. After looking closer, he couldn't even be certain they all had heads. Much of the leathery muscle was encased in scales that simply came up from one pile of leaves, disappeared beneath another, went up into some trees, dropped down again, wrapped around his waist, slithered down his leg and submerged into the dirt. When he looked up again, he found himself staring into the wide, churning brown orbs that could only have belonged to a Mist Born.

Its head was larger than Randolph's. Considering how far back it stretched along a thick tube of a body covered in dark green and darker orange scales, it may have been as big as his own torso. Vaguely snakelike in shape, the head also shared qualities with an alligator. Its snout was long and wide, capped by slits that opened and shut with every breath. Ridged brows met above its eyes and extended all the way back to the smooth bumps that could have been its ears. And after taking all of that in, Randolph was brought back to its eyes.

Instead of a pupil and iris, they contained a thick substance the color of old mud that slowly boiled inside thick glassy orbs. Those eyes took him in as the large, scaly head slowly recoiled and was raised by a body that flowed all the way back into the dense masses of the jungle and was thicker than a cluster of telephone poles.

"Icanchu?" Randolph asked.

The churning eyes blinked and the head nodded once.

Without being asked to do so, Randolph Standing Bear did something he'd never done to another living thing. He did something that had never even occurred to him as a possible course of action in all of the most difficult turns his life had taken. Lowering his head, he averted his eyes and knelt before something that was undeniably greater than he.

"One Full Blood on these lands is a presence I barely tolerate," the Mist Born said in a voice that was neither hiss nor growl. "But you have already been in the presence of one such as I." Icanchu's voice escaped from between lips that barely parted, rolling like fragrant smoke in the back of a throat that could very well have stretched all the way back to the river. His words had the flavor of an accent culled from fifty countries, curling around a thick tongue that was split into three segments.

Randolph shifted his shoulders to feel for the sling. It was still there, but was most definitely lighter than the load he'd carried all the way across the continent. Before he could worry about having possibly lost his trophy during his journey through the treetops, he spotted the withered black wing being dragged by three snakes.

The snakes carried it over to Icanchu and raised it so he could sniff without bringing his nose too close to the ground. A brow arched as he said, "I hope this wasn't intended as a threat. Besting the trickster in a fight is impressive, but not enough to warrant whatever special favor you surely want to ask of me."

"Not a threat," Randolph said. "Merely an offering to show that I am worthy of an audience."

"Spare me the formalities, Full Blood. I have heard of you. I have seen you. I know the only thing you respect is the Balance."

"Y . . . yes."

"You're surprised I know this?"

"You can't hear everything I say," Randolph said. "There is no way for you to be everywhere at once."

"Not everywhere, but I can see more than you know." Icanchu's mouth closed tightly and his eyes continued to churn.

"I already told you," Jaden said. "The Mist Born haven't gone anywhere. There are more than the ones you have seen."

Although Randolph had almost forgotten about his guide, glancing over at her was enough to bring all of his more recent memories to the front of his mind. She smirked at him as if she could hear the wheels turning inside of him. "So," he said to the serpent lord that loomed over them, "you talk to each other."

Jaden nodded and settled into a seated position.

"I know I am correct in what I said," Icanchu told him. "That's all you need to know. I can smell the trickster on you, which means you've spoken to Kawosa before coming to me. The last I saw of him, he was living as a coyote and selling his lies to the natives of the northern continent."

"The Skinners captured him and were holding him captive."

Icanchu's eyes narrowed in blatant disapproval.

Randolph continued at his own pace. "He was simply contained. It was only a matter of time before one of the Skinners either put Kawosa to use or allowed him to escape."

"Instead of that," Icanchu said, "you decided to free him yourself. Perhaps to garner his favor?"

Randolph didn't confirm or deny that, but his silence was more than enough to put a fraction of a grin on the Mist Born's face.

"Kawosa does what he pleases," Icanchu warned. "No matter what he told you."

"He told me where I might find you."

Icanchu's mighty head swung toward Jaden. Several of the snakes that had arisen from the earth also looked in her direction. It wasn't until then that Randolph could see the serpent bodies wrapped around her ankles and sliding beneath her fur. Suddenly, he couldn't tell if she was sitting down or being held fast by fingers springing from the ground itself. Icanchu's face was as tough to read as the expression worn by an oak tree. Randolph couldn't help but wonder what terrible promises Icanchu would have fulfilled if he thought she'd been the one to betray his hiding spot within the Amazonian jungle.

"So," Icanchu said, "why go through so much trouble to find me? Surely you don't think you have anything to gain from attacking me as you did the trickster."

"What I asked of Kawosa was payment for his freedom, and he would not comply."

"Liars are often difficult to bargain with."

"I am not. My terms are simple and I uphold whatever word I give."

Icanchu's body lifted his head high enough for it to hang down from the leafy ceiling and gaze down at the Full Bloods as if they were bugs in a terrarium. "Terms? *Terms?* You come to my home and offer me terms? For your sake, I hope the act of spilling Mist Born blood hasn't given you a swollen head. Kawosa is not a fighter, but even he has not been defeated by one of the mighty shapeshifter immortals. The trickster's biggest fault has always been his soft heart. He likes to deal. Entire human civilizations have disappeared when they spoke out of turn to any of the rest of my kind. And as for your word, the wind passing from a frog's backside means more to me!"

Throughout this entire tirade, Randolph stood tall. Even though he was forced to stare several stories up at Icanchu, he never turned away from the eyes set within the Mist Born's ridged face.

Shifting his glare toward Jaden, Icanchu asked, "What insanity has infected your mind for you to bring this one here?"

"Don't speak to her," Randolph said. "Speak to me!"

For the next few moments Icanchu was speechless. He

looked down at the Full Blood, unsure whether he wanted to show him more respect or strike him down where he stood. Even in eyes as muddled and alien as his, the conflict was clear to Randolph. Finally, Icanchu asked, "What is it you want?"

"I need access to the flow of the Torva'ox."

"If you wanted your share, you should have taken your place at the last Breaking Moon."

"I'm not talking about the trickle given to the others or even the more lingering taste given to those who broke the long-held traditions by gathering near a source."

"You want a taste of the purest waters," Icanchu said.

"Yes."

"No creature has drunk from that well since your forefather cut his swath of blood across the mortal world."

"Gorren was overambitious," Randolph said. "And he wanted to dominate the lesser creatures."

"What would you do with the power that comes from the raw Torva'ox?"

"That's not your concern."

Icanchu didn't like that. The scowl that formed on his face turned him into a vast, unknowable horror from the deepest recesses of a fever dream. His thick body brought his head closer to Randolph's level while retreating so far back into the jungle that even a Full Blood's ears couldn't track where the rustling ended. "Then you can go back where you came from, little dog. You're not the first to approach me with big demands. There is no other being on this earth apart from me that can bend the flow of the Torva'ox, and no other that is more qualified to guard it."

"I want to take a small piece so I can make a change to this world that will set things right again."

"For your precious Balance?"

"Yes."

Icanchu expelled a short, huffing breath. "What sort of change could I possibly be concerned about?"

"One that eradicates those who would drink from the

Torva'ox without caring about tainting the flow. Only the strongest would remain," Randolph explained. "No more cheating or lying to acquire territory. No more machines providing strength to humans that are barely able to defend themselves without them. No more wretches fighting on Full Bloods' behalf. Things go back to how they were meant to be."

"The only way to make a genuine change," Icanchu pointed out, "would be to eradicate Full Bloods. Nothing draws from the Torva'ox more than your kind."

"Only those who were power hungry enough to turn the last Breaking Moon into a farce. The Torva'ox flows to them in a stronger current, while some of us have chosen to only take what we need to live. Surely you can see that just by looking at me. Whatever is put into the flow will go to the power-mad like Esteban first, and to the rest of the shape-shifters next. Those of us who have hardened ourselves enough to live without such an advantage will be able to weather any storm."

"And what of the humans? Even if they don't use it, they draw from the Torva'ox as well."

"I know that. So do the Full Bloods who strive for more than their share. That is why they've spent the days following the Breaking Moon wiping the humans out. The fewer of them there are, the fewer trickles will be taken from the Torva'ox. They are to be slaughtered, and many thousands have already fallen or been turned into wretches. Fortunately, this is after they have played their part in creating the tools I need to harness the single element the other Full Bloods have been lacking. Even tolerating the presence of the leeches will prove to be worthwhile once I cannot only collect more than my share of the Torva'ox, but focus it well enough to require one drink from the purest source to make me more powerful than Gorren himself."

Icanchu's body stretched once more from the jungle. His nostrils flared and a whisper emanated from the back of his wide throat that sounded like steam being released after being trapped in the bottom of a volcano. "You do not carry the Jekhibar with you. That is the only thing ever created that could do what you claim."

"Not the only thing," Randolph said. He calmly picked up Kawosa's severed wing and began pulling it apart. "I have studied the legends. If nothing else, the humans are good enough at telling stories and keeping records for me to piece together much of the Torva'ox lore. What I couldn't learn from them, I got from Kawosa. The trickster loves to talk, and being locked away for so long made him even more willing to confide in someone who was willing to listen." The wing came apart with a great amount of effort, but Randolph kept tearing away the narrow bones until he separated the narrow talons from where they connected to the whole.

"I have been alive for several of your lifetimes," Icanchu said reflectively. "There isn't much of what he says that's worth hearing."

Randolph's hands spread into wider appendages. With them, he was able to strip away the flesh and clean the severed wing down to the bone. Because he'd waited until now, the few drops of Kawosa's blood that had been preserved in the Mist Born's flesh soaked into the skeletal frame to rejuvenate it. When he snapped the wing apart and slipped the talon between his fingers, Randolph could feel it solidify into a lightweight hook that was tougher than iron. "Some of the things he said were stories, but others were true."

"How can you be certain?"

"I trust my instincts."

Sensing the change in the Full Blood's tone, Icanchu clenched his jaws together and hissed, "Do you, now? And which stories do you need me to verify?"

"How about the one that tells where the Gypsies found their Jekhibar? The Travelers never were forthcoming, no matter how vigorously I questioned them. The legends only tell of scavengers finding strange ore scattered in the forests. More obscure tales say it was found in the wake of a great beast that dwelled there. Skinner journals narrow the beast down to a serpent. Historians say many serpents. And finally, after centuries of pursuing my answers, I piece together enough to know of one among the Mist Born who can truly fit all of those tales. Ironic that I needed to approach the First Deceiver for my truths."

"Even more ironic that a beast known for howling at the moon and eating raw meat is the one to spend so many years in such intricate study."

Randolph chuckled as he flexed his fist around the shattered slivers of bone. There was no use in trying to hide his activity from Icanchu, so he appealed to the ancient creature's curiosity by making the process of cleaning the talon even more of a show. "There were plenty of useless tidbits, dead ends, and insulting references mixed in with what Kawosa said, but there was truth buried there as well. If I'd had my conversations with him when I was a few hundred years younger," he added, "I may have been taken in by the lies. As it was, I knew just enough of the picture to know which pieces truly fit."

"And which were those?"

A smile crept onto Randolph's face when he heard genuine interest in Icanchu's tone. To intrigue something like him was no small feat. Randolph tensed and his muscles shifted into a thicker mass beneath the near-invulnerable coat of fur that covered his body. No matter how much he prepared, he knew there was no true way to be ready for what was coming. "He told me that the Gypsies only had a few Jekhibar remaining and that Jonah Lancroft had acquired one of them. I believed him. And when Kawosa told me that the source of the Jekhibar was to be found in the metal pearls that grow beneath the scales of the Mist Born Serpent Lord, I believed that too.

"I've taken a lesson from the Skinners as well. They know how to use their enemies' strengths against them. Now that I see the fear in your eyes," Randolph said as he crouched down and allowed his fangs to grow to their full length, "I see my time was well spent."

Icanchu's interest was no longer piqued. His head pulled away from the clearing and rose into the upper reaches of the trees. "If you trust the word of one known for his lies, then by all means put it to the test."

Despite the urge that built inside of him, Randolph did not howl. His blood pumped vigorously through his body and his muscles tensed to launch his body into a jump that carried him from the leafy jungle floor into the gaping maw of what many believed to be a god. The talon he'd plucked from Kawosa's severed limb was entangled within several layers of fur that had grown specifically to hold it in place.

Jaden shouted something at him, but Randolph was beyond the reach of her words. He'd already committed himself to the path that he knew would either lead him to the destination he'd been seeking for centuries or off the edge of a cliff. For the moment, neither of those outcomes mattered. There was only the fight.

Icanchu reared back and up, which still wasn't enough to avoid the Full Blood's first assault. Randolph landed on the side of his neck, digging in with the claws attached to each of his paws so he could remain in place when the serpent's gigantic body started to thrash. Twisting around, he snapped at Randolph using powerful jaws that sent a shower of sparks through the air as jagged teeth made from a substance resembling petrified stone scraped against each other. He opened his mouth, allowing half a dozen forked tongues to spew out and slap against the werewolf's side.

Now that he was attached to Icanchu, Randolph needed a moment to reorient himself. The world he'd traversed to get into that jungle had been replaced with a floor of thick scales and a skyline that churned crazily over his head as trees smashed into him. He kept his head down low while climbing along Icanchu's segmented torso, and flattened his body against the shifting Mist Born as massive, snapping jaws tried to find him. Suddenly, the trees gave way to a blinding view of clear sky. Icanchu's angry, hissing roar exploded in every direction until hot breath flattened the fur on

Randolph's back. Even though he was moving as fast as he could, the Full Blood knew he had to go faster.

The first bite that found its mark sheared several layers of skin from Randolph's ribs. It was followed almost immediately by a nip that would have been enough to cut an aged tree in half if it hadn't caught empty air. Icanchu began flailing madly, trying to knock Randolph off using either the trees or the side of his head. Much like a tick being swatted by a fleshy palm, the werewolf was tough enough to withstand the blunt attacks and move on.

The serpent's scales were everywhere beneath Randolph's feet, hands, and belly. Once Icanchu turned his head down toward the trees and dove beneath the uppermost layers of branches, Randolph used the talon he'd taken from Kawosa to chip at the edge of one scale. The Skinners knew that humans didn't have what it took to wound a werewolf, which is why they used fangs and blood from fallen enemies to help them in their fight. A Full Blood facing a Mist Born had a similar problem. If there was one thing in the legends that was consistent, it was that the only true threat to a Mist Born was another one of their own kind. As he clung to Icanchu's body, Randolph had to use all of his strength to drive his claws in less than a quarter of an inch. For a creature that was too large for three sets of Full Blood arms to encircle, and longer than Randolph could fathom, Icanchu truly had nothing to fear from any other species.

After climbing down farther along the serpent's body, he found a single loose scale. The Mist Born thumped against the ground with an impact that sent a shockwave through both creatures' bodies and crushed one of Randolph's legs. Bones that should have been turned into powder were instead cracked into pieces before being healed again. Even with his ability to recover from that and much worse, Randolph still felt a pain that surged through him like a raw electrical current. Icanchu lay flat on the ground and started rolling against the earth in an attempt to scrape him off.

All he could do was press his face against the serpent and hang on. At times he felt stumps or rocks tear into him like teeth. Other times he was forced to endure impacts that made it seem as if the earth itself was a fist pounding against his back and head. When Icanchu rolled over long enough for Randolph to catch a breath, the Full Blood drove his stolen talon beneath the wayward scale and levered it away from the serpent lord's flesh.

Suddenly, all thoughts of harming Randolph were pushed aside as Icanchu lifted his head to wail in a voice loud enough to ride the Amazon River all the way to the ocean. The Mist Born tensed as Randolph sank his other hand beneath the scale. When his finger found an irregularly shaped lump of metal, Randolph figured out why that particular scale had been loose. That brief touch was more than enough to send a chill of the Torva'ox throughout his entire body. Before he could pull the metal out, however, he was flattened between the ground and the enraged Mist Born.

Randolph could see only black.

Most of his bones might have been broken, and when he felt the gnawing itch of his body mending itself, he knew it was so.

More darkness came, but then Randolph was able to swallow a few large gulps of air. The paw he pulled out from beneath the scale was skewed in the wrong direction. Because the fingers were crushed, he wasn't able to do anything as simple as make a fist around the lump of metal he'd collected. Since that end of Icanchu's body was thrashing like the tail of a whip, Randolph worked his way farther down the Mist Born's segmented length.

After a few cautious advances, he found a way to move with more speed. As Icanchu thrashed, Randolph shimmied in one direction as if climbing a tree. When one hand gripped tightly, the other stretched forward. He even clamped on with his teeth to keep from being dislodged as the mighty serpent bellowed and flailed. Now that Randolph was no longer digging into him, Icanchu seemed to lose track of where he was. Settling into the lower branches above the jungle's floor, his thick body swayed.

"You're making powerful enemies, Full Blood," Icanchu said in a voice that rolled through the jungle like a foul wind.

Even though he wasn't foolish enough to believe he could hide from the Mist Born, Randolph moved as carefully as he could to keep from drawing attention. Every step of the way, he tested more scales with fingers and toes. He found another that shifted beneath his palm and immediately set himself to the task of prying it loose. The moment he made enough of a gap, he sank the talon in and pulled.

Icanchu roared and lurched into motion. Being farther away from the giant's head, Randolph had an easier time hanging on. Before he could get too used to his more tenable position, however, he felt smaller bodies slithering against his feet and legs. While reaching beneath the loose scale, Randolph shook his leg to try and rid himself of whatever smaller creatures had attached themselves to him during Icanchu's journey through the trees. Little tongues flicked against his skin, and soon fangs sank into him. The pain of those bites was something new to the Full Blood. Teeth, claws, and even knives and bullets were rarely strong enough to pierce his hide. Feeling something as common as a snakebite brought him down to a level he'd all but forgotten throughout years of dominating lesser beings.

After the first bite, another followed. Another and another came after that, piercing Randolph's body at will. Slithering bodies wriggled beneath his fur, burrowing deeper so they could find yet another place to plant their curved teeth. Randolph reached down with one hand to swipe at the snakes. Some of them were instantly severed by his claws, but the rest swung back to wrap around him. They were more than just stray snakes following a command from Icanchu. They were connected to the Mist Born somewhere along his massive body. The serpents that had been shredded by the werewolf's claws were sucked beneath Icanchu's scales like rope being retracted by a reel, while the others were free to move without being impeded by the larger serpent's movement.

Not wanting to pass a chance to claim another stone, Randolph gritted his teeth and absorbed the pain of all those bites. Some kind of venom was being pumped into him, which clouded his vision around the edges and made his ride on the Serpent Lord's back even more dizzying. Another lump of metal was firmly in his grasp, but Randolph had to fight to dislodge it. When it came loose, he reclaimed the arm he'd sunk in all the way down to the elbow.

It wasn't just a Jekhibar. That was something crafted by Gypsy hands and suited to their needs. Perhaps the humans couldn't do anything with the raw ore, but that wasn't Randolph's concern. He was a Full Blood, and the Torva'ox flowed like blood through their veins. Now that the ore was in his possession, he could feel it being drawn to the earth. Perhaps this was why the Gypsies needed to craft it into their Jekhibar. It took all of his strength to maintain his hold on the pieces of metal as the Torva'ox flooded his system.

Rather than clench his fist around that which he'd sought and jump away from the Mist Born, Randolph moved even faster along Icanchu's writhing body. He was no longer concerned with looking for anything, so he was free to scamper along the Mist Born's thickly muscled trunk as it swung back and forth. Some of the smaller snakes chased him, while others appeared to block his path or clamp onto him to prevent him from jumping free. Branches of all sizes brushed against his back and tugged at his fur until Randolph was finally slammed into the river.

He kept his focus on the living plateau directly beneath him. Submerged in the chilling waters of the Amazon, he concentrated on shredding the snakes holding him in place so he could circle around Icanchu's rough cylindrical body toward open air. Breaking the water's surface and filling his lungs, he found more scales that rose above the smooth plane of the rest. Since he was only a short pull away, he dragged himself along the Mist Born and drove the talon beneath one of them to pry it off. Icanchu responded with a renewed series of twisting convulsions. A snarling hiss drifted from the skies, warning Randolph that the serpent's massive head was coming his way. Before he could escape, Randolph spotted something that caught his interest. Without wasting another moment of contemplation, he leapt back into the water and dove straight to the bottom of the river.

Icanchu's head splashed above him, creating a ripple through the Amazon that he could feel as he paddled farther down. The Mist Born's segmented trunk emerged from the bottom of the river, surrounded by several glittering jewels similar to the ones he'd already plucked. There was more of the ore to be had, but even more interesting than that was the moss-covered portion of Icanchu's torso that led into the ground itself.

Like a chunk of rock that had been dropped from the sky, Icanchu's gaping jaws surged toward him. When he glanced over his shoulder, Randolph discovered the Serpent Lord a few inches away, his eyes churning wildly, as if reflecting the mud kicked up on all sides. The Full Blood curled his body so he could turn around sharply and swipe at Icanchu with both rear paws. He drew enough blood to form a hazy cloud around Icanchu's face and followed that with a solid bite to his cheek. Icanchu recoiled and twisted his head away, more stunned than wounded by the attack. Randolph took the opportunity to swim down far enough to see that his suspicions had been correct. The river bottom was cracked open, and Icanchu's body emerged from the hole like a worm from the meatiest portion of a rotten apple.

As he floated beneath the surface, Randolph wondered how far down the Mist Born went. If his body had the same proportions as a snake, it would widen in the middle and slowly taper at either end. As far as he could tell, Icanchu's segmented torso had gotten wider the farther into the water it went. At the spot where it emerged from the cracked river bottom, it was as thick as four tanker trucks lashed together in a bundle.

The rush of water came again. Randolph pushed away

from the river floor using both legs and paddled as best he could with both hands clenched around the lumps of ore. Suddenly, the water around him rippled. A distortion formed on all sides, and before he could change direction yet again, massive fangs pierced his back and chest. They tore into him like broken iron girders, dragging him sideways through the filthy water as his powerful limbs kicked uselessly against the current.

Randolph's mouth opened to unleash a scream that was silent apart from the torrent of bubbles exploding from his throat. Those same bubbles were brushing against his face before being left behind completely. Icanchu's fangs tugged at the flesh in which they were lodged, and before Randolph could figure out what direction was up, he was lifted from the water and tossed into the air.

Even as he sailed without anything solid beneath his feet, he thought to protect the pearls he'd collected. His fists closed around them and he angled his body so his back would take the brunt of the impact when he landed. Wind rushed past his face and roared in his ears, letting him know he was still sailing.

Trees brushed against him and branches snagged in his fur to pivot him in midair. It was still another few seconds before he snapped the larger branches on his way down through the tree line. Closing his eyes, Randolph tucked his chin in tight against his chest and formed a ball of muscle that skidded against the dirt after a solid thump. His ears hadn't stopped ringing when he heard the hissing of snakes drawing closer. Icanchu's voice could be heard above them as it cursed the Full Blood in an ancient language. When Randolph attempted to stand up, he staggered and lurched to one side.

Power surged through his hands, emanating from the pearls that drew their energy from the rawest form of the Torva'ox. Randolph had lived through many full moons when the ancient energies flowed but had never felt the visceral connection to that which fueled everything from the first sparks of life to the whitest core of every flame. He knew if he soaked it in and channeled it through his body, he would become the most powerful shapeshifter on the planet. Even among Full Bloods, he would be a force to be reckoned with. Legends of Gorren told of how the ancient werewolf could rip through legions of wretches and annihilate entire populations of Nymar without their claws or fangs causing more than a scratch. Gypsy clans had been made extinct in the effort to put Gorren down, and cities set to the torch in the smallest hope that he might be caught in the flames. Such legends were unproven, but now Randolph had the means to test them for himself. And unlike those who needed to wait for their share when the next Breaking Moon rose, he would just have to allow the pearls in his hands to recharge.

"Keep that which you took," Icanchu hissed through the mouths of at least a dozen snakes that wriggled toward him through the grass, "and I will be able to find you. Return them now and you may keep your life."

Randolph's fists clenched even tighter as he shifted into a more compact form, one that would allow him to run faster without forcing him to use all four legs. Ahead, Jaden howled in a way meant to show him the quickest way through the jungle. He pointed his nose in that direction and started covering ground in leaping bounds. He only needed to run toward a few more howls before the ground became familiar beneath his feet. Once she'd led him to the river and pointed him north, Jaden disappeared.

He would remember what she'd done.

Chapter Twenty-Nine

Slovakia

They hadn't driven more than twenty or thirty miles after crossing the border, but Cole felt as if he'd been taken into another century. Not only were the roads quieter than those in the States, but they looked as if they'd been that way even before packs of werewolves were such a common sight. Sophie veered onto a path that took them into the forest and even farther from civilization as he knew it.

After emerging in a clearing smaller than half a football field, she pulled to a stop in front of a shack that whistled when the wind blew hard enough to stir the leaves piled on either side. Now that he'd had more than a few seconds to take in the rustic sight, Cole could see the ridge surrounding the clearing. Covered in thick layers of moss, it was too low to be a wall and too high to be fallen logs. Whatever it was, it formed a shape similar to a crater, with the long, rickety shack situated in its center.

Sophie and Milosh approached the shack so she could knock on the door while he scanned the edge of the crater with wary eyes. Paige walked with Cole, while Waggoner stayed behind. Taking a new Skinner under their wing was one thing. Trusting a former Vigilant member with something like this was another. After a few knocks, the door was opened by a tall man who filled the opening almost as much as his solid, muscular body filled the dirty layers of clothing wrapped around him beneath a filthy apron. "Come in," he said with a thick accent. "I trust these are Skinners?"

"Yes," Milosh replied. "And they've done well enough to chase Vasily's dogs back into Prague. Ira, this is Cole and Paige."

"Well then," the large man said. "Not only will I speak English, but they can help themselves to the stew I just made."

Cole and Paige followed the Amriany inside. The shack was at least three times longer than it was wide. The front portion was dominated by a rectangular table cluttered with dirty soup bowls, papers, a checkerboard, some battered paperback books, and a phone that was five generations behind the one in Cole's pocket. At the back of the cabin a stone fireplace crackled, with flames that shed a flickering light on blades hanging from three of the four walls. "Looks like that's not all you've been making," Paige said.

Weapons sat on pegs that had been knocked into the walls or hung from hooks dangling from crude racks. They ran the spectrum from simple daggers and wedge-shaped blades to curving designs even more complex than the sword strapped to Sophie's back. Sizes ranged from a few inches all the way to broadswords almost as tall as Cole. Each of the weapons were encrusted with the same runes as the Blood Blade, but all had the rough, ashen look of metal pulled from a fire and left to gather dust. Once he got over the spectacle of being in a room that stank of burnt metal and being surrounded by so many exotic weapons, he noticed that none of the weapons were complete.

"I was hoping you'd make it out here," Ira said while waddling over to the fireplace. His awkward movements weren't caused by a problem with weight or coordination, but from joints that were even less pliable than the iron he forged.

"Those bastard Nymar swarmed into my summer home and destroyed it!"

"Was that the same place we were at before?" Cole asked. "The place where those Half Breeds attacked?"

"Yes," Milosh said.

"That was a summer home?"

"It is warmer there than here. Can't you tell?"

Ira waved at both of them before reaching into the fireplace that still burned with a large flame. He grabbed a black pot by a curved handle, a whispering hiss coming from his hands. He brought the pot to the table with the heated handle still burning his palms, then set it down so he could blow on his hands as if he'd accidentally touched a hot coffee mug. "I would have fought them myself if you would have left at least one strong arm to help me."

"We don't have anyone to spare," Sophie told him. "Besides, I can't remember the last time you needed someone to protect you."

Holding up a thick, callused finger, Ira said, "I just needed someone to hold a few of them back so I could swing. Not protect me. Is big difference."

"Of course."

Having made her way to one of the walls, Paige reached out to run her fingertips along some of the blades. When she touched one of the shorter swords hard enough to set it swinging into its neighbor, she looked over to the Chokesari as if expecting a reaction. Ira merely looked back at her while spooning some stew into one of the bowls. "Are all of these Blood Blades?" she asked.

"Not yet. Stew?"

"We didn't come all the way out here to—"

Cole interrupted her with, "I'll have some stew."

Nodding with approval, Ira handed over a bowl and stooped down to pull out a bench that had been hiding beneath the long table. "They would be Blood Blades if there were any more Jekhibar around that were . . ." He rubbed his fingertips together as if something vital was slipping through them. After a few seconds he snapped them and said, "Charged. Is that the word?"

Milosh nodded. "Yes it is. All of the Jekhibar we have are drier than my first wife's . . . what are you looking at?"

Ira's face had taken on an expression that made him look almost childish. "What happened to your arm? The last time I saw you, there were two of them."

"Lost to a Weshruuv," Milosh grunted while rubbing the stump that had been wrapped in several layers of torn scarves.

Turning on the balls of his feet, Ira shoved aside a pile of scrap metal with the same ease someone else might push a chair aside. He reached down and retrieved a bottle, then filled several glasses scattered atop the table. There was no label on the bottle, but a tentative sniff told Cole it was probably whiskey. Either very cheap stuff or home brewed.

Ira raised his glass and looked at each of the others as if daring them to do anything but follow his lead. Not surprisingly, they each took a glass and lifted it to the crooked rafters over their heads. "To the flesh we've lost," Ira bellowed, "and the steel to pay it back!"

No matter how bad the whiskey was, Cole drank it all down.

Letting out a hard breath while slamming his empty glass onto the table, Ira moved to the back of the room in his uneven, waddling stride. "I sifted through this soil for days the last time I was here. The only Jekhibar I found were lumps of worthless stone."

"One was found in America," Milosh said. "A Weshruuv collected it and hid it away from the others."

Ira spun around and raised his bushy eyebrows. "Is it humming?"

"I don't know. Ask them."

Although every Amriany eye was pointed at him, Cole looked over to Paige and waited for a nod. When he got it, he dug into his coat pocket and closed his hand around the Jekhibar. Even a direct shotgun blast to the tanned Full

Blood leather wouldn't have been enough to tear through that coat, and yet Cole felt vulnerable just thinking about handing the Jekhibar over. "What do you mean by humming?" he asked.

"The Jekhibar is nothing more than a special kind of rock," Ira explained. "And all that's special about it is that the Torva'ox collects inside of it. Soaks it up like a damn . . ." He winced before brightening again as he found the word he was after. "Sponge! Soaks it up like a sponge. Takes a man like me to get it out, though. There may not be a lot of us left, but we can put the Torva'ox into the steel. Turns 'em into Blood Blades. Only other thing that soaks that juice up more than Jekhibar is Weshruuv."

"That's why the Blood Blades can hurt them so badly," Cole said. "They're connected."

Ira nodded and approached the Skinners. "Used to be legend that it took someone close to a Weshruuv to kill them. Since I've never seen one of those animals hold anyone close enough to care about them, I think this legend is about the Torva'ox. Perhaps something is lost in translation and it is talking about something that is a part of them. Other shapeshifters are part of them and they can hurt each other, but the Torva'ox is part of them, just like she," he said, pointing to Paige, "is part of you."

Cole wasn't about to deny the claim, especially since he and Paige hadn't stopped watching the other's back since they made it to the Hub. He hadn't been aware it was that obvious, though.

"Amriany have always been craftsmen," Ira continued. "So we forge steel into blades. We hammer iron into tools or weapons and charm it with energies stolen from nymphs or other creatures."

Sophie made both of the Skinners jump when she snapped at the blacksmith in a string of barbed words in her native tongue. Ira's face twisted into a tired grimace as he waved her off with his charred hand. "It is true. We can call it whatever we want, but we steal from the monsters so we can do what we do best. Amriany make blades, and Skinners carve wood. Amriany write curses, and Skinners scribble their runes."

Even as Sophie continued to scold Ira, Cole stepped up to him and asked, "What about the runes?"

The burly blacksmith shook his head as Sophie continued to snarl his name as if it was the harshest curse she knew. "Torva'ox is what powers the runes," he said. Once that was out, Sophie threw up her hands and stormed to the back of the room to inspect what Ira had been working on prior to their arrival. "I don't know how they work, because that is savage workmanship. All I know is what I see, and when I see those runes, I know they pulse with Torva'ox."

"Savage, huh?" Paige said. "Seems refined enough to do the job."

Ira seemed confused by the tone in her voice, so Milosh explained, "We call you savages. Just another name for Skinner."

But Cole was too tired to argue semantics. Pulling the Jekhibar from his pocket, he waved it in Ira's face and asked, "So Skinners must have these things too, right?"

"No," Ira replied without making a move toward the polished stone. "You people are crude, just as crude as your country, and it serves you well. You draw on as much of the Torva'ox as any man, which isn't enough for my craft. It is enough for yours, though. As for the shapeshifting wood and blood rituals you do . . . I call them savage. Not another word for Skinner either. *Savage*."

Paige shouldered past Cole until she'd inserted herself into the narrow space between him and Ira. "What do you need the Jekhibar for?"

"You see these weapons I made?"

"Yeah."

Motioning to the walls that practically shone with firelight reflected off of the edges of so many blades, he said, "These can all be Blood Blades. They just need a little juice."

Cole's knuckles crackled as his fingers closed even tighter

around the stone. "You can try to take this from us, but you know it won't be easy."

Stepping away so her back was to a wall, Paige followed Cole's lead as if there were no other way. "Or even possible." The look she gave her partner showed a hint of surprise mixed with a liberal dose of hope that he knew where the hell he was going with this.

Ira hadn't moved, but Milosh cursed under his breath and took half a step forward before Sophie stopped him. "Nobody said anything about taking it from you. I know how valuable these weapons are, but enough people have already died for them."

Cole said, "All I want is to put this historical feuding shit aside for good. Whatever it is between Skinners and Amriany, it's too petty to keep going now. Our country is overrun, and if yours isn't yet, it won't be long before that changes for the worse."

"I was going to give you blades," Ira said. "No need for such dramatics."

"I'm not talking about a weapons exchange. I'm talking about an alliance. A real one."

"Even you don't know which Skinners you can trust," Sophie said. "Why should we trust them?"

"You'll trust the ones we do, just like we'll trust the Amriany that you do."

"And what becomes of our two people then?"

"We form a group that has the weapons and intel of both. With our nymph connections, we can even make it easier for us all to work internationally."

"And you save your proposal until now instead of when we were all talking before?" Milosh grunted. "Very sneaky."

"I only just thought of it now," Cole admitted. "But it's not like I'm asking for anything that will hurt either one of us. Sure, we'll both lose some of the whole secret society thing, but it'll save us having to figure out new ways to tiptoe around each other when the next big emergency crops up."

"And," Paige added, "if we join forces on a larger scale,

maybe those big emergencies won't crop up so often."

"I suppose this starts now?" Milosh asked. "By you Skinners loading up on all the Blood Blades you can carry?"

"Just enough for me and Paige," Cole replied. "Plus a few for us to divvy out to the Skinners on our nice list." When he saw the glances going back and forth between the Amriany, he added, "You know. Like the naughty and nice list? You've got Santa over here, right?"

Ira stomped over to Milosh and slapped a hand on the shoulder that only had a stump attached to it. "Yes, we do, and you are looking at him. I wasn't going to let you walk out of here carrying nothing but those sticks!"

"And I wasn't going to let you leave this country before I proposed something similar to this alliance of yours," Sophie said. She nodded to Paige and then looked at Cole with newfound respect. "I've heard you two were worth watching. Of course we figured there would be good things coming from her, but I wasn't sure about you, Cole. Until now."

"Uh . . . thanks?" he replied, as if unsure whether he should feel flattered.

"Don't worry," Ira chuckled. "She is still not so sure about me either. Let me see what you brought all the way out into this damned forest."

Even though he'd been guarding the Jekhibar with his life until now, Cole no longer had any qualms about putting it into the blacksmith's rough hand. Ira immediately held it to his ear and smiled. Extending the stone toward Cole, he said, "Listen to that one sing! I haven't heard one that good in a long time!"

Rather than take the stone back, Cole leaned in toward it with about as much expectations as someone trying to hear the ocean through a seashell. Unlike that cheap beach trick, however, this one actually lived up to the hype. The sound that came from the Jekhibar was a single, perfect note that resonated only when his ear was directly in front of it, less than an inch away.

"Usually it is a soft purr," Ira explained. "This one couldn't hold more juice if you crammed it in using a bar." He winced. "Crow bar? You know what I mean."

"Yeah," Paige said as Cole moved away. "What do you need to do now?"

Ira turned from the others and walked toward a large workbench while flipping the Jekhibar in his hand like a smooth rock he was about to skip across a lake. "The hard part is done. All that's left is to put what's in here into all of these fine blades."

Once again Cole looked around at the weapons hanging from the walls. He hadn't been able to count them before and surely couldn't do it now. Giving voice to the same thoughts going through his mind, Paige asked, "How long is that going to take?"

Without a word, Ira went to one of the blades dangling from a hook on a rack placed higher on the wall. It was about four inches wide at one end and tapered down to about half that length before forming an angular point at the other end. The hook fit through a metal stem meant to be hidden inside a handle. Ira grabbed that blade and held it up so the Skinners could see it curved to form a subtle wave shape just under two feet long. Gripping the blade in the middle with one hand, he tapped the Jekhibar against its tip and slowly raked it along the flat metal surface while muttering words that didn't sound close to the Amriany dialect or any other language Cole had ever heard. One by one the symbols etched into the blade shimmered, and when the dim light in them faded, that section of the weapon had the imperfect sheen of a silvery lake muddled by murky patches of shadow. It was the same mix of light and dark marking the very first Blood Blade that Cole had ever seen.

"This," Ira said proudly once he'd moved the Jekhibar all the way down the blade, "is for you."

It took Cole a few seconds to realize the blacksmith was

staring directly at him. "Oh," he said tentatively. "I've already got a weapon. I'm kind of attached to it."

"I know you are, but I will make it better. Give it here."

When he didn't move, Cole felt a familiar elbow prodding him in the side. "Go on," Paige said. "You're the one that wanted to build bridges."

Cole drew the spear from the harness strapped across his back. He held it out to Ira, only to have the weapon pulled away with enough force for the thorns to draw his blood. He'd become immune to that pain, but seeing the blacksmith hack at the spearhead using the newly charmed Blood Blade was a whole other kind of agony. "What the hell are you doing?" he shouted.

It only took four chopping cuts, delivered beneath the spot where the metallic varnish had been applied to the tip of the spear and angled upward, to chop off the end of the weapon and leave a neat little point. From there, Ira carved a shallow notch into the point and handed the weapon back. "Concentrate," he said while positioning the Blood Blade so the prongs from which it had been hanging were fitted into the notch. "Close the wood. Grow it back. Do whatever it is you savages do. Just fit the pieces together."

Cole grabbed the spear so the thorns in the handle pierced his palms. Emotions helped when it came to shifting the weapon's shape, and there were plenty of them boiling inside him at the moment. In a matter of seconds the wood flowed up and out, to slip between the prongs and meet again. Ira nodded slowly and watched the process while prompting Cole with a few instructions as to where he should move the spear or which portions needed to be grown out next to envelop the prongs and inch its way up toward the wider portion of the blade.

Paige was so entranced by the gradual little miracle that she jumped when she felt a hand touch her shoulder. Sophie had come up to her and said, "This could take a while. Are you serious about this whole bridge building thing?"

After a moment of consideration, Paige nodded. "Yeah. Like a lot of Cole's ideas, it seems dumb at first but stands up to reason. We need to do something drastic if we've got any chance of coming out of this, and by 'we,' I mean all of us. And . . . by that I mean *all* of us."

Sophie let out one of many tired breaths. "There have been plagues, both natural and unnatural, that have hit mankind, but we come out all right. Some of those seem more like God trying to trim the population. Cruel but necessary. This is different. The Weshruuv have been content to prowl their territories, but now they have committed themselves to an extinction agenda. Even the most bullheaded among us can see our entire species is in danger and that old rivalries need to be set aside."

When she said that last part, Sophie looked directly at Milosh. The one-armed Amriany grumbled and headed for the door. "I will tell the others that we will be in the company of savages for a while longer," he said. After that, his grumblings shifted into his own language.

"Don't worry," Sophie said as she led Paige to the door. "I'm sure Ira's got something for you. Whenever Milosh or Nądya spoke of you to him, he wanted to know about your weapons. Now I see why."

"Kind of like an old college friend of mine," Paige said fondly. "Whenever I mentioned something I liked to Karen, she always remembered it. A little while later—or sometimes a lot later—she'd send a little gift that was always perfectly suited to whatever I'd mentioned."

"She seems nice. Is she a Skinner?"

"No. She was living a normal life when I last saw her, but the way things have gone back home . . . I just hope she's still alive."

Obviously no stranger to the sadness that crept in on those last few words, Sophie steered her outside the cabin and then around its perimeter to the wide field behind it. "How much influence do you have with the nymphs?" she asked.

"A good amount, but we've been kind of pushing it lately.

Things seem to be getting better, though. Why? Looking for some free trips? I'm sure they'll bring us all back to America, but I should be able to get them to extend the courtesy to a few of you right away. Probably won't be an all access pass, but one or two of you should be given a trial membership to the VIP rooms until they get used to you."

"They know us well enough. At least, they know my people. The Amriany have bad history with the Dryad."

"How bad?" Paige asked.

Sophie drew a long breath before replying, "Let's just say it would not be a surprise if our first trip through their temple ended with us being sent into a bad place."

"Like Iowa?"

"Like the bottom of an ocean."

"Hmm," Paige said slowly. "I guess that could be worse than Iowa. We may be able to put a good word in for you."

"We do have something to offer them," Sophie said as she and Paige walked toward the low ridge surrounding the clearing.

Now that she was closer, Paige could see that it was more rounded than what she'd originally assumed, and there wasn't as much dirt on it as she'd guessed. The texture was part of the rock instead of something that had collected in uneven layers on it. Also, the rock was trembling. "Is that what you want to trade?" she asked. "Seems like the kind of messed-up crap the Dryads might be into."

"No. That is the reason Ira works here. He used to find many Jekhibar wedged into this stone. He thinks it is a statue or idol left behind by the nymphs." Sophie climbed over the ridge and headed toward a clearing Paige hadn't noticed until she gotten closer to the trees. Then she noticed another ridge, only slightly higher than the first, was formed around it like a huge, loosely coiled rope that peeled away from the outermost ring to point toward the nearby clearing before gradually angling into the ground.

It took them a few minutes before they reached a spot where the ridge dropped off altogether into a series of cracks that ran so deep they couldn't be filled by the dirt, leaves, and grit that had blown into it. At a spot where the ridge met the cracks, Paige crouched down to lay her hand upon a section that had been rubbed smooth. Wiping the glassy texture revealed something that made her pull her hand away. "Are those scales?" she asked.

Sophie paused just long enough to look over her shoulder. She drew the sword from its scabbard and held it in a loose grip at her side. "That is Chuna."

"I thought we were supposed to talk to Chuna."

"Sometimes it does talk," Sophie said as her gaze drifted upward and into the trees. "This forest is usually full of snakes. They are scarce when it is colder, but usually there are still some around. And in the warmer months, Chuna's real face can sometimes be seen."

"Where did he go? Underground?"

The smirk on Sophie's face showed that she was fully aware of the condescending tone Paige was trying to cover. "This is another Skinner weakness. You rely too heavily on what you can see and touch. Some legends are allowed to slip away."

"Legends are full of too much BS. Paying too close attention to them keeps you from tackling things head-on. Maybe that's an Amriany weakness."

"Or perhaps another reason why our peoples should learn from each other. Chuna is one of two siblings, so the legend says. Our Chokesari have always worked close to this place, which is probably why the nymphs mentioned that name instead of Ira's. The last Chokesari they knew by name was the great-great-grandfather of Ira's cousin's neighbor."

"That explains that," Paige said as she rested her hand on the trembling ridge that led directly into the earth. "What about the rest?"

"Chuna has always been here. The Jekhibar are fashioned from jewels that were supposed to be found beneath his skin. He is an ancient creature that commands the serpents. Or perhaps the serpents are part of him. Maybe only the serpents in this forest are part of him. As you say," Sophie added with a shrug, "legends are not always accurate. It could very well be that this is just some thick, peculiar root that snakes like to use as a home. Whatever it is, it has always been called Chuna and we have never seen its twin brother or sister. I suppose a Skinner would have dug it up to see what it is."

"And if there were a bunch of snakes in there," Paige said as she cautiously stepped away from the ridge, "or one giant one, we might have gotten ourselves killed."

"If we work together, Amriany and Skinners, it must be to make up for our weaknesses without overlooking our strengths."

"Agreed. Now can we get the hell away from this thing? I don't care what anyone calls it, it give me the creeps. Instincts like that are usually dead on."

"Yes. That is true. What I need to show you is nearby."

Paige followed her into the clearing and was greeted by a sight that was so beautiful it nearly overwhelmed her. The trees, grass, and sky were different than what she'd been looking at until now, making every other leaf or cloud seem a poorly made copy. The wind that had once been so sharp and cold now treaded softly through finely crafted branches, delicately brushing the thick green and brown carpet, nudging a few fallen seeds against a fragile ivory lattice that rose up from the earth. She moved forward because there simply wasn't anywhere else she wanted to be. The moment her feet touched the soft ground surrounding the structure, Paige felt a tranquility that had abandoned her the moment she'd gazed into the hateful eyes of the creature that dragged her into the Skinners' world over a decade ago. And yet, because she never would have visited this place outside of that world, she was glad to have endured every bit of pain required to bring her there.

"Is this," Paige breathed as she closed her eyes and savored the fleeting touch of her fingers against a divinely curved archway that rose up to almost twice her height, "a Dryad temple?"

"How did you know?"

"I've been to enough of them."

"But you can't have been to one like this."

"No," Paige sighed. "Not like this. It's more of a gut reaction. It just feels so much like them. There's no getting around it."

Sophie nodded slowly and mulled that over. Something about the way she looked at Paige made her seem jealous—either that she'd seen enough of that kind of beauty to recognize it, or that she had what it took to trust her instincts without question. "This may very well be the first Dryad temple. At least it is one of the first."

"And you won't let them use it?"

"We took it from them. This was long before either of us were born. Way back when there were no Skinners." When she looked at the structure that seemed too delicate to stand upright, letting her eyes drift along the flowing Dryad script that had been written with a perfection to which no human hand could aspire, Sophie paused. She looked away as she said, "Our ancestors took this place from the Dryad, piece by piece, and brought it here. Perhaps they thought to try and figure out how to make it work for themselves."

"Maybe they . . ." Even thinking about what she meant to say, Paige had to take her hand away from the smooth contours of the arch. "Maybe they wanted to hold it for ransom. Force the nymphs to help them."

"The fact that we can even think of such things when in the presence of such beauty does not speak well of us. But yes, that could have been the case. We have maintained this place as best we could, but haven't wanted to approach the nymphs because of our bad history."

"And," Paige said, "you thought that bringing it here and leaving it next to Chuna might charge it up enough for you to use it without anyone's help." Seeing the weary look on Sophie's face, she let her off the hook by adding, "It's something we might have done too. Are you willing to give this back to them, even if it means letting the Dryad so close to Chuna, Ira, and the setup you have here?"

"Yes. Keeping this has never been something I've been very proud of."

"And you've got the pull to make that call?"

"The Amriany have many layers of leadership," Sophie explained, "but I am high enough to make this decision. Nobody will be too surprised by it, and anyone who has a problem will be quiet when they see that we're allowed to use the Dryad bridges just as the Skinners do. I trust you have the pull to make *that* happen?"

Chuckling at how strange it sounded for her to mimic slang that was obviously so unfamiliar, Paige told her, "Yes I do. Skinners don't have any layers of leadership, but anyone who doesn't like it can come to me so I can tell them personally to suck it."

Now it was Sophie's turn to laugh. "I think this will work out for all of us. Our peoples have been apart for too long. When do you think you can make the first arrangements?"

Paige dug into her pocket and checked her phone. Although she knew she wouldn't be able to use it overseas, she looked up a number and committed it to memory. "How's now sound?"

No phone could get much reception that close to Chuna and the ancient Dryad ruins, but Sophie loaned hers to Paige. As soon as she got some privacy, she dialed the number and was immediately connected to the Hub.

"Paige, is that you?" Tristan asked.

"Yeah, I'm using someone else's phone. Is something wrong? You sound like you've been running."

"Things are getting worse here. I know you said not to pay attention to what's on the news, but they're saying the entire East Coast may be overrun by Half Breeds within three days."

"How did they come up with that figure?" Paige asked.

"I don't know. The Army and Marines are fighting in Shreveport. It's worse than ever. Are those the IRD soldiers you talked about?"

"Probably. How bad is it there?"

"People are getting evacuated," Tristan said breathlessly.

"So many are getting killed and even more are being turned that the reports don't even mention numbers anymore. I've heard from someone named Frank. He says he's a friend of Cole's from Colorado."

"Right. What did he say?"

"He just said that he can call for help in Louisiana but it might not be enough. Paige, the people on the news are saying there may be bombers flying down toward Shreveport. What does that mean?"

"It means the military is getting desperate."

"How desperate?"

Lots of things sprang to mind when Paige thought about that question. Some of them involved too many soldiers dying for a lost cause, and others involved doomsday scenarios complete with mushroom clouds and large craters where cities used to be. She hoped she was just getting carried away, but she had been with Adderson for too long to write those things off completely. No matter what scenario was playing out, there was still only one thing to be done. "We need to get to Shreveport as quickly as possible. Remember what you did in Atoka? Can you send us directly into Shreveport without a temple on the other end?"

"I don't have the energy to do it myself, but if you can get to the Hub, I should be able to get you into the city. After that you'll have to get to a temple if you need to be taken out again."

"Just get us there and we'll do the rest."

"Can you get to a temple right now?"

Paige looked in the direction of the forest where she and Sophie had their conversation. "Actually, I've got some pretty good news about that. What about the Memory Water?"

"I've collected more than enough to set one Full Blood back to how it was before the Breaking Moon, but I don't know about the others."

"Fine. Just have whatever you've got ready and we'll pick it up when we see you." After hanging up, Paige looked over to Sophie and asked, "Do you have any idea how the

Full Bloods are changing so many humans into Half Breeds without biting them?"

"They must be tapping into the Torva'ox," Sophie replied. "We've seen people forced into the Breaking who aren't anywhere near a Full Blood."

"How can that happen?"

Sophie let out a strained breath. "Chuna is the source of the Torva'ox, according to our legends, but any of the Mist Born may be able to bend it to their will. Are they still working with Ktseena?"

"If you mean, Kawosa, then yes," Paige told her. "But we haven't seen him for a while."

"It could be possible that Ktseena charmed the Full Bloods. Gave them access to the Torva'ox. There are several legends where the Mist Born trickster gave someone great power in exchange for his soul. He nearly tore apart the Amriany by knowing exactly who to corrupt within our ranks several generations ago."

"Skip the history lesson for now. We have a way to take the power away from Esteban, but it won't do a lot of good unless we can take away power from some of those others."

"What about poisoning the Torva'ox?" Cole asked as he approached the two women. Paige and Sophie both spun around to look at him, "The Full Bloods are all plugged into the Torva'ox," he explained, "so if we can find a way to get what we need into there, it should be passed along to the others, right?"

"We get some of that crap too, you know," Paige pointed out.

"But if it's Memory Water, it'll only help. Besides, we barely get a trickle compared to the shapeshifters."

Paige couldn't think of anything to say to that, so she looked over to Sophie. The Amriany nodded and said, "I have an idea."

Minutes later they were back in the cabin. "Good," Ira said as he held out a callused hand. "I need your weapons next."

After he had Paige's sickles and started hacking off the

blades, Sophie explained the topic they'd been discussing.

"Sounds like you need a divining rod," Ira said.

Paige said, "I need my weapons back before you— *Hey!*" she yelped as the curved blades of her sickles were snapped off and unceremoniously pitched aside.

"Building bridges, remember?" Cole said while grabbing her by the shoulders and holding her in place.

"Isn't a divining rod used to find something?" Sophie asked.

"It is drawn to energy," Ira said without paying attention to Paige's seething glares. "Now that I have such a fine Jekhibar, which just so happens to be empty at the moment, I could build it into something that would draw Torva'ox in and maybe channel it."

"Maybe?" Cole asked.

The smith ground his teeth together and flipped the handles to Paige's weapons in the air. "You want to poison the Torva'ox just for Weshruuv, yes?"

"Yeah."

"Then poison one who is already dipping into Torva'ox . . ."

"Wait," Paige snapped. "Dipping in?"

"Using it," Ira said. "In it. Whatever. I know what I want to say, but there is no translation."

"We know what you mean," Cole said. "Go on."

"Poison a Weshruuv who is dipping into Torva'ox, then draw the Torva'ox through him and into Jekhibar. Then, plug Jekhibar back into the Torva'ox." Snapping his eyes back to Paige, he added, "However you want to say. You know what I mean?"

"I think so," Paige replied.

"I can craft something to hold the Jekhibar and channel it into the Torva'ox," Ira continued. "Once the power you draw from the Weshruuv is mixed in with the source, it should trickle down to the other Weshruuv that drink from it. If the first beast is poisoned, the others should be poisoned too. And since the poison came through a Weshruuv, it should only effect Weshruuv."

"Are you sure about all of that?"

Ira puffed out his chest in response to Cole's question and said, "Of course I am! I am Chokesari! This is what I know!"

Sophie nodded and patted the burly man on the shoulder. "He is the only one in this country who can make that claim."

"I can craft something to hold Jekhibar and channel the Torva'ox for you, and it should be easy," Ira said. "The tricky part will be to draw out the Torva'ox from a Weshruuv instead of a pure source. You would have to do more than stab the Weshruuv. You would have to get the weapon to soak up his . . ."

"To bond with him?" Cole asked.

"Yes. Can you accomplish this?"

Cole stooped down to pick up a portion of his spear that had been chopped off. Most of it was coated in the metallic varnish, but an inch or so of the original wood could be seen. "We're Skinners. That's what *we* know."

A few hours later Paige was standing outside Ira's cabin with her arms folded and her eyes focused on the trees beyond the ridge. Light had pulsed from there ever since Tristan arrived. When the Dryad stepped through the arch and saw the temple, she dropped to her knees and wept.

Now, Cole asked, "What is she doing?"

Without turning to look at him, Paige replied, "There are other nymphs there now. They're all performing some sort of ritual to connect that temple with the others."

"Are they singing?"

She closed her eyes and felt herself drifting off into something between a waking dream and a light, much-needed nap. "Yeah."

Cole's arm settled around her shoulders and drew her close. "It's incredible."

They stood in the freezing night air to listen to the song of joyful nymphs dancing in the Slovakian forest. Of all the things he'd experienced since becoming a Skinner, this was one of the strangest and most sublime. And like most of life's greatest moments, it was over much too soon.

"I am finished," Ira said as he stormed around the cabin to approach them.

Straightening up and forcing the stupid grin off his face, Cole turned to ask, "Sure you couldn't charm a few rounds of ammunition for us?"

"How many times do I have to tell you? There are no silver bullets! That is Hollywood movie bullshit. There is not enough room to write the proper engravings on a bullet, so stop asking. I do have these for you, though."

Cole took the weapons the blacksmith offered and handed two of them over to Paige. Ira's slap on the shoulder was almost hard enough to send him staggering to the ground. He laughed heartily and spoke to the Amriany who had come around the cabin with their weapons.

"Not looking to go back on our truce already, are you?" Paige asked.

"No," Milosh said. "Me, George, and Nadya are coming with you."

"We can use the help, but it's gonna be rough," Cole warned.

"I know that. It's all over the news. We were with you in Atoka, so we will be there for this as well." And before anyone might think the Amriany was getting overly sentimental, Milosh added, "If we leave it to you, the Weshruuv will spread to our country after cleaning out yours."

"Fair enough."

"But one of you must stay behind."

Cole felt the hairs on his arms stand up when he heard that. "We never agreed to that."

"No," Sophie said, "but it is a necessity. I've brought up our arrangement to the rest of the Amriany leadership and they refuse for us to part with so much just so you can go back to America."

"You don't think we'll return?" Cole asked.

"I do," Sophie replied. "They don't. They ask for a representative to stay behind."

"You mean a hostage," Paige snapped. "Screw that."

"No," Waggoner said as he approached the group. He'd been so silent until now that Cole had almost forgotten about him. The expression on Waggoner's face was surprisingly calm when he said, "It makes sense. I'll stay behind."

"I don't know when we'll be back," Paige warned.

Waggoner shook his head. "I know you'll come back. Besides, I don't think these folks will hurt me. I wanna fight, but whatever you're headed into right now . . . I know it ain't a place for someone who's still learnin' the ropes."

Nodding, Sophie said, "This will be acceptable. We can even show him how things are done here as a way to start forging our alliance."

"Just keep him safe for now," Paige said. "You sure you're all right with this, John?"

"Yeah. I still feel bad for signing up with Jessup for the short time I did. This'll go a ways in proving I intend on being more than an overblown hunter."

When Paige looked over to him, Cole said, "Seems like the way it's gotta be. I sure as hell won't be staying behind."

The group walked to the clearing, checking their gear, weapons, and ammunition along the way. Before they could see the Dryad temple, melodious voices drifted through the night air. When they caught sight of the delicate structures, and a soft, green glow, the winter chill evaporated. Cole didn't feel warm or cold when he stepped into the clearing. There was only comfort and peace within the circle of tall, wispy grass that had sprouted since the temple was reclaimed. In that short time the grass had grown tall enough to brush against his waist.

Marissa and Lexi stood swaying on either side of the arch as Tristan knelt before it with both arms raised. They were all naked and their hair flowed around them without a breeze to push it. When Tristan stood and turned to face them, it looked as if she'd just arisen from a lake of the purest water earth had ever known. Her skin shimmered and her nipples stood erect. When she spoke, her voice was carried by the air to slip enticingly into each human's ear. "I can see where you wish to go." Her eyes, without pupils, were a solid, jade green. "I can send you there, but not all at once. This temple is fragile and not fully entwined with the others. I can use the Hub as a Skipping Temple to send you straight into Shreveport, but I can't guarantee both groups would land in the same spot."

"We'll just have to take our chances," Paige said.

The symbols on the arch began to shine, and when they grew bright enough to cast shadows in every direction, a rippling, translucent wave toppled from the apex and came down like a ghostly version of the beads that hung from the entrance of the Dryad bridges Cole had seen before. He steeled himself before stepping through, but knew there was no way to prepare for what awaited him on the other side.

Chapter Thirty

Shreveport, Louisiana

Adderson and his men were dug in at a small park in a residential section of town. Although he started the day on a routine patrol in search of survivors or buildings used as dens by Class Twos, he was no longer concerned with street names or addresses. Once the Class One had climbed to the top of a firehouse and howled loud enough to turn a quarter of a platoon, the IRD was reduced to hit and run tactics just to keep their heads above water.

It was colder than normal, and cloudy enough to reduce the sun to a distant stranger that didn't bother looking in on the city no matter how hard the wind blew. Even though it was slightly above freezing, Adderson felt a chill rip all the way down to his bones. When he lifted the radio to his mouth, he did his best to keep his hand from trembling. "Raven One, this is Hunter One. Over."

The silence that followed was more than enough to send his gut into his boots. Before he got too lost in the possibility of losing another chopper, Hendricks responded amid the thumping of helicopter blades. "Go ahead, Hunter One."

"What's your position? Over."

"About ten klicks south of you, circling over a parking lot. There was supposed to be a pickup, but the unit was compromised. They're gone, so I'm heading back. Over."

"Has there been any word from the Air Force? Over."

"Bombing runs have started in West Texas and northern California. Don't know any specifics. I've been kind of busy. Over."

Adderson tried to narrow it down using what he knew about shifter movements over the last several days. He swore under his breath when he realized things were bad enough in so many places that he couldn't make any guesses as to where those bombs were being dropped. All he could do was hope the cities had been properly evacuated. Forcing his mind back to the present situation, he asked, "How many men are you carrying?"

Asking one question without framing it in proper radio procedure gave Hendricks the go-ahead to speak normally as well. "Just the door gunners, sir."

"Have you spotted the Class One yet?"

"Saw him hopping around to the north. He might have been headed your way. Want me to swing by there?"

Holding the radio away from his mouth, Adderson looked to the closest Marine he could find. "Warren, what's the status on Raven Four?"

She was lying on her stomach on top of a squat cement building containing a set of bathrooms. Under normal circumstances it might have been a disgusting place to set up. Since there hadn't been anyone in that park since the first werewolves had torn up a kids' soccer game there, the only smells coming from that building were rusty water and mildew.

"Visual contact on the messenger, but not with the rest of them," Warren replied.

Every IRD soldier had a radio and at least two other means of communicating with their teammates. Because the wolves were just too damn fast, the most reliable way to keep tabs on another team was for them to leave stragglers behind. Those were called messengers. If the rest of the team was attacked, the wolves wouldn't stop before coming back for the straggler. If that happened, the soldier watching that team would know. Otherwise, they got a thumbs-up from the messenger. It wasn't a very friendly way to go about things, but Adderson had never known the military to be cordial.

"Any sign of the Class One?" he asked.

After taking a sweeping look at the horizon through her binocs, Warren said, "Not yet."

He keyed the radio. "Hendricks, see if you can bring the Class One to my position."

"I've herded that thing into one ambush after another, sir. None of them do jack shit. All I've been doing is wasting a lot of ammo and getting scratches on my bird."

"The attacks have been launched on a diminishing schedule," Adderson said. "That thing is slowing down."

"Slowing down a little, but not enough. We'll have to—"

"Whatever it is, we'll have to do it, Lieutenant. Do you understand me?"

The familiar tone in Adderson's voice had been instantaneously replaced with authority, and Hendricks responded in kind. "Roger that. It's my professional opinion that the ordnance I'm carrying won't be enough to do the job. Over."

"Then we'll have to throw all of it plus what I've got at that thing. We back off now and it'll just get a chance to lick its wounds so it can come at us fresh in the next city. No matter what happens in that fight, it means this city will be completely compromised. Is that understood?"

"Yes sir."

"How many other Ravens are in the air?"

"Last time I checked, three."

"Good," Adderson replied, even though he knew that meant two choppers had either been brought down or crashed when their pilots were turned. "You and another Raven take turns firing at that Class One to lead it to my position."

"That thing can fade in and out, sir. When it ghosts like that, nothing even ruffles its fur."

"Then act wounded and make it chase you. I don't care how, just bring it to me so we can all hit it in one concerted effort."

"All due respect, Major, but we haven't been collecting in a big group like that for a reason," Hendricks said. "What happens when we start to drop?"

It had become habit for soldiers in the IRD to assume any one of them would be turned at any given moment. Not only was it a harsh dose of reality, but it brought out the best in any fighting spirit. Adderson cringed when he heard it even though he'd been pivotal in starting the trend. It was nothing but a cold statement of fact when he replied, "We may drop now or later, but the longer this fight goes, the more of us will wind up turned into one of those things. And the more of us that go, the fewer volunteers we'll have to join this outfit and do what needs to be done."

"That's a load of shit, sir," Hendricks said without hesitation. "And with all due respect, I'd punch you in the mouth for saying it if I was there."

"Good, then prove me wrong."

"Yes, sir."

The connection was cut, and Adderson had no doubt it was so Hendricks could issue orders to the other helicopter pilots circling the city. Times might change and wars might come and go, but certain things remained constant. Sometimes a soldier just needed a good old-fashioned boot to the ass.

He lifted the radio to his mouth but paused before touching the button. Sensing a tremor working its way through his body, Adderson decided to let it pass before it put something into his voice that he didn't want broadcast to the rest of the IRD. When it turned out to be a simple shiver sent by the cold instead of a wave of broken bones sent by a deranged creature, he let out the breath he'd been holding and prepared to speak.

"Hunter One, this is Hunter Three!"

Grateful for another moment to prep himself, Adderson said, "Go ahead, Hunter Three."

"We found at least five packs of Class Twos in an apartment complex and they're being engaged by a team of specialists."

"Say again, Hunter Three?"

"Have found a large group of Class Threes, but there are specialists on site. Repeat, we have specialists on site."

All Adderson had to do was look up to see some very relieved expressions on his soldiers' faces. To Warren, he said, "Get down to the others and rally everyone to join Hunter Three."

"Will we be getting a lift from any of the Ravens, sir?"

"I'll try to arrange it, but we may be humping it across town. Either way, we're going in hot."

"Yes, sir!"

Before she could climb down from her post, another voice crackled through the radio. "Hunter Three, this is Raven Two. Looks like the Class One sniffed out those specialists of yours. It's headed your way. Over."

"This is Hunter One. Are there any Ravens in the area to take me and some of my troops in to meet up with Hunter Three?"

All of the chopper pilots chimed in with their positions. Raven Two was closest, so Adderson ordered them to make a quick pickup and sent the others to gather as many troops as they could before heading into the hot zone. The pilots gave their affirmatives and broke contact.

Less than fifteen minutes later Adderson was sitting on the edge of one of the fold-down seats inside Raven Two's cabin area. The rotors churned over his head as the helicopter navigated the Shreveport streets in a gut-wrenching series of hard turns that culminated with a drop into what could have been hell itself. Even through the noise of the engine, wind, and radio chatter from the cockpit, he could hear the wild howling and hungry snarls scattered amidst the choppy barrage of automatic gunfire. When an unwavering howl rose above everything else, the pilot followed safety procedures by immediately dropping to a safer altitude. Adderson broke some safety protocols himself by unbuckling his harness and grabbing onto one of the rails above his head so he could get a look out one of the windows.

The street below wound back and forth across a small field that could have been used for sporting events or maybe small carnivals or fairs. Adderson spotted plenty of bodies down there, but most of them were lying in gory pools. A few wolves picked at the carcasses and barked up at the helicopter, but the real action didn't pick up until the grass gave way to a parking lot surrounding a small complex of three story apartments. Two Humvees were parked at right angles to each other to provide some measure of cover for the soldiers keeping their backs to the doors. The helicopter's gunners were both still pulling the triggers of their .50 cals, which did nothing to discourage the onslaught of Class Twos pouring out of the middle apartment building.

Placing his finger to the button that would open the connection between him and the pilot, Adderson said, "Bring us in above those Humvees so we can lay down some support fire."

"Yes, sir."

Dusting in above the soldiers forced the troops on the ground to lower their heads and secure their loose clothing, but it also brought a few grateful shouts from the men who still had enough breath in their lungs to cheer. The copter's gunner sighted along the top of his belt-fed machine gun and sent a stream of lead into the encroaching werewolves. Cement and dirt alike were chopped up along with plenty of Class Two flesh and bone. The wolves that weren't cut into enough pieces divided into smaller groups and scattered. Once they got too close to the Humvees, the gunner eased back on his trigger.

"Where's the closest place you can set us down?" Adderson asked the pilot through the helmet radio.

"On one of those rooftops. Any closer and we're risking the bird, sir."

The IRD might have had the support of the United States military, but NH-90s didn't come cheap. And if this battle was going to be won, no available asset could be wasted. "Fine," he said. "Do it."

The helicopter rose straight up and eased over to settle above one of the apartment buildings. As soon as the gear touched down, the door was opened and troops were deployed. Last man out shut the door behind him and the bird was once again in the air and firing at another group of targets. Bing, bang, boom. Now if the rest of the day could run like that, Adderson thought, he would be a happy man. He carried his HK-G36, but some of the other troops had brought along semiautomatic Benelli M-4 shotguns. Several paçes before reaching the door that led into the building, two shotgunners moved forward to take point. They kicked the door in and headed down a narrow set of stairs that led to a maintenance room at the end of a long hall. The next set of stairs was lit by a flickering set of emergency lights. Judging by the boards nailed to the interior of the frames, the residents of those apartments had tried to defend their homes against the beasts that invaded their city.

One of the lead shotgunners stopped and raised a fist so everyone behind him could see it. The entire group came to a halt and waited silently for the next signal. With a minimum of hand motions, the shotgunner told them he saw something ahead and down the next set of stairs. At least two possible threats.

A pair of Marines carrying HKs moved up to join the shotgunners, and Adderson moved back. Once the new marching order had been arranged, he ordered them to proceed down the stairs and assess the situation. It was an open, square stairwell, which allowed the shotgunners to proceed downward and the Marines to cover them from higher ground. Adderson hung back with the remaining team members and divided his attention between the soldiers ahead and behind. There was no way for anything to get the drop on them without being spotted first. Of course, considering what they were up against, spotting the enemy usually wasn't the problem.

At the bottom of the stairwell something heavy smashed through a set of reinforced doors. Adderson could hear the doors being knocked off their hinges, followed by the loud clanging of iron bars hitting the floor. The IRD fire team remained where it was, sighting along their weapons and waiting for a target to present itself. When several rasping growls drifted in from beyond the broken entrance, he knew every one of the trigger fingers around him was tensing. He held up his hand, signaling the team to remain where it was as the scraping on the lower floors reached the bottom of the stairs. They were definitely Class Twos. Adderson recognized the mixture of hunger, pain, and rage in their rasping grunts.

He sent the two shotgunners forward so they worked their way to the next landing and dropped to one knee. By now Adderson and the Marines with the HKs had once again positioned themselves on higher stairs to look down at the shotgunners. The Class Twos were ripping at something. Those sounds, mixed with the tearing of wet meat and the lack of screaming, told him the wolves had found a dead body at the bottom of the stairwell. When one of the shotgunners looked up to him for instruction, Adderson pointed toward the rest of the team and made a sweeping motion that ended by pointing his fingers directly to the bottom of the stairwell. If the wolves decided to pick the wrong time for a snack, there was no reason that mistake couldn't be their last.

The lead shotgunner held up three fingers, ticked them off one by one, then led a shuffling charge down the stairs. All of their steps started quietly enough, but built in pace as well as intensity as the team got close enough to where they knew the wolves would hear or smell them at any second, no matter how stealthily they tried to approach. The chomping downstairs stopped as the first werewolf grunted and then barked up the stairs. By the time the small pack started scrambling upward, they were already being met by a volley of gunfire.

The shotgunners were first, and they unleashed a twelve-gauge torrent that tore into the werewolves' faces in a way that put a smile on the team members pulling the triggers. But despite that gloriously visceral payback for all of the blood they'd seen spilled, the IRD shooters weren't able to put the Class Twos down. That's where the team members on the upper stairs came in. Once the shotguns slowed the wolves down and ripped away enough of their flesh, more precise rounds drilled into the creatures' spines and skulls from a downward angle. For any other living thing, the result would have been instantaneous. Then again, Adderson mused as he pulled his trigger to send bursts into the pack of shapeshifters, no other living thing could have withstood the shotguns. Even though his team performed by the numbers, one of the Class Twos made it to a shotgunner and clamped its jaws around his shin.

Gritting his teeth as the fangs drove in deeper, the man pressed the Benelli's barrel against a gaping wound on the creature's face and pulled his trigger. The shotgun round exploded out through the back of the creature's head, but its grip on his leg only tightened. It took a few more concentrated bursts from the HKs to put an end to that reflex so the shotgunner could kick the dead beast away.

"You all right, soldier?" Adderson asked as he moved to the lower landing.

The shotgunner looked up and nodded without showing surprise that Adderson's gun was pointed at him. "I'm good to go, sir."

"Did the fangs get through?"

"Yeah, but just into the armor and some meat. Not the bone." Pulling in a pained breath, he said, "The specialists said they had to get all the way through to bone before I'd turn, right?"

"Right."

Adderson stared at the messy wound on the shotgunner's leg. Instead of the compassion he'd felt when seeing lesser wounds in other conflicts, he could only think about whether he should take the questionable data gathered by what amounted to a supernatural militia member over the knowledge he'd gained from the battlefield. "Do we have any more of that stuff the specialists mixed up for us to clean these wounds?"

The reply came from one of the Marines above him. "Used the last of it up yesterday, sir."

"If there's more specialists in the city," the other shotgunner offered, "then we could—"

"We could waste a lot of time on a gamble that they're carrying the exact supplies we need," Adderson snapped. Pointing to the second shotgunner and the Marine who'd spoken up earlier, he said, "You two stay here and dress the wound. If he starts to turn, you're to put him down immediately. Understood?"

"Yes sir."

The orders were taken without resentment or a second thought. That didn't mean Adderson didn't feel any pangs upon issuing them, however. Referring to his own troops like animals went against every instinct in his body but was a necessary evil in a world that had been fucked up beyond his ability to repair it. After signaling for the rest of the team to go down the rest of the stairs and sweep the next room, he brought the radio to his mouth and said, "Any Ravens in the vicinity of Zone Four?"

After a brief pause, Hendricks replied, "Never got too far from you, Major. Need a lift?"

"What's the status on that special delivery from up north?"

"Should be arriving within the hour. Over."

"And what about that Class One?"

"Ripping the hell out of a park, but he's awfully mobile. Doesn't seem to want to get too far away from those specialists, though."

"Do you have gunners?" Adderson asked.

"Down one after that last howl."

"Replenish your supply and pick up as many troops as you can. I'm bringing one along with me, so come and get us ASAP."

"What's the plan from there, sir?"

When Adderson pressed the radio's button, he felt like he was ready to crush the device in his hand. "We point every barrel we've got at that fucking Class One and burn it down."

"Roger that."

Chapter Thirty-One

Cole had never been to a therapy session.

Even when things got a thousand miles past stressful at Digital Dreamers, as deadlines crept in and forum trolls were anxiously awaiting a game they could rip apart and criticize while playing it online, he'd never felt the need to undergo any sort of counseling to exorcise his demons. And more recently, when he was introduced to what very well could have been real demons, he still hadn't considered doing much of anything that would be considered therapeutic. Injecting the healing serum into his arm had always gone a long way toward putting him into a bleary, vaguely dizzy sense of mind that was good for a solid night's sleep but was never enough to cool the searing heat that lanced through the base of his skull like a hot knife. That same headache plagued him now in a way that was a strange reminder of his days as a game designer. Funny how building deathmatch levels and running for your life from shapeshifters could trigger the same basic stress pains. And after so much practice with being spread too thin, he'd never come up with a better way to relieve stress other than the few moments of respite he found in the dark with Paige. Getting behind the grips of a belt-fed machine gun bolted to the window of an

NH-90 helicopter flying in low above the streets of Shreveport was a real close second.

The Half Breeds were out in force. Packs ran down every street, exploded from every alley, and roared up at him from nearly every window along what had been a business section of town filled with strip malls and chain restaurants. He'd never been to Shreveport, so he didn't know what that section of town had looked like before the Breaking Moon, but he knew what it looked like now: the best shooting gallery ever conceived. As soon as he saw a four-legged shape come into view, he aimed at it and fired. The machine gun rattled in its heavy frame, making a stuttering mechanical roar that filled his ears and brain with a numbing thump. Glass shattered. Bricks exploded. Cars rocked. Cement cracked. Most important, Half Breeds skidded out of control and were knocked around as if swept up in a powerful wind. As per the instructions he'd been given during his crash course in IRD training, Cole swept the gun back and forth until the Half Breeds stopped moving or fell apart into more than one piece. As the pilot banked steeply to round a corner, he eased off the trigger and caught his breath. Paige sat on one of the folding benches with two other IRD troops, all of whom looked at Cole behind cautiously raised brows.

"I needed that," was all he had to say.

Paige gave him a quick upward nod and replied, "When's my turn?"

"Better save the ammo," the soldier sitting beside her said. "We'll need it once we get closer to the LZ."

"Will we beat the others there?" Cole asked.

"Everyone else that came in with you should be driving straight across town to meet us. They should be waiting for us."

"Driving is faster than flying?"

The soldier nodded once. His darkly tanned face twisted into a mildly amused expression that showed good humor despite the fatigue that wore at every inch of his weathered skin. "When there ain't no traffic or cops around to get upset if you mount curbs or drive through the occasional yard, driving is pretty damn fast. Plus we've got to slow down when that machine gun is blazing away. Gives you better chances to hit something."

"Oh stop looking at me like that, Paige," Cole grunted as he flipped the safety on and set the gun barrel into the bracket that held it in place when it wasn't in use. "I took out plenty of those things."

"No explanations needed, sir," the IRD soldier told him. "Every one of those things were headed toward the primary LZ, which means they meant to put the hurt on the troops already there. We'll need all the breathing room we can get."

"You don't have to call him sir," Paige chided the soldier. "He was probably just pretending he was in a video game when he was firing that thing."

"You specialists may not have an official rank," the man replied, "but we all know what you guys do with them sticks you carry. None of us mind treating you with the respect you deserve."

"Tell that to your bosses," Paige sighed. "I have a feeling our days of going where we please are over."

"Not if the major has anything to say about it. Ever since you left, he's been all over the—"

The soldier was cut off when something slammed into the side of the helicopter with enough force to send it wobbling perilously close to an office building. The others tucked their heads down and secured themselves as they'd been trained to do, but it wasn't a routine affair for the Skinners. Cole and Paige did their best to keep from falling over as the helicopter spun through two complete rotations before it was pulled back onto a steady course. Before the pilot could get them right again, the craft listed to one side as its fuselage was torn open to the screeching cries of metal meeting claws.

Grabbing onto the machine gun's mounting, Cole pressed his back against the wall and looked straight across to the side door. Light from outside as well as streams of cool air poured in through four sets of openings created by the claws dragging through the fuselage. Another set of claws had punctured the metal a bit higher and to one side, only to curl inward as the helicopter launched into a series of tight, waggling maneuvers.

"Hang on," the pilot shouted. "Gonna try to shake it off!"

The only reactions on the soldiers' faces were a few closed sets of eyes and a whole lot of focus as they tried not to think about what was attempting to get at them. Cole couldn't do much more than that because he knew if he let go or allowed his muscles to relax, he'd find himself skidding straight toward the wrong side of that cabin. Before too long the pilot straightened the aircraft's course.

"Are we clear to fire?" one of the soldiers asked.

"That'll just rile it up," the pilot replied. "Let me take her down before you give that shaggy bastard a reason to kick."

Cole didn't take his eyes off the claws lodged in the door. He watched as they shifted so the long pointed ends dug deeper into the steel as the wide, fearsome visage of a Full Blood rose up to gaze in through the window. Its dark gray fur was matted with blood and pressed against its face by the wind. Even more blood was encrusted onto its fangs amid several smaller strips of loose meat and what looked to be part of a shredded uniform. Solid white eyes stared through the window to assess the contents of the military transport.

Cole had only seen Esteban a handful of times, none of which had been the up close and personal interactions he'd had with other Full Bloods. Liam had been a hell raiser and Henry was just plain crazy. Randolph could carry on articulate conversations in between bouts of homicidal rage. Those were far from friendly faces, but at least they were familiar. Somehow, even when facing things torn from legend, it made just a little more sense when he could put a voice to the face or a method to the madness. Esteban didn't bother stating its motivations to the insects he trampled. When Cole looked into those eyes, he knew there was no explanation coming. No time wasted in thought. There was only death to be found as his head phased into a ghostly image that moved through the door as easily as a stone through a cloud.

One claw remained solid, which allowed the Full Blood to launch his smoky body into the cabin. Before he could get all the way inside, Cole reached for the spear strapped across his back and charged at him. In its compact form, the main portion of the spear was just as long as the curved Blood Blade that had recently been attached to it. The charmed metal sliced through the air as easily as it sliced through the hazy image of the werewolf. Esteban opened his mouth in a silent expression that could have either been a laugh or a howl.

"You can't hurt anyone like that," Cole shouted over the thumping of the overhead blades and the whining of the straining engine. "And you're not scaring any of us, so you might as well fight or get the fuck out!"

Anger flashed in Esteban's eyes as he swiped at Cole with a paw that solidified halfway along its journey toward his face. Cole leaned back and reflexively swatted at the incoming paw. When the blade made contact, he felt about three-quarters of the resistance he might feel if he'd parried a normal blow. Rather than slash at him again, Esteban slammed his paw against the floor, dug his claws into the steel and willed himself to take a physical form.

"Fire!"

Paige had given the order as she freed herself from the harness holding her in her seat. Three of the IRD troops already facing the door pulled their triggers without bothering to get up. The soldiers on either side of her had more practice in disentangling themselves from the safety straps, so they were out and turned around much quicker. The gunfire exploding within the confines of the cabin was only eclipsed by Esteban's bellowing roar.

The Full Blood materialized like a bad dream, shrinking down to his more compact four-legged form, which was still almost too large to maneuver within the confines of the cabin with any effectiveness. Unfortunately, he didn't need to worry about being tripped up by posts bolted to the floor or structural elements within the aircraft itself. Steel, glass, and flesh alike all gave way as he lunged directly into the live rounds that thumped into his thickly muscled body.

The IRD troops closest to the door were knocked down with the first swipe of Esteban's paw. One of them caught the blunt side of the appendage while another felt every one of the curved claws dig through his body armor, gouge into his chest, and then emerge out the other side amid a bloody spray. The beast's victorious howl quickly turned into a pained cry as Cole drove the curved Blood Blade into his side. The impact seemed to surprise Esteban more than anything else, and he lost his footing in his haste to pull away from the charmed weapon.

Cole felt the blade carve through Esteban's flesh, but found himself staggering to the floor as the Full Blood shifted into the form he'd acquired during the Breaking Moon. Like a picture being shifted out of focus, the werewolf went from solid to incorporeal in two seconds. The next few shots fired at him sparked against the interior of the cabin before the soldiers eased off their triggers, and the rounds snagged in Esteban's fur clattered onto the floor.

Paige's voice rang out once again. "Bank hard left! *Now!*"

The IRD pilot had enough field experience to keep his cool under any circumstances and more than enough training to follow through on Paige's order. Everything in Cole's immediate vicinity tilted crazily to the right, sending him and a few of the soldiers down and rolling clumsily toward the side hatch. Esteban had a similar reaction, but lacked the physical presence to bounce off something or grab anything else. Instead, he slid along the floor while also melting through it. When he should have hit the wall, his body simply kept going. His progress was only stopped when one of his paws became solid enough to grab the floor.

"One more!" Cole shouted as he crawled over to where Esteban was hanging on. "Hard right!"

It took a moment for the pilot to reach a spot where he

could perform the maneuver, but he did so with even more sharpness than before. Not only did the bodies of the first two soldiers roll into the benches, but Esteban's weight dragged the helicopter down as he shifted back into his normal body. Cole didn't concern himself with that. The Full Blood's paw was solid, and that was the only target he cared about. Having braced himself against the shredded hatch, Cole gripped his spear in both hands and willed it to stretch out to its full length. Then he swung it in a diagonal arc that brought sparks from the floor and dug into Esteban's paw. Paige got to them by sliding on her knees across a floor that was tilting like a funhouse beneath her. The stake that grew from the sickle's handle dug into the Full Blood's paw, forcing him to let go. Esteban's angry howl rolled through the air as his body plummeted to the ground.

"You want me to keep rockin' and rollin'?" the pilot shouted back.

"No," Paige said in what was one of the few times Cole had ever seen her get even vaguely queasy. "For the love of all that's holy, level off."

"That Class One impacted behind us. Should I circle back?"

"Yeah. Just make sure we've got backup."

"Oh, that shouldn't be a problem."

Chapter Thirty-Two

Even after the helicopter had veered onto another course, Adderson's gaze was still fixed on the sky. "Where did that thing land?" he asked.

Warren stood on top of the Humvee, sighting through her binoculars. "I'd say about two or three klicks from here, but couldn't be much farther than that."

"Can you get us to that impact site?"

"Yes, sir."

"Then go!"

He, Warren, and the other troops they'd collected along the way piled into their vehicles and rolled down the street. Adderson still didn't have much of an idea about his location using any sort of civilian terminology. If he ever visited Shreveport again and someone gave him a street address, he'd probably get lost. But when someone referred to the grid that the IRD had set up that allowed them to navigate just about any urban environment, he'd know exactly what they were talking about.

"All Ravens," he said into his radio. "Give me a location on the shifter that was just dropped."

"This is Raven Two. Dropped that bastard into Sector

Fourteen, but I couldn't tell you if it's still there or not. Swung over to have a look, but it was already up and moving."

"Sector Fourteen," Adderson said to the Humvee driver. That was all the driver needed to hear to get the vehicle moving in the proper direction. Adderson scanned the side of the street for movement as he spoke into the radio. "Do you still have those specialists, Raven Two?"

"Yes sir. They're anxious to get back into the fight. Already told them you'd be joining the party. Was that speaking out of turn, sir?"

"Not at all. We engaged a large group of Class Twos in Sector Eight, but they were just wild and hungry. Most of the bigger ones are probably going to meet up with that Class One. All Ravens, deploy your troops and provide air support."

"You'll have it as long as we can stay in the air, sir," another of the pilots said.

"Negative, Ravens," Adderson snapped. "If the ground forces get overwhelmed, you are all ordered to bug out and regroup at the western rendezvous point. Those choppers are too damned expensive to be thrown away. Understood?"

One by one the pilots gave their affirmatives, but none of them seemed happy about it. Adderson tucked the radio away. No troops needed to be happy about their orders for them to be carried out. He knew the IRD soldiers were conditioned well enough to see them through before giving in to the panic that gnawed at all of them. If he thought about his current assignment for too long, he could still feel that panic creeping in at the edges. He shoved it back down and prepped his assault rifle. When the time came, that's all he would need.

The warning sirens had been off for some time. Any civilians who hadn't gotten into their shelters by now were on their own. Half Breeds swarmed through the city, racing through yards, bounding down streets, scampering along sidewalks, and even leaping onto first story roofs before rejoining the main flow that led into what had been designated Sector 14. Milosh looked out of his window as Half Breeds ran past the Humvee that met them shortly after their arrival in town. Some of them even kept pace long enough to glance over and snap at the vehicles. The driver jerked the wheel to the appropriate side to nudge the creatures along, which was enough to buy some space before any tires were shredded.

One of the soldiers who'd met them was a young Asian man with bright eyes and a curious smile. "So what's the deal with you guys?" he asked.

"Deal?" Milosh grunted.

"Yeah. Usually all you specialists carry sticks. What's with the knives and that post?"

Milosh turned in his seat to look at George, who carried his long weapon so the weighted end was resting on his shoulder and the claw was wedged between his feet. "What is the deal with that post, Georgie?"

"Nobody calls me Georgie, and if they do," the Amriany added while shifting so the weighted end of his weapon was on more prominent display, "they don't remember it. This post can make you forget your last three birthdays, know what I mean?"

"He's definitely talking to you, man," the soldier said.

"We are not Skinners," Milosh said. "We are called Amriany. In our language, this means both chosen and cursed. Appropriate, eh?"

The soldier shrugged and readjusted to get more comfortable in his seat. "Whatever. Now I see why the major just calls you all specialists."

From the front seat Nadya chuckled. It had been generations since an Amriany tasted the sweet scent of pure nature energies used by the Dryad. She knew Sophie would have loved to travel that way herself. If things went according to plan, there would be other chances. For the moment, the Amriany couldn't afford to send one of their most valuable assets into a wolf infested city.

The driver of the Humvee spoke on her radio and then

put the handset into a bracket mounted to the dash. "We're headed to Sector Fourteen." Glancing over to Nadya, she added, "Not far from here."

"I figured. Aren't we headed toward the spot where that Weshruuv was dropped like a rock from one of your helicopters?"

The driver's face cracked into a smile, making it seem almost pretty. The effect lasted for a few seconds before the Army shield was up again. "I guess that was a tough sight to miss, huh?"

"Yes."

"So. Wesh-roove. What language is that?"

Without bothering to correct the driver's pronunciation, Nadya told her, "It's a mix of lots of things. More of some and a sprinkling of others."

"My whole family's like that."

"Yes," Nadya said while glancing over her shoulder at the two Amriany crammed into the back with the other soldier. "Mine too."

The Learjet 45XR touched down at Shreveport Regional Airport, where it was immediately met by a military convoy. On any given day a year ago this would have gummed up the works for several commercial airlines and possibly hundreds of commuters. But since most of the people who wanted to leave the city had already done so, and nobody was too anxious to get there, the jet had the landing strip to itself as it taxied to a halt.

One of the soldiers who'd arrived to greet the plane stood on the tarmac with his back to the aircraft. Other soldiers stood alongside him, facing away, their rifles already raised to their shoulders. "How we doing on shifter activity?" the first soldier asked.

"Still a few packs in the airport, but Jeffries and Bukowski are keeping them occupied."

Glancing over his shoulder, the first soldier watched as the jet's side hatch was opened and steps were lowered.

About two seconds later he asked, "What the hell are they doing in there?" Rather than yell up into the jet, he tapped the shoulder of the man beside him and said, "Go up and see what's keeping them. We've got a limited amount of time here."

Esteban's howl echoed from another part of town, causing the IRD troops to shift their focus to the men beside them. It was more of a feral howl than the solid, vaguely melodic tones that infected random humans, and was cut off by the thump of multiple explosives, which ironically put the soldiers on the landing strip at ease.

The soldier who'd been sent into the jet ran up the steps and quickly poked his head out again to say, "It's not ready yet."

"What's not ready yet?"

"I don't know! Should I clear the cabin?"

"Can you do that without compromising any of the assets?"

The soldier at the top of the steps looked back, studied whatever was in the jet for a few seconds, and turned around without being able to disguise his wince. "Can't say for sure."

After a haggard sigh and a muttered curse, the soldier on the ground shot a quick glance to the others, who had formed a firing line in front of the jet's stairs. None of the troops indicated that they saw anything coming from the surrounding area, so the first soldier shouted, "If that aircraft isn't empty in three minutes, you're authorized to clear it by force."

Just as the soldier in the jet was about to acknowledge the order, something caught his attention and drew him back inside. He stepped up to the open hatchway but was shoved aside by a lump of a figure wrapped in a hooded sweatshirt, at least two sweaters, and a parka. Despite the soldier's protests and attempt to stand his ground, he was unable to keep himself from being moved away from the exit hatch so the lumpy passenger could depart.

"All I asked for was another few minutes!" the lump said. Although no hands could be seen beneath the multiple layers of clothing, squirming arms were wrapped beneath a tottering pile of cases, jars, and small coolers. Faded sweatpants led down into a pair of rubber boots that jangled noisily as the unfastened buckles rattled against each other with every shuffling step. "After breaking my windows, messing up my carpets, knocking over my comic boxes, and breaking down my door, the least you could do was let me finish!"

Another man in uniform stepped into view. It was the pilot, who wore a dark green jumpsuit and pushed his way past both the armed IRD soldier as well as the griping passenger. Not even getting jabbed by one of the sharp implements poking out from the bundle in the passenger's arms was going to prevent him from getting the hell off that jet. "If it was up to you, you wouldn't have left that damn apartment."

Daniels poked his head from behind the mound of stuff he was carrying. "I could have worked a lot better there than wedged behind some seats with my eardrums popping out of my skull."

The pilot rolled his eyes, walked down the stairs and patted the first soldier on the back. "They're all yours."

"You might want to stick close to us, Lieutenant," the soldier warned. "Class Twos are in the airport."

"After flying all the way from Chicago with that little jerk, I'll take my chances."

Daniels was escorted down the stairs by the soldier who'd gone up into the jet, along with two other IRD troops. Sally brought up the rear carrying several small cases that were either hanging from her shoulders or gripped in her hands. "Most of the work is done. There's just a few finishing touches, which we can get to on the way over. Is there enough room for him to work?"

"Should be," one of the escorts replied. He addressed her fondly while completely ignoring the Nymar's never-ending flow of gripes. Apparently it was a trick that everyone on that jet had learned, because none of them seemed anxious to acknowledge Daniels whatsoever.

When he got to the bottom of the stairs, Daniels looked up at the soldiers and let out a weary breath. "Where do we go from here?"

"You hear all that shooting and howling?"

Daniels listened for a second before nodding.

"That's where we're headed."

"Her too?" the Nymar asked while glancing back at Sally.

Upon hearing that, the soldiers who had previously been annoyed with Daniels took notice of him again. One was a tall man with thick, angular features and skin the color of burnt clay. The only patch he wore other than the IRD insignia was a faded sampling from an older uniform that read OURAY. "We'll look after her," he said.

"I was told on the way over that this city is just about overrun. Can you keep her safe here?"

"If worse comes to worse, we'll pack her up and fly her to the nearest Green Zone. Those places are the closest thing to safe that this country has anymore."

"Not just this country," Daniels sighed. Reluctantly, he nodded. Sally placed a gentle kiss on his cheek. "Might as well go with them, sweetie," he said. "You'll be better off than being with me."

"If I could help you, I would," she said while framing his face in her hands. "And if I could take you with me, I would too."

"You can still take me with you," Daniels told her. "Just knock out these armed men and hijack that plane."

"Sorry, but I just can't stand the thought of flying again with you right now."

Daniels's laugh was strained beneath the weight of all the stuff he was carrying. He was relieved when the soldiers from the firing line came along to take some of the heavier cases from him and carry them to the waiting Humvee. "I didn't go through this much to be with you just to let you go now," he said. "Just keep safe and I'll see you again real soon."

Ouray escorted Daniels to the Humvee. The Nymar didn't look back until he was inside the vehicle, but it was too late. Sally was already up the stairs and being locked behind the door while an old man in a jumpsuit scrambled to refuel the jet.

Chapter Thirty-Three

"What the hell does that thing want?" Adderson asked after emptying an entire magazine into a pair of Half Breeds that had charged at him without batting an eye at the dozens of other rounds thumping into their bodies.

Cole and Paige stood with their backs to a semi trailer that had probably been sitting in the parking lot behind the large store since before the Breaking Moon. The posts propping it up were rusted and caked in dirt. Cole knew as much because he'd spent the first twenty minutes after his arrival huddled beneath the trailer, looking out from behind those metal supports. Even as he inched away from cover, his foot remained in place, as if his ankle was attached to that post. "Doesn't matter what he wants."

"I thought you guys knew these things. Talked to them."

There were two other soldiers posted near the trailer with Adderson and the Skinners. Both of them turned to look at Cole and Paige.

"This one doesn't want to talk and he doesn't want to deal," Cole said. "Do you really need me to tell you that?"

"What about the one in Kansas City?" Adderson asked. "Didn't you get some help taking that thing down?"

Paige fired the last of the rounds from her Beretta, holstered it, then drew her sickles. "We won't be getting that kind of help here. What's with you, anyway? You were never interested in doing much of anything other than shooting these things before. Now you want to ask about getting help from Mongrels?"

Pointing his assault rifle's muzzle downward, Adderson said, "If siding with Class Threes is what it'll take to clear this city, then that's what we've got to do. Once this place goes down, there won't be much incentive to keep the higher ups from lighting up the rest of the cities that are being overrun."

"How much of the country is overrun?" Cole asked.

"Whatever you've heard on the news, times that by five."

"We stopped watching that crap."

"Let's just say it's bad," Adderson told him. "Even by our standards. Most recent estimates put the danger zones at sixty-five percent of the populated areas."

"Jesus," Paige breathed. "Is that this state or the whole country?"

"That's worldwide. U.S. figures are even worse. Some countries don't acknowledge being attacked by these things, but satellite imagery has been modified to pick up on the shifters' heat signature. They're everywhere. Something's been spreading this infection or whatever the hell it is even faster over the last two days. Whatever you were looking for, I hope you found it, because if this city falls, we might as well find a bunker and take our chances with whatever my bosses in DC decide to drop on us in the next air strike. All I can tell you is it won't be the little fireworks the Air Force has been flying in so far."

Cole gripped his spear and looked down at his coat. Over the last several minutes the Full Blood hide had taken a beating from Half Breeds and stray gunfire alike. Now that there were no more Snapper rounds or Blood Blade ammo flying around, he could run wherever he pleased as the IRD soldiers fired around him. Unfortunately, they'd barely made a dent in the packs that had converged on the parking lot to encircle the perch Esteban had chosen.

The Full Blood paced on top of the wide roof of a big name discount electronics store. Cole's former life flickered in his mind as he recalled a few late night openings he'd gone to in stores just like that one when new games or consoles were released. In those years, smelling plastic wrap was more than enough to get his blood flowing. Now there were other ways to do that job. A small trickle of it seeped between his fingers as he drove the thorns of the spear's handle deeper into his palms. "Has Daniels arrived yet?"

"Landed about half an hour ago," Adderson said. "Troops met his plane and are en route to us now."

"Is he alone?" Paige asked.

"Negative. There was a woman with him, just like you said. Sent one of my best assault teams to his apartment. They reported the place was torn to shit and damn near empty. Nymar had been crawling inside and outside the entire building, tore apart most of the apartments, even killed some of the civilians living there. Most of the stuff you requested was either destroyed or missing, but the team found Daniels and the woman dug in good and tight inside a fortified closet. Hell of a good design as far as panic rooms go. Even Ouray was about to write them off before the door was popped open from the inside."

"Did he bring what he needed to bring?" Cole asked.

"You mean the aerosol containing questionable metallic elements?" When the Skinners glared at him, Adderson told them, "Daniels kept his mouth shut about it, right until a can exploded during the flight. I thought he was smart enough to know about little things like cabin pressure."

"God damn it," Cole grunted. "Did he lose it all?"

"We'll find out soon. Better lay down some covering fire to clear a space big enough for our guests." The soldiers in the immediate vicinity fanned out and fired into the Half Breeds in a series of three-shot bursts.

Now that their attention had been drawn back to the parked trailer, the Half Breeds barked at the soldiers and charged at them with renewed vigor. Cole had been content to focus on the trailer to keep himself from panicking as the night grew darker and werewolves continued to pour into the parking lot from every direction. His conversation with Adderson had been a distraction from the task at hand, but now there was no getting around the reality of what was happening.

The helicopter that brought him and Paige to meet with Adderson had met up with another one, and now both were circling so their machine guns could tear into the Half Breeds. A third helicopter, which got too close to the electronics store, wavered after Esteban's howl and was taken down by a swarming mass of Half Breeds.

Several of the IRD soldiers had been turned during that same howl and were gnawing off the last of their uniforms so they could acquaint themselves with their new forms.

Of the three Humvees that had arrived in the last few minutes, only one remained. It was at the far end of the parking lot, somewhere between 100 and 150 yards away. A gunner in place behind the mounted .50 cal was being defended by the Amriany, who had been brought to the rendezvous point. Light from the few bulbs that still burned atop dented poles glinted off the charmed steel in George and Nadya's grasp. Although Cole could only see the Amriany in fleeting glimpses, he could tell it wouldn't be long before they were either brought down or forced to retreat.

Overhead, the sky had turned an inky black as thick cloud cover rolled, vaguely illuminated by a waning moon. Now that the wave of Half Breeds had caught a new scent and decided to turn away from the faltering IRD squads, they tore at the Skinners with claws that ripped apart the pavement and churned it into a cloud of gritty dust.

There was no more time to waste in waiting for Daniels. Cole and Paige both knew that the Full Blood could leap away any time he chose. There was something keeping Esteban at that spot, which must have also been whatever had brought him to Shreveport.

"This must be where he's drawing from the Torva'ox," Cole said as he set his sights on the Full Blood.

"Give me that divining rod thing," Paige said. Cole flipped open his coat to reach into one of the large interior pockets. The object he drew out was an amalgam of his old spearhead, some pieces of Paige's old sickle blades, and a tool Ira had used to harvest the Torva'ox to be put into his Blood Blades. The Jekhibar fit into a small rack designed for that very purpose near the middle of the tool, which tapered down into a spike about four inches long. She held the Jekhibar to her ear and listened for the hum. "There's a big source somewhere close, all right."

Watching her listen to a shiny rock brought some questions to Adderson's mind, but he decided not to waste the time to ask them. "What do you need from us?"

"When will Daniels be here?" Cole asked.

"Should be any minute. And," the IRD Major added while pointing to the other end of the parking lot, "he should be coming from that direction."

"Keep the Half Breeds as busy as you can, but don't push too hard. Keep them occupied, but don't drive them away from the parking lot," Cole said. "Know what I mean?"

Paige handed the divining rod back to him and said, "Just keep shooting those things without shooting us."

Adderson nodded. "I can do that." Into his radio, he announced, "All Ravens, maintain a perimeter and lay down enough fire to keep any more Class Twos from flanking us. All ground units, protect the incoming Humvee!"

Looking in the direction Adderson was shouting, Cole spotted the vehicle that had just pulled into the lot. It was spouting a continuous stream of fire from its turret as it swerved to join up with the Humvees still being guarded by the Amriany. "All right," he said to Paige. "This is about as good as it's gonna get for us. Let's move."

She holstered the Beretta, slung an HK across her shoulder, and then drew both of the weapons from her boots. The handles were the same as always and bit into her palms in a familiar fashion. As soon as the connection was made, however, Paige gave the weapons a command that she'd only needed since Ira tinkered with them. The Blood Blades he'd attached were narrow and slightly curved so they could lay alongside the handles and still fit within the holsters. Although the metal wasn't pliable, the wood to which they were attached responded as well as ever. The section at the top of the handles flexed like an elbow, causing the blades to spring upward and give the weapons a shape similar to the sickles she was used to. As she jogged to keep up with Cole, she twirled the weapons in a tight circle to get a feel for their weight. The smirk on her face proved that she was a fan of Ira's work.

Cole held onto his spear like he was charging at Gettysburg. The long blade at the end sliced through the first Half Breed it encountered before the werewolf could let out more than a surprised yelp. That was enough to alert the others, and the packs quickly turned toward them. IRD troops entrenched at various spots around the parking lot or on neighboring rooftops took advantage of the moments when the creatures shifted their focus toward Cole and Paige. Bullets thumped into Half Breed backs and heads, sending some of them down for good while softening up plenty more. Paige swung to clip a Half Breed in the face, and the chopping motion she made with her left weapon gave her the momentum to move forward and cut down one Half Breed after another with the Blood Blades. By the time they were halfway to the Humvees, the creatures had pulled back to come at them from different angles.

The werewolves weren't bright enough to put together a complicated plan, but they'd seen enough of their pack mates get killed while charging straight ahead. Now, when one creature jumped at Cole's head, another pressed its belly to the pavement to scurry at his legs. Cole jabbed at the first to impale it beneath the jaw. All it took to free the blade was a sharp swing and the charmed steel cut all the way through, as if the Half Breed was constructed of hot wax. From there he kept the spear moving so he could open the tines of the forked end, shove the lower Half Breed's neck toward the ground to grind it to a halt and then turn the weapon around to drive the blade straight down through its spine. The werewolf let out one last shuddering growl before Cole plucked the blade out and moved on.

Where he delivered slower, heavier hits, Paige's were quick and slashing, coming in a flurry of nonstop movement. With so many creatures attacking, she didn't bother to stop and finish off each one. When a Half Breed was cut down, she went on to the next one that stood between her and the Humvees. She assumed Cole would be with her, and he didn't let her down. Both Skinners made it through the parking lot to meet up with the Amriany.

"You shouldn't have come here," Milosh shouted as he threw one of his knives into the eye of a Half Breed and then filled that hand with a .44 Magnum. "We need to get to that Weshruuv!"

"Didn't come for you," Paige said as she headed for one of the other armed vehicles. Before she could say another word, the door to that Humvee was opened and Daniels spilled out.

"Steph's reclaimed Chicago," the Nymar wheezed. "All of it. Barely got out."

"Great," Paige snapped. "Did you finish that spray?"

"Had to mix another batch on the plane, but yes," he said while handing over a can that still bore the label of a generic oven cleaner. The bottom was heavily taped, making it look more like a crude pipe bomb than anything Daniels normally pieced together for them.

"Glad to see you're alive," Cole said. "What happened in Chicago?"

Appreciating the concern, Daniels said, "Remember how I was always so worried Steph or some of the others would come after me? Well they finally did. And remember how I told you about that new room I fortified?"

"No."

"Well, it held out just fine, even when the Shadow Spore climbed in through the windows. I think they were sniffing us out, but these Army guys showed up and took them out.

Ruined two of my three apartments along the way, but you know. Whatever."

"Yeah," Ouray said from where he knelt so he could use the vehicle for support as he fired a single shot from a sniper rifle. It was modified beyond Cole's ability to identify the make or model. "Killed a bunch of vampires before they harmed a hair on you or your girlfriend's head. Whatever."

Cole extended a hand to the IRD commando and introduced himself. By the time Ouray returned the favor, Paige had finished checking out the spray can.

"You're sure this has a strong enough mix to get the job done?" she asked.

"Sure," Daniels replied, rooting through his satchel. "I tested it on the other phantom Full Bloods that were sitting around my place. Now roll up your sleeves."

Ouray's face didn't look like one capable of registering surprise. That changed when he saw the electric needle Daniels took from his bag. Less than fifty yards away the gunner in one of the helicopters laid down enough fire to scatter a large group of Half Breeds that had been charging toward the Humvees. More fire from the vehicle's turret gave the ground troops a few moments to catch their breath. In that time, Daniels set up inside the Humvee so that each of the Skinners could take their turn getting a dose of the tattoo ink, which had been all but perfected in the last year.

"I'll take a cool snake," Cole said when it was his time to put his arm into the Nymar's care.

Glancing out the window where Paige stood to fight off Half Breeds that made it past the IRD firing line, Daniels asked, "What about a drink? You must be starving." Cole didn't respond. Unwilling to bring up the tendrils directly in the company they were keeping at that moment, the Nymar asked, "Is your stomach hurting?"

"No."

"It will be soon. Then you have to feed them."

"No I don't," Cole insisted. "Just do the damn tattoo, Daniels."

The needle buzzed in Daniels's hand as he hastily scrawled into Cole's arm. There was no design other than a few lines of varying thickness that traced along his veins to make sure the inky concoction and shapeshifter elements bonded to the minerals in the ink would have their desired effect. As long as the stuff remained beneath the flesh, it could pass on some of a shapeshifter's strength and speed into a human and burn off before it did any real damage.

"You seem to have been handling yourself pretty well so far," Daniels said. "But don't push it. Those tendrils will punish you if—"

"I know all about that," Cole cut in.

Daniels nodded and completed another line of ink. Since he wasn't going for anything artistic, it wasn't a long process. Even though he'd taken his finger off the button that made the machine buzz, he left the needle in Cole's arm. "You know, it's not unusual for the newly seeded to be squeamish."

"I'm not seeded," Cole grunted. He wanted to pull his arm away but couldn't.

"Maybe not with a spore, but you've still got Nymar elements inside of you."

"Making it sound clinical doesn't help. Now get that damn needle out of me before I rip it out and put it somewhere you won't like very much."

Either Daniels had been around Paige too long to be frightened by threats or was too determined to give up talking that easily. "However you want to put it, those things need to be fed."

"I know. I'll deal with it."

The needle was jammed just far enough into Cole's skin to catch his attention. When his eyes narrowed into a deathly stare, Daniels held his ground and said, "You need human blood and I know you've tasted it."

"How do you know that?"

"Because you're still alive."

"Nymar blood seems to do the trick just as well," Cole

said in a threatening snarl, even though there was some truth to Daniels's words.

To his credit, Daniels remained steady. "That's because Nymar used to be human. Half Breeds used to be human as well."

"Are you suggesting I feed on those things?"

"Better that than die. Times are hard, right? Isn't that what everyone's saying?"

"It sure is."

"Then you've got to do what you've got to do to survive. You and Paige are doing more than surviving. You're helping the rest of us to survive, and we can't lose you." The pressure of the needle in Cole's skin eased up but didn't subside. "And what's so bad about what I'm suggesting compared to what you guys do all the time? I mean, you wear Half Breed skins, for God's sake. You had an up close and personal relationship with the thing that used to wear the leather that coat was made from, right?"

Cole didn't say anything to that. The fighting outside had died down for a moment, which only meant it would soon intensify.

"The Half Breeds may not be human anymore, but there's human blood inside them," Daniels said. "There's plenty of it around and it may take the edge off."

"But . . . Jesus. I mean skinning them is one thing. Using their claws or teeth is easy enough. But drinking their blood?"

"Being a Nymar may be a lot of things, but sanitary isn't one of them. Just keep it in mind, okay? Think of it as another way of using what they give you so you can keep fighting the good fight. That's what Skinners do, isn't it?"

"Yeah. Speaking of that, I could use some of the healing serum if you've got any."

Daniels's eyes narrowed as he removed the needle. "I'll administer it when this is over. You need to stay sharp."

Even though Cole wasn't hurt and he could produce a certain amount of the serum within his own body, he didn't hold back when he grabbed Daniels's wrist and twisted until the Nymar let go of the tattooing machine. "You're not my doctor. Give me more serum."

"I'm your friend," the Nymar replied through gritted teeth. "And I'm also like you more than you care to admit. I know what I'm talking about, and it'll take more than brute force to make me do what you're asking. The Nymar were putting me through a hell of a lot more than that before you ever knew what they were. Now would you rather waste more time or do you want to let me work on the next tattoo before all of us are overwhelmed?"

Outside, the IRD had launched multiple attacks to keep the Half Breed packs divided. The price of that strategy was paid by the loss of more soldiers than Cole cared to think about, as they were either ripped apart or turned by Esteban's howls. He let go of Daniels, kicked open the Humvee door, and allowed George to crawl into the back.

Chapter Thirty-Four

Even though George's weapon didn't have a blade, it must have been charmed in a similar fashion as the other Amriany edged weapons, Cole decided, because it did just fine against the Half Breeds. George and he took the lead as Milosh, Paige, and Nadya covered their backs. Thanks to the ink introduced to their bodies, their blows landed with enough force to sever limbs or knock Half Breeds aside completely.

Farther out, IRD guns still chopped into the encroaching werewolves without putting much of a dent in the overall Half Breed population. For every creature mowed down by excessive large caliber gunfire, another ran in from another part of the city. As the night wore on and Esteban continued to howl, Shreveport slid even closer to the abyss. Cole knew better than to mourn for the things he hacked apart with his newly upgraded weapon. His blade hadn't been the one to kill those people. That was Esteban's doing or the fault of the creatures that had been set loose. All that was left to do now was see to it that the Full Bloods were prevented from finishing what they started when the Breaking Moon had risen.

A helicopter swung in low to hover over the Skinner and

Amriany team, but before its gunner could find his mark, the aircraft was attacked by half a dozen Half Breeds responding to a guttural bark from the Full Blood perched upon the edge of the roof. As the NH-90 swung out and away from the electronics store to try and shake the werewolves off, Cole could hear the pilot screaming in pain. By the time it crashed, George was smashing his way into the store with the weighted end of his weapon.

The inside of the building was identical to any number of places Cole had visited. There was a group of carts next to the entrance, which he and the others ran past before skirting two rows of cash registers. As they rushed between rows of newly released DVDs, a Half Breed leapt at him from atop a large metal shelf designed to hold plasma screen TVs. Cole caught it with the forked end of his spear, diverting the creature until it slammed down to crack several floor tiles with its body. He removed its head with one swipe of the Blood Blade.

More Half Breeds leapt through and over the shelves, knocking over the single television set that hadn't already been trashed. George swatted one away and went to work on the others by spinning his iron weapon like a propeller. The weighted end pulverized already broken bodies, and the claw opened wounds that wouldn't be healed. Any Half Breeds that tried to get up were finished off by Paige, Nadya, and Milosh.

The parallels weren't lost on Cole when he sent a Half Breed flying into the video game aisle where it demolished a display of *Hammer Strike* action figures and strategy guides. "Where's that Torva'ox coming from?" he asked.

Blinking quickly to make sure the drops she'd put in before breaching the store were soaked in, Paige pointed toward a section of flooring that had been crudely ripped away. "Right here, I think." She looked straight up and then tightened her grip on her weapons. "Yep. This seems like the right spot."

"You sure?" Cole asked.

Pointing up to a massive hole in the roof, she replied, "Again . . . yep."

Since the power hadn't been on for a while, there wasn't a huge difference in temperature when Cole stood next to Paige to get a look at the hole that showed him a cold winter sky. Grit from outside sprinkled down, along with chunks of cement and plaster, as a figure loomed above the hole to peer down at them. An explosion from the battle between the IRD and Half Breeds illuminated enough for him to see a snout, a clawed hand, and part of a furry chest. Then Esteban lowered his face to fix his white eyes upon them, his lips parting to display rows of uneven fangs.

"You have shown yourselves too late to do anything but bleed," the Full Blood said in a rich Spanish accent.

Cole shifted his spear to his left hand so he could reach into his coat with his right and draw the divining rod from his pocket. "Don't mind us," he said, approaching a spot in the middle of the torn-up section of flooring. "We're just here to plug a leak." He pointed the metal end of the rod at the floor and drove it down. The sparks that crackled from the rod weren't as dramatic as he'd been hoping for, but they caught the Full Blood's attention. Even without the drops in his eyes, Cole could feel the electric crackle in the air die down as the Jekhibar soaked up the power the Full Blood was trying to use.

"Gypsy alchemy!" Esteban snarled. "You don't even know why I've chosen this place."

"Don't know," Paige shouted, "and don't care. We're just here to clean up the mess."

Having gotten only a minimum of instruction from Ira about what the divining rod was supposed to do, Cole grabbed the wooden end with both hands and twisted it as if exacerbating a giant wound. More sparks flew and the metal spike sank in a little deeper, which caused some of the glyphs inscribed on that end to pulse with a dim orange glow.

Esteban gripped the edge of the hole in the roof and

swung his feet over the side. He dropped all the way down, clipping a set of broken lights as well as the piping of what was probably a sprinkler system that had been broken due to neglect. His paws thumped solidly onto the shattered floor and his claws sank in through broken tile. "We have stood by too long," he growled. "That is over. Your only hope is to hide and pray to escape our notice until your short lives dwindle to an end."

Paige stepped forward and willed both sickles to fold down so they could be holstered in her boot. Reaching into one of the pockets of the jacket worn over her tactical vest, she said, "Why don't you just disappear into a forest or somewhere scenic like your friend Randolph?"

The Full Blood's face twisted into something of a smile. "You have no idea what Randolph is doing. If you had any sense at all, you'd allow the rest of us to gather our forces so we can better deal with what he is prepared to unleash."

"Like there's anything worse than this?" she replied. Paige's hand emerged from her pocket holding the vial that Tristan had given her. "That's the advantage to being completely screwed. The only direction to go from there is up."

Esteban shook his head as if silently pitying a small child, then shifted into a bulky four-legged form and leapt at the largest group of humans. Rushing forward to join them, Cole took a straight jab at the werewolf with the newly modified tip of his spear. The weapon not only felt better in his hands than the last time he'd swung it, but the wooden section responded fluidly to his mental command for it to grow into something better suited for fighting a Full Blood. The forked end widened so it could catch one of Esteban's thicker limbs, and curved spikes emerged from the ends of both tines, making that end of the spear resemble the talon on a bird of prey. Before his limb could be completely ensnared, Esteban phased into a ghostly image so the weapon as well as a follow-up swing from the Blood Blade could pass through without harming him.

The Amriany spread out to surround the Full Blood.

Nadya wielded a short sword but was obviously more accustomed to automatic weapons. She swung tentatively at Esteban's spectral form, and as soon as her sword passed through it, he became solid enough to rip a set of bloody grooves across her face and neck. She twisted away and stumbled backward, hitting the ground on her side.

After running back to the torn section of floor, Cole drove his spear into the exposed dirt beside him. As soon as the blade was wedged solidly in place, he reached out to twist the divining rod, using both hands. The sparks that flew didn't seem to hurt Esteban, but they drew the Full Blood's attention. Several Amriany blades as well as a few short chopping attempts from Paige passed through his wraith form as he stalked toward Cole. Opening his mouth in a roar that could not be heard, the beast charged.

Claws that were incorporeal one moment and solid the next scraped at the floor. Saliva that dripped from his fangs either dissipated into nothing or spattered onto nearby shelves. Cole stepped away from the divining rod, took the spray can from the pocket of his coat and waited for Esteban to get closer.

Explosions and gunfire from outside faded into a muffled rush.

Flickering lights seeping in through the windows became a dim smear at the edges of Cole's vision.

After all of the hell he'd put his body through to learn how to swing his weapon or trade blows with stronger creatures, it now all boiled down to standing in one spot, waiting for the right moment to push a button. Who said playing video games wasn't going to help him in real life?

Part of Esteban's head and most of his front paws began to solidify in preparation for tearing the unarmed Skinner in half. Dropping down to one knee, Cole pointed the spray can at the Full Blood's spectral lower half and pressed the button that sent a shimmering silver mist into the air. He kept his finger solidly in place as he launched himself sideways into a roll while twisting his body around to put his back to Esteban. Thick claws raked against the shoulder of Cole's coat, penetrating the tanned werewolf hide deep enough to shred through a few upper layers of flesh. He clenched his eyes shut through the pain and continued to roll while hastily calculating how far he was from his spear. Every second that passed, Cole expected to feel the weight of that Full Blood drop on him like a collapsing portion of the roof.

He wound up on his stomach just short of slamming into a wire display rack. Propping himself up, he pulled his feet beneath him to find Esteban still standing in the spot where he'd initially landed. The Full Blood's back was arched and his head craned back and forth. The glittering metallic specks that were added to the aerosol hung suspended in the Full Blood's body like stars in an inky night sky as Esteban was painfully forced back into solid form. His voice returned too, booming with an agony and rage that gave Cole an extra burst as he ran to the spot where his spear still protruded from the floor.

Pieces of his body flickered like a fading television signal, but the aerosol was doing its job by making it next to impossible for him to shift into an insubstantial form. Esteban reared up and screamed as the powdered Blood Blade fragments shifted inside him.

The Amriany attacked from left and right. Nadya was still on the floor but managed to pull a borrowed assault rifle around from where it was strapped over one shoulder. As Paige and Milosh were driving their blades into the werewolf, George joined them. Although some of their tattoos had burned off, there was enough remaining in them to batter Esteban or cut into him with more brutal efficiency than the Full Blood could have expected from any human.

Still, no matter how deeply the Blood Blades cut or how many times he was rocked by a thumping impact from George's iron staff, the Full Blood was too enraged to be put down. He slashed at Milosh, knocking him aside with ease. Paige ducked beneath the claws intended to take her head off, and George blocked that paw with the middle section of his weapon. Cole plucked his spear from the floor and stood so one of his heels remained in contact with the divining rod. That way he could swing and parry as much as he needed without losing track of where the specially crafted tool could be found.

The Full Blood threw a backhanded swipe in Cole's direction, which was diverted by an expertly performed block using the forked end of his spear. Before he could attack Cole again, the Full Blood was swarmed by Paige and George. Overhead, the thumping of helicopter blades blew in through the damaged roof as one of the NH-90s settled into position over the store.

"Move him closer to the opening," Ouray said through the earpiece. "I found a few more of those Snapper rounds."

"They won't do much against a Full Blood," Cole said as he reached back to grab the divining rod. He twisted it again and then dragged it through the ground as he backed up to move beneath the ragged hole.

"Maybe not," Ouray said calmly through the earpiece, "but it might give you some breathing room."

Since he wasn't about to argue with getting backup, Cole shouted, "Over here!" to Esteban as well as Paige and the Amriany. Paige, who also wore one of the earpieces, already knew what he was trying to do, and swung both sickles at the Full Blood. Her eyes glazed over as she hacked at Esteban. She moved with deadly fluidity, ducking and leaning to clear a path for a few attacks without seeming to notice that sections of her tactical vest had been ripped away. Nadya stopped firing, but George and Milosh closed ranks around Paige as one swipe from the werewolf completely shredded the layer of Half Breed skin that was her vest's main line of defense. A clubbing blow from the claw at the end of George's staff that finally dropped Esteban down to all fours.

The glyphs etched into the divining rod were seething now. Cole could smell burnt iron, which meant the Jekhibar had absorbed all it possibly could. Plucking the rod from the ground, he prodded the Full Blood with it to create an even bigger shower of sparks.

Drawing once more on his experience as a game developer when something unexpected and cool happened, Cole pretended it had been his idea. “You want me to stop that?” he asked as Esteban looked at him. “Then come and make me!”

The Full Blood’s thick torso was accented by protruding ribs and a backbone that rose up like a stony ridge from a desert floor. He nipped at George to make him back off. Then he barked and swiped at Milosh to send a spray of Amriany blood through the air. Paige held her ground, staying behind him in case Esteban decided to move too far away from the hole in the roof.

Cole held his spear in one hand and the divining rod in the other. When Esteban was close enough, he stepped forward to jab the sharpened end of the Amriany tool at the Full Blood’s head and shoulder. The reaction between the divining rod and the werewolf was similar to a live wire brushing against a piece of wet steel. Esteban bared his teeth and lifted his face toward the roof as a shot was fired at him from above.

The round cut the air with a deeper hiss than a normal bullet. Esteban’s entire body was pulled to one side when the heavy projectile thumped between his shoulder blades, skidded against his flesh and lodged in his fur. Cole was close enough to see the blood-smeared round poking out from his coat. When Esteban turned to bite at the thing lodged in his fur, the humans renewed their attack. The Full Blood slammed the side of his head against Cole’s shoulder, knocking him off his feet, to sail several yards through the air and into a case filled with empty display boxes of games that were current before Shreveport had been overrun.

Although he couldn’t see her, due to the huge werewolf blocking his line of sight, Cole could hear Paige over the earpiece when she asked, “How many more rounds do you have?”

"Just one," Ouray replied.

"Take it!"

"Fine," the IRD commando said, and worked the bolt of his rifle.

Cole pulled in a breath and focused on what needed to be done. It looked as if they were already down by two. Nadya wasn't up yet and Milosh was struggling to get away from Esteban so he could catch his breath. The only one occupying the Full Blood was George, who slashed at the werewolf or pounded against his ribs, depending on which end of his weapon he was using. There were a few more stages of the plan that needed to be carried out, and if one of them didn't happen, the whole thing failed. And if the plan failed, everyone who'd died in Shreveport would have done so for nothing.

Tossing away his spear, Cole grabbed the divining rod in both hands so he could more effectively use it as a weapon. When he found a wound that had been opened by a Blood Blade, he attacked it using the splintered points of the broken Skinner weapons Ira had attached to the divining rod. The thorny protrusions made contact with the wound and completed a circuit that gave the stored Torva'ox energies somewhere else to go. Even though Ira insisted that's what would happen, Cole had been skeptical. But the energies flowing through fragments of a shattered Blood Blade had caused Esteban's body to twitch and the open wound on the side of his neck to pulse with enough raw energy to illuminate the crimson texture of his muscle tissue.

"I know that hurts," Cole said. He was close enough to see that the Full Blood's eyes weren't completely white after all, but more like smooth ivory circles resting on multifaceted ice crystals. By the time a rifle cracked over the rotors churning above the building, the Full Blood was shifting into his upright form. Cole heard the distinctive hiss of the incoming round as if it had been fired into a vacuum.

For the next heartbeat the path of that round was all that mattered.

It needed to hit the breach in Esteban's natural armor to give the Skinners enough time to deliver the Memory Water.

Cole thought about all of this in the time it took to blink. Meanwhile, Esteban snapped a hand up so the bullet could slap against his palm with its distinctive *snap.* He crushed the dart and threw the pieces away before leaning forward to spit a defiant growl into Cole's face.

It was all Cole could do to jump aside before the Full Blood's jaws clamped shut around his head. Already Esteban was shaking off the effects of the aerosol as well as the jolt from the divining rod, and Cole knew it wouldn't be long before he shifted into something that couldn't be harmed by bullets or blades, no matter how charmed they were.

When Esteban stood up and roared, every Half Breed outside joined him. The chorus was drowned out by a wave of heavy gunfire mixed with the screams of soldiers whose bodies were broken down into those of wild animals. Even though his system was inoculated with more than enough serums to protect him from changing, Cole could feel the Breaking tug at his skeletal structure. He held onto his weapon, ran at the Full Blood and shouted, even though he couldn't hear his own voice.

Esteban batted away one of Milosh's blades and tore open a messy gash across his neck with a swipe that was hardly more than a blur. Before Milosh dropped, Esteban turned and snapped at George. The Amriany held his weapon horizontally so the werewolf could clamp down on it instead of anything vital. With one powerful twist, George yanked the staff free and slashed Esteban's face with the weapon's sharpened claws. The werewolf pivoted before Cole could drive the Blood Blade into his side and knocked him down. Esteban's claws shredded his coat but were unable to go much deeper. Paige stepped in to snag his wrist using the curved blade of her sickle before the killing blow could be delivered, but he swung at her with enough force to rustle her hair when she ducked beneath the savage blow.

The beast's fangs glistened with saliva and his breath

stank of blood as he leaned forward to sink his teeth into the portion of Cole's chest that was exposed, thanks to the shredded coat. Less than an inch before he got there, the weighted end of George's weapon thumped against Esteban's face and diverted his bite a few vital inches to the left. That reprieve, however, only lasted until the Full Blood's vicious backhand sent George into one of the shelves in the next aisle. Cole took a straight shot with his spear but the weapon was knocked aside before its blade could draw another drop of blood. Esteban's mouth yawned open. His fangs dug into Cole's temple and chin. Somehow, the Skinner leaned back so those teeth only gouged him and sent a flow of blood down his face. From there, Cole nearly tripped over himself in his haste to put some distance between himself and the werewolf.

Esteban trembled as a few drops of Cole's blood dripped from his fangs onto his tongue. He strained to get closer so he could take a real bite, but was restrained by something that caused his eyes to clench shut and his head to arch back. Paige clung to his upper back, hanging onto the grips of her weapons as the curved blades came around the front of his neck to keep him from getting any closer to Cole. Roaring as the Blood Blades cut into his flesh, Esteban reached up to grab her arms in an attempt to pull her off.

Cole held his spear in a two-handed grip and jammed the blade into Esteban's chest. The charmed metal cut deeply, but there were several layers of solid muscle as well as bone that could very well have been cast iron beneath it.

"Not yet!" Paige screamed. "Don't kill him yet!"

"Shut up and get down from there," Cole replied through gritted teeth.

"Just get that divining rod ready!" As she spoke, Paige struggled to keep from being pulled in half. The only thing that allowed her to put up any sort of resistance was the last bit of tattoo ink flowing through her muscles. The enhanced-strength bought her leeway to squirm within Esteban's grasp. When his fingers closed in even tighter, she needed to resort to more creative measures. Her fists were poking out of his clutches, and the sickles had been moved away from his throat. Just as her body was pulled to its limit, she willed the sickle handles to bend so the blades snapped down as if they were about to be holstered. They cut into Esteban's fingers deep enough to force the Full Blood to let her go before his hands were mutilated.

Since his weapon wasn't able to go in any deeper, Cole removed the spear and stepped back before he could be cut down by a wild bite. When Paige didn't hop down from Esteban's back right away, he shouted, "You all right?"

She didn't answer, so Cole hurried around the Full Blood in the direction George had been thrown. The Amriany wasn't on his feet yet but was propping himself up using his staff. Nadya was nearby, laying completely still in a growing pool of blood. Milosh was gone. His body lay in a heap that hadn't shifted so much as an inch since he'd been cut down.

"Paige, jump away!" Cole shouted.

She tossed a sickle, used that hand to grab some fur on Esteban's back, and drove the curved blade of her other weapon in deep behind one of his shoulders. That strike came just when the Full Blood was reaching back to grab her, and caused enough pain for him to abandon his attempt so he could howl up at the broken roof.

"I said be ready with that damn Jekhibar!" she shouted. "We're only getting one chance at this."

Since he knew his partner well enough to be certain she wouldn't listen to him no matter how many times he tried to convince her, Cole rushed back to where he'd left the divining rod. Outside the store, everything seemed quiet. Even the helicopter that had been hovering overhead was gone. Unlike most conflicts, however, the lack of gunfire and shouting wasn't exactly a good sign.

"What do you want me to do?" George grunted. The Amriany had gotten close enough for Cole to take half a swing at him when he was shocked by the sound of his voice and realized who he was.

"Just keep her alive and don't get killed," Cole said. "In that order." Then he Cole carried the divining rod to the spot where Esteban stood upright, swaying and snapping on empty air while snarling in a baritone that drifted between coarse Spanish obscenities to primal animal grunts.

The Full Blood had grown to his full height, between eight and nine feet tall. Paige was still on his back, hanging onto one sickle with her right arm like a mountain climber dangling from a vertical slope. Even though she and Esteban were in constant motion, Cole could see that her arm had been stripped down to muscle hardened by the first batch of tainted ink. Now that her tattoos had burned off, that arm—the skin been peeled away, revealing tissue that looked like chipped, wet rock—was the only thing that kept her from being tossed through a wall. Paige's grip would not be loosened, no matter how many times Esteban's claws slashed at her. She winced and sweat rolled down her face as Esteban slashed at her again. Anyone else would have lost their limb or let go by now, but she hung on.

Cole pushed himself harder than he thought possible as he stabbed Esteban with the Blood Blade. The effort tapped into the last of his tattoo ink but wasn't enough to inflict a mortal wound. But it succeeded in distracting the Full Blood before he ripped into Paige again.

"What are you doing?" Cole shouted.

Grunting as she pressed her body against Esteban's back, she said, "That wound is still open. Just . . . give me another few seconds!"

"Get the hell away from him! We'll think of something else!"

"No, I . . . *got it*!" As she said that, Paige braced her feet against Esteban and lifted the vial of Memory Water that Tristan had given her before sending them all through the temple in Chuna's clearing.

The Full Blood roared, clenched a fist, swung it at Paige, and was stopped short by a gleaming length of charmed, Amriany iron. George's effort had burnt away the rest of his tattoos, but the clawed end hit Esteban's arm to rip out a sizable chunk of flesh and bone. The weapon even smashed apart a section of the floor on its downward trajectory. That bought Paige enough time to get a solid grip on the vial and drive it into the wound on Esteban's back. Glass shattered and the mystical fluid seeped directly into the werewolf's body. Some of the Memory Water might have even worked its way in deeper when the Full Blood pivoted around to hit George with a blow that knocked the iron pole from his hands. Cole heard the wet crunch of breaking bone and watched helplessly as George crumpled to the floor like a broken doll.

"What have you done to me?" Esteban snarled.

"Paige!" Cole shouted. "Get away fr—" The rest of his plea was lost in a gust of air that felt as if it had been pulled from the lowest reaches of his lungs. His feet were no longer on the floor, the roof no longer over his head. He even lost sight of Esteban until the Full Blood's savage face swung across a portion of his peripheral vision. After that, everything in his sight became a jumble of cascading shapes, blocky figures, and shades of black as he toppled through the air. Esteban must have thrown him twenty to forty feet with a blow that no human eye could have seen. Cole was reminded of the first time Randolph had tossed him aside in Canada when his back slammed against something solid and unforgiving. Even with his coat absorbing a good amount of damage and the serum pulsing through his veins, he had to fight to stay conscious.

Opening his eyes just in time to see Esteban rear up, Cole heard the beast shout, "Skinner bitch!" The towering creature tried to stand up straight, but his wounds weren't healing and blood poured from the multiple places he'd been stabbed. Since he couldn't move well enough to swipe at Paige anymore, Esteban threw himself toward a shelf and turned at the last moment to mash her between himself and the flimsy metal structure.

"Cole!" she shouted. *"Now!"*

Without pausing to think about the pain that lanced through his body, Cole climbed to his feet and ran across the room. Along the way he felt a jolt through his back that clouded his vision and made him feel as if he were still sailing through the air. Bones were cracked. He knew that for certain. Blood had seeped into almost every inch of his clothes, but he was still alive. By the time he found the divining rod again, Esteban had pushed through another row of shelves and would have crushed Paige against a solid cement wall if she hadn't used a sickle lodged in his shoulder to steer him into a sharp turn. Now that Daniels's spray had worked its way through his system, he tried to shift.

Esteban remained solid. The Memory Water had done its job. Unfortunately, the Dryad mixture was also healing his wounds.

Cole picked up the divining rod and ran toward the Full Blood. He had a substantial amount of ground to cover, which left the Esteban with just enough time to finally pull Paige from his back, grab her by the front of her tactical vest, and slam her against the cement wall.

She can take it, Cole thought. She's tough. She's had worse.

Paige was slammed again. This time Esteban snarled at her while chips of cement fell away behind her. Blood dripped from his claws as he pulled that hand back and allowed her to slump to the floor. Before the Full Blood could touch her again, Cole stuck him with the Blood Blade. Esteban tried to swipe at him, but Cole followed that attack with a second. The moment he pulled the spear out from between the werewolf's ribs, he jammed the wooden end of the divining rod into the wound. That end of the weapon was a mass of sharp edges created either by splinters from the forging process or points of the weapons from which it had been made. He clenched his fist around a sharpened piece of one of Paige's old sickle blades and immediately felt the bond form between himself, the hybrid weapon, and the Full Blood.

Images from the Full Blood's thoughts rushed through Cole's mind.

Knowledge he'd never gleaned came to him.

Memories of unknowable power flashed behind his eyes in a murky haze.

As much as he wanted to soak up more of those wondrous visions, Cole staggered back and found the large patch of ruined floor. Keeping his grip on the divining rod, he used the rest of his strength to drive the metal end into the ground.

The sparks that had flown before were nothing compared to the flash that pulsed through Cole, Paige, Esteban, and every other living thing within miles of that store. It ended quickly, snapping back into the rod before rushing through the earth along a current that Cole could only see for a fraction of a second. It was a sight as beautiful as it was terrifying.

Esteban dropped. Rather than allow himself to be seen in such a weakened state, he stood up and pulled in a haggard breath. For once, a Full Blood sounded as bad as Cole felt. His exhalation was a wheezing strain on his entire body. His muscles twitched but weren't able to shift the way he wanted them to. The werewolf's frustration was palpable as he looked over to the wall where Paige was still resting. When Esteban turned to look at Cole again, he seemed somewhat appeased. He leapt up to the hole in the roof, where he scraped to get a grip on the jagged edge and pull himself out. His footsteps were heavy and uneven on top of the store, and when he leapt away, a rush of movement from the parking lot followed him.

Chapter Thirty-Five

Milosh was dead. Judging by the amount of blood on his knives and the number of times he'd thrown them, he put up more of a fight with one arm than some who had an army behind them.

Nadya still lay where she'd fallen early in the fight. Esteban's claws had hit her along an artery. The expression on her face made it seem she'd fallen asleep and simply failed to wake up.

Cole thought the third Amriany had joined the other two, but George was still feeling good enough to throw a shaky wave at him when he called his name. But those were secondary concerns as Cole shoved past some toppled shelves to get to Paige.

"Taking a breather?" he asked. "Get your lazy ass up before the Half Breeds come sniffing around again."

She sat with her back against the wall, her legs stretched out, and her arms wrapped tightly across her chest. When she started to laugh, she winced and allowed her arms to droop toward her stomach. "Did your stupid plan actually . . . work?" she grunted.

"First of all, it was our plan, and second, it wasn't stupid."

"Did it work?"

"There was a big flash, so the stick must have been charged up with something it took from that Full Blood. Didn't you see the lights?"

She blinked but kept her eyes closed. When she started to get up, she grunted and coughed up some blood that trickled down from her lip. "Think I blacked out for a few."

Cole tossed his weapons and dropped to one knee. Reaching down to place a hand on her shoulder, he asked, "Are you all right?"

"Sure. Just give me a second."

"You're bleeding."

Paige used her tongue to get some of the blood from her mouth, pulled in a breath and opened her eyes. "This isn't over, Cole. Those Full Bloods are still out there, but they're weaker. And Randolph . . ."

"I know. We'll find him."

She cut him off with a fierce glare that he hadn't seen since their first sparring sessions, when he would still get distracted by the sight of her in tight sweats and a sports bra. "Listen to me! Randolph wasn't here, and he's always been around. With everything that's been happening . . ." Cole started reaching to help get her to a more comfortable spot, but she slapped his hands aside and added an even sharper edge to her voice when she said, "With everything that's been going on, he's got to be doing something. He wasn't here, but he was somewhere putting something together. You need to figure out what it was."

"We will. Just take a moment to breathe."

Rather than try to get up, she settled against the wall and closed her eyes again. "The IRD's wiped out, aren't they?"

"It's pretty quiet out there." With a low growling tone better suited for cheesy movie trailers, he added, "Too quiet."

"Are there any left?"

Cole's tired laugh faded as a helicopter thudded overhead. "I just heard from Adderson. Frank brought a few more Squams from another part of the state to help keep the Half Breeds from converging on this spot."

Paige's face showed intense concentration, quickly followed by frustration.

"You're still grabbing your side," Cole pointed out. "Did you break some ribs?"

"Maybe."

He reached down to move her arms, careful to hold the right one someplace that wasn't torn up too badly. Too much blood had soaked into her clothing to have just come from her arm. "Holy crap," he said, looking at the tattered remains of her tactical vest. "Looks like that big bastard got you worse than I thought."

"Yeah. I think so."

Tugging at one of the straps holding her vest in place, he found four quarter-sized holes that had been punched through it, above a fifth that hadn't managed to pierce her body armor. He thought back to when Esteban slammed her against the wall. Now he could see that the Full Blood had drilled his claws straight into her chest like four railroad spikes.

"Oh my God," he whispered. "Are you . . ."

When she forced a chuckle from the bottom of her throat, more blood seeped from the deep chest wounds. "You ask me if I'm okay and I'll smack the shit out of you."

"Keep your eyes open and I'll get some serum!" As he started to turn away, he saw the first hint of desperation he'd ever seen in Paige's face. When she grabbed hold of his coat to keep him from leaving her, he took another look at the wounds in her chest. Two of them went straight down into her heart or damn close to it. There wasn't enough serum to fix that and not nearly enough time to administer it if there was.

"What should I . . ." Rather than finish the question, he lowered himself onto the floor so he could sit beside her. The moment his leg settled against hers, she lifted her foot so she could drape it over his shin. Since that seemed to have sapped a good portion of her strength, he reached down to pick up her hand.

"I don't . . . want to leave you," she said.

After all he'd seen and all the pain that had been heaped on him that night, this was the first time his vision blurred so badly that he couldn't see anything at all. He cleared it with a few blinks, squeezed her hand and said, "I know."

"I'm sorry about when I was a bitch to you. Sorry about dragging you into this whole . . . Skinner thing."

"What about trying to stake me through the heart?" he asked.

"Nah. That was the right call."

"I guess so."

Her hand turned inside his so she could hold him a little tighter. "Do you forgive me?" she asked.

Cole turned and put his face close enough to hers so they could hear each other without having to raise their voices above a whisper. He didn't care about what else might be out there or creeping into that store to sniff out fresh meat. The only thing on his mind was the feel of Paige's cheek against his and the little bit of warmth he could still feel from her body.

"There's nothing to forgive," he said. "Thank you for everything you've shown me. I'm a better man because of you."

When she nodded, Paige bumped his forehead a few times. Her skin was becoming cool and clammy. Her words were strained even though they could barely be heard. "I love you, Cole."

"Love you too. So much."

"Are you sure I can't stay?"

"What?"

Then, Cole could tell that she wasn't talking to him. He doubted she even saw him when she smiled and sighed, "All right."

Her body slumped against him.

Every one of Cole's muscles tightened until he felt like a fist was clenching inside his head to wring the tears from his eyes. He wrapped his arms around her, buried his face against her neck so he could feel the touch of her hair against his skin, and screamed until his throat was raw.

If there was anything nearby looking for a chance to attack him when his guard was down, he wished they would just hurry up and get there.

A hand dropped onto his shoulder but he didn't react. When that hand started pulling him away from Paige, he swung back with one arm to knock aside whoever or whatever was attached to it.

"Come on," George said. "We have to go now."

"Then go."

"There isn't any time, Cole. She's gone."

He was right. Paige was gone. She was just . . . gone.

As his grip around her tightened, Cole felt once more like he was being thrown through empty air. "I can't leave her here!" he said in a voice he barely recognized. "She's not . . . I can't . . . I can't just . . ."

George grabbed his shoulder and tried to pull him to his feet. "We have to go!"

Cole jumped up, pulled away from the Amriany and took a wild swing that George didn't even try to evade. "I'm not leaving her here," he snarled.

Blood trickled from George's lip. Testing his jaw, he winced with pain as he said, "We're not leaving them here, Cole. But we have to go."

Cole's breaths came in frenetic bursts. The pain filling his head became even more dizzying when he tried looking around. "Where are the others?"

"We're the only ones who survived," George said. "And that won't be for much longer if we stay here."

One helicopter hovered over the store, and it landed in the parking lot by the time Cole and George stepped outside. Soldiers were scattered throughout the lot, most of whom were either laying flat on their backs or waiting for medical attention. At the perimeter a few humanoid shapes passed a pair of Humvees and disappeared. Cole guessed they were the surviving Squams.

"The Class One ran away," Adderson said in a tired yet solid voice. "It tried to howl a few times, but that was just a bunch of noise. When it ran away, the Class Twos scattered."

Cole nodded and did his best to just keep breathing.

"Eyes in the sky say that the bigger packs have broken up," Adderson continued. "We did enough damage to keep the bombers away from Shreveport for a while."

Now was a time where Paige would have said something to put things into context, let him know they'd done good. Instead, there was only silence.

Despite the noise of the helicopters, the cries of the wounded, the distant gunshots, the sporadic growls from stray Half Breeds, and the engines of approaching Humvees, for Cole there was only silence.

Chapter Thirty-Six

Nine days later
Somewhere in the Rocky Mountains
Montana

The wind was colder than it should have been. Randolph sat near the peak of the mountain range in his shaggy, two-legged form, feeling the fierce gusts tear through his fur. To the north was the Canadian expanse of his self-imposed exile when he'd wanted only to run free without a thought about human civilization or the schemes of his own kind. Now, most of the world was a cold, quiet place. If the insanity inflicted by his brethren had a perk, that was it. Unfortunately, there was a lot more that had gone wrong.

Esteban had been the downfall of the entire Full Blood siege. Where Liam was wild and unpredictable, the Spaniard had always been proud and stubborn. Now all of the survivors had to pay for those flaws. Perhaps the one to take Liam's place would be more reasonable.

The wretches ran wild now. That had always been the case. As Randolph sniffed the air, he could tell they had scattered to cover this continent just as they'd covered all the others. Their numbers would grow, but there was no longer the singular howl to unite them. And even more devastating for the Full Bloods, the link to the Torva'ox had been severed. He didn't know how the humans had managed to do that, but he'd felt a cool pulse flow from the earth that wiped away everything forged during the last Breaking Moon.

The humans would not be overrun and they would not rest. Doing so would be the end of them. Since the wretches were now left to their own devices, the remaining Full Bloods would need to reconfigure their territories. Esteban had been the most prominent enemy to the humans, but the others had done their part in spreading the wretches to every corner of the world. It was only a matter of time before they would meet again to fight for dominance in a bloodbath that would have made the mighty Gorren smile. Now, even that simple strategy would have to be reconsidered. There was still a newly arisen Full Blood to be found, and the war sat perched upon the brink of becoming a true nightmare just as he sat crouched upon the edge of his craggy mountain slope. Instead of being washed away in a timely manner, the humans had chosen to subject themselves to a lengthier conflict with an enemy they only just met.

Fortunately, his brethren would not be without guidance. The pearls he'd stolen from Icanchu were not from the stream of Torva'ox that nourished every other living thing. They were pure and untainted by whatever had knocked the other Full Bloods from their perch. As he allowed some of that power to trickle into his flesh, Randolph could taste a difference between it and the Torva'ox the Skinners had so recently polluted. It was as distinct as lapping up water melted from a hidden glacier instead of drinking from a rusty spout.

The wretches would eventually fall back into step with the Full Bloods. That was the natural order of things.

Now that they had a foothold once again, the humans would struggle to climb back up from the brink of extinction. That too was the way it had always been.

The next big change, as always, would come from the Full

Bloods. One would have to rise above all the others when the human retaliation came, and that one would have to be strong enough to stand against the Mist Born when they inevitably tried to reclaim the power that had been taken from them. Old ones like Icanchu had been content to lie in their native lands even as others like Kawosa and his sister roamed among the humans and shapeshifters. And NOW that he had seized his prize, the Mist Born would no longer be so willing to sit idly by and let the mortals conduct their business.

The early days of this war had been ugly, but the humans had survived. Randolph hadn't expected them to be so resilient. Bloodier days were coming. The humans would need to fight a lot harder to see more than a few of them.

Chapter Thirty-Seven

Onekama, Michigan

The sky had a deep purple hue as the sun breached the eastern horizon. The only sounds came from a restless breeze that shook a few branches in the trees lining Northwood Highway, a few struggling trucks attempting to brave the elements near the homes on the other side of a small inlet of Lake Michigan, and the methodical scraping of a blade against near-petrified wood. There were two cars parked along the shoulder of the highway, one of which was still ticking after having just pulled to a stop behind the other.

George left his vehicle, pulled his coat tighter around him and walked past the trees on that side of the road. Once he stepped beyond them, he could see a wide expanse of partially frozen water leading out to the Great Lake itself. The sun's rays against the clouds smeared overhead gave them a bright glow, and were reflected off the icy waters to either mesmerize or blind anyone looking at them. He used his iron weapon as a walking stick, keeping the clawed end down so it could dig into the ground whether it was covered in snow, ice, or concrete. It wasn't long before his steps were muffled by dirt. He stopped, allowed the echo of his arrival to drift away and drew a long breath of frosty morning air. "I didn't guess you were a morning person," he said.

Cole sat on a bench with a back that had been partially snapped off by the same creatures that scratched the hell out of the nearby street. He didn't acknowledge the Amriany's presence with anything more than half a shrug and continued sharpening the forked end of his spear.

"Mind if I sit down?"

Cole shook his head.

After leaning his weapon against the bench, George reached down to clear off a space. Paige's sickles sat next to the Skinner and an empty urn rested by his feet, so George moved around to the other side where he only had to move a few bags of fast food away. "These feel warm," George mused. "You found a place that serves breakfast?"

"Life goes on."

"Mind if I have some? It's been a week since I've had anything other than bagels or powdered eggs before noon."

"Must still be riding with the IRD," Cole said.

"They needed help regrouping. Those Vitsaruuv that left Shreveport tried to take a run at another city. I don't know its name."

"They all run together after a while." Looking up, Cole admitted, "I'm not even sure what this place is called."

"I guess that's why it took three days to find you." Now George picked up the fast food bag, sat down and dug out a sausage egg and cheese muffin. "Looks like the Vitsaruuv were here not too long ago."

"There was a Half Breed den by the lake. I cleaned it out."

"By yourself?"

"Yeah."

"Isn't that dangerous?"

Cole stopped what he was doing, glanced down at the sickles and continued his sharpening.

"If you don't know what town this is, why did you come here?" George asked.

"I could ask you the same thing."

"I asked you first."

After a sigh, Cole said, "I heard it was quiet here. When I got here, there were Half Breeds just like every other goddamn place on earth, so I cleared them out. Now it's quiet."

"Who told you it was quiet?"

"The nymphs that run the strip bar outside of town."

"Ahh," George said through a mouthful of breakfast. "So that is how you got here and why you didn't even know where 'here' is."

After a few seconds Cole said, "One time, Paige told me she wanted to be cremated because the whole burial and funeral thing was creepy. When I asked where she would want her ashes scattered, all she wanted was someplace quiet."

"So, have you mourned her enough?"

"I don't know. Have you already forgotten about Milosh and Nadya?"

"There is forgetting and there is mourning," George said. "Mourning is something we can't indulge in for too long. Forgetting is something I doubt either of us will ever do."

"You got that right."

"Since you did some work before coming out here to sit on your butt and look at the sunrise, I suppose I can forgive you."

Cole chuckled as he looked up. The sun was now casting more orange than purple onto the icy water. "Didn't even realize it was sunrise. What time is it?"

"Time to get back to work."

If his spear had been made of normal, untreated wood, it would have snapped beneath the force he used to whittle down the forked end. "Adderson's been talking to me every couple of hours. If my fingers weren't so freaking cold I would have turned my phone off by now."

"Cold fingers?"

"Yeah. The touch screen works off of heat. I can push a button to answer the call, but the screen doesn't respond too well. Paige would have given me no end of crap about that one," Cole said with a tired laugh. "She always loved to point out when my tech stuff didn't work right."

"Is that so? What did she say when it did work?"

"She'd say, 'give it a few minutes.'" Cole started to laugh in earnest, but the effort became too much for him so he turned his attention back to the spear.

George finished his breakfast sandwich in a few overzealous bites and then leaned forward to glance down at the large plastic mug near Cole's feet. "Is that coffee?"

"Yeah," Cole replied. "My coffee."

"Can I have some?"

"If you don't mind my backwash."

George shrugged and reached down to grab the mug. "We've fought and bled together. We've lost dear ones on the same night we both nearly died. I think I can stand to drink some of your coffee."

"What about the backwash?"

"There was probably worse things in the fast food you insist on buying."

The whittling stopped and Cole's hand drifted to the sickles. Rather than pretend he was doing something else or busying himself with the spear, he picked them up and set them upon his knee. The blades were folded down against the handle, which he touched gingerly, as if he was once again afraid of the thorns.

"She's a hero," George said. "Everyone who knows what happened in Shreveport knows that."

"Yeah."

"The Weshruuv continue to howl, but nobody breaks like they used to."

"That doesn't mean it's over," Cole said. "There are still more Half Breeds than ever and they can still make more by attacking humans."

"But the planes no longer drop from the skies," George pointed out. "The IRD can fight them. Armies across the world are fighting them."

"Adderson said it was close, but the ones above him in the chain of command aren't talking about nukes anymore."

"They were considering nukes?" George asked as the optimism he'd been injecting into his voice dissipated. When Cole nodded, he took another sip of coffee.

"The IRD took some major losses, but they're recruiting from every branch of the military to make up for it. They're even splitting into international groups now."

"I know. I already heard from the IRD UK." Seeing the question in Cole's eyes, he added, "That's the United Kingdom."

"I know. I just didn't know they knew about the Amriany."

"I've been trying to drag the clans into the new century for a while now, but they all just want to stay quiet and bitch about you Skinners. I think Shreveport brought us together in more ways than you know. That was Paige's doing also."

Leaning back, Cole looked at the water and closed his eyes. A lazy smile drifted onto his face and his eyes pinched in at the edges. "I can still hear her voice. I don't ever want to forget that sound, but I can't think about her face for too long before . . ."

"Before you want to break something," George said. "I know."

"Killing those Half Breeds helped."

"Well there are plenty more out there."

"Plenty more of them along with the Full Bloods and the Nymar." Cole opened his eyes and tightened his grip on the sickles. "The bloodsuckers have been cleaning their own houses and already started trying to sneak into ours. Tried to get a Shadow Spore into the IRD. One of Adderson's boys shot the son of a bitch and burned him alive before the antidote rounds could do their thing. Wish I could have seen that."

"I think you'll be seeing plenty of that sort of thing for a while. Every country is under some sort of lockdown because of the damn wolves. Eight of our cities back home have fallen to Vasily while the Amriany turned their attention elsewhere. And if you would believe it," George added, "things continue to become stranger. In Peru and Colombia they say the snakes are reclaiming the rain forests."

"Snakes?"

"Uh-huh."

Cole ran his thumb along the edge of his Blood Blade. "Esteban is still out there. Lots of Full Bloods are. The Nymar have just been waiting, and now they've got a chance to sink in even deeper."

"That doesn't mean we can give up," George said.

"Give up? That's never really been an option, and now I don't even want to hear anyone say those words. This is a war, but it's because of Paige that it's no longer an extermination. It was only a matter of time before the shapeshifters either turned or killed most of the people in the world. The ones that survived would have been caught in the cross fire as the military kept trying to kill Full Bloods using the wrong weapons."

George rubbed his eyes and stuffed the wrapper from his sandwich into the bag with the others. "For a while even we didn't have the right weapons for that."

"Now we do, but this fight's got a long way to go. The Nymar will make another move. The Full Bloods aren't finished. The Half Breeds are always hungry."

"And the snakes," George sighed. "Don't forget about those snakes."

Cole grinned. "Paige died to make this war winnable, so I'm going to win it for her. The Amriany can help me. The IRD can help me. Nobody can help me. I don't care. I'll find a way to win."

"Do you know someone other than the IRD or Amriany?"

"There are some assholes in Louisville I plan on visiting."

"You need someone to come with you?"

Standing up, Cole put his spear into its harness and then collected the sickles. "Check back with me in a few days. There's one more stop I need to make."

Epilogue

St. Louis, Missouri

Cole felt strange going to the cathedral in the section of St. Louis known as Dog Town. The last time he'd been to St. James the Greater was when people were still worried about the Mud Flu. Lancroft's plague seemed like a fond memory compared to the circumstances that brought him back to that chapel on Tamm Avenue. When he tried the door, he found it was locked. His knocks were answered by a stout, balding man wearing glasses that were thick enough to be bulletproof. As soon as the man laid eyes on him, he flashed a wide, friendly smile.

"I remember you!" he said. "Looks like things've been rough since we last met."

Cole's hand drifted to the three fresh scars that ran down his left temple and picked up again to form three similar gouges on that side of his chin. Since touching the scars would only make them itch, he pulled his hand away and asked, "Can I come in?"

"Where's Paige?"

Cole twitched but was too tired to react more than that. "Mind if I come in?"

The man with the glasses nodded and opened the door

the rest of the way. "Probably a good idea. Nowadays, Dog Town really lives up to the name. Had to keep the place locked up so the wolves wouldn't get in. Hasn't been too bad for a little while now, though."

It was cold, but the layers Cole wore beneath his stitched-up coat kept away the chill. He walked straight through a small room filled with chairs and folding tables to the cathedral, pausing as soon as he got a look at the familiar stained-glass windows and statuary. Even the smell brought back memories. When he clenched his fist, he swore he could feel Paige's hand in his grasp. "I shouldn't have come here," he said.

The man behind the glasses rubbed Cole's shoulder. "Don't be silly! What's this place for if not to give shelter to a fella like you? You're not about to sprout fur and fangs are ya?" he asked with a subtle St. Louis drawl.

"No," Cole replied with an uneasy laugh. When he felt his strength start to ebb, he lowered himself down onto one of the pews.

"I didn't catch yer name," the man said as he sat down beside him.

"Cole."

"I'm Bill. Can I get something for you to drink? We've got coffee, or maybe something stronger?"

"No thanks."

After folding his hands across an ample belly, Bill sat quietly for a few seconds before saying, "Paige won't be coming, will she?"

That one almost broke Cole all the way down to the center of his chest. He pushed back the pain so he could shake his head without falling apart. "Nope." Once he pulled himself together, he asked, "How did you know?"

"I could see it on your face. You want me to get one of the priests to have a word with you?"

"You knew Paige?"

"Yeah," Bill said fondly. "She didn't come in a lot, but she was busy. Especially," he added in a guarded whisper, "with all the important work she was doing."

"You knew about that too, huh?"

Bill nodded. "I had a close call myself with one of those wolf things long before they showed up on the news. We would talk to each other because 'most anybody else around here would think we were nuts." Gazing up at the altar, he said, "She once told me that she would be fine with . . . well . . . passing on, just so long as it was for a good cause. Always wanted to go down swingin', you know?"

"I do."

"Did she?"

"Oh yeah."

Bill nodded, smirked, and then pulled a handkerchief from a pocket so he could dab his eyes.

Cole sat there, looking at the murals Paige had enjoyed, hoping to draw strength from the same source that she'd gone to when she needed it most. He even thought about praying for the courage to walk even further into the fire that had already burnt him so badly. When he found he wasn't able to go through those unfamiliar motions, he just closed his eyes and let the soft, funny memories rush in along with the painful and annoying ones. For the moment, that's all he owned and all he needed.

The fight would still be there when he found the strength to stand up.

And because of Paige, he had more strength than he'd ever thought possible.

MARCUS PELEGRIMAS's

SKINNERS

HUMANKIND'S LAST DEFENSE AGAINST THE DARKNESS

BLOOD BLADE

978-0-06-146305-1

There is a world inhabited by supernatural creatures of the darkness—all manner of savage, impossible beasts that live for terror and slaughter and blood. They are all around us but you cannot see them, and for centuries a special breed of hunter called Skinners has kept the monsters at bay, preventing them from breaking through the increasingly fragile barriers protecting our mortal realm.

But beware...for there are very few of them left.

HOWLING LEGION

978-0-06-146306-8

TEETH OF BEASTS

978-0-06-146307-5

VAMPIRE UPRISING

978-0-06-198633-8

THE BREAKING

978-0-06-198634-5

EXTINCTION AGENDA

978-0-06-198638-3